I0788542

# Ma Guy
## GHOST DEVIL

A.J. Morano

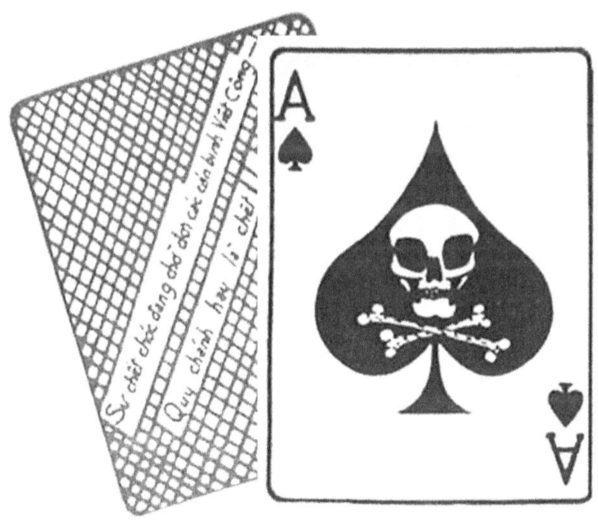

WALDEHOUSE PUBLISHERS, INC.
WALDEN, TENNESSEE

*Ma Guy: Ghost Devil*



Disclaimer: This is a work of fiction. Names, characters, descriptions, businesses, places, events, locales, and incidents are either the products of the authoru's imagination or used in a fictitious manner. Any resemblance to actual persons, living or dead, or to actual events is purely coincidental.

Published by Waldenhouse Publishers, Inc.
Printed in the United States of America
ISBN: 978-1-947589-18-6
Library of Congress Control Number: 2019948071
  In first-person, fictional protagonist Pauley Walker tells the story of his mafia life in New York City, Las Vegas, Florida and Cuba and then recounts his experiences as a "tunnel rat" severely wounded in Vietnam during the 1960's. - Provided by publisher
FIC050000 Fiction/ Crime
FIC027260 Fiction/ Romance/ Action and Adventure
FIC000000  Fiction/General

# *INTRODUCTION*

This is the story of a man's life – his great joys and devastating sorrows.

He served in Vietnam in a long-range special operations unit where he and his partner effectively killed the enemy without ever being seen. The Vietnamese searched for a platoon of GI's. They never knew it was only two Special Forces tunnel rats, named *Ma Guy* by the Vietnamese. The English translation is GHOST DEVIL.

Vietnam played a major role in his life, but not as much as the Mafia. Destiny foretold his life in the Mafia.

# *CHAPTER 1*

One day I came home from school to find my mother crying at the kitchen table. It wasn't just tears down her face, it was uncontrollable bawling. I sat with her until she stopped sobbing and could tell me what happened.

My father had been fired from his job for drinking. His addiction to alcohol had become so bad that he was rarely sober. My mother said he was passed out on the floor in the bedroom and asked me to help her get him into bed. Once Dad was tucked in Mom told me she didn't know how we were going to pay the rent and the electric bill, buy food and ice for the ice box – we didn't have a refrigerator. I told Mom not to worry, I'd come up with something. I asked her how much she needed each month. She told me. After that day, I was never a kid again.

I rode my bike to Kelly Street, about five blocks away. A New York City block is long. Kelly was a different neighborhood, stores instead of apartment buildings. At the far end of the street was Tony's Bar and Grill.

Whenever we got some extra cash, my friends and I would go through a side door and sit at a table. We'd order a large pizza and share it, the best pizza in the world. A man would serve us. There were times when one of the guys would disrespect him. I looked at that man and saw my father trying to do a job to earn money, and I always treated him with respect.

At Tony's I asked the bartender if I could talk to the owner. He pointed to the back where a gentleman was sitting at a table, looking at some papers. I approached him, feeling nervous. I had to get this job or let my mother down, and that's something I never wanted to do. I told him I was sorry to bother him. I needed to ask for a job. He looked up, and it was the guy who had waited on us.

He said, "The respectful kid! Sit down and tell me what's going on." I told him everything, and that I needed to make $25 dollars a week to give to my mother. I told him I'd do anything. If he gave me the job, I'd be indebted to him for the rest of my life.

He sat back for a couple of minutes then said, "You have the job. I'll pay you the $25 a week for your mother and $10 for you. You'll start tomorrow after school."

Under no circumstance was I to quit school. Tomorrow he would explain the job to me. His daughter would take me shopping for clothes, and I was to burn the worn-out shoes and rags I was wearing. I was to go home and tell my mother about the job, so she could feel a little better. I'd be eating dinner at the grill at night, so she wouldn't have to worry about me.

"I know your name is Pauly. My name is Tony DeAngelo. You refer to me as Mr. D as everybody else does. Get outta here."

I walked out, looked to the sky, and said, "Thank you." As I was heading home I was thinking: *Why the fuck do I need to burn good clothes?*

The next day I got home from school, said hello to my mother, dropped off my books, then anxiously walked to the bar. As I walked through the door, I heard, "Hey, Pauly, come here" Mr. D was sitting at a table waving to me.

I sat down and said, "Good afternoon, Sir."

Mr. D looked at me and asked. "You OK?"

I replied I was. Then he started telling me about the job. I had to sweep the serving area and eating area, then get a cleaning bucket with water and a rag from the kitchen and go over the tables, chairs and counters. I was not to do anything at the bar – I was not to go near the bar. The kitchen help would clean the kitchen, not me.

"When you're done with the grill, you'll get on the El and take it to the 116th Street Lenox Avenue stop. Walk two blocks to 118th to a store on the corner, Kingfish Locks. See Gary, the locksmith. He'll hand you a small brown bag that you must conceal immediately. Never carry it in the open. Then get back on the El and bring the bag back to the bar. Be careful. I don't like doin' business with those fuckin' niggers. Gary's OK. He'll get the word out that you work for us. Most everybody would be afraid to screw with you, but the niggers are doin' drugs, and ya never know."

I didn't want to look stupid and didn't say anything, but I didn't know what "doing drugs" meant. I also didn't like people being called niggers but didn't say anything about that. Mr. D asked if I was alright with it. I said, "Sure."

Mr. D told a guy named Vince to pick up his daughter and take both of us wherever she wanted. Vince and I walked down the block and into a side door of a decrepit building with garage doors on the front. Inside was a fantastic three-car garage. Vince told me to get in the back seat of the Lincoln. He got behind the wheel. Some guy came over and opened the garage door, and we pulled out and headed north. After about a half hour, we were in Yonkers on a street with nice, modest homes. On the corner was a young lady. Vince pulled up to her, got out and opened the back door for her.

She got in and said, "Hi, my name is Maria. How are you?"

I was numb, couldn't get a word out. I had never seen or been that close to such a beautiful girl. I just couldn't stop staring at her. She said, "It's OK. You just relax."

She told Vince where to go. She broke the silence by telling me she knew my name and that I was all her father could talk about. "He'd been talking about you before you came in for the job and was happy when you did. My mom and dad had me and they were trying for a boy when she died. He thinks of you as the son he never had."

"Thank you for that and I'm sorry for staring at you. I've never been this close to a girl as beautiful as you are." She blushed.

The car stopped in front of a clothing store. Vince got out, opened the door on Maria's side, and helped her out. I got out on my side. Maria and I walked into the store, and Vince returned to the car. We spent about an hour shopping. Maria picked out everything for me. When we were done, she paid with a hundred-dollar bill. I had never seen one before. Maria helped me carry my stuff out of the store. Vince saw us, bolted out of the car, and took what Maria was carrying. We put everything in the trunk.

Maria said, "Let's go into Bloomberg Apparel next."

I was tired of this shopping crap but being with her a little longer was great. After we finished, Vince drove Maria home first. When we got to her street I told Maria, "Thank you. This has been the best day of my life. Not just for the clothing but for you." She leaned over, kissed me on the cheek, and got out of the car. I think I came in my pants.

During the half hour drive home, nothing was said. I was exhausted. Vince pulled up in front of my apartment house. Vince helped me carry everything to my apartment. I thanked him, and he left. I didn't know how he knew where I lived. It didn't matter.

The next morning at school I didn't see any of my friends, probably because I was running a little late. In my homeroom as

I was walking to my desk, I noticed all my classmates staring at me. Probably because I was late. As I got to my desk, Ira and Rob came up to me and blurted out how great I looked, and that it seemed as if I changed. Where did I get the clothes?

I told them it was a long story, that I had a job, and I wouldn't be seeing much of them after school anymore. I said that and looked at my friends. We were friends, and would probably always be friends, but differently. The past two days changed me. I outgrew my friends.

Everything at school changed for me. It wasn't that long ago that I was eager to learn. I was like a sponge soaking up whatever I could. I remember a couple of years ago, I was reading a book in class and I heard my name from the back of the room. I turned around and saw a guy I knew. He started whispering something to me, but I couldn't hear what it was. Then I heard, "Mister. Why are you talking in my class?"

I turned around, told the teacher "I was not talking. I was looking at the back wall."

"Who were you talking to?"

"No one. I told you I was looking at the back wall."

I guess my teacher felt that she wasn't getting anywhere and had made her point, so she went back to her desk. I turned and looked back at the guy who was giving me two thumbs up. I reached behind and gave him the finger. Two girls giggled.

Now I would say, "Yes, I was talking," and nothing more. I no longer gave a damn. Nothing mattered anymore.

After school I went to the bar. Mr. D was sitting in his usual spot. I walked up to him and said, "Good afternoon, Sir. Thank you for all the clothes. With due respect, I would like to say you have the most beautiful daughter in the world, both inside and out."

He looked at me and said, "Thanks. She is just as her mother was." I could see tears well up in his eyes. I turned and walked away, thinking *I really like this guy.*

Spring came and went, uneventful except for my getting my job down pat and loving it. I never thought people could earn money so easily. Summer came, and life was good. I would sleep in, get up, get dressed, eat something and go to the bar. I didn't see much of my father. He was either sleeping it off or out somewhere boozing it up. My mother told me he was getting better, and she was looking forward to the day he would kick the addiction. She was a good woman. I didn't think most women would have put up with his shit.

I got to the bar, and as always, greeted Mr. D. This time he told me to sit with him. He wanted to talk to me. I was afraid he was going to fire me. I sat and waited for him to start talking. It seemed like hours but was only a few seconds.

"Pauly, as far as I know you're doin' a great job. I'm increasing the money I'm giving you to $25 dollars and keeping the money for your mother the same." I thanked him. He asked if I ever looked in the bag.

"No, but I could feel there was a bundle of money." I told him whatever was in the bag was his business and none of mine.

# *CHAPTER 2*

"Good. I want to tell you all about my business and who and what I am."

Before he could continue talking, Larry hollered, "Mr. D, you have a phone call."

"Tell whoever the fuck it is to call back in an hour."

Larry hesitantly said, "It's Mr. G from Queens."

Mr. D got up, walked over to the bar, grabbed the phone, and said something in Italian. He told Larry and the guys sitting at the bar to go somewhere, get lost. With his back to me, he said something into the phone in Italian and then stood there listening.

I got up and started to do my job. Mr. D finished his telephone conversation then hollered out to his guys that they were going to take a trip and take care of some business.

Vince pulled in front of the bar in a limo. He opened the front passenger door for Mr. D; the guys piled in the back. I went about my job and went home.

The next morning my mother asked me to pick up some things at the market for her. On the way, I passed a small newsstand in front of the candy store. The stand was covered with early-edition *Posts* with a big headline: *Mafioso Killed in Brooklyn.* There was a picture of a guy lying on his back with a fish on his crotch. I picked up what my mother wanted, and passing the candy store, I bought a paper and went home.

I had plenty of time before work, so I read the article. The victim was found in a Brooklyn junkyard on the hood of a car, with his penis and testicles stuffed in his mouth. He was Joseph

Stinzano, a made-man in the Genovese family. A made-man is like an officer in a mafia family. The murder, according to the article, was mafia-style for a man who raped or abused a woman. Because the mafia code protected a made-man, the cops felt it was a murder made to look like a mafia hit. The police didn't care because they saw it as a sleazy wop was off the street. I didn't understand how a man could abuse a woman.

A couple of years ago, we were sitting at the kitchen table. My father, mother, I and my brother who was sitting facing me. My brother was older and stupid, beyond stupid, whatever that would be. My brother had been sickly as a kid; my parents favored him. He learned to take advantage of it as he got older. Today he wanted to get my father's favor. He started to rank on me. At first, I just shrugged it off and didn't say anything. He kept it up – there was no stopping him. I was hoping my father would say that was enough, but he didn't. He never did. I just sat there and put a deaf ear to it. It was meaningless, stupid shit. After a while I had had enough. I looked at my brother and snarled, "Shut your fuckin' mouth!"

A hand came across my face and knocked me off the chair. I got up holding my cheek – it hurt. "Don't you ever talk like that in front of your mother or any other woman again!"

I stood looking at my father, stunned, and then I turned and glared at my brother. It was a look that promised *I'll tear your head off and piss down your throat, you son of a bitch*. I grabbed my coat and headed for the street. I was mad, raging mad, mentally cursing everybody and everything.

Suddenly I stopped, sat down on the curb and thought. My father was right, not in hitting me, but using that kind of language in front of my mother. It was disrespectful and wrong. I vowed I wouldn't, and no one else would ever disrespect my mother again and get away with it. I returned to the apartment and went over to my mother. I told her, "I'm sorry for using that kind of language in front of you. I love you and would not disrespect you for anything in this world." I walked over to my father and said, "Sorry," and went to my room.

At work I didn't say anything about the hit in the paper. Someday, when the time was right, I'd ask Mr. D. I felt he would tell me. Time went on and nothing new or exciting happened at work, or at least nothing I was aware of.

One day as I was walking back to the train with the bag from Gary, I could see a cop coming up behind me. He was a big guy and moving fast. I thought he was going to pass me on the sidewalk, so I just kept walking. I didn't do anything wrong, had nothing to worry about. Then I felt a hand on my shoulder and the cop told me to stop. I turned around and was looking at a huge belly covered with a cop's uniform. I looked up and there was this sweaty, round face looking down at me. I figured if things went bad, I'd punch him in the nuts and run for the subway.

In a strong Irish brogue, he asked what a white kid was doing walking in the middle of Harlem. I told him I got off on the wrong stop and was trying to get back on the subway.

"That's bullshit. What are you doing here?"

"I told you."

"You're here to buy dope."

"No, I don't know what dope is."

"You little piece of shit. Tell me what you're doing here."

I had enough of this, and one way or the other, I was going to end it. I said, "I have not been disrespectful to you, and you don't have a right to disrespect me. Get out of the way so I can get back on the subway."

I watched his face for a reaction. Before he could try something, I would get my punch in. The cop smirked at me and said, "Get the fuck out of here … and say hello to Mr. D for me."

I got back on the train and tried to calm down. I was wondering what "Say hello to Mr. D" was about. Was it some kind of test? I didn't think Mr. D. would do that to me. The cop knew Mr. D, so he knew what I was doing there. He also had to know what Gary was doing and didn't do anything about it. I couldn't wait until tomorrow to ask Mr. D.

At the bar I handed the bag over. I didn't feel like eating anything, so I went home and went to bed.

Next morning was the same as every other except I was pushing it to get to work. I walked into the bar. Instead of greeting Mr. D and heading for the kitchen to get the broom, I walked over to Mr. D.

"Good afternoon, Sir. I had a little problem yesterday and wanted to talk to you about it."

Glancing up from some paperwork, Mr. D said he knew about the little problem. It was nothing, and he would explain it to me one of these days when we got a chance to talk, and for me not to worry about it. I walked to the kitchen, got my broom, and started sweeping. *This sucks,* I thought. *I'm not supposed to worry about it? Bullshit!*

The summer passed. I went back to school. Fall flew by and it was winter.

I was cold, so fuckin' cold my teeth were chattering. I couldn't wait to get to the bar where it was warm and comfortable. I'd pace myself, doing my job, never goofing off, just taking my time so my body could absorb the heat. Made the run. The day ended.

School was nothing. I had a problem concentrating. I never did homework. I never studied, yet it all seemed to be so easy. All I could do at school was think about work. I didn't know how I was getting by.

One day as I was headed for the broom, Mr. D waved me over to his table. I walked over and said, "Sir?"

He reached under the table and handed me a navy pea coat saying, "Maria got this for you." I took the coat. It was heavy.

"Thank you, and please tell Maria thank you, that I greatly appreciate it."

I knew it was Mr. D. Maria probably picked out the coat and bought it, but the coat came from Mr. D. He just wouldn't take credit for it. Some years later I found out I was wrong – the coat was all Maria.

I finished cleaning, put my coat on and headed for the El. I couldn't believe how warm I felt. Deep down I think I felt a little warmer knowing that Maria held the coat and somehow was still holding it as I wore it.

# *CHAPTER 3*

Before I knew it, it was Christmas. On Christmas Eve Day Mr. D called me over. He told me the bar and all his businesses would be shut down until January 2, so that everybody could spend time with their families. Fuck the family. I needed the money.

Then he told me that every Christmas he invited everyone who worked for him and their families, his family and friends to go to Mass then celebrate with a great dinner, drinks and fun.

"I know how your family feels about Christmas. Don't come."

Mr. D told me that he gave his guys bonuses at the party. "Here's yours." I thanked him and walked away.

I was feeling bad. I felt like an outsider looking in, like I was just sliced off. I also didn't know how my parents felt about Christmas, or how Mr. D knew so much of my shit. I thought we didn't celebrate because we couldn't afford to, and that we didn't go to church because we didn't have nice clothes. Then I realized most families had a crucifix hanging on a wall, but we didn't. I also didn't remember Jesus Christ ever being mentioned in the house. I needed to find out what was going on.

I finished up in the bar, did my run, got back to the bar. I gave Luigi the bag and sat down to eat something. Just as I was leaving, about to walk out the door, Luigi hollered out, "Pauly, have a merry Christmas! I'll see you tomorrow at the party."

I turned and said, "Sure, same to you," and walked out. As I was walking home, I remembered the bonus. I had forgotten all about it with all the Christmas crap on my mind. I reached in my pocket, took out the envelope and opened it. I was stunned. I was looking at five one hundred-dollar bills. *Holy shit! I'm a rich fuck!* I stuffed the envelope back in my pocket and went home.

My mother was sitting at the kitchen table, staring at nothing. Said hello and kissed her on the forehead. I stood over her, just looking at her. She was a petite woman who was extraordinarily beautiful – flawless olive skin, lustrous brown-black hair.

I told her I got a bonus at work and wanted her to hold on to it. "We'll add to it when we can and call it our *gruzzolo,* our nest egg." I handed her the envelope.

She looked inside, and her eyes got big, and all she could say was "OK". I told her I needed to know about us and Jesus Christ and the church, and how come a guy named Tony D'Angelo knows more about us than I do. She looked into my eyes and asked if that was who I worked for.

Before I could answer, she told me, "Be very careful. I can't lose a son. I know Tony, and he knows me very well. During the week, when you have time, I'll tell you all about it. It's a long story, and I'm tired now. As for the church and Christ, when Christmas is over with, and the church isn't busy, go down to St. Michael's and ask to speak to the priest. He'll tell you everything." She said good night and we went to bed.

The next day was Christmas. I sat around depressed and pissed off. I wanted to go to the party, to feel that I belonged, and to get a chance to see Maria. Vince had told me once that Maria was unapproachable. Mr. D would cut the balls off anyone who hit on her. I felt looking and feelings are not "hitting on" and are OK. Maria was a year older than me; she had a different lifestyle. Despite that I was drawn to Maria. I couldn't get her out of my head.

Thinking about Maria made me horny. I went into the bathroom and jerked off. When I got done, I walked out and told

Mom I was going outside. As I stood on the sidewalk deciding where to head, someone tapped me on the shoulder. I turned to see Rich, a friend that I used to play with, one of our little gang.

Rich said he had seen me at school a couple of times, but I was always preoccupied, so he didn't want to bother me. He asked how I was doing. I told him I was doing good, and asked about him. "Nothing new, same old shit." I asked if his younger brother would want my bike. He said yes. I told him Lenny could have it.

Rich was standing there shivering. I snapped, "Why the fuck don't you wear a heavier coat than that rag?"

He gave me a you-moron look, "If I had one, I would. This is what I got."

"Shit, Pauly," I said to myself, "You're fuckin' stupid." I forgot how my teeth used to chatter before I got the pea coat. I told Rich, "Let's go down the basement. I want to ask you something, and you can get out of this cold."

In the basement, I asked Rich if all the other guys were in the same boat – asses freezing off. Yes, with another you-moron look – deserved. When I asked if he liked my coat, he moaned he'd give his left nut to have a coat like mine. I told him I had one more question for him. I just wanted a yes or no, and forget about the fuckin' looks. I asked if he thought the other guys would like it. The response was yes.

"Do me a favor and meet me back here at noon tomorrow. I might have a way of handling things." Rich walked to the back of the basement to look at the bikes. I went back to the apartment.

Mom was working in the kitchen. I touched her arm, wanting her attention. I told her I was going to spend some of the rainy-day money. "I want to buy coats for my friends. It's bitter cold outside and these guys are freezing." I wasn't asking her permission, just telling her what I intended to do.

With a big smile on her face, Mom reached up, put her hands on my cheeks and pulled my head down to her. She kissed me on the forehead then turned away.

I went to my room. I needed to think. My priority was this coat thing, and then I needed to get to the church, and later sit down with my mom and talk. It would be great to get all that shit off my mind.

I decided I was going to call Mr. D in the morning to explain what I wanted to do. I'd ask him if he could have Maria and Vince come here and take everybody to the store where she bought my coat. Both car and limo would be needed. I'd buy the same coats for all of them. The only problem I would have to overcome with Mr. D was how he felt about my friends who acted like big shots and were disrespectful to him when he waited on us. I felt I could handle that. If my friends knew who that waiter was, they'd shit their pants.

I slept well, woke up early, and waited for a good time to call Mr. D. Someone answered the phone. I told the guy who I was, and I needed to talk to Mr. D. He told me hang on. After a while I heard, "Pauly, how you doin'? You OK? What's a the matter?"

I was taken aback by his concern. I composed myself and told him I was sorry to bother him. I needed his help. It was not a major thing; it was something I needed to do.

We spoke for a while. At the end, he said he would ask Maria. If she didn't have a problem with it, she and Vince would be in front of my apartment house at eleven o'clock tomorrow. I said thank you and hung up. I knew he would make it happen no matter what.

At noon I met Rich in the basement. I told him to get ahold of everyone and be in front of my building at a quarter to eleven. Someone was going to pick us up, and we were going to get coats for everyone. He, Mick, Nana, Frankie, Joe, Pete, Rob and the other guys; everyone could bring their kid brothers and his brother, if they wanted coats also.

Rich was excited, "Oh, my god, this is unbelievable!" He raced off to tell everyone.

I went up to the apartment and flopped down on my bed. I was bored. I missed the hustle of work. I couldn't stop thinking of Maria. I used to think of her as that beautiful girl that fucking would be great. But now she's that beautiful girl I wanted to spend the rest of my life with. I wanted to hold her, smell her, and touch her beauty. I wanted to be loved by her. I just wanted this beautiful goddess so bad. I was at an age when horny was the thing. I was a virgin. I had never even kissed a girl, never felt up a girl, and I wanted to do all of that. In my dreams I did, and a lot more. I lay there hoping that Maria wanted to see me as much as I wanted to see her. I couldn't wait until tomorrow.

Mom woke me up for dinner. I ate and then told her I was going for a walk. I needed to get rid of some of the pent-up energy, feel free. It was bitterly cold, and I was the only person on the street. The exercise was relaxing me. After a while I walked back to the apartment and went to bed.

The next morning, I got up, dressed and sat around. Mom fixed me eggs and toast. I was getting antsy and hoping things would work out. I decided to go down to the street. In front of the apartment building, there was a mob, standing silently. I walked over and said, "What the fuck are you guys doing here this early?" All I heard from them was they didn't want to miss out.

I told them to go into the apartment hallway and get out of the cold. "If anyone tells you to get out, just leave, and don't give them shit." As I waited on the sidewalk, I realized I should have a talk with these guys. I didn't want anything to fuck this up. If anyone could, it would be them.

I went into the building and told everyone, "The people who are picking us up are very special. There is going to be a beautiful girl and a limo driver. Everyone is to be on his best behavior. No horsing around. In fact, no talking unless one of them speaks to you. Be respectful always. Do not talk to or go near the girl unless she talks or goes near you. I'm going to ride in the front seat with the girl, you three in the back, and the rest of you in the limo. Whoever is sitting behind her when we get where we are going gets out of the car and holds the door open for her."

Just as I finished I saw Maria's car and the limo pull up. I turned and walked out. I turned again, and they were standing there. I told them, "Come on, and don't forget what I said."

I was going to stop at the limo first to tell Vince thanks, but decided that could wait. I wanted to see Maria. I opened the door and my heart was pounding. I sat down. Looking at Maria, I said Hi, and she said Hi.

We sat there staring at each other. I was melting away. I snapped out of it and realized these three guys were in the back seat. I introduced them to her, telling them that this is the very special lady I told them about. Maria said, "Hi." In return, almost in unison, they said, "Hi, glad to meet you." I thought to myself: *Where did these shits come up with that?*

Maria headed for Yonkers with Vince right behind us. I couldn't keep my eyes off Maria. Occasionally she would glance at me then look back at the road. After a while, she switched from driving with her right hand to her left. She put her right hand on my leg and whispered, "I missed you, Pauly." I sat back in the seat, closed my eyes, thinking I died and went to heaven and was touched by an angel. We pulled up in front of a store that looked familiar. Nana got out and opened the door for Maria. As Maria was walking toward the store, Nana ran to the door, opened and held it for her.

Three clerks were carrying boxes from the back. An older woman said, "Good morning, Miss DeAngelo. We have what you requested. What won't be needed we will keep in our stock." The clerks fitted each guy with a coat. After Maria approved, the guy was asked to wait outside or in the limo because we were a crowd in the store.

After everyone was fitted and left the store, Maria and I were standing at the register with the older woman. "Miss DeAngelo, that was sixteen coats,"

Maria said "Fine."

Reaching in my pocket, I said, "I'm going to pay for those coats. What's the total? Out of curiosity, how did you know what and how many we needed?"

"Miss DeAngelo called yesterday and told me what she wanted. The clothing had to be here by 11:30 today. Later Mr. DeAngelo called, said to bill him for the coats. Sir, you're not going to pay for them."

Maria saw I was getting a little irritated. "I am going to pay for those coats, not Mr. DeAngelo. I don't want him to pay for them!"

The woman said, "Whatever Mr. DeAngelo wants is the way it is. I cannot accept your money."

Maria gently touched my arm. "He wants to do this. Let him."

As we were walking out, I stopped. Maria, "Thank you. I feel blessed to know you. I know how your dad feels about anyone approaching you. Please keep this between us. I love you with all my heart."

She whispered, "I love you, too, Pauly."

Maria drove in silence to our block. When we stopped, I got out, walked back to the limo and thanked Vince. The guys had already thanked him for the ride and were by the car thanking Maria for the coats. Vince said, "Mr. D wanted it."

I shrugged and walked to Maria. Standing by the door I wanted to reach in, hold and kiss her, but I couldn't. Vince was right behind us, watching. It had nothing to do with fear of Mr. D. It had to do with disrespecting him, something I would never do. Maria looked at me, and understanding, said, "Bye, my love" and drove away.

I handed the money back to my mother and told her everything went great except the store wouldn't let me pay for the coats because Tony insisted on paying for them.

"I knew he wouldn't let you use your money for the coats. That's the way he is."

I went to my room and sat on the bed. My head started to go haywire. The coat deal was done. I didn't care about it anymore. But Maria – 1 couldn't get her out of my head. I relived holding her, and my whole body tingled, experiencing the moment she whispered in my ear that she loved me. I became light-headed and had an overwhelming feeling of happiness. I stretched out on the bed and fell asleep.

# *CHAPTER 4*

I awoke and thought this would be a good time for me to go to the church and talk to the priest. Grabbing my coat, I told Mom where I was going. Once inside the church and looking around, I became a little hesitant, nervous, but I had to find out what was going on.

I walked down the aisle gaping around. I had never seen so many statues and crucifixes in my life. Some guy wearing all black with a white strap around his neck asked if he could help me. I told him I needed to talk to the priest. He asked why. As I started to tell him, he interrupted, saying he was the priest, and knew all about it. We needed to go in back, sit down. He would tell me all he knew.

He was a soft-spoken mick with a typical Irish brogue. In the small office he sat behind a desk motioning me to a chair in front. He started out by telling me his name was Father O'Rourke and asked mine. He knew about my mother and father's experience with the church because the priest that he replaced had told him the story. He told me Father Boyle had resigned his priesthood. Father O'Rourke sat back and told me what he knew, paraphrasing what was said.

"The evening Father Boyle was leaving the parish, the two of us decided to celebrate. Being Irishmen, we were doing it right. … and Father Boyle told me the story."

"Your mother and father came into the church and asked for an audience with the priest. They met with Father Boyle in this very office. Your mother started speaking. This threw Boyle back a little because women usually sat back while men did all the talking. Talking was the man's job – women were supposed to be silent. Your mother began by saying they were Catholic and wanted to have a church wedding. She wanted his blessings and asked what would be involved.

"He told them he could not give his blessings because this was a mistake, a grave error on their part. 'You are a beautiful, smart Italian lady, and he is a dumb Polack,' is what he told her. Your mother's fierce look was an if-looks-could-kill glare.

"Ignoring your mother's scowl, Father Boyle went on to say that they were two different people. He quoted the Bible: '*An oxen with an uneven yoke cannot walk straight.* The two of you cannot walk a straight path. You're different in every way: background, heritage, intelligence, et cetera. Your marriage would never last. In the Catholic Church divorce is not an option. You would live a life of regret and anguish. If you ever brought children into this world, what would they be like?'

"Boyle told me he sat there watching this beautiful woman cry. It was disgraceful! He kept berating her – he enjoyed seeing her anguish. He told me he enjoyed it so much he had an erection.

"Then he said this little woman stood up, wiped her tears with her sleeve, and said, 'Fuck you! You can stick yourself, your church, and Jesus Christ up your ass. I don't believe in any of this anymore, and don't want anything to do with it.' She grabbed your father's hand and they left.

"Somehow the word got out on the street. Father Boyle told me it was a couple of weeks later when a young, fierce-looking man came into the church and asked for him.

"He said, 'I looked into his eyes and it was like looking at stone-cold death. The wop said he had a proposition for me, my choice. I could resign my priesthood and get out of New York, or I could leave the church in a coffin. This was not an idle threat

– this was going to happen. So I told him I would resign. The young man said Good and walked out.'

"The day I arrived, Boyle told me he'd be on his way. He was heading to New Jersey to see what life had to offer. I said, reluctantly, 'Good luck' but thought to myself, *You're an ass*."

Father O'Rourke said, "Paul, that's the story. I don't know if that's what you wanted to hear, but that's what I was told."

I thanked him and left. I went home, told Mom I just finished with the priest at St. Michael's. I kissed her on the forehead, hugged her, and said, "You're a great woman." Knowing my mother, all the time I was gone she worried about what my reaction would be. I guess I was trying to tell her I was OK with it.

I lay on my bed thinking, *That fuckin' priest was so wrong. My mother is going through a period of anguish right now. She feels it will end, and life will be good because she has always loved my father and still loves him, and he her. In life that's all that matters – loving someone and having them love you in return. Everything else is a freebie.*

My mother's spirituality was a big part of her life. She began to explore different religions, teachings, beliefs. She combined them with the Native American belief that God was an energy that permeated everything. She also felt good about many of their beliefs. She excluded man's embellishment and the dogma associated with all the known religions. My mother developed her own religion. She maintained a strong belief and connection to her God. She spent a lot of time talking to me about it; and she made all the sense in the world.

The next morning, I didn't see my father, which was nothing new. My mother made me breakfast. When I got done, I asked her to tell me about Tony DeAngelo. She told me OK she would.

I told her I'd be back. I went into my room for a pack of Lucky Strikes. I lit up a cigarette and went back to the kitchen.

Then as if I got hit with a bolt of lightning, my mother's Italian temper rose up and struck. With a voice that wasn't motherly she flared, "Don't you ever smoke in this house again … and I want you to stop all together."

I walked over to the sink, ran water over the cigarette, and threw it in the trash. I worried I screwed up and she wouldn't tell me about Tony now. Mom sat down. I gave her a sheepish look.

She said, "Only if you promise me you'll quit smoking."

I gave her a half shrug. She knew I wouldn't lie to her.

# *CHAPTER 5*

Mom began, "I had five brothers and a sister. We lived in Naples. My father was Italian aristocracy. His name was Barnardino Dominic deDomenico. He was also *capo-di-tutti-capi* of the Mafia in Italy, that means is he was boss of bosses. My brothers were boss, *consigliere*, under boss, and *caporegime* of a family that controlled the port of Naples, everything in and out. They had their hands in everything: racketeering, extortion, gambling, prostitution, and anything where they could make a quick lira. My father, your grandfather, was receiving tribute from eight other families across Italy. We lived a very affluent life. My father's wealth was unsurpassed, we wanted for nothing.

"As time passed, everything stayed the same except my sister and I, who were the youngest in the family, grew up. My father put out the word that we were unapproachable unless he gave his permission. If you were not at least a *caporegime* or in today's Mafia, a made-man, you shouldn't even ask for permission. A woman's role in the Italian society was to bear children, preferably sons. Once the childbearing time ended, it was a life of servitude, nothing more.

"One day a young man came to our house and asked my father for a job. My father gave him work as a gardener and let him live in a shack a little way from the main house. There were times I would look out the window and see him. On occasion we would look into each other's eyes until he looked away and continued his work. This went on for a while until one night I left the house while everybody was sleeping and went to the shack. He was flabbergasted by my presence and couldn't speak. I told him, 'My name is Seravina.'

"He finally spoke and said, 'My name is Mateo DeAngelo.'

"We talked for a while, then I took his hand and I had him hold me in a corner of the shack on the floor. We stayed that way till I got up and went back to the house. There was something about him I liked. He was gentle, courteous, caring, and respectful – nothing like the *Mafiosi* that I was accustomed to seeing at the house.

"Time was moving fast. I yearned for Mateo, but rather than take the risk of being caught and his losing his life, I stayed away. One summer night my father had all his sons come to the house for dinner to talk about a business problem. All the men were sitting at the dining room table drinking wine and talking. My mother told me she was ready to serve and sent me to ask my father if it was OK. When I entered the dining room, everyone stopped talking. I told my father that I was sorry to disturb him, but mother told me to announce that dinner would be served when he cared to eat.

" 'Thank you. We'll eat now.' I nodded and went back to the kitchen to help my mother and sister serve dinner.

"Suddenly it sounded like lightning was striking the house many times. My sister got really scared. My mother grabbed both of us and shoved us into a corner cupboard on the floor, and she lay over the top of us. We didn't make a sound, just lay there. After a while somebody walked into the kitchen and then left. It sounded like footsteps were leaving the house. It was very quiet, and we stayed in the corner.

"The back door flew open. Mateo entered the kitchen; we came out of the cupboard. Mateo told my mother that he saw a mob of guys break into the house, and then he heard the shotgun blasts. He had not looked yet but suspected the master and her sons were dead.

" 'We need to leave. We can all go to my shack and I'll come back.'

"My mother said OK, but she was going to come back with him. My mother wanted to make sure Mateo's shack was safe for my sister and me.

"On the voyage to America, Mother told me how wonderful Mateo was. All he wanted was for us to be protected. He was a great help to her after they left my sister and me in the shack. She told me what happened when they went back to the house.

"They walked into the dining room. My father and brothers were lying on the floor in puddles of blood. They were dead.

"She took Mateo by the arm and led him into Dominic's study. She had Mateo move a wall cabinet aside, then remove a false wall. Glowing back at them were stacks of small gold bars. She told Mateo to fill the two satchels that were sitting in the corner. She went to the kitchen and found a large, empty bag used for flour. She and Mateo began filling the bag with bars. When the satchels and the bag were full, she told Mateo to fill his pockets.

"Mother went to her room and emptied a large trunk that was at the foot of the bed. She put three blankets and some of our clothes in the trunk. She took the trunk to Mateo and asked him to remove the contents, fill it with the rest of the gold, then replace the clothing and blankets. She returned to her room, grabbed two corsets, and went back to the study. As Mateo was finishing, she threw the corsets in the trunk.

"She had Mateo replace the wall and move the cabinet back. She picked up a satchel in each hand. The strength of sturdy Italian peasants was in her blood. She asked Mateo if he could lift the trunk, set it on his shoulder and lift the flour bag. Mateo tried. The trunk wasn't a problem, but the flour bag was too heavy. She told Mateo they would carry what they had to his shack, and that Mateo would return with a wheelbarrow for the bag. When Mateo got back to the shack they were done.

"My sister and I were sitting on the bunk bed. Mother sat on a chair and Mateo sat on the trunk. Mateo told mother he overheard the men talking as they were leaving the house. 'They sounded like Sicilians. After they killed the patron and sons, they probably spent the night killing all the bosses and their families. By the next day the Sicilians will control families in Italy and Sicily. It is likely they will be back to kill you because they fear that someday your sons would come at them for vendetta.'

"Mother agreed with everything Mateo said. She had a plan to protect her daughters. She asked Mateo to go back to the house, and in Dominic's desk drawer he would find a lot of lira notes. 'Take them and go to the port. Buy three steerage tickets on a ship leaving for America.' Her plan was that she and the girls would leave for America as soon as possible, Mateo would follow later.

"From a list Mother would give him, Mateo would load his buggy with things from the house. He was to find a carpenter to build a shipping crate. Once the crate was packed, he'd take it to the port, pay for the freight and his ticket with the remaining lire from Dominic's drawer. Eventually we'd all be together to start a new life.

"Mateo though the plan was good. Before he left, he asked permission to speak to me. Mateo ask me to step outside. Once outside, Mateo took me into his arms, hugged and kissed me. 'We'll be together soon. I love you and I'll take care of you for the rest of your life.' I told him I loved him and always had.

"Mateo left for the port, and I went back to the shack. Mother had us take the clothes and blankets out of the trunk, fill the trunk with bars from the flour bag until we couldn't lift the trunk, and then replace the blankets and clothes. Gold bars from the flour bag were stitched into the corsets. Mother did the same. Whatever gold remained in the bag was put under the bed for Mateo.

"Back from the port, Mateo gave my mother the tickets and the leftover lire. She said she didn't know how she'd change the gold to American money yet, but it would be easy to change Italian lire notes to American money. Mateo had a friend who was a seaman on the ship we were going on. He'd ask his friend to help us on the trip, and then get in touch with his older brother Tony. Tony would help us exchange the gold.

"Mateo put the two satchels in the trunk, loaded the trunk into the buggy, then helped me and my sister onto the back. My mother rode on the seat with Mateo. When we got to the ship, Mateo found his friend.

"My mother, sister and I presented our tickets, and then followed Mateo who was carrying the trunk, following his friend to the steerage. When we got there Mateo introduced us to his friend who was very nice.

"Mateo asked me to step outside, so he could say good-bye. As soon as we were out of everybody's sight, he kissed me very passionately. He said, 'We'll be together soon. Please be very careful.'

"I answered, 'I will, and you be careful. *Ciao*.'"

# CHAPTER 6

"When we arrived in America, Mateo's friend helped us depart the ship and took us and our things to an apartment. It was small and dirty, in a poor, run-down neighborhood. He told my mother it'd be the best place for us now – we would be hidden. The houses separated a poor immigrant Italian neighborhood on one side from a poor Jewish neighborhood on the other. He thought that my sister should shop and do whatever we need to in the Italian neighborhood because she was the least recognizable. After a while, once we learned to speak English, we could shop in the Jewish neighborhood and avoid the Italian neighborhood. He told us he'd contact Mateo's brother, who'd help us with anything we needed and look after us. Mother told him she didn't know how to thank him for all that he had done. He told her Mateo's friendship was thanks enough.

"We cleaned the apartment. My sister shopped, and we waited for Mateo's brother and then Mateo, so we could begin a life.

"It was a while before Tony became involved in our lives. Word came to Tony from Italy that Mateo had been killed by the same Sicilians who killed my father and brothers. Tony was consumed with grief, anger and hatred. He raged, spending days and nights yelling and cursing, and beating walls with his fists. And then he stopped, as if someone or something stopped him. He began to think about what the friend of Mateo told him, what Mateo wanted him to do. He needed to make arrangements to exchange the gold for cash. He wouldn't be cheated or taken advantage of! He needed to protect us and guard me with his life. He felt that doing what Mateo wanted of him was a tribute to his brother. Being close to the one that was Mateo's love would bring him close to Mateo. He also knew helping and protecting us would take his mind off what was burning in him, and he could become less of a monster.

"Tony wanted to make the gold arrangements first before seeing us. He needed to be able to discuss it with my mother to get her approval. He went to south Manhattan and made discreet inquiries into buying and selling gold. All the inquires pointed to a Polish-German Jew. He sought out the Jew – he didn't have a problem dealing with Jews. He felt in this situation it probably would be the best, but he needed to find out as much as he could about this man to determine for himself if he was honest. If he was an honest man, he wouldn't take advantage of them.

"In the Jew's apartment, he started, 'My name is Tony DeAngelo and your name is?'

"The reply was, 'Hyman Finkelstein.'

"Tony said, 'I have a business proposition for you that will be very lucrative. But first I want to know all about you.'

"Hyman shook his head yes, sat back and started to talk. As he spoke, Tony could see pain in his face and eyes, eyes that had seen hell. Hyman told Tony of his childhood in Poland, and that when he was old enough, he went to Frankfurt, Germany to learn the jewelry trade in the Jewish community. At the same time a wealthy family moved to Frankfurt from Switzerland. The father had bought a bank that was having problems, turned the bank around, and was prospering.

" 'I came upon a deal for diamonds that was 40% below wholesale. I looked at it as an opportunity to finance my own jewelry business. I could wholesale some and keep the rest for retail. I went to see the banker; we got along well.'

" 'The banker extended me the loan and invited me to dinner. The banker was playing matchmaker with me and his daughter. His daughter was a beautiful blonde-haired, Aryan-featured girl.

The banker and his daughter were also Jews. It worked. After some time, courting, we were married. My business was prospering. In time, we had two daughters. As the two girls got older, they mirrored their mother. It was in the genes. Then Hitler and the Nazi movement became very big in Frankfurt. The SS took over the bank and killed my father-in-law.

" 'Almost simultaneously the SS invaded the jewelry store. They overpowered me, bound me, and forced me to take them to my home. Some of the SS took everything out of the store, killed the clerks, and burned the store. Others put me in a corner of the master bedroom, punched me several times, and I fell to the floor, dazed. The SS brought my two daughters and my wife into the room. They tore their clothes off. One by one they took turns raping the girls. They were young girls, virgins. The rapes were brutal. They had my wife bent at the waist. One of them began to do her from the back. Another grabbed her head and told her to open her mouth. He put his penis in her mouth and forced his body against her head. She was choking. After a while he pulled out, reached under her and began squeezing her breast. She started screaming, then fainted. They let her fall to the floor.

" 'Then they shot and killed her and my two daughters. As they came to kill me, they saw what looked like a body in a zombie state. The officer said, 'Leave him. He's no longer a man … he has no soul.' After two days, I freed myself, kissed my wife and daughters, and left.

" 'The Jewish community helped me get to America, and then the community in America took me in and nursed me for a year. I became a middleman between Jews who brought jewelry and gold here and buyers. I've been doing this for some time now and I can help you.'

"Tony reached over and hugged Hyman. Their individual pain bonded them and Tony felt compelled to hold Hyman.

When they stepped back he said, 'Good, we will do this. I will contact you.' He left to go to our apartment, and Hyman went for a walk.

"Tony told me the story Hyman told him about your father. Hyman was walking, staring at the sidewalk, thinking how much he missed his beautiful wife and daughters. Walking toward Hyman with his face down was this little boy. The two collided. The boy apologized in Polish and Hyman acknowledged his apology in Polish. The boy looked up and said he had been looking for someone who spoke his language. He had just arrived in this country and needed food and water. He was sick because he hadn't had anything to eat in days. Hyman told the boy to follow him.

"As they were walking to Hyman's apartment, Hyman realized the grief he brought upon himself telling his story gave him a strong feeling for this boy in need. He would help him. Once inside his apartment Hyman gave the boy water and told him to drink slowly, a sip at a time. He heated up leftover chicken soup and told the boy to eat slowly. Hyman sat beside the boy and asked if he was a Jew. The boy said no, he didn't know what a Jew was.

" 'No matter. If you want, you can stay with me, and I will take care of you.'

"The next day Hyman took the boy to Ellis Island. They stood in a long line for hours before they finally reached the front desk. Hyman told the uniformed man the boy needed citizenship. The man took a form from a large stack, picked up pen, said, 'Name?'

"Hyman asked the boy in Polish, the boy responded then Hyman repeated the name several times. The exasperated official said he didn't get it. 'The hell with this. I'm hungry, I'm tired and don't want to put up with this shit.' To control his impatience, he stared out a grimy window. The passersby inspired him, 'I've got it! Your name is going to be Walker.' For the first name, he shuffled through some finished forms, then said, 'Nathan - your given name will be Nathan.'

"The official would answer the questions on the form for them. He looked at Hyman for approval, Hyman shook his head yes. The man filled out a large form and a smaller one. He handed the forms to Hyman and told him to sign Nathan Walker at the bottom of each. Hyman did and gave it back to him. He stamped both forms and handed the small form to the boy. 'Congratulations, Nathan Walker. You are a legal resident.' Hyman told the boy what the man said, and the boy smiled. It was the first time he had seen him smile.

"Tony told me about meeting us for the first time. I told him how we felt. When we opened the door, we saw this very muscular Italian young man. With a square chin and a face that looked as though it had been chiseled out of stone, he was a fierce-looking man. We were afraid till he introduced himself. We were so glad, so relieved to see him. Tony later told me that he looked at me and thought to himself, *This girl is beautiful. She's an angel. Someone you could hold in your arms and never let go.* He understood how Mateo could love me.

"Tony told us about Hyman, that he felt he was the one to help with the gold exchange. He suggested that we try him, and if he didn't work out, he would take care of him and find someone else. If we agreed, he would bring Hyman by the next day to discuss the details.

"Focusing on me, Tony paused then quickly his voice choked up. 'Mateo ... Mateo was murdered in your home by the same mob that killed your father and brothers.'

"I screamed. Tears poured down my face. I doubled over, clutching my body, with a soul wrenching pain. Tony began to cry, covered his face with his hands. Mother put her arms around both of us, and Sis did the same.

"After the tears tapered, Tony said he would be back tomorrow. Then Tony told us he would protect us and insure that no harm would come to us. He looked at me and told me he would protect me and those close to me from a distance for the rest of his life and, if need be, give his life for me.

"The next day Tony brought Hyman and Nathan. After introductions Mother, Hyman and Tony went to a corner to talk.

"Because of the language barrier, we sat in silence, Sis on her bed, and Nathan and I on the floor in a corner. Nathan would look at me, and then look away. I would glance at him, then look away. Nathan wondered why I had so much sadness in my eyes. I thought Nathan looked like one of those Jewish refugees: drawn, thin, pale – almost like the walking dead.

"Tony told me Mother felt good about his choice to have Hyman handle the gold. She gave Hyman a bar. Hyman and Nathan left.

"Hyman and Nathan went home. After supper, Hyman told Nathan that he was going to teach him English. He needed to learn how to be able to talk to people in America. Hyman pointed at an object, said the word in Polish, then English. He had Nathan say the English word until he had it right. Hyman would have him repeat both words over and over. They did this day and night for months, adding descriptions to the objects. The more he learned, the easier it became.

"Nathan asked Hyman if he could do what they were doing with the girl in the apartment, so he could talk to her one day. Hyman thought that was good, and they could do it with everyone who wanted to learn. He would find someone who spoke Italian and English. He was thinking a lady. He wouldn't have to pay her much.

"On the next scheduled visit, Hyman brought Nathan and an Italian lady. With the lady interpreting, Hyman started talking to mother. The weather has been nice – Mother knew he was talking about gold and not the weather. She answered 'Yes.' Hyman asked if she was enjoying the weather so far. She answered 'Yes.'

"Then Hyman told her about his plan to teach everyone English. He told her, as he did Nathan, 'You will need to speak English to be able to talk to people in America.'

"Hyman had everyone seated on the bed, with Nathan standing in front, and the lady by his side. Nathan was going to teach us English the same way Hyman taught him. Nathan would repeat what he learned. It was good for him, and teaching would bring him out.

"Mother thanked Hyman and asked if the lessons could continue. Hyman said until everyone could speak English, or until she wanted him to stop. Time passed. Everything was going well. On one of the scheduled visits mother got Hyman aside and gave him an envelope and said in broken English in the envelope is $1,000. She told him $500 was his, the other $500 was hers, and that he should invest their money, so they could start making money on money.

"Hyman asked Tony if he wanted to put $500 in, and he would invest the money as a lump sum. As time went on, learning English became easier and easier. Hyman enrolled Nathan in public school and set his scheduled visits for late afternoon. Nathan would be talking to me and Sis, while Hyman would talk to Mother about all kinds of things. She enjoyed his knowledge and the gentleness of his manner.

"Tony would visit to ensure that everybody was all right, and to find out how I was getting along. He noticed that I seemed to be comfortable talking to Nathan. Hyman began referring to mother as DD, shortened from Mrs. DeDomenico. She liked it. I became Sera instead of Seravina and Sis was Jenny. We liked Americanizing our names."

My mother finished her story. I looked around at the kitchen where we sat and thought, *What the fuck? I've never heard any of this shit before.* It really opened my eyes.

# *CHAPTER 7*

It seemed time was moving very fast. I was a senior in high school, starting to think about my future. My father had been sober for a while now. He was working. My mother was happy. I missed Maria and wanted to see her so badly. I was miserable

One day I went to work as usual and said, "Good afternoon, Mr. D."

He waved me to his table. "Pauly, it's time you and I talked." I thought I could find out how he knew so much about me.

"I'll tell you about myself and my business. I'll have Vince pick you up at your place Saturday at two o'clock. We can talk while you have dinner with us."

The only thing I could think about was that I would see Maria. The week both dragged and went quickly. On Friday when I walked in, Mr. D called me over. "Forget about the cleaning today. I want to take you on a tour of this place since we're going to be talking tomorrow."

He walked up to what looked like a closet. He stepped inside, pushed on the back wall. It opened! I followed him. My immediate reaction was: *holy shit, this is something different.* It was a very large room.  There were at least twenty guys sitting at desks, talking on phones. On the walls surrounding the open area were glass-enclosed offices with guys sitting at desks.

"Mr. D, there have to be 30 or 40 guys in here, and I never saw any of them. They sure as shit don't live in here. How did they get here?"

He told me he owned all the property, street to street, around the bar. He had his construction company build a large metal building and attach it to the bar and a concrete parking lot. The sign on the building reads Muraso Distributing. Everyone here comes and goes through the Muraso building.

We walked over to one of the offices. He opened the door and introduced me to the gentleman seated behind the desk. We exchanged greetings. When we walked out he told me that was his *consigliere*. Mr. D. motioned to the glass offices and said, "These are *caporegime*. Each one controls one of our businesses. They are all made-men." He would explain everything to me to-morrow. We continued down a hall and he opened a door, to a dining room for everyone. He pointed to a door on the opposite wall and said this is the head. Further down was a conference room. The last door was his office. I looked in and thought this was some magnificent room.

We went back to the bar, Mr. D to his usual spot. I picked up the bag for Gary and did my run. When I got back and was sitting at the table eating, I realized why the kitchen in this little bar and grill was so busy. They were feeding everybody, and it was hard to believe how good the food was.

The next day I got up, showered, got dressed in the nicest clothes I had, and sat around pushing time. After a while my mother hollered lunch was ready. In the kitchen my father and brother were sitting at the table. I said "Hi" and sat down. My father was seated opposite me; my brother was sitting to my right, and my mother was going to sit to my left. I was sitting there looking at my father, and my brother started his putting me down, pulling my chain, instigating a fight. I said to myself I had enough of his crap. I turned to him and cheerfully said, "*Non rompermi 1 coglioni stronzol.*" I turned to my father and assured him, "It wasn't bad; it was a greeting."

I looked at my mom who was out of sight of my father. She was shaking her head. I gave her an I'm-sorry look and she shrugged. I had told my brother to stop breaking my balls and called him a piece of shit. I knew he didn't understand Italian – but I wished he did.

I didn't know why my brother had to put me down in front of my parents. I thought it was his way of showing my parents he was better than me, and his way of getting their approval by showing them a bad side of me. There were probably a hundred reasons; most important was that he was just fuckin' stupid.

I was sitting there looking at my father, and I was wondering if he liked me or disliked me. He never said, and I couldn't read him. I started thinking: *What happened to you? You were the strongest man in the world to me when I was young.*

He once told us about his life.

His parents were peasants in a small village on the Polish-Russian border. His father was a carpenter, his mother cleaned fish, and he had a sister one year older. They played together constantly. Aside from being brother and sister, they were best friends. They slept in the same bed in a tiny room. His sister slept facing the wall and he slept on the outside. In the middle of the night, when she had to go to the bathroom, she would climb over his feet to get out of the bed. Unintentionally she'd wake him. He'd get dressed and escort her to the outhouse. He wasn't told to do it but wanted to do it to make sure she was all right.

When he was ten years old, the family endured a severe winter, and soon after his father and sister died. He was grief stricken. He became moody and depressed, missed his other half. His mother came up with the idea that he should go to America, earn money, and bring her to America. She thought he needed to get away.

Somehow, he made his way to a port and stowed away on a ship going to America. He arrived in the United States malnourished, dehydrated and very sick. He got off the ship and started walking. He came upon some guy and asked where he could get water. The man didn't understand him, probably thought he was begging for money, so he pushed him away. He kept walking, staring at the ground. He felt terrible, thought there was no more hope, and just wanted his life to end. Accidentally he bumped into someone. He apologized. The man replied in Polish! After they spoke for a couple of minutes, the man took him in and cared for him. They developed almost a father-son relationship which lasted for many years.

I was thinking back about what my father had told us and thought what balls he had. I couldn't do what he did and didn't think anyone else could. When he left home, and crossed the Atlantic as a stowaway, he was only a kid, an eleven-year old kid. I looked at him and thought I truly loved him.

I ate some of the spaghetti and meat sauce my mother prepared, told them I had to talk to the man I worked for, and would probably be home late. Downstairs I waited only a while until Vince showed up in the Lincoln. I got in and said, "Hi Vince."

"Hello Pauly, how you doin'?"

That was a first. We made some small talk, and before I knew it we were in front of Mr. D's home. I got out and Vince took off. I walked up to the door and knocked. Some guy opened the door, said hello, and motioned me in. I was struck by how this modest-looking home could look like a classy mansion inside.

Then I heard, "Pauly, it's good to see you. I'm glad you could make it. Come over here."

"Good afternoon, Mr. D."

"In my home I'm Tony. Forget the Mr. D. Sit down. I need to get something out of the way." He told me he didn't get to where he is by having a blind eye. "I see and know everything that goes on around me."

*Oh shit, I'm fucked. That's what this is all about.*

He continued, "From now on you have my permission to talk and get close to Maria. The no-approach is off for you."

I stood there, numb. *This must be a dream, but if it's real, it's the best thing that has ever happened to me.* "Thank you, Tony. I won't disappoint you, and would you mind if I talked to Maria for a minute?"

Tony hollered out, "Maria, come down here."

Maria walked down the stairs and stood at the bottom. I got up, guided her to a hallway, and told her that her father gave me permission to approach her. She said she knew. I kissed her and said, "I love you with all my heart."

"And I you."

We stood silently holding each other. I told Maria I had to get back and hoped we could spend some time together later. I walked back to Tony and thanked him. We were sitting in an alcove on the most comfortable leather chairs I had ever sat in. I noticed that on the wall were two large framed pictures of my spectacularly beautiful Maria, each in a slightly different pose and a different dress. I asked Tony why he had two pictures of Maria hanging on the wall.

"The one on your left was my wife; the one on the right is Maria."

I sat there, staring at the pictures.

"I want to tell you about my business – all of it, and to tell you about my plan. If you agree with my plan, that would be good. I am the boss of a large Mafia family. There are five families in New York City; each control a borough. Mine is the strongest and most diversified. The other families are not like us. Above me in the whole organization is a *capo-di-tutti-capi*, the same as your grandfather was in Italy. Our *capo* handles payoffs to the state and city officials. He does payoffs where it does good for all the families. Each family does their own where it directly affects them.

"I pay off the police captain of the precinct where you make your run. I don't know why that cop stopped you. They all knew about you and were told to leave you alone. I wanted to look into it for two reasons. First, I pay these fuckin' micks a lot of money not to bother you, Gary, and some other things I have going on there. Second, where did this cop get off saying to you, 'Tell Mr. D hello.' I had a *consigliere* that is not a made-man talk to him. The cop is a fool with a wife and two little kids. If it wasn't for those kids, the cop would have had an accident and been dead. Because of those two kids, he's not on the force any longer and works in some company."

"Back to the *capo*. He enforces and governs our code. The Mafia code is our way of life. An exception can be made with the approval of the *capo*. He mediates problems between families but has no power over the families. He advises the families on matters that affect our business, and he resolves disputes. The five bosses take orders from no one. We report to no one; we are responsible for our own family.

"I will get an exception to the code from the *capo*. It used to say a made-man had to be full-blooded Italian. It now says as long as your father is Italian. With your grandfather and your mother's brothers, I won't have a problem with an exception."

"This is as good a time as any for me to explain our code. The code is simply rules that govern our way of life and protect us. Over the years there have been additions; the code has grown. I'll tell you about the parts that are meaningful, so you can get the idea."

"The code pertains to made-men only. You cannot introduce yourself or enter into a conversation with another made-man directly. There must be a third party who can verify who each of you are. You can never be seen with or talk to a cop. You cannot be a part of a family if a relative, no matter how distant, is a cop. You must obey *omerta* – silence. You cannot discuss anything that happens or anything about the family with outsiders. If you do, you will be killed. You must never look at another man's wife. You must treat wives with respect. You must always be available to the family, even when your wife is giving birth. You cannot harm or kill another made-man. You cannot go to pubs, bars, or night clubs unless owned by your family. You cannot have facial hair. You cannot engage in any form of lurid sex or be serviced by a prostitute. The code is simple: it is Mafia first – before God, country and self."

"We are having good times right now, but I feel that will change, and we must be ready for the changes. The Sicilians will try to take over the families, which will result in wars that will hurt everyone. The government will try to crack down on crime to show the people they are doing something. The papers will build it up and make more of it than it is. The Sicilians will take over New York. There won't be a Mafia in New York City – it will be La Cosa Nostra.

"The Sicilians are a stupid, brutal people bent on power and control. They are the scum of Italy. I will not let anyone in my family get hurt. I will negotiate with the other Mafia families to buy my businesses. If they choose to join in with the Sicilians or fight them, that will be their business, not mine.

"I am involved with a very large financial business that has nothing to do with the family. I plan to move it to Vegas. My good friend Hyman started it. I plan on your mother and father joining Hyman in Vegas and being a part of the business. I plan to move the *famiglia* to Las Vegas and start over. I will also satisfy my vendetta against the Sicilian family that killed my brother and your grandfather and your uncles.

"I want to see what kind of man you are and will become. I know right now you are street smart and have good common sense. I want to take that further. When we move to Vegas, I want you by my side, and we will run it together. For now, I want you to work at a salvage yard in the Bronx. You will start at the bottom. Very hard physical work, it will break your balls. I want to see what kind of man it makes of you. At some point, we will go through the ritual of making you a made-man, and you will have to make your bones. Tell me what you think. Is this something you would want to get involved with?"

I knew that making your bones is killing someone who is hurting the family. I wanted into this *famiglia* for real. I could follow this code. I said, "You're giving me my future. You're giving me something that most guys would give their left nut for. I think it's fantastic. Yes, I want to more than anything. I want to do this."

Tony reached over, kissed me on the cheek and said, "Thank you."

I didn't know what to say or do. I just sat there. Finally, I said, "Tony, before you continue, I have something that's been bugging me. A few years ago, we were talking, and we got interrupted by a call from Mr. G, then you and the guys left. The next day I saw a headline in the *Post* 'Mafioso killed'. Was that you?"

"Yeah, and I'll tell you about it. Mr. G is Vito Genovese. He is boss in Queens. He said he had spoken to the *capo* and got an exemption to the code to talk to me and put a hit on Stinzano, a made-man. The only thing is, it had to come from another family and that no one was to know who."

Then he told me the story Vito told him. "Stinzano and his daughter were engaged to be married. She was this warm, caring, gentle girl. She was also a good Catholic, and a virgin who was not going to do anything till after marriage. Stinzano was a good kid. He respected and cared for her; they were a good match. They were engaged for a while. How or why I don't know, Stinzano got into drugs. Out of the blue one day he beat her and raped her. When Vito found out about it, she begged and pleaded with him not to hurt him. He said he would not.

"Stinzano was thinking that because he is a made-man, our code wouldn't allow Vito to bump him off, because the code is important to him. Vito felt this bastard is not going to get away with it. He will have his vendetta, he will enjoy seeing him dead, and he will piss on him in his coffin. He said to me, 'My friend, I need a favor from you.' I told him, 'You have it, wouldn't be a problem.' Veto thanked me and said he would be indebted to me.

"We found Stinzano in a coke house in Queens. Took him out, bound him and threw him in the trunk. In the condition he was in, it was easy. We drove past a market, and Joey ran in and bought a fish, and then we drove to one of our auto salvage yards in Brooklyn. We laid him out on the hood of a car. I shoved a rag in his mouth and said, 'This is for someone very special, you fucking freak' and spit a glam in his face. Carmine cut his trousers, and then sliced off his dick and balls. He shoved both down his throat. Stinzano was dead.

"The fish in the crotch is symbolic. It means he now swims with fishes. That's kinda a hard story to hear, but you have to believe me, he deserved it. I don't care how screwed up someone is, there is no reason to do what he did."

Tony paused, then continued speaking. "Since I mentioned auto salvage to you, I'll tell you about our auto salvage business. We have three yards, one in Brooklyn and two in the Bronx. They ship their car bodies and ferrous steel to our processing plant on Bruckner Boulevard in the Bronx. We can load barges from there. We also have a large metals recycling plant in the Bronx where we reclaim the lead from batteries, and we clean radiators for brass and copper cores. We recycle all of the metals and sell trailer loads to smelters. We also have two yards in Queens. We salvage parts and sell them to body shops, auto repair shops, and to the public.

"We pay off three guys from the top three auto insurance carriers responsible for the disposal of totaled autos. We acquire titles and wrecks for right money – almost no money. We pay off two cops who run the impound yards in the Bronx and Brooklyn. The yards hold an auction for abandoned cars that have been impounded for more than sixty days. By law the auction must be posted and open to the public. We have worked out a way to get around it. We are the only bidder at the auction. We also own two large used car dealerships. The whole thing is a big money maker and it gives us a way to wash money."

I didn't know what he meant by that, but I didn't say anything.

"Let's take a break. Would you like something to drink? What would you like? We have everything."

If I asked for wine, beer or booze, I'd probably fall asleep while he was talking to me. I didn't feel like a soda so asked for water.

"How about I have Maria join you on the back patio? I'll have someone bring you out a couple of iced teas and the two of you can talk for a while."

"Thank you. That sounds better than water."

In a couple of minutes Maria arrived on the patio with the tea. She put the glasses on the table and slid into my arms. I put one hand on her cheek, the other on the back of her head, and I kissed her, a beautiful kiss. I wasn't an experienced kisser. I never had much of an opportunity to kiss. We remained in the embrace, enjoying the moment.

I had a hard-on. If I came, I would stain my pants and be embarrassed to hell. I pulled back a bit and gazed at her face. Gorgeous. Radiant. Her eyes were closed, and her expression said she was experiencing the greatest pleasure in the world. "My beautiful Maria, I love you so much."

She opened her eyes, blankly stared at me, then said, "I love you. I'm sorry, but I have to go now. I'll see you later."

I picked up my glass of iced tea and went inside. Putting my glass on the end table, I sat down opposite Tony. He was smoking a bent little cigar and asked if I wanted to join him smoking a rope.

"No thanks, but if you have a cigarette." I had heard that the first time you smoke a Dinobli cigar, you turn green and puke your brains out. This wasn't the time or place for me. Tony got me a pack of cigarettes. I lit one, sat back, and listened.

Tony started by telling me that the family was a large family. "We have our hands in many things, some legit and some not so. If something gets shut down, it won't hurt the family. We are all over the city. We pay a tribute to each of the other families for their protection and their permission to operate in their borough.

"Shit, I almost forgot – I bought you a Mercury. It's not brand new, or flashy, but it's a good car. I titled and registered it in your name and have insurance in your name. Tomorrow

Vince will pick you up and teach you how to drive it, and then take you for a driver's license."

I thanked him.

"When we walked in the back, and you saw the bull pen. Those guys are taking numbers and booking bets from a select clientele across the country. And we are middling bets from Vegas. It's really a fast-moving, hectic place. We also control the ports of New York, everything in and out. We are the Longshoremen's Union. We are also the Teamsters Union. We control the loading and offloading of the ships. A lot of it is in ocean-going containers.

"We have four construction and two asphalt companies. The construction and the asphalt companies do all the city-let contracts. There's a cement plant in the Bronx and an asphalt plant in Brooklyn and the Bronx. We also deal in a lot of other things that we'll get into. I am into a legit business that cannot be tracked back to the family. I'm a one-third owner of a corporation, SHT, Inc. It's an umbrella corporation. Under the umbrella is Sehyto Investments, Inc. and Sehyto Holding, Inc., which owns a lot of companies and is a major stockholder in more than I can count. None of them have a connection to the family in any way.

"We are also Amalgamated Insurance, Inc., the insurance carrier for the unions, the bonding agent for the construction contracts, and the insurer for the companies. It also insures ocean and land freight. It's a fully-- rounded insurance company, large in its field. The corporation was started years ago by Hyman as a way for DD, himself, an' me to make money on money. After your grandmother died, Hyman made your mother a one-third share owner, and Jenny and your father limited stock holders. Today, by himself, Hyman has built a multimillion dollar financial empire.

"It was by chance I was sitting at a table in the grill when you came in to ask me for a job. Since then I have always managed to be there only when you came to work. I liked 'Good afternoon, Mr. D'. I liked seeing you. Your mother and my younger brother Mateo were very much in love in Italy. He was killed before he could join her in America. I vowed I would take care of your mother for the rest of my life. When you came along, you kinda fell in with that. I have known you all your life. Your mother is a very wealthy woman. She doesn't know it. I will make your mother aware of her wealth when I feel your family is in order and after I have a long talk with your father."

# *CHAPTER 8*

"Hyman Finkelstein, is the man who took your father in when he came to this country, gave him anything he wanted. Took care of him, educated him, Americanized him and made sure he grew up right. Your father looked at him to be his teacher, his mentor, his father, and his god. Your father followed in Hyman's footsteps. Hyman dealt mostly with Jews, your father dealt with the Irish and Italians. Your father looked to Hyman for advice, and each success your father had gave Hyman joy.

"Hyman told me the story. Your father came upon a deal where he could make a lot of money. He needed a lot of money that he didn't have. Your mother and father were courting. They developed a love that was very strong. Your mother's appearance changed. The grief-stricken look disappeared, replaced by a glow about her that made her look even more beautiful.

"Your father was not uncomfortable in asking his future mother-in-law to invest in him. Sera, Hyman and DD sat down with Nathan and discussed the deal. Your father wound up borrowing $200,000 with the promise to repay with interest. DD gave your father everything they had, and Hyman made up the difference.

"I was excluded from it all, probably because I didn't approve of your father with Sera.  If he was Italian, I would have. I don't know what went wrong with your father's deal. Maybe he was conned or maybe it was just circumstances that happened, but your father lost all the money. No one would ever tell me what happened. I was told not to do anything to Nathan and to stay out of it.

"Hyman told me that Nathan came home, sat Hyman down, and told him everything. Nathan promised that if it takes him all of his life, he would repay him. And with that he began crying. Hyman held Nathan and told him to calm down. Money wasn't a big deal to him and things like that happen.

Hyman advised Nathan to tell DD what happened. He didn't think she would take it well. He told your father that although DD is very intelligent – exceptionally perceptive, clear-headed, quick-witted, it is dangerous to deceive an Italian woman. She becomes a fierce animal – vicious. And DD would feel defrauded, swindled. Hyman cherished DD's friendship and he would help your father repay DD. Your father was not to tell DD that any money came from Hyman. I loaned Hyman the money to give to your father.

"Hyman went with your father to tell DD and give her part of her money back. She reacted as Hyman expected, violently. She told Nathan never to set foot in her house again, never to see or speak to Sera again. If he went against her, she would have him killed. Nathan handed her the money and left, a broken man. Hyman tried to comfort DD, then said good-bye to everyone.

"Sera did not say anything to her mother in front of Nathan or Hyman out of respect for her. When they were alone, Sera told her mother she knew how she felt, but she was wrong in the way she handled it. Nathan didn't intentionally want to hurt her, and he would repay her. Sera said when the loan was repaid, she was going to marry Nathan. DD didn't say anything.

"One-day Hyman told Nathan he had heard through the Polish community that Nathan's mother had passed away. Nathan was distraught over the news. He could have brought her to America, but was so caught with everything, he waited…and now it was too late. He felt such gilt. Added to his failure with the business and his isolation from Sera, Nathan was disheartened with life.

"The next time Hyman stopped by to visit, he brought duplicate sheets of paper that had the amount Nathan owed her and the payments. Handing DD some money, he asked her to initial each payment, so they could keep track and there would be no questions. DD agreed and hugged Hyman. It was the first hug in all the years. It was her way of saying she was sorry. Hyman felt relieved. He had been so afraid that what had happened would end their friendship.

"After several visits, DD asked Hyman to bring Nathan on the next visit. Nathan was overjoyed transformed into his old self. At the apartment DD greeted both with a hug."

# *CHAPTER 9*

"One day by chance I was visiting DD when Hyman was there. I asked for their advice. I had been made boss of the Bronx *famiglia* and didn't like the way things were done. Racketeering, extortion, prostitution, and all the hardass shit were old school and penny ante. I wanted to have us do things that were big bucks."

"DD, your grandmother, started telling me about your grandfather. He and your uncles controlled the ports of Naples. They were paid for every ship that docked and every ship that departed. They were paid to unload and store freight, and then load freight onto carriers. They were paid to load ships and fuel ships. They were making lots of lire while the people that worked for them made a pittance but were happy to get something.

"The port of New York is one of the largest ports in this world. The shipping companies control their own docks. If someone was to get the shipping companies out of the dock business and organize the whole port, they would make a lot of money. Hyman suggested I start with one line. Make them a proposition they wouldn't be able to refuse, then acquire one after another until I had them all. Taking control of the splintered Longshoremen's and Teamster's unions would be good.

"Hyman pointed out there was a lot of home building going on in Long Island. The City would have to let contracts for streets, sidewalks, sewer and storm drain work. The City needed to have the east and west side drives widened, approaches to the bridges widened. There was probably twenty years of work, and there was not a company big enough to take it on.

"I thanked them for their advice and decided that was the direction I was going in. I also wanted to get into the auto salvage and waste business. I began building my *famiglia* by finding smart guys to work for me. Slowly we started businesses; we acquired businesses; we took over businesses. We did whatever it took to build what we have now.

"Monday at eight in the morning I want you to start working at the Beacon Street yard. You will need to see, Sam, the foreman. I'll call him and tell him what I want him to do with you and that you won't be on his payroll. Your salary will be $300 a week, under the table – you're not to tell anyone how much you're making. Do you have anything you want to ask me?"

"No."

"Do you need anything?"

"No."

"If you have to use the john, it's down the hallway on your left. Here's a $100. Tomorrow, after Maria gets home from church, the two of you ought to go out to eat at a nice joint. I'm gonna go upstairs and send Maria down, and the two of you can spend some time together."

"Thanks for everything. You're one hell of a man. I'm gonna miss seeing you every day."

Maria came down. After a brief kiss, she led me to the patio where we sat and talked for hours. I told her about Tony wanting me to learn the business, and she told me about herself. I was mesmerized by her beauty and eloquence as she spoke. I realized how lucky I was to love and be loved by this beautiful angel.

We made plans for Sunday. I asked Maria if she would like to stop by my place and meet my mother. Maria said she was eager to get to know mom because she had heard so much about her.

Sunday was a great day. My mother and Maria hit it off; chatting as though they were lifelong friends. I had never seen my mother talk as much to anyone as she did with Maria. Mom told Maria about herself, how she met, grew to love and marry my father. She described her life and how Tony's close friend Hyman helped look after her and her mother and sister, and the great friendship her mother had with Hyman. Tears formed when Mom reveled how much she missed her mother who had died of a heart attack in Hyman's arms.

Maria said that she missed her mother also. The two of them were crying and hugging, consoling each other. I was sitting and just listening and thinking it was good for both of them. To share their joys and sorrows.

My Mom and Maria decided to go shopping together the next day, then cook dinner when they returned. My mother was a great cook, and Maria had been taught by the chef that Tony hired to fix their meals. It would be an opportunity for them to talk some more and for Maria to meet my dad and brother.

I was feeling left out and getting antsy. I suggested we go to the Cathay House for some Chinese food. I told them at least I could be eating while they were talking. I almost said "bullshitting" instead of talking, but I couldn't say that in front of my mother and Maria.

After a good meal, I dropped Maria off. As Mom and I were on our way home, she said, "Maria is very nice. I like her a lot. You did good."

I said, "She likes you, and it's good for her to have a mother in her life."

Hesitantly, Mom said, "Pauly…I need a favor from you".

"Sure, anything".

"Your brother wants to go to college. I need to use our nest egg money, and I need you to ask Tony to get in touch with Hyman for me. So, I can borrow some money from him. I'll pay it back."

"That's OK. I'll handle it for you. Don't worry. This thing bothers me. This didn't just happen with him. He's known about college for a while now. Why can't he get off his dead ass and get a job?"

My mother didn't have an answer for me. As I drove I figured out what I was going to do. When we got home I called Tony. Some guy answered the phone and I said, "This is Pauly. Can I speak to Mr. D, please."?

After a little while I heard, "Hey gumba, how you doin'?"

"Good, Sir. I need a favor from you. My mother asked me if I could get in touch with you to ask Hyman to call her. She wants to borrow some money from him.

My brother is pushing her to pay for college. I thought you told me that my grandmother left my mother some money. You didn't want her to have it until my father got straight and you talked to him. I think my father is straight. And he's got a good-paying job with a construction company. At the beginning, he came home dripping with sweat and dirty, now he just comes home dirty. He's starting to look fit and good. Did you have anything to do with his job? Is that your construction company?"

"Yes, and I've had someone watching him from the time he leaves home till he returns. I have even had someone bait him into drinking, and he politely refused. It's time I talk to him. Ask your mother if it would be OK if I stopped by tomorrow at one o'clock. I'll have your father's foreman tell him to take the day off."

I asked my mother, then told Tony she would be looking forward to seeing him.

Tony told me after he spoke to my father, he was going to have Hyman ask my father to work with him running the financial business. He would make more money than he ever dreamed.

"I'm going to give your mother the money your grandmother left her, plus the money Hyman made on that money. Your mother will never have to worry about money again, and you won't have to worry about your mother anymore."

"Thank you. Have a good day." I hung up and told Mom what was going to happen and told her to act surprised.

# *CHAPTER 10*

The next morning, I got up early, dressed, and drove to the salvage yard. I parked by the fence, locked my car, and walked through the gate. The first thing that hit me was how many junk cars there were in the yard. They were three high, thirty rows across and ten deep. A couple of guys walked past me as if I wasn't there.

I hollered out, "Hey, where can I find Sam?"

I got back, "Who the fuck wants to know?"

I said, "Nobody. I just need to see him, and if you would stop fucking with me, I'd appreciate it."

He said over there, in the building. I went to a small building and walked in. Like everything else with Tony, the outside looked like shit that belonged in a scrap yard, the inside a great looking office.

I heard, "Can I help you?"

I said, "I'm looking for Sam."

All of a sudden, this huge guy was standing over me looking down at me. He said, "I'm Sam."

I said, "Good morning, my name is Pauly. Mr. D told me to see you. He was going to call you and tell you what he wanted you to do."

Sam said he did, and he was OK with it, with anything Mr. D wanted. "I'm going to pair you up with Joe. He knows what he's doing. The two of you are going to be stripping bodies and loading them on transports. He'll show you what to do. Come with me."

We walked outside, and Sam hollered out for everybody to get over here. Guys started to come out of buildings and from the yard. There was a mob.

Sam hollered out, "This is Pauly. He's a friend of mine. Each and everyone one of you is to make sure nothing happens to him and you're to watch out for him. Joe, I want you to take Pauly to the east side yard and start stripping, cutting, and loading bodies on the transports. Everybody get back to work".

A guy came up to me and said, "I'm sorry for what happened earlier."

I told him it's OK.

Joe grabbed me and said, "Let's take one of those boom trucks over to the yard. I'll show you how to drive it"

On the way to the yard Joe said, "We'll pull down six bodies, pull the tires, drop the gas tanks and then flip them on their sides. We'll cut the drive shaft, transmission mount, motor mounts and the exhaust at the motor and any linkage. We'll cut the four brake housings off, the radiator, heater core, and any die cast or aluminum parts, the battery, and any wiring we can see. Did you ever use a torch?"

"No."

"I'll show you, and we'll do the first couple of cars together. Climb up to the top of the pile. I'll swing the boom to you. Break a hole in the windshield at the top with the hook and hook the roof. I'll lift the bodies off and set them on the ground. We're goin' to do it six times because that's all the transporters can hold."

I climbed up the cars to the top, and Joe swung the boom to me. I busted the windshield with the hook, and I set the hook and got out of the way. Joe lifted the car off the pile and set it on the ground. After we had the six cars lined up, I got down and Joe handed me a lug wrench and a bolt cutter. He said he was going to take one side and for me to take the other.

"We'll take the lugs off the tires. Be careful that the tire doesn't come off on you."

When I was finished with the tires, I was to open the hood and cut the battery cables, lift the battery out, and set it on the side. Joe was done with his side ahead of me. He got into the first car, sat on the back seat with his feet against the rear window and kicked it out. He pulled up the back cushion looking for anything of value, then under the front seat and in the glove compartment.

Joe set the boom hook into the roof of the rear window and lifted the ass end of the car up. He hollered out to me to take the two rear tires off and stack them out of the way and get the bolt cutter. He showed me the two screws for the straps that held the gas tank up. He told me to cut the screw furthest from me first and then the one closest to me, and to be careful because the tank was going to come down. He said that sometimes it would get hung up by the rubber hose on the neck and I'd have to break it lose with a bar. I cut the two screws and the tank came down and hit the ground. Joe told me to set it off on the side away from the car.

He got back in the boom and lowered the car down and told me to hook the front. He lifted the front up and told me to take the tires off and put them with the others. He let the car down and told me to hook the side. He lifted the car, flipping it on its side. He got out of the boom truck and told me to follow him.

We walked over to an area that had a half dozen two-wheel dollies with tanks on them and a large cabinet. Joe opened the cabinet and handed me a pair of gloves and safety glasses, and then he took out gauges, hose, and torch. We walked back to the dolly and Joe attached the gauges to the tank.  When I got there, Joe told me to check and make sure the knobs on the torch were tight and then turn on the knobs on the tanks.

He said, "This is an oxyacetylene cutting torch. I want you to wear the glasses and the gloves until you learn how to cut. Once you know what you're doing, if you don't want to wear them, you don't have to. At the beginning, you're going to get a lot of hot slag blown back at you.

"Shit I forgot something. Turn off the tanks and grab the bar. We have to open the trunks."

We busted the lock and the trunk lid opened. We looked inside and there was a spare tire. Joe told me to get the tire out and put it on the stack of tires.

Joe told me to wheel the dolly to the car about fifteen feet away. We then went back to the torch. Joe showed me how to light the torch and how to cut. He cut the drive shaft at the rear end and then in the middle. The two halves fell to the ground. He cut the cross member holding the transmission, the front motor mounts, and the exhaust pipe at the motor. The motor slid down.

Joe shut the torch off, laid it over the tanks, and got in the boom truck. He told me to hook the motor in the exhaust man-ifold. I did. Joe engaged the winch, and the radiator, motor and transmission pulled out. Joe set the motor on the ground and told me to cut the clamps on the radiator with the torch. I lit the torch, cut the clamps, shut the torch off and pulled the radiator from the motor. Joe lifted the motor and transmission and set it on the side and told me to put the radiator by the tires. He got out of the boom truck and told me we had to cut out the heater core. He took the torch and cut out a box on the right side of the firewall and a core fell out. He told me to put it by the radiator.

He then handed me a pair of side cutters and told me to cut any wire I saw and throw it in a 55-gallon drum that was close by.

"That's it. We'll do six and then load the bodies on the transport. Think you can handle it?" Joe said.

He was going to get Matt to help me. "Tell him what you want, and he'll do it. I'm going to get another boom truck and start working six others. We'll see who beats who."

Joe came back with a young guy and said, "Matt, this is Pauly. Whatever he says, you do."

I nodded to Matt and Joe took off. I asked Matt if there were a couple of empty five-gallon buckets lying around. I decided to take a break and smoke a cigarette. Matt came back with the buckets. I asked him if he wanted to take a break and a smoke. He said yes, but he didn't have any. I offered him one. I told Matt that when we finished our cigarettes, I wanted him to get a lug wrench and take off the lugs on the five cars and throw them in a bucket instead of on the ground. I wanted him to be careful that the tire and wheel didn't pop off and hit him. I started breaking open the trunk and taking out the spare and anything that was good. Then I kicked out the rear windows, pulled up the rear cushions and looked under the front seats and glove compartments. I found a lot of change and a few bucks and tossed everything into the bucket. Matt was finished. I told him to set the hook in the rear bumper of the second car, after I lift it, to take the rear tires off and put them on the stack of tires, then throw all the rear widows into the cars.

Matt and I stripped the cars easily. I walked over to Joe and asked him where I should empty the gas from the tanks. He told me to tell Matt to go up front and get a flat truck that has a tank on it. "He can empty the tanks into it; then you can use it to haul everything to the shed," I told Matt. He left, and I sat on a motor and lit up a cigarette. I was thinking about getting Matt to dump the gas tanks and load up the truck while I'd load the transport trailer.

I noticed there was a guy in a suit walking around. I walked over to him and asked if I could help him.

In a heavy Spanish accent, he said, "I am looking to buy Ford flathead motors and for you to take them to the ship for Peru."

I said, "I'll take you to the boss." Matt drove up, and I told him to put the money that was in the bucket in his pocket. "Dump the gas tanks in the tank on the truck. Then load the tires and radiators and batteries on the truck and leave room for the motors."

I told the suit to come with me. We walked over to the office. I told him to wait in front, and I went in.

Sam was sitting behind a desk. He said, "Hi Pauly, what's up?"

Some guy was walking around in the yard. I asked him if he needed help, and he told me about a deal that sounded good to me. I told him he needed to talk to you. I've got him outside.

"Tell him to come in and thanks." I walked out and told the suit to go in.

Matt had the truck loaded and the gas tanks emptied. I told him to pick up everything on the ground and throw it in the cars along with the empty gas tanks. I started loading the motors on the truck. Matt helped me finish it, and I told him to pull the truck out of the way. I swung the boom around to the first car and told Matt to throw the hook through the front windows and hook it back into the cable on the roof. I lifted the car and set it on the transport. We loaded the five other bodies. I told Matt to take the truck up front, ask someone if they could pull the loaded trailer out and back an empty in, and for him to take a lunch break.

"You coming?"

"I'm not hungry and want to start on another six cars."

"If it's the money, what you told me to put in my pocket could buy you a pretty good lunch."

"No, it's not the money. What I told you to put in your pocket is yours. I just want to get some more of these cars done."

"Hell, I'm not hungry either, and we can eat something after the next load." We took the cars off the piles, worked them and loaded them on the transport trailer and cleaned up. It was getting late. I thanked Matt for his help and told him he probably needed to get out of here.

I heard, "Pauly, come in here."

It was Sam. I walked over to his office and went in. Sam told me to sit down. He said, "Considering this was your first day, you did a great job. You ever do this before?"

I said, "No. Joe was a good teacher."

Then he said, "For as long as you're going to be working for me in the yard, you take a half hour lunch and you drink a lot of water. The guy you brought in to me could be a good deal. We just have to work out some details. He said he'd be back. When he does, I want you to sit in on it with me. You got anything to say to me?"

"I just have a couple of suggestions. I know it's my first day and I really don't know shit. There are some things that are just logical to me. An air compressor and gun, pulling the lugs would be a lot less time. If we had a boom truck that had a magnet on a separate winch from the hook, it would be a one-man job instead of two. If there was a way to press the cars, we could get 12 on a transport instead of six. Matt is a good man and hard worker."

Sam said he knew, he had been watching us work. "Why did you decide to have him put the lug nuts in a bucket instead of leaving them on the ground?"

"They could get thrown on the steel pile."

Sam said, "Mr. D was right. You're a smart kid. Have a good night. See you tomorrow".

I drove home and went upstairs. I was beat tired, just wanted to eat something, take a shower and go to bed. My mom grabbed me and said, "Thanks, thank you for everything."

"You don't have to thank me, but if you have something to eat, I'm starving." I ate, took a shower, and slept like a baby.

Next morning, I drove to the yard. Everybody was standing around a food truck. Joe came up to me and said, "Morning. How about a cup of coffee and something?"

"Thanks. Just coffee, light and sweet." Joe got the coffee for me and told me Sam wanted us to work together again.

"He wants eighteen bodies today, and as we pull them off the pile, to separate the Fords with flathead motors and keep them on the side. They also have a compressor and gun out there for the lugs. Sam told me they were working on a boom truck, installing a magnet for us. I don't know where they came up with this shit, but somebody finally got their head out of their ass."

Joe and I started pulling cars off the piles. We left the Fords and lined up eighteen cars in a row. I started taking lugs off and Joe did the trunk, rear window, and pulled the batteries. We finished what we were doing almost at the same time. Joe got in the boom truck and we lifted the rear of the first car. I took the tires off, got the torch and cut the tank off. Joe let the car down and told me to hook the second car. He lifted it. I pulled the tires and dropped the gas tank. Joe let the car down and we flipped both cars on their sides. Joe told me to start torching them. He was going to go down the line dropping gas tanks. I finished the two bodies, and I hollered to Joe, "Let's take a break. You need to show me where I can get some drinking water."

"OK, follow me." We went to a building next to Sam's office and went in.

Joe said, "Get some water out of the refrigerator and we'll sit at the table and take a break."

We lit up a couple of cigarettes and were making small talk when Sam walked in and sat down. "How you guys doing?" We told him good. Sam said, "Pauly, the suit called. Tomorrow at eight. I want you to make the deal with me." He also said, "I'm glad to see you're drinking water. Take a thermos of it with you."

Joe and I went out and worked the first six cars together and were going to load the transport trailer when Sam hollered out, "Joe, take that boom over to the shed and bring the one with a magnet on it back. Let's see how it works."

Joe came rolling up with this good-looking boom truck. It had two winches, one with the hook, the other with the magnet. It had about two tons of weight mounted on the front and a seat that turned around, so you could control the winches and see what you were doing. Joe positioned the truck, played around with the controls a little, then set the magnet on the ass end of the first car. He lifted the car and set it on the transport trailer, then the five others.

He got out of the boom and hollered, "Holy shit this is fantastic, Pauly. I'm going to lift the next one with the magnet and take the tires off. I'll set it down and lift the magnet out of the way, drop the hook down, and we'll flip the car. We'll do them all like that."

Together we finished all the cars off. I walked over to the shed, asked if we could get someone to pull the transport trailer out and bring an empty one. If Matt could bring the flatbed truck over, we could get rid of all the shit.

Joe came up to me and said, "Sam wants us to clear the main aisle out, gate to gate. You use the boom and I'm going to use the fork truck.

"What the fuck do we have to do that for?"

"You'll see… and because Sam said."

We got it done. It wasn't too long after that the rear gate opened, and a semi-trailer was backing in. I turned around and an ocean-going container was backing in the front gate. They backed the two of them close to each other and opened the trailer door. It was empty. They cut the seal on the container and opened the doors; it was full of cardboard boxes on pallets. They moved the load out of the container into the trailer. I didn't ask what was in the container; I figured Tony would tell me at some point.

The day was over, and I went home feeling good about the way the day went. I walked into the apartment, said hi, and went to my room. My mother knocked on the door and told me to throw my clothes out, so she could take them and some other laundry down to the washer in the basement. "After you shower, and we eat something your father and I want to talk to you and your brother." I said OK.

We were sitting in the living room and my mother was telling us about the visit from Tony and Hyman. Most of it I already knew, but I played along like it was all new to me. Then my mother told my brother and me that she and my father were moving to Las Vegas. My father was going to work with Hyman again, and she was going to be doing something at the casino.

She asked my brother if he wanted to go to college here or in Vegas. He said Vegas, so he could live with them while he was going to school. My mother asked what I wanted to do.

"I'm going to stay here. If things work out the way they're supposed too, I'll join you in Vegas in a few years." I asked her when all of this was going to happen. I was told in a couple of months.

"Good, that will give me enough time to get a place."

My mother said, "Pauly, we have more money now than I have ever seen in my life. I want to give you the *gruzzolo* with some that I added to it. I want you to put it away and use some of it to take Maria someplace nice or buy her something. I really like that girl. Don't lose her."

"I won't Mom. She means everything to me."

My dad came over to me and asked if we could go for a walk. We started walking on the sidewalk and he said, "I'm sorry. I haven't been much of a father to you. I want to make it up to you. I also want to thank you for everything you did for the family. I know that all the good things that have happened for me were in a lot of ways because of you."

"You don't have anything to make up to me for. I'm so glad to have my dad back; I missed you and need you. I have always felt you were the strongest man I ever knew. The good things that happened to you were because of you, no one else."

We stood there and just hugged each other without saying a word.

# *CHAPTER 11*

I got to work early. I had been thinking all night how I would handle the deal with the suit. I walked into the office and Sam said, "Good morning, Pauly, you doin' alright?" "Morning to you and I'm doing great."

"Grab a cup of coffee and we can talk before this guy gets here."

"Tell me something before we get into this. I'm curious. Did Tony want me in on this deal or was it you?"

Sam said, "The only thing that Tony knows about this is that some spic wants to buy Ford motors to ship to Peru. You being in on this deal is all me. I'm going to introduce you. Ask him a couple of questions and tell him you're going to work out the deal with him."

We were making some small talk, and somebody yelled out, "Sam, there's some guy here to see you."

Sam went to the door, opened it, and said, "Good morning. I'm glad to see you. Come in. I'm sorry, I forgot your name."

The guy said, "My name is Juan Hernandez."

"I'm Sam Dawson, and this is Pauly Walker. Would you care for a cup of coffee or something to drink?"

"No thank you."

Sam said, "Let's go into the conference room and talk this thing out."

We walked into this neat room. It didn't look like it belonged in a junk yard. We sat in some comfortable chairs. Sam started it off by saying, "Juan, we have the 50 Ford flathead motors that you want. I need to know if you are the buyer or you're an agent or employee of the buyer. Either way it's OK. It just has to do with making decisions on the details."

Juan said, "I understand, and I apologize for not offering you my business card." He handed Sam and me a card. I looked at it and read: Juan Hernandez, President and CEO Auto Internationale.

I said, "OK, you're the man. It's good to deal with the boss. Sam asked me to work out the details, and if it's OK with you, let's get to it. I understand you want fifty motors. Are the motors for you just blocks, or complete with starter, fuel pump, carb, fan, distributor, and generator? Do you want motor and transmission?"

Juan told me that he wanted the complete motor and transmission. I told him that transmissions could be automatic or manual. Was this OK?

"Yes."

"We can guarantee that there will be no external damage. We can't guarantee anything else in the motor or transmission. We're interested in a long-term relationship with you and feel that we are men of honor. If a motor or transmission is totally not usable, we'll replace it on the next shipment. We'll remove the carburetor and generator and box them with the motor. We'll separate the transmission from the motor. I plan to mount the motors and transmissions on skids, frame the skids and stack them two high, both the motors and transmissions. We'll make arrangements for two ocean going containers. We'll load them and take them to the port. Is there anything I missed, or you want to ask me?"

Juan said, "No. Just how much is it going to cost?"

$550 a motor and trans, delivered to the port in ocean going containers.

Juan sat back, looked at Sam and then at me, and said, "We have a deal."

"Good, I want $10,000 up front and the balance when the containers are at the port. I can make arrangements to load the containers on a ship and can get insurance a lot cheaper than you'll be able to, I think. I'll find out and let you know. If you want me to handle it for you, I will, or you can make whatever arrangements you want. Sam, you OK with all this?" Sam said yes.

I asked Juan if he could write us a check. He said yes. I asked Sam to draw up an invoice for Juan and show the $10,000 as a down payment.

Juan shook my hand, saying, "Thank you for everything."

"You're welcome and thank you for the business." I walked outside, lit up a cigarette, and was trying to work out the easiest way to do it. Juan said good-buy as he left.

Suddenly I heard, "Pauly, get in here." I walked in and Sam told me to sit down. "Where the fuck did you come up with that shit?"

*Did I fuck up? I'm in some kinda shit now.* I said, "Sam, what was so fuckin' wrong?"

He said, "Wrong?  There was nothing wrong! I've been in this business twenty years and have never seen as good a deal. You're fantastic. It was like you've been doing it all your life. You handled it like a pro."

"Sam you're a piece of work." We both sat there laughing at each other. "Sam, I suggest we clear out an area in front of the shed and pull the motors there."

"I already have that figured out. I'm going to have Joe and the crew do it, and I'm going to explain to them how I want the motors pulled. I want you to go over to the shed and ask for Mario. He runs the shed. I'll call him and tell him to do whatever you want. Just tell him what he needs and how you want it done, then get back here. I've got a job I want you to help me with."

I walked over to the shed and asked for Mario. Some guy pointed out this square looking guy with baggy pants. I walked up to him and thought, *This fuck looks like a wop that just got off the boat.* I said, "Excuse me. My name is Pauly. Sam told me to see you, and he was going to call you."

"He did. Follow me. We can sit down, and you can tell me about this deal and I can make some notes."

Mario asked if I would like something to drink. Before I could answer he said, "I've got water, pop or beer."

"Water would be great." I told Mario the whole deal. He just sat there listening, didn't interrupt me once.

When I finished he said, "Seventy-five 2x4's and twelve 2x6's, 100 small cardboard boxes and 100 small bags. I'll borrow a nail gun and compressor from one of the construction companies. I've got a drill, but I'll need a hundred 1/2x2-1/2 lag bolts and a hundred 1/4x2 bolts. That should do it. You got anything to add?"

"No, but I'm amazed at how you just did that."

"Not as amazing as the deal. Don't worry. We'll get it done right."

"I know you will. Bye."

I walked out and thought, *My mother is right. She always says that you can't judge a book by its cover. Now I know what she means.* I went back to Sam's office.

Sam said, "How'd it go with Mario?"

"Good, he's a good man."

Sam nodded his head and said, "Yeah, he is. Tony wants me to give him a lot layout. He wants to get a crew in here and pour a pad for a car crusher he's buying. I want your help doing the layout."

"This is fucking great! Before Tony told me about you and that from now on he was going to be my boss, I had this guy who didn't know shit about auto salvage. He was afraid to do anything or ask for anything. He was afraid of Tony. We operated under unsafe conditions, the way it was done for years. Now things are going to be great."

"Sam, Tony is not going to want to run this show. He's got too much other shit going on. Why don't you ask him for the job?"

"No, Pauly, for two reasons. The first is you have to be a wop to be in that job, no disrespect intended."

"No disrespect taken. I understand."

"The second is that I like my job. I like being in the yard and not in an office. I like the action and hustle. Let's get to the layout. And you have to call Tony. Hernandez called and asked me if he could talk to the big boss. He wants to invite you and the boss to dinner to discuss another deal."

I called Tony and told him about the Hernandez call. He told me he would call Hernandez and accept the invitation for both of us. We did the layout; it was easy. I suggested to Sam that he ask for two good size boom trucks with magnets to load the crusher and to unload it on to the transports. We needed them because the layout was designed to flow and eliminate the stock-piling of the junk cars.

# *CHAPTER 12*

I called Tony, saying, "Good afternoon, Sir." He laughed and said, "Still got your shit, Pauly." He told me he had accepted the Hernandez dinner invitation. We were going to eat in the hotel where Juan was staying, the Waldorf Astoria.

"I want you to take tomorrow off. You and Maria go shopping for clothes. I need you to look the part. Maria will know what to buy. She'll pick you up at nine in the morning. That'll give time for alterations. Then Vince and I will pick you up in the limo tomorrow night at eight."

I was waiting at the stoop. When Maria pulled up, I got in and sat down. Maria leaned over and we kissed. She told me, "I missed you so much. Dad's been telling me about what you've been doing. He also told me that his lifelong friend from Italy, Mario, thinks you're the sharpest guy he's seen in that yard."

We pulled up in front of a store. The sign on the front read: Fine Tailoring from Italy. We walked in and this little Italian guy walked up to us and said, "Hello, Miss DeAngelo. Nice to see you again. Mr. DeAngelo called and told me what he wanted. If you could have your gentlemen friend stand on this platform, I will be able to take his measurements."

"Sir, with all due respect, if you would like me to step on that platform, then you need to address me. Otherwise, it is fuckin' impolite."

The guy didn't know what to say at first, then he apologized to me and didn't stop apologizing. I finally told him it was alright, and we needed to get on with it. While I was standing there, and this guy was measuring every part of me, I started thinking how on earth could I have said "fuckin'" in front of Maria. I was agonizing over saying it. I wanted to pound the little shit in front of me into the ground for making me say it. Then I realized it wasn't his fault – I said it.

The guy finally got done and asked if I would like to see the material Mr. DeAngelo chose for my suit. I said no. He said, "I will close my shop for the day and will wait for you to pick up your suit at five o'clock." I reached for Maria's hand to leave and the little guy said, "Good-bye Miss DeAngelo. Good-bye, Sir."

Once outside I blurted out how sorry I was for using that kind of language in front of her. "It will never happen again." I just kept telling her I was sorry, over and over.

She finally stopped me and said, "Pauly, it's OK. I would have stopped you sooner, but I was enjoying watching you grovel. I love you and that doesn't matter."

I told her, "I love you more than anything, and it matters to me."

We shopped for shoes, socks, a belt, a tie and a white shirt. Maria picked out everything. We decided to get something to eat. Maria suggested we go to The Grill and have some good pizza.

I said, "I don't know about The Grill."

She told me it would be OK. Don't worry. Let's do it. We got to The Grill and sat down at a table. Some guy came running out of the kitchen and went to the bar. He told the bartender something, and the guy got on the phone. I had not seen the bartender before. He must have been a new guy.

As I was wondering what was going on, I heard, "Good afternoon. What can I get for you fine people today?"

I turned. It was Tony. I said, "We would like one of the pepperoni pizzas this fine establishment is famous for. And two Cokes. Please."

Tony brought the two Cokes, and in a little while, the pizza. As Maria was eating, I was watching her, thinking how terrific she is. She saw me staring and said, "I have a great idea. After your dinner tonight, how do you feel about my getting Dad to let you stay in our guest bedroom? You could go to work in the morning."

"Sure, if it's OK with Mr. D."

After a while I heard, "How is your pizza? Does everything meet with your satisfaction?"

Maria said, "The pizza was magnificent, and the service could not be better. May I speak to you privately?" They stepped away from the table. I could see Maria talking, and Tony standing there nodding.

Maria came back to the table with a big smile on her face. "Dad said it would be OK if you spent the night in the spare bedroom. When we leave here, we'll go over to your place. After we visit with your mother for a while, you can take your work clothes with you, follow me to the tailor, and then home."

"Sounds like a plan."

We were finished. I walked over to Tony, told him thanks. "That was great. Can I please have the check?"

Tony said, "It's on the house, and the waiter wasn't worth shit, so don't leave him a tip." I thanked him and told him he was wrong about the waiter.

I followed Maria to the tailor shop. The little guy said, "Good evening, Sir. Please step in back where your clothing is hanging and put on the pants and jacket." I walked in back, changed clothes, and then returned.

Maria said, "Pauly, come over here under the light so I can see how good you look.  My god...you look fantastic! That suit fits you like a glove. I don't know if I should let you go out in that suit. I'll have to beat all the women off of you"

I just looked at her and smiled. Then the guy had me step over to the mirror to see if I approved. I looked in the mirror, told him it looked great. After changing into my other clothes, I handed the suit to him. He put it on hanger and then into a suit carrier.

Maria said, "Dad wants to take care of this, so let's go."

We walked out, and I said, "Sweetheart, I need to pay my own way. I need to talk to Tony about this."

"Pauly, there are a couple of things involved here. First, the suit and stuff today are all about business. It's so you make a good impression. The second thing is the suit is a $2,000 suit. I want you to save your money for us."

I followed Maria. We drove first to my mother's and then home. We began taking my stuff out of the car. Some guy came running out and asked if he could take the packages. Maria told the guy to put the packages in the guest bedroom and told me to follow her. The room was a large, very nice room.

Maria told me she was going to hang up the clothes, put everything away, and then take a short nap. "Dad is home. Why don't you find him and the two of you can do some talking."

Tony was sitting behind this huge desk. The minute he saw me he said, "Hey Pauly, how you doin'?"

I replied, "Great, and good afternoon, Sir."

"Same old shit. One of these days you'll get over that crap."

"I don't think so. It's my way of showing respect to someone I respect more than anyone – Sir."

He asked if I would like something to eat or drink, anything.

"No, thanks, but if you don't mind, I'd like to have a smoke." I didn't want to all day because of Maria. I lit up and said, "Thank you for the suit. It's my first suit. It fits great, looks terrific, and the material is out of this fuckin' world."

Tony said, "I know. I've got one just like it, and you're welcome. About our dinner tonight with Mr. Hernandez. I've had some people checking out Juan. I don't like doin' business with someone I don't know. I want to find out everything I can. How he makes his bucks. Can he afford to do business? His strengths and weaknesses. If I read this guy right, long before he did business with us he checked me out. After the two of you did business, he checked you out. You're a fuckin' mystery to him. My people have told me our boy Juan is the real McCoy. He owns the largest rebuilt American-made auto parts distributing company in South America. He has used car lots in Peru, Columbia, and Mexico. He has a mansion in Peru, a nice home in Mexico, and a very large ranch in Columbia. On his ranch, he has peasants growing poppy and weed. They harvest and process it in plants on the ranch. He sells his shit in California. My gut feel is this guy wants to talk to us about distribution for the East Coast and the rest of the country. I don't mind doing the auto business with him. I don't know if I want to fuck with the other shit. We'll see what he has to say."

"By the way, his father is Ramon Hernandez, a military general who runs the country. Sonny boy gets away with all the shit he wants. We need to be careful dealing with him. We don't want to get in over our heads. We have a lot of time before dinner. I'm going to get some shit done. Why don't you go upstairs and spend some time with Maria? She misses you."

I went upstairs and knocked on the door. Maria said, "Come in." When she saw me, she hopped out of bed and jumped on me.

We kissed. She was only wearing her bra and panties. She said, "Come back to bed with me. You can take a nap and I'll wake you in plenty of time to get dressed for tonight."

I got undressed and we got into bed. We were kissing and holding each other. Maria said, "Pauly, we're going to get married someday. I appreciate your respecting my wishes not to have sex till after we're married."

I must have dozed off because Maria was tugging me, telling me I had to get up. I showered, dressed, and went downstairs. Tony was waiting for me. He told me I was lookin' good.

I said, "Not too shabby yourself." He jokingly commented, "Some respect!"

We got in the limo and greeted Vince. Once under way I asked Mr. D if it was OK to discuss today's talk. He shook his head yes and said, "Hold on a minute. Vince, close this window."

"With all due respect, I would like to give you my opinion on something you said about Hernandez checking us out. If he only got as far as who you are and what you have on the surface, not bad. If he ties Hyman to you, then through Hyman, my mother and I become weaknesses. If they go back and find the Sicilians, then there's a whole new ball game. If he's as good as you think, I'm not a mystery. If he's as smart as you think, he knows the Sicilians are going to try and take over. My gut says he'll join with them and kick us in the ass. We need to find out in a diplomatic way what he knows. As long as we know what he knows, we can control the situation in our favor."

Tony said, "I'll find out during dinner. If he's a bragger, he'll boast about it. If not, we have ways to find out. Don't worry about that part. He's going to build a good-size parts business with us, and then build in the drugs. We need to take advantage of the parts deals, then listen to the dope deal and think about it. The deal may be good for us. I just get the feeling that he's going to try to use us temporarily. He's gonna have us do the shit work. Tonight, we act as if we are the best of friends. We are doing business together, and we treat him right."

Vince pulled up in front of the hotel. He couldn't get close to the curb. There were cars everywhere, people coming and people going. Guys with red hats on, carrying bags. Guys pushing racks with bags. The place was a fuckin' nuthouse.

Tony told Vince the two of us are going to stay at the hotel tonight. "You stop by my house and pick up Pauly's suit carrier, work clothes, and boots. Bring them to me tomorrow morning by seven."

# CHAPTER 13

We got out of the car and walked to the hotel entrance. Tony told me to have breakfast with Hernandez then go to the yard to finish doing business.

At the front desk, there were good-looking chicks and some guys taking care of people. One of the guys walked up and asked if he could be of assistance to us. Tony said, "We are here to see Mr. Hernandez."

The guy said, "One moment please." He looked in a book and asked, "Are you the DeAngelo party?"

"Yes."

"We are so glad to have you at the Waldorf. You will be having dinner in the Hernandez private suite in the penthouse." Then the guy hollered out, "Boy, show these gentlemen to the penthouse, the Hernandez suite."

We followed the guy to the elevators. He walked over to one that was off by itself and unlocked the door with a key. I had never seen anything like that before. I always thought you opened an elevator door by pushing a button. We got in and were going up when Tony asked the guy why the fag called him "Boy?"

The guy answered he didn't know, that's just the way it was, and he needed the job.

Tony said, "I plan on giving you a good tip if you do something for me. If you don't want to or can't, I won't give you as good a one. I want you to tell that fuckin' fag that I didn't appreciate his announcing to the world where we were going, and he needs to stick his boy-shit up his ass."

The guy smiled. OK, but he might like that. Tony handed him a hundred-dollar bill. He thanked Tony as the elevator door was opening.

Hernandez was standing there. He said, "Tony, Pauly, glad to see you! Come in and make yourselves comfortable. How about we have some wine and talk a little before dinner?" Hernandez walked over to a waiter standing in the corner.

A minute later the guy came toward us carrying a tray with glasses and a bottle of Chianti. He opened the bottle and poured a little in Tony's glass. Tony smelled the wine, then tasted it and said, "Good." The waiter poured glasses for everyone and left. He came back with a tray of crackers with all kinds of shit on them.

Just then the phone rang, and the guy came back. "Mr. DeAngelo, you have a call. I can plug a phone in for you here." Tony thanked him. The guy plugged a phone in and handed it to Tony. Hernandez and the guy left the room.

I heard Tony say, "Yeah, it's OK… OK, forget about it. OK." He hung up. Looking at me, Tony very slightly shook his head 'no' and rubbed his ear, pointing to it. I understood Tony knew they were listening to us, and he wanted to keep them guessing.

Hernandez came back in and asked if everything was OK. Tony said, "Yes, it was nothing. I shouldn't have been bothered with it at all." Tony had known the front desk guy would call. All in the guessing game. We toasted and started drinking wine. Tony said, "Juan, what all is Auto Internationale and Juan Hernandez?"

Juan took the lead and began telling us the shit we already knew. Then told us how his father had a protective curtain around him in Peru. He could do anything he wanted to and get away with it in Peru. His fear was this country – he did not have diplomatic immunity. If he got caught doing something wrong in the States, he'd go to jail and couldn't get help from his father. The US government didn't recognize his father as the leader of Peru. My brain did back-flips. We just got a weakness!

I reached over and picked up a cracker and took a bite. The cracker had on it these little balls in gel that had a salty-fishy taste. Not bad. I could get used to this shit with Chianti.

Tony and Juan were drinking and bullshitting. I'm drinking and scoffing down crackers with all kinds of shit on them. I was thinking, *This is one fucked up dinner*, when Juan said, "Let's eat something; then we can talk business."

*Huh? Where the fuck was you before I ate all those fuckin' crackers? I'm full and dying of thirst. I'm at a point where all I want to do is go to sleep for a while.*

We finished eating and were back relaxing and talking. Juan offered after dinner drinks. Tony accepted, and I declined. I felt if I had any more to drink, I'd have to pry my head out of my ass.

Juan said, "Pauly, let's talk business. I've got a long shopping list of shit I want to talk to you about."

"Juan, with all due respect, you need to be talking to Mr. DeAngelo. He's the man."

Tony said, "It's OK, Pauly. You handle it."

Juan began: "I want 500 of each of these starters, generators, fuel pumps, water pumps, and distributors with cap and wiring. I want 500 fans and all the spark plugs. I also want 200 drive shafts with the two universal joints. I don't care if any of it works. They must all be from US cars, no external damage, and I need you to tag each unit with year and make. Can we do business now, or do you need to do some studying?"

I said, "We can do it now. I just need a pencil and paper to write the stuff down."

I began: "The starters and generators would cost $17 each, the fuel pumps $7. The water pump and fan would be one unit and cost $18 each. The distributors would cost $22 each, only because we would have to crate them differently to protect them for shipping. The spark plugs would be zero cost, and the drive shafts would be $9.

"We'll tag each unit and insure no external damage. We'll provide the shipping crates. Everything will be crated – nothing will be loose in the container. I can make arrangements for the containers and loading, but that would have to be at your expense. I just had a thought on two more things you might want that weren't on your list, oil pan and oil pump, $12 for both."

Juan asked me for the paper and started reading, line for line. Then he sat back, looked at me for a little bit, and said, "OK, we have a deal on everything. Make the arrangements for the containers and the loading, and I'll pay you at the port."

"I'll have Sam draw up an invoice tomorrow. Can you write a check for five grand downstroke?"

Juan said he could and went on, "The next things I want are titled used cars at wholesale. I want sixty for my lots. I want a T-bird for my daughter. I need two late-model Cadillacs. I want two late model, top-of-the-line Lincoln limos. They can be hot. I can title them in Peru. What do you think gentlemen?"

Tony said, "I don't see a problem with any of it. Tomorrow after you and Pauly go to the yard, the two of you can go over to Royal Auto Sales. I'll have Tom Meaghan, who runs the lot, and his boss, Mr. Fanarssi, go over the cars and costs with you. Don't mention anything about the limos in front of Meaghan. Fanarssi will handle it. Pauly, I want you with Juan to ensure everything is right, and we take good care of Mr. Hernandez."

# *CHAPTER 14*

Juan said, "I'm getting tired, but I've got a bunch more I want to talk to you about. How about we do this again tomorrow night?" Tony agreed.

"Good. There's a large hot tub out there. I'll have three ladies join us, and we'll play around in the tub and drink some more. You gentlemen are going to spend the night here and might as well have some company. There are bathing suits and bathrobes in your rooms, if you would care to use them."

Tony said, "That sounds good. I've never been in a hot tub, and a lady sounds even better right now. How about you, Pauly?"

I said I'd like to try it. In my room I put on the bathing suit and bathrobe and hung up my suit. I really felt like shit. My head was spinning, and I was tired. I walked into the bathroom, splashed some cold water on my face and took a piss. It didn't help. I still felt like shit.

Tony, Juan and three women were already in the tub. I put my robe on a chair and joined them. It felt good. I sat on a ledge and had water jets hitting me from both sides. I leaned back, closed my eyes and was just relaxing when I felt a hand rub my cheek. My eyes popped open. Standing in front of me, holding two glasses of wine, was this cute girl. She asked if I would like to join her and have a glass of wine. She handed me a glass and said, "My name is Carly."

I told her my name.

I heard a woman say, "What kind of a name is Pauly?" It wasn't said in a nice way. I turned and saw Juan with his arm around this good-looking spic.

"I don't know what kind of name it is, but I do know it's my fuckin' name!"

Carly said, "Don't let her bother you. She's had a little too much to drink."

I said, "How about you?"

As I said that, I realized this girl had huge tits, and I must have been staring at them, because she said, "You talking to me or them?"

"I was talkin' to you ... I've never seen tits as nice as those. I'm wondering what they look like without the bathing suit covering them up."

"Let's have some more wine. If you're a good boy I might let you see and hold them."

I didn't care for the 'good boy' bit or that 'might let me' shit, but I let it ride. I was feeling too woozy to screw with it. She got up and refilled our glasses. We continued drinking. Finally, I had enough and was just sitting holding my glass as she drank.

She looked over at me, took the glass out of my hand, put our glasses on the tub's edge, and moved against me. She reached in her top and took out a tit and put it in my hand. She leaned over. Her tit was hanging down and my hand was clutching it. The feeling was wonderful. I began to gently squeeze and rub while she put her hand on my cock and began moving my dick around. I let go of her tit and took her hand off. I told her, "This feels great, but the room is spinning, and I feel funny. I need to get in bed."

She said, "I'll help you."

"I don't think you can." I hollered out, "Tony, sorry to bother you, but I need some help. I need to get out of here and into bed."

Tony waded over to me, jumped up on the ledge. He told the girl, "I'm gonna lift him up so he's sitting on the ledge. As I'm holdin' him, I need you to move his legs around so their hangin' outta the tub. Then get out and stand down there. I'll lower him down. You make sure he doesn't fall over."

It worked fine. The last thing I remember was Tony carrying me to the bedroom. I must have passed out. I don't know how long I slept.

The door opened, and the light woke me. I watched the girl close the door and walk over to the bed. I closed my eyes and fell back off. I felt her hand on my face, her tits on my chest. Her breath smelled from wine.

"Wake up. Come on, wake up, you stupid bastard. I need to get you off, so I can get paid."

My eyes opened to a squint. I grabbed her by her tits and pushed her away, then sat up on the edge of the bed.

"You're nothing but a two-bit fuckin' whore! I wouldn't let you touch me with a ten-foot pole. Where do you come off calling me 'boy' earlier and now 'stupid bastard'? Who the fuck do you think you are? Get the fuck outta here!"

I went into the bathroom, took a piss, and decided I was going to shower to get the chemical smell from the hot tub off me. The bathroom door opened, and the girl came in. She was standing there crying, telling me she was sorry, asking me to give her another chance, not to throw her out. She really needed the money. She was sobbing; her body was shaking, and she looked like shit.

"OK. Everything's gonna be OK. Stop crying and calm down. Go get your stuff and grab a robe. Bring it all back here." As she started for the door, I said, "Hey, put your tits back in your bathing suit! You don't need to be walkin' around like that."

Showering felt great. I dried off and put on underwear and a robe. I walked out of the bathroom, and she was sitting on the bed with all her shit. "Get your underwear, the robe and anything else you need, and take a shower. I don't care if you put on makeup."

I tossed her stuff on a chair, pulled the cover off the bed, and got in on the sheets with my back against the pillow.

When she came out, I thought, *Not bad.* "You look pretty good. You look younger. Get in here. We need to talk." She got in bed, started jabbering and shaking. I told her to calm down. "I told you everything was going to be OK. Just relax."

She started telling me that she was sorry for everything she had said. Because she was so nervous, she put on an act to cover up her nerves. She was a student and a virgin, and she had never been with a man before. She desperately needed the money she was promised from Mr. Hernandez. He told her and her friend that if they took care of us, they would get a good tip because we were wealthy.

She said, "I guess the tip is out."

I didn't answer her. Instead, I said, "How did you get involved with Hernandez and this shit? Before that, do you have a driver's license and something in your purse that says you're a student? I don't like being bullshitted."

She went over to her purse, rummaged through it, and handed me her driver's license and a student identification from the Julliard School of Music.

"OK. So far, so good. You're a kid and a student. Now tell me how you got into this shit with Hernandez."

"I'm hurting for money. I live with a woman, Gloria, who is a better friend to me than anyone has ever been. She's a nurse at the hospital. Her husband was killed by a drunk driver that hit him on the sidewalk. Gloria has been having problems paying rent and utilities. She took me in as a roommate to help with the expenses. I need the money for school and for her."

"A student who knew Hernandez asked if I wanted to make some money being an escort. I told him I'd do anything for money right now. He said he needed two of us. I told him I would get someone. I spoke to Gloria, and she agreed to do it on the condition that any money she made she'd give to me." She said, "I really don't know Mr. Hernandez."

I said, "What are you studying?"

"Music. I'm a singer and I write music."

"Are you any good?"

She said, "I'm still learning."

"Don't give me that shit, I asked if you were a good singer."

"I am."

"Why aren't you making bucks singing, if you're any good?"

"It's really hard to get an audition with anyone without experience, and I don't have any."

"Could you sing at a bar if you had to?"

"Yes, that would be a great start for me."

"Yeah. It also could be good bucks, so you wouldn't have to fuck with this shit. Now what we're going to do is. …"

Before I could say another word, she started shaking again, I reached over and grabbed her arm. "I told you everything is going to be alright. You don't have anything to worry about. You need to relax. I don't like to see you like this."

"I'm sorry. I'm just so worried. I can't do sex. It's not you, it's me. I don't know how I got myself into this mess. I can't have sex this way. I'm sorry."

"You don't have anything to be sorry about. I didn't plan on having sex with you. I'll handle Hernandez. As far as your taking care of me, I'll give you a $1,000 tip for the way you took care of me."

She smiled and leaned over and kissed me on the cheek and thanked me. I had never expected anything like this. I never expected her to be like this.

"I need your phone number. Someone will call you tomorrow and set up an audition. If you're good, he's going to offer you a job. And then no more of this shit, ever, especially with someone like Hernandez."

She said, "Why are you doing this for me?"

"For a bunch of reasons. I can't stand to see a good-looking girl so upset she's shaking. I called you a fuckin' whore, and I'm sorry about that. I see a young kid trying hard to make it, who deserves a break. And some day when you're a big shot, I may need a favor from you."

I told her to get dressed and get her shit together. If she wanted the robe, to take it. I was going to take her home. We dressed, went downstairs, and out of the hotel.

We were standing in front, and I looked around. There was nothing – it was like a ghost town. I asked Carly how far she lived from here. She said, "Not far. We can walk it."

We started walking, and I noticed she was carrying this little duffle bag. I said "Gimme that. I'll carry it." I took the bag and asked her if she got the robe. In a shy soft voice, she said, "Yes, and a bath towel."

I reached my arm around her and said, "Good."

After a while she said, "This is it." We were standing in front of a brownstone building. "Pauly, thank you for everything. You're the nicest man I've ever met. I'd like to see you again and spend some time together."

"Carly, I'm sure we'll see each other again sometime. But I am deeply in love with the most beautiful, wonderful lady in the world. I'm going to ask her to marry me and then get permission from her father. If it wasn't for her, I could really enjoy spending time with you."

She kissed me on the cheek and said good-bye.

Back at the hotel I went to the front desk. Nobody was there. I looked at a clock on the wall. It was 4:30! I was tired. I needed to sleep. I hollered out, "Hello." From a room in the back a guy came out and walked toward me. I noticed he walked funny, swishy, and held his hand out with a limp wrist. *What the fuck do I have here?*

He said, "What can I do for you at this hour in the morning?"

"I'm sorry to bother you. I really need your help. I need to get back to the Hernandez penthouse and get some sleep. Just open the elevator for me."

In this high-pitched, faggy voice the guy said, "Gee, there is no possible way I can do that. It's against regulations. You'll have to sleep somewhere else."

I repeated: "Please open the elevator."

He warbled, "Noooo, I won't do it."

"Open the fuckin' elevator for me, or I'm going to come over this counter and tear your fuckin' head off."

He stood there looking at me with this funny expression on his face. Then he came out into the lobby, strutted to the elevator and opened it.

I walked up to him and happened to notice the front of him was soaked, from his dick down his pants. "If you weren't such a horse's ass, you wouldn't have to spend the rest of your shift in your piss."

I got in the elevator, went up to the penthouse, got to my room, hung up my suit and fell in bed. I don't know how long I had slept before someone was pushing me and saying, "Pauly, wake up."

I groaned, "Go 'way."

I got another push and a "Get the fuck up!"

I opened my eyes. It was Tony, standing over me.

I said, "Hi, good morning, Sir."

I heard a muffled laugh and a "How you doin'?"

I sat up on the edge of the bed and said, "I'm sorry about last night. I don't know what happened to me, but I was out of it."

"You had a lot of firsts last night. You ate a lot of caviar on those crackers. That got you thirsty. Then the dinner added to it. I never thought you could drink as much wine as you did. Combine that with the heat and chemical smell of the hot tub, I'm surprised you didn't puke your guts out. How'd you make out with the girl?"

"She was a nice girl who needed money bad. I really didn't want to do anything with her because of Maria. She really was afraid and didn't want to do anything either. We just talked. I need a favor from you. The girl is a singer. I need you to get Vito to give her an audition, and if she's as good as she says, hire her."

"Sure, no problem."

"Thanks, and if you don't mind, how did you make out with the lady you were with?"

"I don't mind. After Maria's mother died, I felt that I didn't want to be with another woman. Ever. The lady last night and I just talked. Her name is Gloria. I didn't do anything either. I found her to be just as my wife was. She's kind, considerate, loving, and a nice person. I like her."

"That's good. The girl I was with is her roommate. She said the same about her. The other good thing is neither one of them have anything to do with Hernandez."

"I asked Gloria to go out to dinner tonight and thought you could join us." I agreed and suggested he ask Maria to join us.

"Yeah, that would even be better. Here are your clothes. Maria threw some shit in a bag for you: toothpaste, toothbrush, hairbrush, a change of underwear, and I don't know what. That girl really looks out for you."

"Yeah, ain't it great?"

# *CHAPTER 15*

Tony told me to have breakfast with Juan, if I wanted. "Then the two of you go to the Beacon Street yard to go over the deal with Sam and Mario. Then go to Royal Auto Sales and go over the cars with Meaghan. I'll have Fanarssi there. Be back at the hotel by three o'clock.

"Vince will pick up Maria and Gloria, then us at six, to go out for a nice dinner. I'd rather do it that way than do another meal with Juan."

Tony asked if I knew how good a deal that parts-deal was. "Yeah, most of it we scrap when we strip the motors for the blocks. I'm going to try and add on crankshafts and camshafts, and I'll throw in push rods."

"You are a smart fuck. Have a good one, and I'll see you at three."

I took a shower to try and wake up, and then I got dressed. I was sitting around thinking about the deal when the phone rang. Juan invited ne to join him and two of his employees for breakfast in the penthouse.

In the dining area Juan and two guys were sitting at a table. As soon as I sat down, a waiter was standing beside me and asking if I would like coffee or orange juice or both. I chose coffee.

Juan said, "Pauly, I would like you to meet Emilio and Punta. Emilio runs my used car operations, and Punta works for him." I nodded. Emilio looked like a first-class act. The other guy looked like a typical low-life spic.

"Unless you have some objection, I'd like to take Emilio and Punta to Royal Auto Sales. They can walk the lot and pick out the cars they want. While they're at the lot, you and I can go to the yard, finish our business, and then join them. That way we can get everything done and be back here by 3:00 as Tony wanted.

"Sounds good to me. Did you tell Tony what you wanted to do?"

"No, the thought came to me after Tony left."

"That's OK. I need to borrow a phone. You guys start eating and I'll catch up."

I called the Muraso Distributing number and asked for Mr. Fanarssi. After a little bit, I heard Alfredo Fanarssi. I said, "Good morning. This is Pauly. I know that Mr. D told you about Hernandez and the cars. This morning Hernandez told me how he wanted to handle it. I thought you should know so we'd be prepared."

I didn't hear anything one way or the other, so I just kept going. "He wants to drop two of his employees at the lot this morning to look over the cars and pick out what they want. Hernandez and I will go to the Beacon Street yard and finish up with Sam, then return to the lot. We need to be finished by 2:30.

"I have a suggestion. Have Meaghan make up two copies of the inventory sheets and a copy of the list of cars that are not on the lot. Get ahold of Sam and tell him to expect us."

There was still silence. "Are you still there, Mr. Fanarssi?"

He said, "Done, gratis."

I hung up the phone, thinking I can't wait to meet this guy. After a quick breakfast, we left. Emilio and Punta were talking as I walked past them toward the elevator. Punta did a slight head movement toward me and said, "*Mar icon.*"

When I was a kid, some of my friends were Puerto Rican, and we use to rank each other out with *mar icon.* Nothing better than calling your friend a fag – kidding. At the elevator door I leaned over to Punta, and snarled, "*Eguts mar icon.*"

Emilio, Punta, and I got out of the car and entered Royal Auto Sales. Located in Queens, Royal Auto Sales is the largest used car dealership on the East Coast. The cheerful and spacious lobby is something I'd expect in a new car dealership. Meaghan was pointed out as the gentleman sitting at a desk in a glass-enclosed office. Emilio and Punta followed me to the office. Before I could get very far, Meaghan was up and rushing toward me, in a typical car-salesman voice and attitude.

After he greeted us, I said, "I would like to introduce Mr. Hernandez's employees to you. Emilio is your counterpart in Peru, and Jerkoff works for him. Good-bye. I'm leaving."

At the Beacon Street office, the door opened, and Sam said, "Good morning, Juan, it's good to see you. And Pauly, it's great to see you again. Come in and have a cup of coffee." While we drank coffee, I gave Sam my notes on the prices and explained the specifics of the deal.

"Juan, I was thinking about two more motor parts that would be really good for you. The crankshafts and bearings, and the camshaft and push rods. The crankshaft $25 each, the camshaft $15 each." He ordered a hundred of each.

"Sam, please add them to the invoice. Juan is going to give you $5,000 down-stroke. We're kind of pushing time, so I'm going to go to the shed, fill them in, and be back. When you're done, we'll be outta here."

At the shed Mario took me into his office and asked if I wanted coffee or something to drink.

"No, thanks. If I have any more coffee, I'll be pissing my brains out. I just wanted to give you a heads up on the parts deal that Sam's writing up. Hernandez is buying a bunch of motor parts. They all are going to have to be crated. The cranks and cams might be a problem."

Mario said, "No problem."

"The distributor and cap, water pump, and fan?"

"A little tricky, but we will do something."

"Good. I knew you could. It's good seeing you again. You take care of yourself."

Mario clasped my shoulder saying, "You, too. You, too."

As I walked into Sam's office Juan and Sam were shaking hands and saying good-bye. "Sam, I forgot to mention something that I want on the invoice. We're giving Juan all of the plugs and the camshaft pushrod for nothing."

Sam noted it on both copies of the invoice.

On the way to Royal, Juan and I made small talk. Mostly he was telling me how beautiful Peru is and how great the women of Peru are. He rattled on and on.

At the lot, we found Meaghan at his desk talking to this big, rough-looking wop. I said, "Good morning, gentlemen. This is Mr. Juan Hernandez. Mr. Hernandez, this is Mr. Fanarssi and Mr. Meaghan."

Meaghan got up, and with his typical car-salesman attitude was all over Juan. Fanarssi just sat there, silent.

"Juan, your people are still in the lot. Let's go into the conference room and talk. I have a list of high-quality, top-notch cars which are not at the lot but might interest you, and we can discuss them." Meaghan took the lead with Juan by his side, and Fanarssi and I followed. *What's with you, asshole? I gave you the courtesy of introducing you to Hernandez. You could at least acknowledge me.*

In the conference room Meaghan and Juan started into it hot and heavy. Fanarssi, for the most part, listened, jumping in occasionally. I sat back. If this wasn't business, I could be taking a fuckin' snooze right now. It wasn't long before Juan suggested we go to lunch. Fanarssi said he knew a good joint close by. I declined "I'll pass and stick around here. I'm not hungry."

They left, and I walked over to the showroom. The same cute young lady that had pointed out Meaghan earlier asked if she could help me. I asked if she could direct me to the restroom, she did. I felt I had to piss badly. That fuckin' coffee! My eyeballs got to be floating. The john was a great relief.

Back in the showroom the same young lady came up to me and asked if I was alright. After I said yes, she asked, "Can I help you with something now?"

"Yeah, do you have a desk in this place?"

She motioned me to a small cubbyhole and sat behind the desk. "Can I interest you in any particular car?"

"No, I'm not a customer. You and I work for the same company. I was kind of hoping you'd tell me about your job."

She hesitated, then said, "It's a good job. A lot of it has to do with the people I work for." She paused, then continued, "My boss, Meaghan, is a sleek salesman. His boss, Alfredo Fanarssi, is a down-to-earth, smart, nice guy who makes up for Meaghan's bullshit. I met Mr. Fanarssi's boss once for a short time. I didn't get his name, but he was the kindest, most caring, considerate man I have ever met. Working for people like this is terrific.

"I get a salary that's not great, but I only have my son to support, so I don't need a lot. I also get a commission for sales. Selling cars here is so easy. We have a couple different kinds of customer. The first are guys that come in pick out a car they like, no hassle on price. They pay cash and leave. My thought: wise guys from all over the city.

The second are men and women who pick out a car they like. We have so many that there's a car for everyone's pocketbook and likes. Price is never an obstacle. We don't lose sales. We carry our own credit. If they don't pay for the car up front, they pay for it in interest and fees, and feel good about it. What's funny is I feel safer here than I do at home."

Just then I could see Juan, Meaghan, and Fanarssi come through the door, followed by Emilio and Punta. I thanked her and left. When everybody got in the conference room and was seated, Meaghan commented, "You missed a good lunch, Pauly. You hitting on my salesperson?"

"No. She's a very nice lady and hitting-on is not my style." Out of the corner of my eye I could see Fanarssi had a guarded grin.

Meaghan said, "Mr. Fanarssi, I would like you to meet Emilio, who is my counterpart in Peru for Mr. Hernandez, and Jerkoff, who works for Emilio.

Punta jumped up and protested, "My name is not Jerkoff. It's Punta."

Meaghan didn't know whether to shit or go blind. He couldn't apologize enough. He said he was sorry – he must have misunderstood when they were introduced. He glanced at Fanarssi with a fearful look. Fanarssi had a blank expression. Clearing his throat, Meaghan said, "OK, let's get to it." I looked at Fanarssi from the corner of my eye. He now had an unguarded big grin.

They went down the inventory list, and, for the most part, agreed on price. There were some exceptions, and Fanarssi jumped in and handled them. When they finally got done, Juan said there were three other cars he wanted off the other list. Two Cadillacs, and a Thunderbird for his daughter. With a lost look on his face, Meaghan looked at Fanarssi. Fanarssi gave Juan a price for the Cadillacs, which was OK, and then said the T-bird for his daughter is a gift from us. Juan thanked Fanarssi for the Thunderbird and for how easy he made this deal.

Fanarssi thanked Juan for his business then asked Meaghan to take Emilio and Punta to the lunchroom and buy them lunch. As soon as they were out the door, Fanarssi said to Juan, "I understand you want two top¬-of-the-line black limos. I don't remember if I was told Lincoln or Cadillac."

Juan said Lincoln would be good. Fanarssi gave him an agreeable price.

Then Fanarssi said, "I'll invoice you for the 62 titled cars and expect to be paid in full when we have loaded them on the ship. The invoice will include the cost for the loading and shipping. I won't invoice you for the two limos. You'll pay for the limos, the containers, shipping and loading in cash."

Juan agreed and thanked Fanarssi. After they shook hands, Juan left, going to the lunchroom to talk to his men.

Fanarssi asked if I could handle the shipping. I said, "Sure… and with all due respect, what's your fuckin' problem?"

He winced, paused before saying, "I am Sicilian. I know how Tony feels about Sicilians. Although I am loyal to Tony and this *famiglia*, I can't talk to Tony without an, intermediary – so I distance myself from him. I know of the connection between you and Tony, so I felt it was best if I distanced myself from you."

"I understand, but I think it's wrong. You're a good man, and you're good for this business. You handled that deal today great. You're a class-act and that saleslady thinks the fuckin' world of you. I'm goin' talk to Tony and maybe get this straightened out."

Fanarssi said grazzi, leaned back in his chair, and closed his eyes. I said ciao and walked out. I caught up with Juan and his guys as they were leaving the lunchroom. We got into the car and started back for the city. It was about a half-hour drive. Emilio and Punta were sitting in the front with the driver. Juan and I were in back. The car was set up like a mini-limo, having a window separating the front from the back.

Juan started by saying how he enjoyed doing business with me – it was easy. He liked my attention to detail – it made for fewer problems. He liked my don't-take-shit attitude. He liked my mind. I thanked him and responded with, "Doing business with you for me is also easy because you know what you you're doing and because you are a class-act."

"Pauly, I want you to work for me. No, I want you to work with me. I want to make you my partner. You can have homes here and in Peru. You'll be a multimillionaire. You can have anything you want. I told you how beautiful Peru is, and how the women are beautiful. You can have your choice and as many as you want. Women have been taught from childhood to worship their men, to take care of them in every way, to do only as they are told, and to never ask for anything. They are your property and you do with them as you want. What do you think, Pauly?"

"That sounds out-of-this-world. I thank you very much for offering this to me. I'd be a fool to say no to you. I want to finish our business and think about it a little. I have a loyalty to Tony. I owe him a lot, but this could be the greatest thing in the world. I just need to think"

"I understand, Pauly, and I'll await your answer."

At the hotel, Juan told the driver to take Emilio and Punta to the airport then return. It was 2:30, and if I knew Tony, he'd be there exactly at 3:00 for the meeting. I had a half hour to kill.

We took the elevator to the penthouse. There, sitting in a lounge chair drinking something, was Tony. So much for my knowing this man!

"Good afternoon, Sir. You're here early. Everything went very well today." He said he knew. "We have a lot of time till the meeting. I've been sitting so much; my legs are cramping. How about we go for a walk?"

While in the elevator I told Tony, "Today has been a great day. I spent time with Sam and our friend, and I always enjoy it. They're a great crew. I also had a good time at Royal Auto Sales. While everybody went to lunch, I had time to speak with a saleslady who tried to sell me a car. She told me about her job, how great it was to work there. She was telling me about her boss, Fanarssi, and the headman. She didn't know the headman's name, but thought he was the kindest, most caring man she had ever met – he's just a great guy. I can't think of who she was talkin' about."

Tony came back with "Fuck you."

Outside, we started walking along Fifth Avenue, and were immediately caught up in a swarm of people. Not in a rush, we weren't moving at a fast pace as were the tide of pedestrians. Because Tony is an imposing body, people coming at us did side steps. The people behind us were another story. We got pushed and shoved and elbowed. Someone was jabbing me in my back. I had it! I turned around to swat the motherfucker. There was no one there! I looked down to see that the battering ram was this little, old, gray-haired lady. I turned back to Tony and said, "Let's get out of this shit. We can stand against the building. I need to talk to you."

"Fanarssi handled the deal with Hernandez perfectly. The guy is good, and he's good for the business. The salesgirl who thinks you're the greatest thinks Fanarssi is fantastic--a down-to-earth guy who cares, a guy who is smart and offsets Meaghan's bullshit. The girl feels safe at work. That's not because of Meaghan – that's because of Fanarssi and you.

"Fanarssi understands and respects your hatred for Sicilians. He hit me with it because he knows of our connection. I didn't understand what was going on till after the deal, when I confronted him about it. We talked. I like the guy. He has loyalty to you and the Famiglia. Yeah, he's Sicilian, but he's one of the good guys.  You're fuckin' wrong. You need to make it right!"

Tony considered the issue "What happened to respect?... You're fuckin' right, and I'll straighten it out." I was overcome with relief. I grabbed Tony and hugged him.

Only in New York City could you have two guys standing by a building hugging. Most people walking by didn't give a shit; they're caught up in their own little world. Those that did notice figured we were two fags and didn't give a fuck. You could have a heart attack, be lying on the sidewalk. No one would stop and offer help. New Yorkers would just step over you and keep going, except for the slime ball that would swipe your wallet.

As we walked back to the hotel I told Tony all about Hernandez's proposal to me. "I didn't believe Juan's line of crap for a minute. He's full of shit, but we might be able to use it someday to our advantage."

Tony put his arm around my shoulder, saying, "You're one fuckin' smart guy. Let's get back upstairs and hear what he has to say."

Juan suggested we drink Chianti while he told us what he needed, what he wanted, and how he was going to change our world. We didn't say anything, just sat down and toasted with a glass of Chianti.

Juan said that he wanted to set up a network to distribute his coke and weed. He had a route on the West Coast but needed to expand his distribution because he had too much product. New York City would have the most dealers in the country and be the hub for the distribution routes. He wanted to set up a network from New York to Newark to Philadelphia and down the East Coast to Miami. Then from New York to St. Louis to Memphis to Little Rock to New Orleans. And from St. Louis north to Chicago. And from New York to Buffalo.

He wanted to deal only with the Families. He needed Tony to figure out the best way to do it. He intended to buy a large multi-floor warehouse in the city, spec out the modifications, and have Tony's construction company do the work. The warehouse would have shipping and receiving docks, warehousing and offices. It would house the corporate offices of JH Rebuilt Auto Parts.

Juan visualized that the sign on the front would read JH Auto Parts Distribution. The business would be a legal, perfectly legitimate. On the other end of the building, above two large overhead doors, there would be a sign: JH Auto Parts Redirect. Redirect would have two internal shipping and loading docks. The walls would be concrete with heavy steel doors. There'd be no windows in the area. The Redirect would receive specially marked containers.

The distribution center would receive containers of rebuilt parts from Peru and distribute them across the country. The Redirect would receive containers of auto-parts crates containing pot in bulk, then package it for whatever the market would bear for resale. The Redirect would also receive containers of crated motors containing coke.

"I'll require ten Chrysler Hemi motors. The motors would be totally gutted internally to be a container. On the outside, they'd appear to be a rebuilt motor. You will retrofit the Cadillacs to my specifications. They'll be the carriers of the coke to the different locations. I'll pay you for your expertise to spec both parts of the warehouse. I'll pay you for the construction. I'll pay you for the gutted Hemi motors and the retrofit Cadillacs. At today's street value the dealers would make a half million on each shipment. The distributor would make a million. These amounts will grow as demand dictates a higher street value.

"I'll need to know to what extent you wish to participate in this. I need you because of your control of the port. If you choose to decline, I'll set everything up elsewhere with a different family that controls a port. I enjoy our business relationship and would hope to continue it. On the other side, I plan to build two plants in Lima, Peru. They will rebuild motors and transmissions to be distributed in South America and here through JH Auto Distribution. I'll buy motors and transmissions from you and continue to buy used cars and expand my used car outlets." Juan ended his pitch with, "Tony, talk to me."

"Juan, as you have heard many times before, we appreciate your business. I enjoy doing business with you. We can provide you with everything you want and need without a problem. As far as the distribution, it is something new to us. I'll need to seek the advice and opinions of my family as to our involvement, and then the involvement of all of the other families. In one week, we'll have dinner, and I'll give you a distribution network with the hub in New York. If it's not my family, it'll be another."

# *CHAPTER 16*

We left. Vince had the limo parked at the curb in front of the hotel. Tony and I got in. I said "Hi", leaned over, kissed Maria and told her she looked terrific. Tony and Gloria were talking. Vince took off.

The restaurant wasn't far, but the traffic at that time of day was a killer. The street was a sea of yellow cabs, maneuvering in and out, hustling for fares. Vince was good. He went with the flow and handled the cutoffs well because we were sitting in back. If not for the ladies, there would have been road rage from hell in Italian.

As soon as we entered Polcari's, a sharp-looking older Italian gentleman walked up to Tony, hugged him., "Tony, my good friend, welcome to my house. It's so good to see you. And to everyone, welcome. Enjoy your dinner."

Tony said, "Angie, I would like you to meet Gloria."

Angie reached for Gloria's hand, kissed it, and said, "Welcome. It is my pleasure"

Tony next said, "I would like you to meet Maria, my daughter, and her fiancé, Pauly."

Angie told me I was a very lucky young man. Turning to Maria, he apologized if his staring made her uncomfortable earlier. "At first, I thought you could only be Tony's saintly wife, risen from the dead." He looked up and made the sign of the cross over his heart. "Maria, you are as beautiful as your mother was. I wish you a long and happy life."

The maître d' showed us to our table which was set with glasses of water with lemon and a basket of breads. The waiter took our drink order: mixed drinks for Gloria and Maria, a bottle of Chianti for Tony and me. Tony ordered appetizers that we all would share. They were portions of steamed clams, antipasto, sautéed stuffed mushrooms, calamari, and scungilli.

The food was great. Although I knew better, I overate. I sat back in my chair, wondering how I was going to get the rest of the meal in me. I stood up, excused myself, and went to the john. I opened the door and saw this guy with a towel over his arm. This was not going to work for me. I told him I was sorry and left. I exited through the front door, lit up a cigarette and started walking down the block. I stopped and began a phony cough to hide a fart. The fart was so loud, with so much force, that I thought I blew a hole in my pants.

Finishing the cigarette, I returned to the restaurant. The table was covered with plates of food – there wasn't a bare spot. I sat down, and Maria asked if I was OK.

"I'm good, just needed a cigarette and some air."

"Pauly, take off your suit jacket and drape it over the back of your chair. Spread your napkin over your lap. No matter what anyone thinks or says, I want you to unbutton your top button and tuck this napkin in your shirt and let it hang down in front of you."

I didn't give a shit what anyone said. *If this is what Maria wants, that's all that matters.* I thought how wonderful it is to have someone who cares about me.

We dug in and started eating. The food was beyond belief. I took a bite of something. I don't remember what it was. I chewed and didn't want to swallow it. I wanted to keep the taste in my mouth, and then I went to the next. I was thinking the guy who made this meal had to be a culinary artist; everything was prepared to perfection.

After the table was cleared, the waiter said "Mr. DeAngelo, I trust the food was to your satisfaction and you enjoyed your dinner. May I bring dessert and an after-dinner drink for everyone?"

Tony told the waiter, "We'll pass on the desert; bring expresso for everyone. Give my compliments to the chef as usual. He has done outstanding work."

Turning to me Tony said, "Pauly, tomorrow you can sleep in. Spend some time with Maria and then go to the Beacon Street yard. Talk to Sam about the Hemi motors and Mario about the gutting. Be sure to tell Mario that the cavity is going to have to be as large as possible and will have to be polished, no rough edges at all.

"I need you at the Muraso conference room by three o'clock. I am going to have everyone there; I'm even flying Hyman in. I plan to explain our new business venture and get everyone's opinion on our involvement. Based on our meeting I will make a decision on what we will do. Vince will take you and Maria home; Gloria and I will take a cab. After tomorrow's meeting Hyman will stay at the house. He wants to discuss some other business with me. On Thursday, the three of you will shop for a wedding set and band.

"Maria, pick out what you want. All that I ask is it be as beautiful and magnificent as you are. Price doesn't matter. It's going to be my gift to you. Hyman will guide you. He knows more about diamonds and jewelry than anybody. That business is a scam. Unfortunately, people don't find out till much later how bad they were taken and regret it."

Handing me a gold neck chain, Tony said, "This is for you." It had a gold-plated key on it. I looked at it and thanked him. He advised "Wear it always and never let it out of your sight. The key is to a safe deposit box at Manufacturers Trust Bank. I have started a *gruzzolo* for you. There is $100,000 in cash in the box." I sat there dumbfounded.

Tony said, "Let's get out of here."

As we were walking out, I stopped Tony, put my arm around him and whispered, "Thank you for everything. You're something else."

Once we got into the house, Maria asked if I wanted anything.

"No, I feel drained and just want to go to bed."

"That would probably be best because I have a big day tomorrow, too. Would you mind if I slept with you?"

"Mind? Never." We went to the spare bedroom, undressed, and jumped in bed.

Maria tenderly kissed me and said, "Good night." I was conked out. I must have slept like a log. Then I felt gentle little kisses on my cheek and a very soft voice saying, "Pauly – it's time to get up – come on, Pauly – wake up."

I wrapped my arms around Maria and pulled her down on top of me and we snuggled. The overwhelming feeling of contentment was too brief. Maria pushed off of me, stood up, and said, "Let's go downstairs. What would you like for breakfast? I feel like a glass of OJ, and if you want one, or a coffee, or something to eat, we can get it."

"Only coffee, please. I still feel full. I don't know if I'll ever be able to eat again."

"Me, too. Let's sit out on the patio and talk."

We put our robes on and went downstairs. Maria said, "Go on out and I'll bring you your coffee." She came out, put the OJ and coffee on the table then went back in the house. She returned with a pack of Luckys, a lighter, and an ashtray.

We discussed last night's dinner, how much we enjoyed Tony and Gloria's company. "Dad really had you there for a little bit when you asked permission to marry me."

"Yeah, you're right, he did."

"I knew he was playing with you. He's wanted this for years."

I said, "I have gotten to a point that I feel very close to Tony, more so than just working for him. I enjoy the two of us going back and forth at each other. It reminds me when I was a kid – razzing and joking with friends, the companionship and laughter."

"Tony is the greatest father a girl can have," Maria sighed. "And he's a magnificent man and a perfect parent. I could go on forever telling you how wonderful he is."

"I know. I'm truly fortunate he is in my life."

"Pauly, I've been thinking about our wedding. This is what I would like. If you feel differently, just say so and we'll do it the way you want. I would like to wait about a year – it would take probably that long to work out all the details. I would like your mother to be my matron of honor. Dad and Gloria are hitting it off so well. I want to find out if Dad is going to ask Gloria to marry him. If he is, I would like to have a double wedding. What do you think?"

"I think it's great, and the best part is I'm going to marry a very smart lady."

Maria jumped up and kissed me. "I'm a lucky girl. One more thing before you get out of here and go to work. Last night when we were leaving you whispered something to Dad. What did you say?"

"I told him, thank you for everything and said he was some-thin' else."

"OK, go upstairs and get dressed. You need to go to work."

After I got dressed, I found Maria, I told her I was going to spend that evening with my parents. "I want to tell them about the wedding and Mom's being matron of honor, and to just vis-it. I was thinking about something and want to know what you thought of it. I'd like to ask Tony if I could move into the spare bedroom permanently till everything works out. Mom and Dad are moving to Vegas, and I'm going to have to find a place. Living here would be great."

"Sure, that would be wonderful. I know Dad wouldn't mind."

# *CHAPTER 17*

"Pauly, it's good to see ya. Come 'ere."

"Sam, I need your help. I need ten Hemi motors. I don't care if they're Chrysler or Desoto. Can be any year."

"I know we got four here. I'll have to check with the other yards and Royal Auto Parts, and maybe a couple of outside yards. How fast do you need 'em?"

I said, "As soon as you can. It's a done deal and we're going to have to do some work on them." He told me one way or the other, he'd have them there fast.

"Thanks. One of the good things about this job is my visiting you. I've got to talk to Mario about working the motors."

Mario was at the shed. He told me to follow him into the office. I got the same warm welcome as from Sam. The welcome was always sincere. No bullshit. It gave me a good feeling.

"Mario, we're going to have to work ten Hemi motors. From the outside, they should look like rebuilt motors. The inside will have a cavity, and the cavity must be as large as possible. I figured we would gut the motor, then machine the block and heads. Mario, I'm sorry about that. I didn't mean to sound – I don't know."

Mario interrupted me, "It's OK; it's OK. I know. I'll handle it."

"Tony told me to mention that we'll need to polish the cavity so there are no rough edges at all. Do you have a ballpark idea of how much we can charge for working the motors?"

Mario sat back and after a little bit said, "$1,250 would be good."

"Can you work one motor, so I can get Hernandez's approval, and then we'll do the rest?"

"Yes, good idea. It's none of my business. I'm just curious. How much you gonna charge for the motors?"

"I think I'm going to give him a break even though you're gonna bust your balls on it. I have had a number in my head from the beginning, I'm gonna stick with it - $4,650 a motor." We just sat there grinning at each other.

Mario said, "I'll see you at 3:00. Tony wants me at the meeting."

"Good. Tony's a smart guy. You've got the best mind in the *famiglia. Ciao.*"

# *CHAPTER 18*

I got to Muraso a little early and walked into the conference room. There were three guys sitting at one end of the table, talking. Fanarssi, sitting at the other end by himself, motioned to me. "Pauly, come here and join me."

I walked over, sat down, and said, "How are you? How is everything goin'?"

"I'm good and things couldn't be better. How are you?'

"*Menza menz.*"

"Talya, my salesperson, asked me who you were. All I told her was you worked for the company. She asked me to tell you hello if I saw you again. I guess you made a good impression."

"She's a nice lady. Did Meaghan have anything to say?"

"No, I didn't think he would. I think he wants that all buried. Let's get something to drink, and I want to introduce you to these guys." We stood up walked to the other end of the table.

Fanarssi said, "Gentlemen, I would like to introduce you to Pauly. Pauly, this is Salvatore Manzella, Joseph Valachi, and Frank Nolan. Sal and Joe are *consigliere* to the *famiglia*. Frank is an attorney for Amalgamated and some other financial businesses. I heard Hyman was coming in. That's why you're here, Frank?" Frank nodded.

I said, "Gentlemen, it is my pleasure to meet you."

Fanassi and I walked out, got ourselves a couple of drinks, and sat down at a table in the lunchroom. We made some small talk before Fanassi advised. "When we go back in, don't sit at the conference table; sit in a chair by the wall. There is a lot of tradition involved with this meeting of the *famiglia*. Only made-men can sit at the main table. Out of respect for the tradition, do it. It's the right thing."

As we were heading back to the conference room, Fanarssi said, "One more thing. I owe you. I owe you big."

In the conference room there were a lot of guys sitting at the table. Fanarssi joined them. I walked to the back of the room to sit beside Mario. "I thought for sure you'd be sitting at the table."

"No, it's a long story. Someday I'll tell you."

Tony came into the room, followed by an older gentleman. The old guy said something to Frank Nolan, who then got up and left the room. Tony and the old guy walked to the back of the room where we were sitting. Mario and I stood up as they neared. Tony hugged Mario, "Mario, you know Hyman."

Mario replied, "Yes, it's good to see you again."

Putting one arm around my shoulder and the other around Hyman's, Tony grinned from ear to ear. "Hyman, do you recognize this guy? He was a bambino when you left town. This special guy is Nathan's son, Pauly, my future so-in-law.

Hyman's face lit up. "Paul, my… Nathan's baby. You've grown into a handsome young man. I should have been coming home on visit to watch you mature. My apologies for my neglect." With tears in his eyes he clutched his arms around me. "I'm so happy. I wish you every happiness, good health. Congratulations. *Mazel Tov.*"

"Thank you, sir. It's a pleasure to meet you." I had no idea what he said to me after congratulations, but it had to be good.

Every eye in the room was on me. It probably began when Tony and Hyman approached me, and Hyman embraced me. Tony's the boss; it's understandable. Even though Hyman's a Jew, he's a major player in the *famiglia.* I just got a step up.

Hyman was only a name to me. Meeting him woke me up to his importance. This is the big-hearted man who took in and raised my father. My first impression of just an ordinary old guy, changed quickly. Hyman's demeanor and knowing-eyes radiated strength, warmth, and a superior intelligence.

"We will see each other tomorrow," Hyman said as he sat down beside me, "and get caught up on a lot."

Tony stood at the front of the table. He greeted everyone and said something in Italian. I missed it. Then he said, "I have asked all of you here because I have been given a proposition that will change our business and our *famiglia*. I respect your thoughts and your opinions, and that's what I want. There is no right or wrong here. I want your honest opinion." Tony laid out on the table everything Hernandez told us, omitting nothing. Then he concluded "That's it. I want to hear from each of you."

Manzella started. "Our business is good; we are doing very well. We have always maintained that we would not be involved with prostitution or drugs. I think we should stay with that."

Valachi said, "I have had experience with drugs in another *famiglia*. I think it is good and we should do it."

Everyone was giving his opinion, some for and some against. It was going nowhere.

Fanarssi was the last made-man to give his opinion. "I don't know if we should get involved or not. The only problem I see is there is a lot of money, and we will be involved with the other families. Greed is a dangerous thing. If one of the other families gets greedy, our *famiglia* could be in danger."

"I appreciate all of your opinions. It's not going to be an easy decision. I would like to hear what Hyman thinks."

Hyman stood up. "I agree with everyone's opinions for or against. They are all valid. I will tell you drugs are the future.

More money will be exchanged for drugs than for alcohol or to-bacco. If we don't get involved, someone else will, and we will miss out on a lot of money. If we do not do this, we will be left behind, and that might hurt us more."

"Pauly, I'd like your opinion."

"I agree with what Hyman said. Mr. Fanarssi made a good point, except I feel that our danger is not just the other families, but Hernandez and the Sicilians. If we get into this we must al-ways be aware of the possible dangers. If there is as much money as everyone says, I don't see how we cannot do this drug busi-ness.  Another family doing it would overrun us."

Tony thanked everyone. "Take a break. I want to talk to Ma-rio in my office."

I turned to Hyman. "You're a very wise man. I hope we can spend some time together, but now I want to smoke a cigarette and don't want to do it near you."

I got up and walked outside and lit up a Lucky. I was think-ing that with all the bullshit from these guys, why was the only mention of danger to the family from Fanarssi and me? I didn't think I was wrong. My gut was saying that Hernandez and the Sicilians were our danger, not so much the other families. But Fanarssi's point about greed was a good one. I walked back into the room just as Mario and Tony were returning. Mario and I sat down, and Tony walked to the front of the table with a smile on his face. Mario elbowed me and whispered, "It's good there's one smart guy in this room." Hearing that from Mario made my day.

"You talkin' about yourself?" I shot back.

Tony said, "Gentlemen, I have made my decision. We will be in this business. I intend to give this a great deal of thought, to plan all of our moves. I agree that this business breeds danger, and if we cannot handle it, I will pull us out. I'll not permit our *famiglia* to get hurt. I will also tell you I do not see this as a long-term deal. I'll speak to you individually about your specific involvement. I thank each of you. Go home and be with your families."

Tony asked Hyman to get Frank to meet in his office. He walked over to Mario, hugged him, and whispered something to him in Italian. Mario walked out. Then he turned to me and said, "Pauly."

"Sir?"

Tony smiled and asked me to join him with Hyman. "Maria got ahold of me, and it would be very good if you took the spare bedroom as your new home."

We were headed for Tony's office. Fanarssi rushed up, "Mr.D, may I have a word, please?"

"Sure, Alfredo. Pauly?"

"No problem. I don't mean to bother you with this, especially now, but it's something that's eating at me. Hernandez came out to Royal, and in private, handed me a bundle of money. He said it was for me, for the way I handled the deal for him. I told him I was doing my job and couldn't take the money. He insisted, kept pushing. I told him I appreciated it, but I really didn't want the money. He kept it up. I thanked him and kept the money. I had decided I was going to do what I'm doing now and give you the money."

"How much cash is it?"

"A hundred grand."

"That's a lot of dough. Aside from giving him the T-Bird for his daughter, which, by the way, was good business, did you do anything else?"

"No, nothing else."

"The fuck is buying you. Let me know if he pulls any more shit. As for the money, you did right by telling me, Alfredo. Most guys would have pocketed it and not said anything. You're a good man. Keep the dough – it's yours. Have a good night."

When Tony and I entered the office, Hyman and Frank were sitting and talking, Tony asked, "Hyman, you don't mind if Pauly joins us, do you?"

"No, not at all. He's as smart as his father, with a quality his father doesn't have. He has street smarts and savvy. At your meeting, he made your men look like *manichinos.*"

Where does this Jewish old man come up with an Italian word? He called them dummies. I glanced at Tony and he was smiling. I think Hyman could get away with anything because of Tony's love for him.

Hyman said, "Tony, I want your permission to make some changes. We have a lot of excess money. A lot of the legit big shots are hiding their money from the feds in a place in the Caribbean called the Grand Caymans. The accounts are safe and can't be touched. I want to open three accounts there. You and I have talked about your goal to someday have a villa in Italy where you can kick back, smoke that shit you smoke, drink that crap you call wine, and enjoy life."

Tony interrupted, "We are going to do it together. You are going to drink that faggy wine, Manischewitz, and eat that cardboard crap."

Hyman said, "Yes, payback is hell. Anyway, I want to open two Swiss accounts – one in your name and one in mine, so we can enjoy that carefree lifestyle. The accounts in the Caymans will be Anthony DeAngelo, The DeAngelo Family, and Sera

Walker. They will be set up so you can access all three accounts, and Sera Walker will also be able to access her account. Can I have your permission to do what I want?"

"Sure. Sounds good to me. The only thing is when we are lounging in beautiful Italy, you have to drink Chianti with me."

Hyman turned to Frank Nolan and asked if he saw any problems or if there was anything he missed. Frank said it sounded right to him and he couldn't think of anything else.

Hyman continued, "I only have a couple of more things. A long time ago we set up the scrap yards to wash money. It was good in its time, but times are changing. We own a casino and it's a natural for washing money. The scrap yards will give us trouble, the casino won't. OK, Tony?"

"Good, you're right. It would be better."

Hyman turned to Frank "Thanks for coming. Return to work or go home, whatever you want."

Frank got up, said goodbye, and left. As soon as Frank was out the door, Hyman said, "In light of your meeting today, I would like to get ahold of Steve at Manufacturers, see if he can hide an account, the DeAngelo Family. When the account reaches a certain amount, transfer money to the Caymans account."

Tony said, "You got any more, or is that all the hot air you got?"

"I'm done."

"Thank you, my friend. As always, you are the best. Pauly, what do you have to say about all this?"

"You're a lucky man to have this man in your corner. Everything I heard about money sounds right to me. Hiding money, the way Hyman has described, it's genius."

"That's it?"

"No, but I don't think you want to hear the rest."

"Pauly, you know me better. Don't give me that shit."

"OK, what I'm going to say is from my gut. I don't have anything to back it up. I don't like Frank Nolan. I don't like that he knows so much about the money. I feel he will fuck you someday." I paused then said, "You want more?"

Tony answered yes. Hyman was sitting, listening intently.

"I think you have the wrong persons as your *consigliere*. My opinion is the smartest guy in the organization, the guy with your best interest at heart, is Mario. He should be your *consigliere*. I've got a problem with everyone else in the room except Fanarssi. All of these guys are your leaders; they must be loyal to you. They are men of honor, but to be a leader, you have to be smart. You have to be able to think on your own. You have to be able to think things out. I didn't see anyone who was smart or could think anything out. It was almost as though they were saying what they thought you wanted to hear."

"Fanarssi, on the other hand, said he didn't know if we should do it – he was honest. It took balls to say it. Fanarssi brought up a possible danger to the *famiglia*. You agree. Where the fuck was everybody else?"

"Tony, with all due respect to you, I know you know I mean that sincerely. When you think this out, give some thought to your people. The right people, and we will live longer. The wrong people will be our end."

Tony and Hyman sat there staring at me. I was feeling uncomfortable. I didn't know what to say or do.

Then Hyman spoke, "I listened to what you said at the meeting. I heard what you said about the money and this. I would like to know where you gained your insight and your intelligence."

"Sir, I don't know. It's in me and it just comes out."

"For many years I have regarded your father as my son, and now I have a brilliant grandson."

"Sir, it is my honor to be your grandson."

Tony said. "You're fuckin' amazing. Maria got ahold of me while you were talking to Mario. She wants to have your mother and father, Hyman, you, and me and Gloria for dinner tonight. She wanted to know about Gloria, and I told her I asked Gloria to marry me. Maria didn't seem surprised.

"Tomorrow after Hyman, you and Maria are finished, I need you to go to Royal Auto Parts. See Luca – he runs it. Go over the specs I have from Hernandez on the Cadillacs and spend time with Luca going over the business. Tomorrow night you, me and Mario will have dinner at Muraso, then we'll spend the night talking in my office."

I drove home. Vince took Tony and Hyman home, then went to pick up Gloria and my parents. I beat them home. Maria grabbed and kissed me, asking, "Did Dad tell you I called him?"

"He did. He told me everything. It's good. It's all good. I had a day. I'm going to lie down for a little to rest." I went upstairs and stretched out on the bed. I wasn't tired, I just needed to relax and get some of the day's shit out of my head. Before long I heard a lot of laughing and talking coming from downstairs. I went down to join in.

The first thing I saw was my mother, Gloria, and Maria yacking and laughing. It was good to see my mother laugh, good to see the three of them having a good time. Dad and Hyman were sitting at the table. Hyman was so excited his voice was a high shrill. My dad was intent on what Hyman was saying. Sitting in a comfortable chair in the corner was Tony. He was laid back and taking it all in.

*"Bueno sera, Capo. Posso sedermi conte?"*

"Sure, Pauly. Sit. Have a glass of Chianti with me." He poured me a glass. I tapped his glass and said, *"Salute."* The both of us just sat back and relaxed. Even though it seemed that Tony was at ease, I had the feeling his brain was working a mile a minute. Tony looked at me and smiled.

The veal parmigiana dinner was terrific. The conversation was all about congratulations and well wishes. Gloria accepted everything graciously, as did Tony. Maria was excited and glowing.

Hyman said, "Sera, I have always thought of Nathan as my son. Because of that, I told Paul he is my grandson."

My Mom replied, "Thank you. I have always loved and respected you, think of you as family, and this strengthens our family."

With tears running down his face, Hyman said, "You are as astute and gracious as your wonderful mother was."

After the evening ended, Tony helped Hyman upstairs to his room. Gloria was going to spend the night with Tony, and Vince took my parents home. Maria and I went upstairs. We had a big, busy day tomorrow and needed to get a good night's sleep. As we went to our rooms, I turned to Maria, "If you get up before me, wake me up and we'll have breakfast together."

# *CHAPTER 19*

Hyman was already at the table drinking coffee when Maria and I entered the dining room. I wanted a jolt of coffee for breakfast. Maria went into the kitchen and returned with a cup of coffee and a glass of orange juice. Hyman told us the way he wanted to handle the ring buying. We agreed.

"I'm going to go outside and smoke a cigarette." I lit up and noticed Vince was in front of the house. I knocked on and opened the limo door. "Good morning. How are you? Have you had any breakfast or anything?"

Vince said, "No, I haven't had the time. Tony wanted to get to work early; then I had to be back here for you."

"C'mon inside. We'll round up some kind of grub for you to eat." I asked Maria if she could get Vince breakfast.

"What would you like, Vince?" He just sat and stared at her, looking bewildered.

"OK. How about OJ., coffee, a couple of eggs, bacon, and toast?"

He finally spoke, said it would be great. Maria left and returned with coffee and juice and asked Vince how he would like his eggs. Back to the blank stare. Smiling, Maria said, "Over easy it is."

Returning immediately from the kitchen, Maria sat beside me. I leaned over to her and whispered, "You are wonderful!" Hyman decided to go upstairs to get dressed. By then Vince should be done and we could leave.

The kitchen helper brought out Vince's food and more coffee for me. Vince ate up, Hyman came down, and we took off.

While he was driving, Vince kept thanking Maria. By the third or fourth time I grumbled, "Where's my thanks?"

Hyman said we were going to go to the largest manufacturer and wholesaler of wedding sets in the country. "This man has his own designers and production, buys sets from all over the world. He sells to all the chain jewelers and the independents. No matter where you buy a wedding set, it came from here. His customers are buyers. He doesn't sell retail, so don't expect a typical jewelry store."

We were on the lower east side of Manhattan, distinctly a Jewish neighborhood. Hyman told Vince to stop in front of a small apartment house. At the front door Hyman pushed a button. A voice came over a speaker. Hyman said his name and something else. In a few seconds we heard a series of clanks, like cylinders were sliding, then the door popped opened.

I reached over and opened it wider, so we could walk in. What a difference! From the outside, the door looked ordinary. Opened, it was a solid, six-inch steel door. In the small foyer, Hyman walked over to a corner and waved at a camera in the ceiling. A buzzer went off and another door opened.

Standing in the doorway was a short, elderly, heavyset man wearing one of those little Jewish caps. Hyman and the man hugged and started talking. I couldn't understand a word they said. Maria and I followed them into a room that looked like a secondhand junk store. I wondered what we were getting into. We went through a small doorway into a room that was at least fifty feet by a hundred feet. There were rows and rows of showcases glittering with jewelry. Men and women were sitting at desks talking on phones. The guy had gutted and renovated the floors of the apartment house to accommodate his business.

"Paul, Maria, I would like you to meet my friend Carl."

"Nice to meet you. This man is not just my friend, he is my lifelong friend; he is my best friend. He has done more for me than anyone in this world, and I love this man. Maria, I have a special selection of wedding sets I would like to show you. These sets were designed for the hand of a woman as exquisite as you."

As we passed by a row of showcases, Maria was trying to look in each one. At the back-wall Carl opened a safe, and removed a tray, and set it on top of a case. There were twelve wedding sets in the tray. Maria was transfixed by one set. She leaned over to Hyman. "The second from the left in the first row. What do you think?"

Hyman put the ring on Maria's finger. "Now what do you think?"

Maria sighed, "It's beautiful."

"It's the finest you can buy."

Hyman said something to Carl in Jewish and handed him the set. Carl took a small box from under the case, put the set in it, and gave it to Hyman who put it in his pocket.

Then Carl inquired, "Paul, what are we going to do for you?"

I told him I'm not a jewelry kind of guy. Something plain.

He said, "For someone who is not a jewelry kind of guy, why the gold neck chain?"

"To me, it's not jewelry, it's something else."

"Your gold band can wait until the three of you come back. I have an idea on something."

I thought, *Come back? Shit! I need to get this over with.*

We said our good-byes as we made our way out. In the limo Hyman told Vince where he wanted to go next. He asked Vince if he had heat. Vince said yes, a .38 Smith & Wesson. "Good.

When we arrive, please walk with us to the door. When we leave, escort us back to the car. Bring your piece, and keep your eyes peeled."

We went three blocks and pulled up in front of a rink-looking storefront that had Jewish writing on a sign, and in much smaller letters it read "jeweler". Hyman said, "Like Carl, I have known this man for years. He buys diamonds from all over the world. Most are raw diamonds which they clean, cut, and polish here. The cut diamonds are brought in from Israel. A lot of diamonds are sold to Carl for wedding sets."

"A diamond is judged. In the trade it's called the 4Cs: cut. carat, color, and clarity. Even with flawless, top-color white diamonds, the cut is all-important. If a stone is cut for maximum brilliance, it returns more sparkle to the eye.

Vince accompanied us to the front door. After Hyman said something into a speaker box, a buzzer opened the door. The door was the same as any store door except it had heavy steel bars on it. The windows also had bars. Is this what jail is like? Should I have worn my pinstripe suit?

A guy standing behind the counter said, "Welcome." The guy was dressed in black, with a fancy white shirt, and a fancy little cap on his head. He had a lot of facial hair and long curly sideburns. To each his own.

A back door opened, and a guy hollered out, "Hymie, my Hymie, it's so good to see you!"

"Jacob, it's good to see you again. How many years has it been?"

Jacob invited, "Come, come." Here was another Carl's place, but with far fewer showcases. Guys sitting at workbenches had high-intensity lights above them and magnifying glasses that swung around on arms. On the far wall was an enormous safe. The fuckin' thing looked like it belonged in a bank.

Hyman and Jacob started talking. I was thinking, *This jabbering shit is going to go on forever.* I was also thinking that these guys must belong to the same club. All wore the same little cap.

Hyman and Jacob ran out of words and Jacob came over to us, "Thank you for coming to my place of business. It is my honor that you are here, and *mazel tov.* Come, come, please, follow me."

He led us to the back wall, to a room to the right of the safe. "Please come in and be seated." It was an office as elegant as Tony's.

Jacob put a piece of blue velvet on his desk. Hyman took out the wedding set and placed it on the velvet. Jacob stood over the desk looking at the set. In Jewish he said something to Hyman and Hyman replied.

Jacob turned to Maria. "Miss, if you have your thoughts on the diamonds for your set, I can do whatever you wish. If not, I have a suggestion for you."

"No, no, please, your suggestion."

"We should place a large diamond in the center and surround it by ten small diamonds. It will look elegant" Maria agreed. Jacob said, "Hyman?" Hyman nodded yes.

Jacob swung a magnifying glass over the desk, flipped a switch, and it lit up. From a drawer of his desk he took out two small trays of diamonds and a fancy pair of tweezers. Using the tweezers, he picked up a diamond looked at it, put it back in the tray. He did this four times. The fifth diamond seemed to take forever to examine. With a big smile on his face, Jacob placed the diamond next to the wedding set. Then he checked out the smaller diamonds. Some were put back, but for the most part, the selection went quickly. He arranged the small diamonds in a semicircle around the larger diamond.

He said, "Hyman?"

"No, I don't need to."

"Please. It would make me feel good." He handed Hyman the tweezers and stepped aside. Hyman picked up the big diamond and began studying it from different angles. He set it down, turned it with the tweezers, picked it up, and examined it again. I didn't have the foggiest idea what he was looking at except it was a diamond. Putting the diamond down, Hyman said, "My friend, this diamond is magnificent…Maria, do you approve?" She nodded.

"Miss," Jacob suggested, I will have my best man fit and set the diamonds while we have some lunch. Maria thanked him.

Jacob took us to a small dining room. The table was set and there were pitchers of water and iced tea. Before I knew it, they brought out platters of crackers with stuff on them, little hot dogs with dough around them, and all kinds of little things. I saw the same stuff on the crackers as Hernandez had served, the fishy stuff Tony had called caviar.

A guy came out and poured wine for everyone. Jacob raised his glass, "A toast to my company. I wish you the best of luck. *Maze Tov.*" Hyman said something I didn't understand. Maria and I tapped glasses with Jacob. The wine was a little too sweet for me, but good. Everybody started eating. Maria picked up a hot dog and I picked up a cracker with salmon and cream cheese. The salmon was smoked, and the combination was tasty. I picked up a cracker of caviar and leaned over to Maria. "Taste this. Tell me what you think."

She took a small bite and said, "Pauly, I like caviar."

Jacob said, "We're going to have sandwiches for lunch. The meat is good, and the rye bread is out-of-this-world. The server said, "We have pastrami, corned beef, tongue, roasted turkey, and smoked turkey."

Hyman asked for hot pastrami. Maria chose smoked turkey.

Pointing to Hyman, I said, "I'll have the same as he's having."

Jacob said, "Corned beef for me. We also have coleslaw and pickles. You'll like your sandwich."

There was enough meat piled onto the sandwich for three good-size sandwiches. I broke off a little piece of the bread. I was sure there was no way this was going be as good as Italian bread. It was better. Jacob was right. This had to be the best bread I had ever eaten. "Jacob, what kind of bread is this?" Jewish rye was his answer.

Jacob said, "Maria, while we're eating, if you don't mind, I'll have someone measure your finger. We can size the set for you. I have already picked out a band for you, Paul. If it's OK with you, we'll measure your finger, too." After we finished the sandwiches, Jacob told us to come to the showroom.

On a piece of blue velvet on the case was the wedding set and a great-looking gold band. Hyman said, "Maria, let me help you put the set on your finger. It will feel a little heavy at first. You'll get used to it."

Maria held her finger out then looked at the ring from all directions. She was having a hard time controlling her excitement, exclaiming, "This is the most beautiful, glorious, fantastic thing I have ever seen in my life. It's as if it was given to me by God."

Hyman and Jacob began talking in Jewish while Maria and I stood examining and admiring our rings. Hyman and Jacob hugged, kissed each other on the cheek, and then continued talking. A woman came up to us with two beautiful boxes and asked if she could put the rings in the boxes for us. After she did, she placed the boxes into velvet pouches, then put the pouches into a small brown paper bag and handed it to me.

We exchanged good-byes. Maria's was very emotional. "Thank you, Jacob. Thank you for everything. I really don't know how I can ever thank you enough." She asked if she could hug him.

"Maria, I thank you for that. But my religion will not permit me to touch you. I'm sorry. Good-bye and be well."

Vince met us at the door and walked us to the limo.

Maria gasped, "Hyman… we have to go back to Carl. We never thanked him."

Hyman said he had handled it and that now we needed to go home. He added, "Maria, the wedding set is as you are, beautiful. It is something you should hold very dear because there is a lot of love there. I'd value the set at the wholesale current price at $150,000. The center diamond is flawless and very rare. Before you know it, that set will appreciate ten times."

"This whole thing has been amazing. Carl and Jacob are great men, and most of all, you, Grandfather, are an amazing man. How did the money transaction go down?"

"Paul, Carl and Jacob were survivors of the Holocaust. Carl was a superior, experienced jeweler, and Jacob was a diamond cutter in Europe. They chose to come to America instead of Israel to pursue their trade. They lost all of their families in the concentration camps."

"They arrived here alone, with nothing. I have helped them over the years, and we became the best of friends. They still have no family. Their businesses are their lives. They donate money, mostly to Israel. I believe Tony, Carl, and Jacob are equal in their net worth. Carl and Jacob decided they wanted to give you the wedding set and band as a wedding gift. I tried talking to them, but they refused to listen to me. I think they see the two of you as an extended family."

Maria said, "I don't know what to say. That is so much more than anyone could ask for or expect. It would be a great honor if they accepted us as an extended family. Hyman, if they were invited, do you think they would come to our wedding?"

Hyman thought they would.

Once we were in the house, I turned to Hyman and hugged him. "Thank you. Thank you for everything, but most of all, thank you for being my grandfather."

Hyman told us he was going to be around for three more days, so we would have time to catch up on our lives.

# CHAPTER 20

On my way to Royal Auto Parts I wondered what this yard and Luca were going to be like. I had gone over the specs Hernandez had given Tony for the Caddies and couldn't see any way it could be done. How would I overcome the static I would get about doing it from this guy? I had it in my head I would be going to a shithole and dealing with dickheads.

Some guy cut me off. I gave him the finger, cursing like a madman. The guy took off like a bat out of hell. I stayed on his ass. That was dumb, losing my cool over nothing. "You're a stupid prick, Pauly!"

I finally got to Royal. My first impression was good. There was a concrete parking lot with about 20 parked cars, a long metal building with a sign on the door saying "OFFICE", and a good-looking high metal fence around the lot. I looked through the locked front gate. A metal building was along one wall and another halfway across the back wall. The yard was all concrete, with rows of tall metal racks. The racks were compartmentalized with car body parts, noses, and rear ends. Some of the compartments had cars in them. There was nothing on the ground. In fact, it was spotless – no trash, no dirt. I was impressed.

I walked through the door that had the office sign on it. Behind a long counter were three guys sitting on stools. Two were talking on phones. Like the yard, this was spotless. Normally, in a place like this, there are parts all over. Parts on the floor leaking oil. Parts stuck everywhere. Not here.

The phone free guy asked, "Can I help you?" I told him I was looking for Luca.

"Who's looking for Luca?"

"My name is Pauly." The guy got up and said he'd find him for me; it seemed like quite a while but really wasn't.

This lanky, tall, handsome wop walks up to me, sticks out his hand. "Hi Pauly, I'm Luca. Heard a lot about you. Come on back to my office and we can talk." Luca asked if he could get me something to drink. I noticed a coffeemaker against a wall with a pot of coffee in it.

"How about a cup of coffee? Light and sweet."

We started with small talk. Luca commented, "Those guys at the scrap pile think a lot of you." I knew he meant Beacon Street. I told him I liked Sam and Mario.

"In this business most guys are dumb shitheads. Those guys are the exception. Mr. D wants me to look over some specs you have to modify a couple of Caddies for some guy. He also asked me to show you around and explain the business to you, everything."

I handed him the specs. Luca studied the sheet. He asked if I understood this shit.

"Honestly, no. I can't make heads or tails outta it."

"It looks more than it is. This guy wants to take the front seat and back seat and make four hidden compartments. Look at it again." I took the sheet and looked at it. I still didn't get it.

I thought about what Luca just told me, and it popped right out at me, "Holy shit!" I exclaimed. It was so easy once I knew what to look for. I handed the sheet back to Luca.

"This isn't going to be that easy," Luca explained. "We have to make the benches and backrests, in the front and rear, into large compartments, and then reupholster them so they look like Caddy seats. We'll build the front, so it can move forward and back, but not up and down. I have a suggestion on the back rest in the rear. I could move the box seven inches back and the bench fourteen inches back. It will look like a shelf in the back of the trunk, won't even be noticed."

"I need to get ahold of Mr. D and see if he can get an OK from this guy to change his specs."

Luca showed me the phone. I called the Muraso number. In a couple of minutes, I had Tony. "Good afternoon, Sir." I heard the usual chuckle. "I'm at Royal with Luca. We're looking over the specs for the Caddies. Luca has a great suggestion for a change. How about I tell you about it, and you get ahold of Juan for an OK." Tony told me to handle it and gave me Juan's number.

I told Luca I had to call the guy about his suggestion. "I want to give him a cost to do it at the same time, and get an OK on both." I asked Luca to name a price. Luca got a pencil and paper and started writing down numbers.

"Pauly, the biggest expense we're going to have is the re-upholstery work. It's going to have to look original, and we're going to have to do some optical-illusion stuff, so it doesn't look weird. Our cost is about $2,500 for both."

Juan had time to talk to me, so I explained Luca's suggestion. He thought it was great, especially because it would give him a lot more room. I advised the biggest cost we would have was the upholstery. We could do it a couple of ways. I repeated to him what Luca told me: We could do it for less, but it wouldn't look original or quite right. I knew Juan would want the original, and he did.

"The two of them would cost $11,000 for what you want."

Juan said do it. I told him, "We will have a motor finished in two days, and you should approve it before we tackle the other nine."

"Sounds good. When it's ready, give me a call and we'll get together."

"One last thing. No invoice. No check. Cash! OK?" Juan said it was no problem.

A stunned Luca said, "How did you go from $2,500, our cost, to $11,000?"

"It's the Walker magic"

# *CHAPTER 21*

Tony said, "Mario, you and I have been friends forever. When we were kids, you were always the brains, no matter what it was. You'd think it, I'd do it. That's the way it was. You got us to this country; you got us in the junk business. When I wanted to be in a *famiglia,* you decided you didn't want to and stayed in the junk business. Now, my friend, I need you; I need my brainy friend. I need you to be my *consigliere.* Please."

"Yes. For my friend, yes."

"Mario, I'm worried about Manzella. He's old and knows all of our business. He's vulnerable and could be a threat to us. I'm going to have to put a hit on Manzella. Valachi is different. He's been in the dark on most things, kinda stupid. I'm going to see if Vito would take him into his family. He owes me a favor. Mario, what do you think about Pauly's gut feeling about Nolan? That he knows too much about our money?"

"I agree a hundred percent with his gut feeling. But before we do anything, we need to find out if he talked to anyone about it. Anyone else who knows becomes a loose string for us."

Tony said, "Hold on." He picked up a phone and started talking to someone. When he finished, he hung up and said, "I'm having our people find out what they can about Nolan, then we'll decide what to do. They'll call back before we're done."

"Pauly, what about Fanarssi? The more I hear about this guy, the more I like him. I was thinking about Fanarssi running the whole auto show rather than just Royal."

"I don't think he knows a lot about scrapping. I think he's lucky to have Luca at Royal Auto Parts. I don't think he gets much involved. I do think he's doing a good job where he's at. If you make him boss over scrapping, you'll wind up in the same boat you were in before you took it over.

"It's time to change the thinking, or at least make an exception. Sam Dawson at Beacon is a good man. He's smart and has the respect of everyone in the yard. He knows the business inside out – he's a born leader. He doesn't think he could be a boss because he's not Italian, and only Italians are bosses.

"We should be thinking about people. If someone is smart and can do a job, that's all that should matter. It shouldn't make a fuckin' difference what nationality he is."

Tony just sat gathering his thoughts. Then he said, "Mario, what do you think? Aside from being *consigliere*, you're closer to this shit than anybody."

"An Italian being *capo* is tradition, Mario replied. "It's been the same for hundreds of years. I don't think we should change our tradition, but an exception can be made. Dawson is the right man."

Tony said, "I agree with both of you. I'll talk to Sam."

I interrupted, "Sam told me one thing he didn't like about being a boss was he'd have to spend his time in an office. It seems to me he could be out all the time at one of the locations, as long as he's available to you."

Tony said he'd handle it.

The phone rang. Tony picked it up and listened. It seemed like someone was rattling on forever. Then Tony said, "Forget about it... you're fuckin' kidding me... Thanks." He turned to us and said, "Our boy Nolan is a fag. He's got a wife and no kids, and he has a lover. The wife is for show. Neither has relatives.

"Mario, talk to Luca and see if he can get close to Nolan to find out who he spoke to about the money. And find out who his lover is. Luca is a good-looking guy. He needs to know he's dealing with a high-priced attorney-fag, and he needs to dress for the occasion.

"Pauly, I want you to get close to his wife. Find out if she knows about the money, and who she might have spoken to about it. Handle it anyway you want. I'm hungry. Let's get something to eat."

I was sitting at the table, beating myself up, trying to figure how I could get close to Nolan's wife. I had no fuckin' idea. I didn't want to let Tony down. I couldn't just hit on her. I was really struggling.

Then a thought occurred to me. What if Amalgamated wanted Nolan and his wife to have executive life insurance policies? Agents would have to have appointments to fill out the paperwork. That's how I could get close to his wife!

"Tony, I've figured out how I can get close to Nolan's wife, and it would work with Nolan, too. Have Hyman tell Nolan that Amalgamated wants executive life insurance policies on him and his wife. Two agents will be contacting them for appointments. The policies will be for one million dollars each. Nolan would own the policy and Amalgamated would pay the premiums.

"If he has half a brain, he'll realize it's a good deal. Hyman will need to get us phony IDs and the paperwork to open a life insurance policy."

Tony said, "Done."

The next morning, I drove to Beacon and went to Sam's office. "Just wanted to say hi and see how Mario is coming along with the motor."

"Mario finished the motor, and he has the other nine motors in the yard."

"What are the motors worth?"

"Getting $400 a motor would be good."

In Mario's office I got the usual greeting and a cup of coffee.

"You OK with what went down last night?"

"Yeah, for as much as I've always wanted to stay away from that shit, and for as much as I like the junk business, it's the right thing to do now."

I asked if he had a chance to talk to Luca.

"Yeah, and it was OK with him."

"Sam told me you had a motor done. How did it come out?"

Mario told me, "Good – we spent a lot of time polishing the cavity."

I told Mario, "You have to build shipping crates for the motors. The crates are going to have to be very sturdy, so they can be used over and over again. You got a feel for how much I should tell this guy for the motor work and crates?"

"I'd put it at $2,000 for a motor and crate. We'd come out good."

I called Hernandez and told him we had a motor ready. He said he'd be at the Beacon Street yard in a half hour.

Mario showed me the motor. It really looked good. We sat around talking. The more time I spent with Mario, the greater respect I had for his intelligence. It wasn't long before I heard Sam holler out, "Pauly, Mr. Hernandez is here to see you."

I introduced Mario and Hernandez to each other. Juan looked the motor over. "It's good, very good. It's just what we need. You do excellent work."

I told Juan we'd build ten heavy-duty shipping crates that we can use over again. The motors and crates would cost him $7,000 each. He said OK.

"Mario, Sam has the other nine motors. Juan and I are going to Sam and have him make out an invoice."

As Juan and I started walking to Sam's office, I stopped and asked him to tell me about coke. How do you use it? What do you get out of it, and how hard is it to overdose?

He gave me the whole guided tour. I asked if he had any with him that I could buy. He walked over to his car and came back with a small brown bag. He handed it to me. "It's free. Try it." I thanked him as I put the bag in my pocket. The bag had some weight to it.

We walked into Sam's office. I asked Sam to make out an invoice, and have it state payment-in-full at port.

"Juan, as usual, it's great seeing you. Thank you for the business. I have something I have to get done, so I'll get going."

Juan said, "Pauly, why don't you come to my place with me and we can do the thing together."

"Thanks, sounds good, but some other time. I've got to get something else handled."

# *CHAPTER 22*

I drove to Muraso, walked into the bullpen. Someone handed me two packages. One had my name on it; the other had Luca's. I sat down at an empty desk and called Luca. He said the plan I had come up with for us to get close to those people was fuckin' genius. I told him he had a package at Muraso for the plan and asked if he could get away. He said he'd be right over.

I opened my package. There was a classy briefcase with an Amalgamated ID card on top, and a very sharp-looking pen set. The name on the card was William (Bill) Watson. In the briefcase there were a couple of file folders containing forms and a loose sheet of paper which had the name Sylvia Nolan and a phone number. I called her, introduced myself, and asked if she was aware of Amalgamated's desire to insure her and her husband. She was. I asked if I might have an appointment to go over the paperwork with her.

"Yes, tomorrow morning, 10:00, at my place." I thanked her and said I'd be there.

As I hung up, Luca walked in. I told him I just made my appointment with Mrs. Nolan. I asked him to open his package. I was curious what name they gave him. His ID read Gerald (Jerry) Holmes.

I said, "Someone at Amalgamated has a sense of humor. Holmes and Watson. Plus, they're efficient and a class act."

Luca asked if he could use the phone to set up an appointment with the mister. "Go ahead. Don't forget your name is Gerald."

He nodded and got on the phone. A little bit later he hung up. "I have an appointment tomorrow morning at his office. His calendar is clear for the entire morning."

Sylvia's address was on Manhattan's upper west side, a high-class area. I rang the bell. A butler opened the door. I introduced myself and told him I had an appointment with Mrs. Nolan. He asked me to wait then returned to say, "Mrs. Nolan will see you in the study. Please follow me."

Seated in the study was a good-looking blonde, nice body, very well-dressed. I said, "Good morning, Mrs. Nolan. My name is William Watson. I'm with Amalgamated."

"Good morning. Please call me Sylvia."

"Sylvia, it would be a lot easier if we worked at the table." I sat at the table, and she sat beside me. I thought for sure she'd sit opposite me. We went through Form A, which was her resume. Form B was emergency contacts and included personal friends, business and social contacts. Under emergency contacts she listed Freddie Costa. Under friend she listed Freddie Costa. She had no business contacts. She told me Freddie was her hairdresser and makeup artist. They were fiends, partied together, and he sometimes wore her clothing.

We went through a couple of more forms. One was consent for a physical exam. Another was a request for doctors she had seen in the past ten years, their specialties, phone numbers, and authorization to release records. She signed the consent for the physical, listed the doctors, and signed the authorization.

"There is one more short form and we're done. I'm going to ask you some questions. Please answer yes or no. Do you smoke?"

"No."

"Do you exercise?"

"Yes."

"How frequently?"

"Three times a week."

"Do you take drugs?"

"Yes, prescription."

"Do you drink alcohol?"

"Yes."

"How much?"

"Socially."

"Are you sexually active with your husband?"

"No."

"Are you sexually active with someone else?"

"No."

"Do you plan to have a family?"

"No."

"Do you plan to travel?"

"Yes."

"That's it. We're done. You just have to sign the affidavit on the bottom." She asked if I was going to leave now.

I said, "If it's alright with you, I'd like talk to you off the record. If the physical comes out OK, you'll have the policy. Us talking about things won't matter."

She said, "I'd like to get to know you. Are you married?"

I told her no. I asked her if she did coke.

She said, "Off the record, I do."

"Why don't you have sex with your husband?"

"I have a screwed-up life. My husband is a full-blown fag with a lover, his intern Brian. I'm a showpiece for his wealthy clients. We have nothing together."

I asked if he ever discussed business. "No, just money. He told me about this Mafia boss hiding money in the Grand Caymans and all over and laundering money at a casino."

"Did you tell your friend about it?"

"No. Frank told me not to say a word to anyone or he'd kill me."

"Do you think he would actually kill you?"

"Yes."

"I'm done. Do you have any questions?"

"Yes. Am I the beneficiary of my husband's policy?" When I said yes, she smiled. "We could have a good life together with the mil." She leaned over to me, purring, "I want to kiss you." She did, leaned back, and said, "Thank you, God. Bill, how about you and I make it for a little bit? I'm so horny!"

"Sure. You're beautiful, and you have great tits. I'd give a lot to make it with you. I don't want just a little bit – I want it all. We could do a little coke, and then fuck our brains out."

"Tomorrow. I can give the servants off." She leaned over and started to rub my dick. I reached in her top and gently began squeezing a tit.

She squeezed my cock, not too gently "I want to suck on this."

"Tomorrow. We'll do it all tomorrow."

Reaching her hand under her dress, she started playing with herself. After a while she took her clutching fingers off my cock, started moaning then leaned back. "I'm sorry," she gasped. "I told you I was horny."

"Don't worry about it. Tomorrow you'll be moaning and groaning all day."

"I can't wait. Tomorrow we'll start the same time as today."

At Muraso Luca was standing in the hallway. I asked what he was doing. "I don't know. I finished with the mister and his boy. I got what I wanted and thought I'd see Mario. I can't find him."

"Let's see if Tony is busy. If he's not busy, we can talk to him about the deal." I knocked on the door and heard, 'Yeah.'

"It's Pauly and Luca. We were wondering if you had some time for us."

"Sure, come in." As we walked in, Tony walked out, saying, "Sit down and relax. I'll be right back." In a couple of minutes, he returned with Mario.

"We got close to the Nolans and found out what you wanted. Mrs. Nolan is a good-looking blonde with a great set of bazongas. She has to be the horniest bitch in the world. She does coke and knows every detail of what was said at the meeting. Nolan warned her if she told anyone, he'd kill her. She said she didn't tell a soul."

Luca said, "Nolan said he told only his wife and Brian his lover. Brian thought it was all bullshit and told me he didn't repeat it to anyone. I believe both."

Tony "Whatever you decide to do, it should be soon. These three are loose strings, especially the missus. She wants to spend the day with me tomorrow at her place. If you decide to off her, a coke overdose would work. Before you decide to do anything, I think we should find out if any of them made a recording or wrote something down as insurance against each other or anybody else."

Mario said, "That's smart. We didn't think about that. I wouldn't put it past Nolan."

Tony said, "Pauly, find out from her if she or her husband wrote or recorded anything. If she says no, go through the place. Then off her with an overdose."

"Luca, you to do the same with Nolan. Check his office and diplomatically see if his secretary typed anything about it for him. Find out if he has a safe deposit box. If he has one, get him to take you to it. If wifey has one, you do the same, Pauly. At five o'clock Vince is gonna pick up Nolan and his boy and take them to the East Side Drive. Nolan and his bitch are gonna be part of the concrete retaining wall. Pauly, do whatever you want with her body."

I headed home, beat tired. This shit really was taking its toll on me. I walked into the house and embraced Maria. Holding her close to me felt good.

Maria studied my face, "You look terrible. Why don't we go out on the patio? I'll make us a drink; you can smoke; we can relax until dinner. After we eat, you should go to bed."

Maria came out to the patio with two glasses. "This is a little different. It's called Long Island Iced Tea. It has some extra stuff in it, and no tea."

I smoked, we talked, and I drank my iced tea. My brain became foggy. "I'm not sure what that extra stuff is. I feel woozy. Gonna pass on dinner and get in bed."

Maria helped me get upstairs.

The next morning, I felt refreshed. Downstairs Maria said, "Good morning, Sleepyhead. You're running late. How about some coffee?"

"Thanks, that sounds good. And how is the most beautiful girl in the Bronx doing this morning?"

"Good and thank you."

In Manhattan I lucked out and found a parking spot close. I walked up the steps and was about to ring the doorbell when the door flew open. Sylvia was standing there with a robe on. She locked the door behind us. "Bill, I'm so glad to see you. I thought about today all night. I'm ready for you." She opened her robe. She was naked.

I stared. Wow, what a great body! And those fuckin' tits! I said, "Sylvia, you're gorgeous... and a fuckin' tease. Close your robe. We need to go into the study, and get some business done. Then we can get high and fuck all day. Amalgamated is insuring your valuables along with the life policy. It won't cost you anything. The valuables have to be inventoried. Anything that's big bucks will have to be appraised."

"Sounds good to me. We can start with my jewelry, then Frank's, the safe, and I know he has some things in his desk."

"Thanks. That would get me off the hook with the company."

I followed her into the bedroom. She pointed to her dresser. The jewelry box looked like a miniature dresser on top of a dresser.

"Sylvia, we're just going to inventory insurable jewelry, not costume."

"Bill, all I have is pricey. I don't have anything that is not insurable."

"This is going to take forever. How about you inventory your stuff for me, and I'll inventory Frank's and the safe. That way we can get this done, and then have some fun."

She blurted out, "Let's get this get this started and over with. I need a fix." After she showed me where Frank's jewelry was, she opened the safe,

I asked, if she kept a diary or journal.

"No, I don't have the patience to write and don't have a life to write about."

"Did you write down what Frank told you about the Mafia guy and the money?"

"No, I was afraid to. Frank would kill me"

"Did Frank write it down or record it?"

"Maybe Frank taped it on a little recorder he keeps in his desk."

"Let's get back to work. We have a long day ahead of us. One more thing. I need to use your phone and talk to my counterpart at Frank's office." Once she went back to the bedroom, I called the number she gave me. It was a direct line to her husband. I asked to speak to Mr. Holmes from Amalgamated and was connected to Luca. "Morning, how's your day going?" Before he could answer I told him to get me the watch Nolan was wearing. He agreed then disconnected.

Nolan wore a $10,000 Rolex. I figured Tony could use it. If he didn't want it, I'd wear it. I emptied everything out of the safe and jewelry chest into my briefcase. The desk didn't have much except a mini-recorder and four tapes. I played the tapes looking for the right one. The second tape had what I was looking for. I put the recorder and all the tapes in my briefcase. I left the brief-case in a corner and went to the bedroom.

"How you doin', good-looking?" I put my arms around her and began feeling her up. "How about stopping? We can finish it up together later. Let's have some fun now." She turned around, slid off her robe, and flung it on the bed.

"OK, Billy Boy, let's do it."

A good-looking blonde with great tits and body. She was a fuckin' dream come true, and I was horny. I got undressed and screwed her. After we got done humping, I suggested we get high and asked if she had any.

"I don't have enough for both of us."

"That's OK you start, and I'll catch up with the gift I have for you. Where do you do it?"

"On the bathroom counter. What's the gift?" I took the brick out of my jacket pocket, handed it to her. "Wow, I've never seen this much shit at one time in my life."

In the bathroom she opened a drawer, took out a mirror, a playing card, a straw, and a small medicine bottle. She dumped the medicine bottle in a little pile on the mirror and began moving the powder around with the playing card. She made three rows of powder, then put the straw in her nose and inhaled a row. She stood up, kind of shook it off, and then went down and did the second row. She switched nostrils and did the third row. She was bent over the counter; her tits were swaying back and forth. I couldn't take it anymore.

I turned her around and pushed her to her knees. As I held her tits and began squeezing, I shoved my cock in her mouth. "Suck, bitch, suck." I went down her throat and began squeezing harder. She moaned, and I came. I got her up, told her to open the brick I gave her and make six sticks, three for her and three for me. "Before you do it, start a tub. I always wanted to get laid under water." I went to the bedroom and dressed.

She had snorted some of the shit and was out of it. I took the straw out of her nose and put it on the mirror alongside the coke. I found a plastic bag that had some stuff in it, dumped it out in the drawer, and put the brick in the bag. The tub had filled. I turned off the water, got behind her, lifted and carried her to the tub, and laid her in it. I shoved my hand in her mouth, grabbed her tit with my other hand, and pushed her underwater.

There was no fight, no struggle – she just lay there. I took my hand out of her mouth, kept holding her down, by her tit. After a while I let go.

I went to the study, got my briefcase, put the inventory sheet and my pen in the case along with all her jewelry. I walked back to the bathroom. She was still under. *Arrivederci, dope testa di cazzo.* I put the coke in the case and left.

I was driving back to the Bronx thinking this coke that we're going to get into is some badass shit. I'm never going to do it. That woman was a fucked-up cunt because of it. Then I remembered Juan telling us the coke we'd be getting had to be cut. The brick wasn't; she sure as fuck overdosed.

I headed to the Bronx. With three hours to kill, I decided to go to Beacon and visit with Sam. Once I parked in the lot I thought I had better check out the briefcase. I took the brick out, shoved it under my seat. I put the inventory sheet on the passenger side and piled her shit on it. There was a mountain of stuff – between the gold and diamonds, my car was sparkling. I figured I'd ask Tony what he wanted to do with Silvia's crap. If he didn't care, I'd give it to Maria.

Next was the shit from the safe. I had reached my arm in the safe and raked everything into the case. I hadn't paid any attention at the time. I started going through it, bundles of cash, and small bars of gold. I examined a stack of papers. The front of the stack read 'ten-thousand-dollar bearer bond.' I didn't know what a bearer bond was, but $10,000 for each of these papers was a lot of money. I got down to Nolan's personal shit. There were two watches that looked good. If Tony wanted the Rolex, I'd wear one of these. There was a lot more gold, and the recorder and tapes.

I tossed her stuff back in the case on top of his, then I put the briefcase in the trunk. Passing a 55-gallon drum with burning trash, I threw the inventory sheets in and watched them disappear.

I asked Sam if he had any good coffee in the joint. We sat around shooting the breeze until I finally ran out of patience. "Well…you gonna tell me if you took it, or is it a secret?"

"Yeah, I took it. Tony didn't want anything said till he told everybody at the same time. The thing I like most is going to be dealing with Luca. I don't know why I'm even telling you this shit. You're probably responsible for getting me into this crap."

"Me? Fuck no. This is the first I'm hearin' about it. Who are you going to replace yourself with?"

"You remember Joey, the guy I had you work with? He's smart and a good worker. With a little training, he could do a good job."

"Sounds good. Bye, thanks for the shit coffee. I'm gonna see how the motors are doing."

I left Beacon, drove to Muraso, grabbed the briefcase out of the trunk, and went to Tony's office. Luca was sitting there. "Sorry to interrupt you guys. I can come back."

Tony said, "Fuck no. We've been waiting for you. How'd it go?"

"It went well. Before I tell you about it, I have something for you. Nolan was wearing a Rolex. I had Luca get it for me. I want you to have it."

Tony protested, "Thanks, but you keep it. I don't like watches."

"Mrs. Nolan overdosed on coke and decided to take a bath. She didn't write or record anything about the money out of fear, but she heard Nolan record it. She showed me the recorder and tapes. The one you're looking for is in the recorder." I handed

Tony the stack of papers. He glanced at it and put it to one side. I handed him the two bundles of cash.

He said, "Luca, catch," and threw him a bundle, and then one to me. There were also some small bars of gold along with the jewelry. That's it.

"Take the briefcase home and ask Hyman to fence everything for you."

I told Tony I was thinking about giving her shit to Maria, because it's all top-of-the-line. Tony told me no. "Don't ever do that, and don't ever talk to Maria or anyone else about what goes on or what you do. Ask Hyman to pick out one piece for Maria and one for Gloria, then have him fence the rest. What he gets for it, you keep. Both of you have had a hard day, and you did a good job. I thank you. Go home and get some rest."

I drove home, took the briefcase to my room, then found Hyman on the patio. After I explained the details of what went down, we went to his room. I locked the door and emptied the briefcase on the bed.

Hyman had me put the gold bars back in the briefcase, as he started putting other stuff in. He picked up an earring and looked the diamond over closely. We found the matching earring, put the pair on the dresser. He kept picking up pieces and putting them in the briefcase. A necklace that had a diamond broach was set aside, and I put it on the dresser.

Then I heard, "Oh, my God, Paul! Do you know what you have here?" He was holding a watch. "This is a Sondrio, from a company in a small town on the Italian-Swiss border, the town of Sondrio. They employ extremely skilled Swiss and Italian craftsmen to make handmade watches. These timepieces are built to the highest standards – every part is precision made, the jewels are the finest you can buy. This is a collector's item, worth ten times the Rolex you're wearing."

I asked him if the other watch was a Sondrio. He checked. "Yes, this one looks like it was made in the same year as the first."

"Sir, please do me a favor and tell Tony what you told me. Tell him if he doesn't want it in time he can give it to a grandson, and insist he take it. You keep the other one for yourself."

Hyman told me he couldn't. Please! He said OK.

Everything else went into the briefcase. Hyman would handle it tomorrow, including picking up boxes for the necklace and earrings which would be cleaned and polished. He thought the earrings would be appropriate for Maria, and Tony could give Gloria the necklace.

I walked downstairs looking for Maria and bumped into Tony. He wanted me to go over to the Astro Concrete field office on 125th Street in the morning. I was to see the boss, Benny, who would tell me about the concrete business. Tony had just talked to the *capo* and got an exemption for me to be a made-man. "It seemed at one time the *capo* worked for your grandfather. He said he was a great man, and he owed him a lot of favors. It's a small fuckin' world we live in."

I was to be at Muraso at seven tomorrow night for the ritual to make me a made-man. The Nolan thing was my bones.

Everyone sat down to dinner. Hyman told Tony about the Sondrio watch. He knew Tony didn't like to wear a watch, but this was one Tony needed to collect. Someday when his future grandson was old enough, he'd give it to him as a gift. Tony thanked him.

# *CHAPTER 23*

I took the Triborough Bridge to Manhattan. As soon as I got off, there was a huge billboard: Astro Concrete Corporation. Under the billboard were trailers, garages, a bunch of buildings, and a lot with at least twenty cement trucks. I drove onto the lot and pulled in front of a trailer. I knocked on the door, heard, "Whadda ya want?" I asked for Benny. The guy said, "Benny's in the other trailer."

I knocked on the other trailer door and heard, "Yeah?"

"I'm looking for Benny."

I heard, "Benny's in the other trailer."

"I was just over there, and I was told he was in this one. I don't appreciate your game, so where the fuck is he?"

The door opened. A guy covered in cement dust said, "I'm Benny. So, you don't like my fuckin' game? Neither do I. Come in, have some coffee with me." He fixed me a cup and told me to follow him.

We walked out a sliding door onto a deck, and then up a flight of stairs to a second deck. The deck had a couple of chairs and a view of the whole operation.

I put my cup on a table that was between the chairs and lit up a Lucky.

"Tony called me, told me to explain the operation to you. He also told me all about you."

"The city put out a multi-million-dollar, multi-year contract. Astro Concrete was awarded the contract. We have to widen the approach to the Triborough and reinforce the river side of the East Side Drive. During rush hours, the drive gets really backed up, people trying to get out of Manhattan. The Harlem River has eroded the East Side Drive so bad it's gettin' dangerous. We're setting concrete retaining walls along the drive and will wrap the walls around to the bridge to widen the approach.

"See those two big barges with the cranes on them? They're pounding beams into the silt every ten feet. The cranes on the drive are also pounding I-beams every ten feet, exactly opposite the others, with six feet between them.

"We'll secure twenty-four foot-wide by twelve-foot-high re-inforced steel forms to the beams. The forms will be four feet higher than the drive, while the beams will be the height of the drive. It takes two cranes to lift a form in place. It looks like the cranes are bending, the fuckers weigh so much."

Benny asked how I was doin'. "Good. It's a complicated thing, but the way you're explaining it to me, it sounds simple, and I'm really interested."

He continued. "The beams have to face in the same direction, so the forms can be attached to the meat of the beams. We secure the beams to each other with two-inch all thread. On top of the all thread, running the length, are four sixteen-foot, two-inch rebar. We build grids of one-inch rebar to secure the sixteen-footers and give the wall strength. The two-inch rebar extends from one section to the other. We pour the concrete four trucks at a time. When the forms are full, guys will stand on two-by-eights and scree to float the top. Then we'll wet it down and let it cure."

I told Benny, "There's only one thing I don't understand. You're hauling the concrete from the Bronx plant. You have more than enough land here to put up your own plant. Why don't you do that?"

"The city leased us the land for a dollar a year. You're right! You're fuckin' right. I never thought of it because it's the way we've always done it, and I'm stupid."

I told him he sure as shit wasn't stupid. "You should call Tony and talk to him about it."

"How about we go down to the site and see how they're coming along? I'll get you a hard hat."

They had over three hundred feet of wall done and were working two forms. We walked up to the first form and onto a platform. Looking around, the place was amazing. Guys were everywhere, working on something. It was a beehive. The pounding of the beams, the cranes swinging, and the rumbling of all the motors made it feel like everything was moving to the same beat. We walked to the edge of the platform and looked down into the form.

Benny hollered out, "Franco, you need to get your crew going. You're holding up everything. Form two is way ahead of you."

Franco said, "Sure, boss, sure."

Benny shouted, "I'm not fucking with you. If you can't get the job done, I'll get somebody who can."

We started walking back to the truck. Benny was pissed and muttering to himself. "That fucking asshole. That stupid prick. I've got to get rid of him."

We drove back to the trailer. Benny pulled up in front, turned to me, and started telling me about a guy Tony had wanted him to hire some years ago. "I was to pay him good bucks and work his ass off. The guy was a recovering alcoholic. I worked him for the first few days, and then I didn't need to anymore – he did it himself. That guy was the hardest working laborer Astro ever had. I wish I had him back on this job. He asked if I knew who he was talking about.

"Yes, and thanks for everything you did for my dad, and thank you for today. I'm amazed at what and how you do this stuff. Don't work too hard, take care of yourself. I'm gonna get going."

I drove home, went upstairs, threw my clothes in a laundry basket, cleaned off my shoes, and took a shower. By chance Hyman was standing at the door to his room and motioned me in. He handed me my briefcase. "Paul, here are Maria's earrings and Gloria's necklace, in boxes, and $630,000."

"I need one more favor, Grandfather. I need to know how much money my father owed you that you gave him as a wedding gift. He told me $70,000. Between us, I want to repay that to you. I know you let him off the hook. You did so much for him, and now so much for Maria and me. Please let me even the score."

Hyman agreed.

"I'm going to give the money to my father; then he'll repay you. How much did Tony kick in?" Hyman said Tony forked over the other $70,000. "I knew my mother had the money, but my father was too proud to ask her for it, and the owing continues to bother him."

I caught Tony coming upstairs. "I've got the thing for Gloria, and I need a favor. I know you gave my grandmother $70,000 for my father, and then let Dad off the hook with the wedding gift. I know he feels he still owes you, and it bothers him. I want to even the score."

"You already did. The bearer bonds you gave me were worth $400,000."

"No, that's different. That was business. This is personal. I'm going to give my father $70,000 to give to you. Please take it, and don't mention me, and tell Hyman not to either."

I drove to my parents' place. They hadn't left for Vegas yet. My mother and father were eating. Mom saw me first. She jumped up and began hugging me, and my father joined in. They wanted me to stay for dinner. My father was going on about what a great cook my mother is, and that I'd been missing out on some good food.

"Thanks.  I'm sorry to interrupt your meal. I need to get something done, then I have to get back to work. Mom, I know you have Grandma's money, and you're saving it. Dad, I know you're making good money now. The two of you deserve to have a good life. The $70,000 that Hyman and Tony gave to you as wedding gifts was letting you off the hook. I know it bothers you that you owe the money."

I took $200,000 out of my case and put it on the table. "Dad, give Hyman and Tony the $70,000 each, and keep sixty for yourself. Do whatever you want with it."

My father hugged me, whispered in my ear thank you, and started to cry. I held him for a couple of minutes; then I reached for a napkin and handed it to him. "I'm happy to see both of you, but I have to get to work. Before you leave for Vegas, we'll spend some time together." I kissed my mother and said bye.

# *CHAPTER 24*

In the Muraso conference room, Tony was seated at the head, Mario alongside him, and the seat by Mario was the only empty one. I headed to the back of the room. On the way, I saw Benny. He gave me a guarded smile. Next, I saw Fanarssi, with the same suppressed grin. I got to the back of the room and sat against the wall.

Tony started, "Tonight, by tradition, we welcome a man to our *famiglia*. Pauly, stand here by Mario. Gentlemen, as you know this is Paul Walker. His grandfather was Dominic DeDomenico, *capo-de-tutti-capi* of the Neapolitan families. His uncles were *capos* in Italy. I've known Pauly all his life. He's become an honorable man. He'll be welcomed by all to our *famiglia*.

"Pauly, pick up the picture of the Virgin Mary and hold it in your hands. Mario will stick your trigger finger with a dagger then set the picture on fire. As the picture is burning, and your blood is dripping on it, you will repeat what I say."

Mario did his thing. Then Tony spoke, "As burns this saint so will burn my soul. I enter alive and can only get out dead. I will never betray the oath of *omerta*."

With that, everyone said in unison, "*Benevito trovato anche in queste voci*." One at a time, they stood up, came to me, kissed me on each cheek, then left. Tony picked up a small trash can and brushed the ashes off the table. Then he reached in a sideboard and took out three glasses and a bottle of Chianti. He filled the glasses, lifted his, and said, "This day requires a toast. I toast you Pauly Walker, I toast you." Tony, Mario, and I linked our glasses and said *salute*.

Tony reached under the table and took out two attaché cases. He opened one. There were neatly stacked bundles of hundred-dollar bills. He told me the money was mine, and I was to put it in my safe deposit box. He opened the second attaché. It had two pistols, a silencer, four clips, and ammo. The pistols were a .45 and a .22. The .22 was threaded for the silencer. He told me to take them home and put the pistols in a closet. We'd go over them some other time.

"Pauly, tomorrow morning you need to get ahold of Hernandez and arrange to have him meet you at the port. We have two 40-foot containers with the limos and Chevys, two 40-foot containers with the motors and parts. Eight car carriers will be there in the morning. Get an invoice for the cars and his notes for the limos from Fanarssi. Fanarssi's invoice will list the cost of transporting and loading the cars. He'll have the Beacon invoice for the motors and parts. Sam made out a blank invoice for the motor gutting and the Chevy work you and Hernandez agreed to. Put a number on the invoice. Add to it Fanarssi's notes on the limos.

"You and Hernandez go into the office and make out the manifests. The parts: Royal Auto Parts is the shipper. The cars: Royal Auto Sales is the shipper. Sign the bill for the containers and loading. Have Juan make out the manifest for the cars and pay for the containers and loading. Customs will be a rubber stamp – the office will handle it. Remind Juan to bring his checkbook and cash.

"Try to finish up with Juan by 2:00 or 3:00 and get back to Muraso. Mario, you and I need to finish our talk. Go home. It's been a big day for you. Don't forget *omerta*. As hard as that is going to be, it does apply to Maria."

"I won't forget it and never will. Thank you. Mario, thank you for being you and a good friend."

The next morning, I phoned Juan to inform him we needed to meet at the port to make out manifests and get squared away. "The containers are there, and the cars are going to be loaded. Bring your checkbook, and cash."

"No problem. An hour and half be OK? ... Good. See you then."

I got dressed, took the attaché and briefcase downstairs.

Maria saw me and said, "Good morning, handsome. How about a cup of coffee?"

"Good morning, Sweetheart. I'm sorry. I can't. I'm running late and have a big day. I'll see you tonight for dinner."

I drove to Manufacturers Bank on Jerome Avenue. This was the first time I had been in a bank. I didn't know what to do. There were three lines of people waiting to talk to ladies behind a counter. I didn't have time to wait in line. I noticed there was a guy sitting at a desk in the corner.

"Sir, I'm sorry to bother you. I need to get into a safe deposit box. I'm not sure what to do."

The guy said, "You'll have to wait in line like everybody else. A teller will help you."

"You don't look real busy. You can't help me?"

"That's not my job."

Remembering Tony said the manager was a friend of his, I pushed, "Can you get the manager for me?"

The guy got up and told me to wait. He returned with a guy in a suit. I thought to myself, Maybe I didn't dress for the occasion. The guy extended his hand to me, and said, "Good morning, I'm Steven Mariani, the manager. May I be of service to you?"

"I asked this guy how to get into a safe deposit box. He told me I had to wait in line. I don't have the time. I asked him to help me out, and he told me it wasn't his job. How do I get into a box without waiting in line? I'm about to take my business to a different bank if I can't get help with this."

He asked what name was on the box. I told him mine, Paul Walker.

"The DeAngelo family Paul Walker?" I nodded yes.

"I'm so sorry. Please follow me and we'll open the box." As we were walking away, I noticed the manager give the guy a hell of a dirty look, I thought, You're up shit's creek.

At the vault the manager asked for my key. He took out a master key and turned two locks simultaneously. He slid a lidded box out and put it on a table. When I was done, I was to slide the box in place.

"By the way, your grandfather was in yesterday. Like Tony, he can't say enough about you." As soon as he left, I opened the box and looked in. There was a lot of money in it. Typical Tony. Not just the money, but the box itself was one of the largest in the vault.

I stacked the money in the box, closed the lid, and slid the box in place, and removed my key. I walked past the guy sitting at the desk. He said, "Have a good day." I didn't respond, just gave him the birdie as I walked out.

At the pier they were driving the cars on board the ship. Juan had not arrived yet. I wandered over to our containers. I wanted to make sure the seals were all on and not broken.

A voice yelled out, "Hey! You! Get out of there." As I returned to the car, Juan pulled up.

"Glad to see you. Let's go in this office." We made out our manifests. Juan paid for the containers and loading, and I signed for ours.

The guy standing behind the counter said, "That was you earlier at your containers? I'm sorry about that."

"Don't be. I appreciate your looking out like that."

Juan asked me to join him in the limo so we could square up. I handed Juan the Royal Auto Sales invoice and told him I needed the check made out to RAS, and then the same for Royal Auto Parts invoice. I gave Juan the sheet that had all the cash deals. "This is what we agreed on."

Juan took four bundles of money out of the glove compartment. "This should cover it all. Pauly, we're going to be doing business for a long time. I want to show you my appreciation up front. He reached behind the seat and lifted out a black duffle bag. "This is for you. I won't take no for an answer."

"Thank you. It really isn't necessary. Our doing business together for a long time is all that matters." I put everything on the front seat of my car and headed for Muraso.

# CHAPTER 25

I realized I didn't know how much he gave me for the cash deals. I wanted to make sure he didn't shortchange me. I pulled into a parking lot and started counting the cash. I counted it twice. Juan had given me $20,000 more than he should have.

I put everything from Juan in the attaché. At Muraso there were construction guys all over the place. I walked down the hallway to the bullpen. The same construction shit here too.

With the attaché in one hand and the duffle in the other, I had a slight problem knocking on Tony's office door. "It's Pauly. Good afternoon, Sir." I didn't get the usual response. I thought: OK. I put the attaché on the desk, popped it open, and handed Tony the invoices and checks, the sheet with the cash deals, and the cash. I said the checks were good, and the cash was $20,000 too much. I told him how it went down.

"Don't worry about it. We're gonna see Juan tomorrow. If he wants it back, we'll give it to him. For now, just leave it." Tony got on the phone. "Dino, get in here. I need you to do something for me."

Dino walked in, sat in the chair beside me, didn't look at me, or say anything. This skinny, coke-bottle, horn-rimmed glasses fag at least could have said hello.

"Dino, I need you to go to the bank. Deposit this check against this invoice to the Royal Auto Sales account, the same with this one for Royal Auto Parts, and this cash against this sheet to the family account." The guy picked up everything and left. Tony said, "I want to see how the family deposit is going to be. If he doesn't count it before, the teller will. Somewhere the $20,000 will come out."

"Juan gave me this duffle bag. Because we'd be doing business together for a long time, he wanted to show his appreciation up front. He wouldn't take no for an answer. Here's the bag"

Peering into the bag the bag, Tony exclaimed, "Holy fuckin' shit, Pauly! Did you look in here?"

"No."

Tony closed the bag. "That fuckin' Juan is tryin' to buy everybody in the *famiglia*. Besides you and Fanarssi, I wonder who else he's gotten to. Keep this shit."

There was a knock on the door. It was Dino. "This is the deposit slip and invoice for RAP, this is for RAS, and this is for the family account. If it's OK, I'll post it to each account."

Tony got up and stood beside Dino with his hand on his shoulder. "Dino, did you count the family money before you made out the deposit slip?" He said he didn't. "When the teller counted the money, did she come up with the same amount as the deposit?" Yes, she did.

Tony slid his hand around Dino's neck, lifted him out of the chair. "You little prick. If you asked me for the money, I'd have given it to you. Where the fuck is it?"

Dino, shaking, said, "In my desk drawer." Tony had him get it. He returned and handed Tony the cash.

Tony told Dino to sit down and asked him why'd he taken the money. He had no answer. "How much more have you taken? I'll find out. Make it easier on yourself. Tell me."

He told Tony, "This is it."

"I'm gonna give you a choice. You can tell me now or tell me in more pain than you ever had in your life." Dino admitted to $100,000 over the years. "Where is it?"

"I keep it in a safe deposit box."

Tony asked if he did his banking at the same bank. Dino nodded yes. Tony handed me an attaché that had a pistol with a silencer in it. "Close out his accounts and the box. Dump it all in the attaché so Dino can have a fresh start somewhere else."

On the way to the bank Dino came out with. "Tony is really a good guy. For a minute I thought I was a dead man."

I didn't say anything. After we handled the banking, in the parking lot, I did it. Vince bagged Dino and threw him in the trunk. He dropped me off on his way to Benny who would know what to do. I did it and didn't mind at all. It was easy. I got back to Tony's office, handed him the attaché. He put it under his desk and sighed, "Never a fuckin' dull moment around here."

Tony said, "Come on, I'll show you what I'm doin' to this place. The entry's going to have a small office. It's gonna have two-foot-wide by eight-foot-high concrete walls, and a small, sliding, bullet-proof window on the front. The office is gonna be manned twenty-four hours a day."

"The inside entry door is gonna have an automatic lock that the guy in the office controls. You'll only be able to get in if the guy identifies you. The old conference room is going to be converted into two good-sized offices." In the bullpen Tony told me he sold the bookmaking operation to the Luchese family. "The operation in Vegas is doing better than expected, and we don't need both."

Tony was going to put in a high-class conference room, half dozen offices, and a dining room. "The main entry, the grill entry, and the hallway will have cameras, as well as the front outside. The guy in the office will be monitoring all of this. What do you think of it?"

"Sounds good to me."

"It should. This was all your idea! We need to get together with Mario and finish our meeting. Tomorrow we're goin' to see Hernandez."

Mario, Tony, and I were in his office drinking Chianti. Tony and Mario were smoking ropes. I had my Lucky. Tony told Mario about the Dino deal then said he wanted to make Vincenzo the bookmaking boss, the treasurer of the family, and let him hire a bookkeeper. He also wanted Vincenzo to run something else. The payroll for all the companies would come out of here. He wanted to make sure all the taxes were paid, only because taxes could bring the Feds and State on our asses quicker than anything.

Mario thought it was a great idea.

Tony continued, "Vincenzo's good with people. He can run a deal like that. He's also good with numbers, and he's trustworthy. Sam Dawson is in place and I've told everyone concerned he's the boss. I want to do something different. I want to let Sam run Royal Auto Sales, too, freeing Fanarssi to run the dope deal. It's going to be big, and I want someone we can trust."

Tony clasped my shoulder. "Pauly, one of the two offices I'm gonna build, where the conference room was, is gonna to be for a new under-boss. The other for Mario. The three of us will run this *famiglia*. Pauly, you're gonna be the under-boss. Aside from being everyone's boss, you'll be the only one besides me who will be in direct contact with Hernandez. I don't trust the prick.

"Tomorrow at 2:00 we have a meeting with Hernandez. I'm sure everything will go well. As soon as you can, I want you to get together with Fanarssi and go over everything. Then I want Fanarssi to visit the families in the network. They can get to know him and who they're gonna be talkin' to.

"While I handle the four families in the city, you'll go to Miami. You'll have an introduction to Meyer Lansky from Hyman. They're good friends. Lansky runs the family. Santo Trafficante is the boss. He and I are old friends, and he knows about you. The three of you can work things out. Miami is going to be a big one for us."

The day was still young. I decided to drive home, get the duffle bag, and put the money in the bank.

"Hi, Beautiful, how would you like to go out to dinner tonight to a nice joint?"

Maria kissed me and said, "How about we have dinner here tonight? Then we can spend the evening together… alone. I haven't seen a lot of you lately." I agreed.

In my room I got the duffle out and dumped it on the bed. The money on the bed was in bundles of hundred-dollar bills. I counted a bundle and then multiplied it by the number of bundles. There was half million on the bed! I put $200,000 in my closet, and the rest in the duffle, and headed for the bank.

The bank was empty. I walked up to a teller and asked if I could talk to Mr. Mariano, the manager, came out of his office. "Pauly, how are you? What can I do for you?"

"I'd like to talk to you in your office." I told him I had a lot of cash that I didn't want to stick in the safe deposit box. I wanted to put it into something that would make money for me. I told him I needed his advice on what to do. He asked me how much I had to invest. I told him $800,000.

Mariano suggested I put the money into a twelve-month Certificate of Deposit that would earn 7% annually. "The CD is considered confidential, meaning no person or agency can gain access or have knowledge of it." I asked if he minded opening my safe deposit box for me. I needed to add $500,000 to what I had. After everything was done and the CD was in my safe deposit box, I was on my way home.

Maria and I relaxed on the patio before dinner and were talking. She spoke of her thoughts for our future, her plans. She knew I couldn't talk about work. For me, that was all that consumed my mind.

"Maria, I had been thinking about a new car. How about I buy you one?"

"Thank you, but I love my car. But if you want a new car, go for it. Dad's company owns a car lot. You could get a good deal."

"I feel bad about living here, mooching off Tony. I want to give him some kind of payment."

"I understand how you feel, but he won't take money from you."

"I have a lot of money right now. I want to open a checking account in your name. You'll be able to buy anything you want. And if you decide to buy Tony a gift, it would be a true gift, not something he's paying for. Be OK?"

"Yes, Pauly, that would be wonderful."

After dinner we went back to the patio, to talk and make out. The evening flew by. Maria took my hand and said, "I'm beat. Let's go to bed." As we were heading toward the stairs, the front door opened. It was Tony. He asked if we wanted to join him in sharing some Chianti. Maria pleaded exhaustion. "But Pauly can if he wants to."

Tony broke out the Chianti and two glasses. We toasted. He took out a rope, and I took out a Lucky Strike. "Tony, thank you for today, and thank you for everything. I know you know I truly mean all that. There's one thing that bothers me. I love living here, I love being close to Maria, but I feel like I'm mooching off you. I want to pay you for room and board."

"No, Pauly, I can't take money from you for living here. Besides, after today, you and I are partners in our business. Partners don't take money from each other."

"OK, but I don't give a fuck about what you say. There's still going to be a 'Sir' in there once in a while. For now, I'm going to need your help till I get a good feel and really see how things go. I need to know if everyone in our family knows who I am, and if the other four family bosses know."

"Everybody knows. The other family bosses knew before you."

"I need to talk to you about something. There's a good-size lot behind the shop building at Royal Auto Parts. I don't know if we own it. Either way, I'd like to build a big shop, and tie it into the body shop. There could be small single-car garages across the front and back walls. I want to hire some guys to go out buying totals from insurance companies we don't do business with. Amalgamated is getting big in auto insurance. As a sales tool, they could offer to replace an insured's car with a new car, same make, as long as the accident was not their fault. The other guy's insurance will be paying for repairs. The difference between new and repair in most cases isn't that much. I want all of Amalgamated's wrecks.

"I want to put a Royal Auto Sales in Brooklyn, and one off the Long Island Expressway. I'm going to talk Juan into opening a parts distribution center and a mega car lot in Miami. We can ship cars by rail to him and still make good bucks. What do you think?"

Tony considered all the ideas for a minute, then said, "I think it's all terrific; it's fuckin' terrific. We own the lot behind

Royal, and we'll work on it together with Sam. I'll have Fanarssi, who has some free time right now, set up the lots in Brooklyn and on the Expressway."

"Tony, I have one more thought then I'll let you go to bed. Somewhere in South America there is a lot of dough floating around from this dope shit. I was thinking I'd see if Juan wanted to set up a used car lot of high-end cars. Foreign and American sports cars that he would title there. We could ship them to him and make a lot of bucks."

"Try him. Tomorrow we have a meeting with Juan at his place at 2:00. I'm going to need you to drive yourself. I'm going to get some shit done after the meeting, and I'll need Vince."

# *CHAPTER 26*

I awoke dead set on a new car. At Royal Auto Sales I found what I was looking for – a black Corvette. I looked it all over and tried the door. It was locked. Then I heard, "Sir, can I help you?"

I didn't answer or turn around. When she came up to me, I turned and said, "Hi Talya. I'm going to buy this car from you if you let me sit in it."

"Pauly, I'm so glad to see you. You can't imagine how glad. Wait for me. I'll be right back with the key." She returned, opened the door, and I eased into the Vette. No doubt about it; these wheels are mine.

I got out and said, "It's mine, Talya; let's do the paperwork. I'm paying cash, and I've got a trade-in." She didn't respond.

"What's wrong? What happened to the wide-eyed, happy, saleslady I used to know?"

"I've got a big problem and don't know what to do." She told me about a customer who wanted to buy a car from her on the condition she spend the night with him. She told him she would love to but couldn't because she had a son at home who needed her care. "The guy told me to forget about the car, that he was still gonna fuck me. He groped me as he left."

She mentioned it to Meaghan, who told her to handle her own problems. He didn't have the time to fuck with it.

"I'm afraid to go over Meaghan's head and talk to Mr. Dawson. Is there any way you can help me? I don't know what you do in this company. I just need some help."

"I'll help you. You're too nice a person to have to put up with stuff like that. You should always be able to get help in this company. Did you happen to get his name and address or phone number?" She nodded yes. I told her to get it, then to meet me in Meaghan's office.

I walked into Meaghan's office and told him to get Sam Dawson on the phone. "Ask Sam who I am."

After listening to Sam for a couple of minutes, Meaghan put his head on his desk and started rambling on how he was so sorry, so sorry that he kept screwing up with me, so sorry. I thought to myself: I can't beat this guy after this. I was telling him to lift his head up as Talya walked in.

I assured Meaghan everything is going to be alright once we had an understanding. "Neither you nor anyone else here is to use vulgarity in front of Talya. You are to treat Talya as if she were blood. You are to insure she is happy at work. Agreed?" Meaghan gulped and nodded.

"I didn't hear you." Meaghan said, "Yes, oh yes."

"Good. Talya, you have anything to add?"

"No, here's the man's name and a phone number."

I asked Talya what kind of car she drove. She had an old Ford that was on its way out. "How about we trade cars? My Mercury is in good shape, and Mr. Meaghan can have your old one towed to Beacon Street. I don't need a trade-in. I just want to get rid of it."

"Thanks. That would be great. How much do you want for it?"

"It's a gift. When we get finished with the Vette, and I get some business handled here, I'll give you the keys, title, and registration, and I'll get my stuff out."

I called Tony and asked him to find out for me everything about Tito Scolari. I thought he worked for Mr. G. It took Tony about ten minutes to call back. Tito was an underling in the Genovese family, not a made-man. He was a wife-beater and a cheater. His job was pickup man on extortion and numbers runner.

I asked if he had the wife's name and phone number. He gave it to me. Tony said the guy had $10,000 checking and $15,000 in a savings account. I asked Tony if he could ask Mr. G if he would have Tito here at ten o'clock to meet with me. I also needed Vince and Stusi. I'd have them back long before he needed to leave for Juan. Tony said OK and hung up.

I phoned Tito's wife. At first, she was pleasant but hesitant; then she opened up. She told me if she wasn't afraid of getting caught and doing prison time, she'd have killed him a long time ago. She told me her life was a living hell. I asked if she had a driver's license. She did. I asked if she had a choice what kind of car she would like. She told me. The next question was did Tito have any cash at home. She told me he had a bag in his closet with cash. She never went near it for fear of him. I told her to dump the bag and to let me know approximately how much was there. She got back on the phone and said about $100,000.

I told her Tito was going to have a fatal accident today. That money belonged to Tito's boss, and I would call her back and tell her what to do with it. I asked if she could get a ride to Royal Auto Sales that afternoon to pick up her new car. When she said she could, I told her to see a lady named Talya.

I phoned Tony about the money. I asked if it would be alright if I called Mr. G to see if he wanted the money back, or if I could let Tito's wife keep it to start a new life. And get Mr. G's permission to off Tito.

"Good idea, Pauly. Do it."

After a greeting, I was told to call him Vito. Tony had told him all about me, and he was glad I called. I told him about Tito screwing with Talya and the beating of his wife. I told him about the money, and that with his permission, I would give it to his wife to start a new life. I asked his permission to off Tito.

Vito had a hard-on for guys like Tito, and a soft spot for the women because of his daughter's deal. Vito said, "Sure, do it. Make the bastard suffer. And yeah, let her keep the money."

"Sir, thank you. Have a good day."

I called Mrs. Scolari back and told her the money in the closet was hers. She could do with it as she wanted, but to never tell anyone about it or about our conversation. She promised. I told her good-bye and I hoped she had a good life.

I found Meaghan talking to Talya and asked him for a private office. I advised Talya that a woman would be looking for her that afternoon to buy a blue late-model Chevy, and I'd give her the cash for it. I told Talya that Tito would be there soon to see me, and I warned Talya to keep out of sight.

Just as I was about to tell them I was expecting two gentlemen, in walked Vince and Stusi. In the office, I told them about Tito. Their job would be to escort Tito to the bank, have him close out his checking and savings accounts, and bring him and the money back there. "After that, Stusi, ride with Tito, and follow Vince to the dock. The prick is going to accidentally get run over by the container trolley. Can you handle that?" Both answered yeah.

"The money you're going to bring back here will be $25,000. I'll take out $5,000 for a car for Tito's wife, and you two will split the $20,000." I reminded Vince to be back to Tony in enough time to take him to a meeting we had downtown at 2:00.

Just then there was a knock on the door. It was Meaghan., "Sir, the gentleman you were expecting is here."

"Tito come in and make yourself comfortable. My name is Pauly. This is Vince and Stusi. We work for the Bronx *famiglia* that owns this lot...did you know we owned it?" Tito shook his head no.

"We were told you were interested in buying a car, and, as we do with everyone, we checked you out. We know you work for Vito, and that you have $25,000.00 in the bank. We know it's Vito's money. I spoke to Vito and he feels that if he gets his money back everything would be OK. Vito must think a lot of you. He told me he wanted to give you a new car because you put so much mileage on yours for him.

"We have a new Caddy at the pier that was bought and paid for by this guy from Peru. Unfortunately, he has met an early death, so we're stuck with the car. We gave it to Vito. He wants you to have it.

"That's not bad, a new Caddy for nothing. Tito, trust me, this is the best way. Vito gets his money and has no hard feelings, and you get a new car. What do you think?"

"Yeah, great, and thanks. You saved my ass."

"Vince and Stusi can keep you company going to the bank. It's pretty neat riding in a limo."

I called his wife and told her she'd be getting a call from the cops. They were going to need her to identify Tito and take his personal effects. She had to do it, act like a grieving widow.

I walked out of the office and caught Meaghan and Talya. Both had to forget they ever saw or heard of Tito, and they needed to destroy anything with his name on it.

Talya had the paperwork done on my car; she took her commission off the total. I told her to redo it and put her commission back in. Talya came back with a new invoice. I paid her.

She told me she would do the registration and title work for me. She asked if she should use Pauly or Paul and was the address on the registration I was going to give her good.

"Use Paul and the address is good."

"It's really great to have a friend who is a big shot in the company."

I told her it was great to have a friend, but she needed to forget about the big shot and company.

Tito, Vince, and Stusi returned. We went to the office. I asked how everything went. Tito said OK and handed me the money.

"Good. You guys better get going so Tito can get his new Caddy. Stusi, drive with Tito and follow Vince." As they were walking out, I counted five grand off the money. "Tito and Stusi, go ahead. I need to talk to Vince for a minute."

I handed him the $20,000 and told him to leave Tito's car at the pier, and not to take anything off of him. Have someone at the pier report an accident.

I walked out and found Talya. I asked her to make out an invoice for the Chevy and have it total five grand. I handed her the cash. "The woman is Tito's wife. Aside from everything else, he beat her for years, so please treat her good. Let's go to your desk. I need to use your phone, and I'll need you there."

I called Amalgamated, told them I needed to insure a car, and to change the owner on my other car but keep the premium payment as it was. I requested the automatic annual renewal on both. Talya provided her information, and then she gave them what they needed on my car.

She finished and asked what was with the insurance? I explained she'd be getting a policy that was top-of-the-line. She'd never have to pay a premium as long as she owned the car. The company that she didn't know exists would pay the premium. "I'll drive the Vette to the front alongside my car. Please meet me there with a paper plate and a large envelope."

I drove the Vette to my car. Everything from the trunk and front, including the dope was thrown into the duffle. Talya taped a temporary paper license plate in the rear window then handed me the envelope. I gave her the keys and asked her to get the title and registration out of the glove compartment and wait there a minute.

I took the money out of my pocket, counted out $20,000 for Juan, and then I counted out $3,000 and put it in the envelope. I walked over to Talya and asked if everything was OK. I told her no matter what, she and I are friends, and if she ever needed me, I'd be there. I handed her the envelope. "This is for you. Do with it what you want. I suggest you put it into a Certificate of Deposit for your son's education. He's going to need a good education to be something in this world and have a good life. Good-bye, have a good day, and take care of yourself."

# CHAPTER 27

I drove down the Parkway thinking *I really like this fuckin'
car. It handles great. It's spotless inside and out, and I'm going to
keep it that way.* I pulled into a White Castle. I hadn't been at one
for a while, but I really liked those burgers. I used to order a sack
of twelve for a dollar. I ordered a sack of twelve and was told it
was now a sack of ten, and it would cost me a dollar and a half. I
pulled up to the window got my sack.

The girl said, "Nice ride. It suits you."

I took off for Manhattan, eating the White Castles. They still
tasted the same. We used to call them fart burgers. *It's going to be
interesting – sitting at this meeting – farting my brains out.*

At the hotel I didn't see any place to park. I was standing in
front trying to figure out what to do. A guy came up to me and
asked, "Valet parking, Sir?" I took the ignition key off the ring
and handed it to him.  He gave me a ticket. After putting my
duffle bag in the trunk, I started for the hotel but realized I had
an hour to kill. I didn't want to spend it with Juan, so I lit up a cig
and wandered uptown. I wanted to walk the White Castles off. If
I farted out here, so what.

After three or four blocks, the sidewalk emptied out and it
became a nice walk. I felt a tap on my shoulder, turned to see a
pretty Black girl dressed in gaudy clothes and high heels. "Hey
stud, how would you like a date?"

"That would be great, except I'm running late and have to get
back to the precinct." The hooker took off like a bat out of hell.

I walked back to the hotel and went up to the penthouse.
Juan offered me a drink and told me Tony had not arrived. I

suggested we just sit on his deck, get some fresh air, and relax. At long last Tony showed up. We sat at the deck's patio table with a bottle of Chianti and three glasses.

"Juan, before we get into business, I need to give you $20,000. You overpaid the invoice I gave you."

"I didn't overpay anything. I knew exactly what I was doing, and you keep the money." I guess I just passed Juan-boy's honesty game.

Tony started by telling Juan the DeAngelo *famiglia* was in and would handle everything. He explained the network, and that next week I was going to visit Trafficante in Miami. He was going to sit down with the other four families in New York while Fanarssi visited all the other families in the network.

Juan laid out the costs of the coke and pot. His people at the Redirect would package the pot because it would be coming in as a bale. The coke would be virgin. Either the distributors or their dealers could cut it. No matter what, the distributors must all pay the same. "If you discount to anyone, you'll open a door you won't be able to close."

Juan asked, "Everything alright? Do we have a deal?"

"Yeah, we have a deal," Tony answered.

"When the first shipment arrives, the Redirect will unload the motors then ship them back to Peru. When the second shipment arrives, they'll do the same, except you will fill a couple of motors with my payment for the first shipment. You will always be one payment behind."

Juan asked Tony if he could meet him tomorrow with some of his construction people to look over a building he was thinking of buying for the parts and Redirect. Juan asked me for two more Caddies, the same as those that went to Peru. He told me he'd pay the same. The two that went to Peru would run his West Coast network out of Mexico. The two new ones would run our network out of the Redirect.

I told Juan he didn't have to pay anything for the Caddies. I'd use the $20,000 and we'd be even. I asked Juan what he thought about a new car lot, all high-end cars in an area where there was a lot of money. The cars would be foreign and American sports cars, top-of-the-line. The cars wouldn't have titles. He could make a lot of money on them.

"That's a good idea, Pauly, and I know exactly where I can put the lot."

This could be a biggie. It didn't matter what the car was, we still would only pay $100 delivered.

Tony stood up, "I've got to go and get something handled," and he left.

Juan invited me to have dinner with him. We could discuss this car deal and talk about some parts he had in mind. Juan asked if I would like to try a good Peruvian wine. He really didn't like Chianti, but since Tony and I liked it, he drank it. I told him I'd stick with the Chianti.

As we sat down for dinner, Juan told me he planned to set up a shop in Peru to boil out and repair radiators. He would want specific radiators and heater cores. He also wanted specific windshields. Both would be for South America only.

We started eating dinner, which Juan said was a Peruvian specialty. It was good. I didn't know what it was, but I was too embarrassed to ask.

I told Juan there were parts he needed to get into for South America and here. Brake parts and front-end parts.

"Yes, what did you have in mind?"

"I thought we'd ship brake assembles intact: drums, shoes, springs, hold-downs, and cylinders. The master cylinder and all the front-end linkage. The brake assemblies would cost $28, the master $25, and the linkage $32.

"OK. Everything tagged like the other parts."

I told him we'd pay for the crating, container, loading and shipping. Juan wanted three hundred of each. Before I could say anything, he said, "Change that to five hundred brake assemblies."

"Deal. And so we're together on this: three hundred master cylinders and linkage, and five hundred brake assemblies."

"Yes, and what did you figure on the windshields and radiators?"

"It would depend on the specific ones you want. I will take care of you. I just need a list."

After we dinner, we went out to the deck, and Juan offered me a Cuban cigar. I told him no thanks. He took one out, bit off the end, and lit it up.  It smelled good. I told him I thought there were a lot of guys in South America like him, with a lot of bucks that would enjoy a sports car. "We can get you new or low mileage untitled cars. A variety including: Porsche, Ferrari, Jaguar, Alfa Romeo, Facel Vega, Lotus Elan, Mercedes, MG-A, Austin Healy, BMW, Corvette, and Thunderbird." He'd have a fantastic lot.

Juan told me he was going to Peru for a week, then to Columbia on business – first Medellin and then to look at Buenaventura. Both cities have high rollers with megabucks, and he'd be OK with two new lots in Colombia. When he got back, we could go over the cars and the shipping. He really liked it and would probably take a couple, one for himself and one for his father.

"Unless you have any other business to discuss, we're done. How about I get a couple of my lady friends out here? We'll smoke some joints."

"It sounds great, but I'm going to need a rain check. I need to get home and get some rest. I've got a big day tomorrow. Thanks for the great dinner."

I got to the front of the hotel and found the valet guy. I gave him my ticket. He came pulling up with my Vette. He got out, handed me my key, and said, "That will be $35, Sir."

"Bullshit. $35 for what? Get your boss out here!"

"I'm sorry, it's $15. Please don't get my boss involved. I need money bad and thought you were a high roller with a car like this."

I asked what he needed the money so badly for. He has two kids, one at home, the other is in a hospital, very sick. He needs the money for the kid's medical bills, and this is a second job for him. I asked him to write down the name of the hospital and the kid's name. I gave him $100, all I had on me, and told him this was for the parking and to keep the rest. I opened the door to the Vette, and the odor of the White Castles was overwhelming.

I hollered to the guy, "Do you like White Castles?"

He said yes. I threw him the sack. I started driving cross-town thinking, *So much for my new car. This is fuckin' terrible.*

When I got home, Maria raced up to me but quickly backed away. "What is that smell?"

I said it could be a couple of things. I needed to get out of those clothes and take a shower. Maria said showering could wait. She wanted to show me something.

"Dad told me you were promoted and are an executive. I got you some things to celebrate. Come up to your room." On the bed was a classy attaché case. I thanked her. She said there was more and told me to look in the closet. Except for my suit, my old clothes were gone. Alongside my suit was another suit, four different blazers, slacks and a dozen shirts on hangers. On the floor were pairs of shoes. I was dumbfounded. I said she was terrific and thanked her.

"Hugs and kisses will happen after the stench is off."

We met later on the patio. Maria explained she bought everything with her new credit card, and she wrote out a couple of checks. I told Maria about the valet guy. I gave her the paper with his kid's name and the hospital, Mt. Sinai. I asked Maria to call the hospital and find out how much the parents owed. We'd pay it and any future bills.

I'd been thinking about how we could repay Hyman, Carl and Jacob. I thought we could visit Mt. Sinai and talk to the head man about opening a wing of the hospital that would be devoted to kids, and it would be free. "Between the money we have, and a friend of mine has, and Tony, we could do it and fund it for a lot of years. The company could take it as a tax write-off."

"We could call it HCJ Hospital for Children, with Hyman Finkelstein, Carl Grossberg, and Jacob Goodman as the benefactors. It would be their hospital. It'd be our way of showing our ongoing gratitude to these men. To me a kid doesn't deserve to be sick. Old people, it's another story, but not kids. If we can be a part of healing kids, we'll feel good about it.

"Down the road, you could be the hospital's spokesperson. With your looks and charm, you could get people and businesses to donate money, and they'll want to be involved in a good cause. What do you think?"

"I think it's terrific, and wonderful, and we can do it. Dad told me a little of what you've said and done at the business, and I agree with him – you're brilliant."

"That's what I love about my wife-to-be." We went to bed feeling good about our talk.

In the morning I told Maria I had planned on us going to the hospital in my car, "But it stinks. I'm going to Royal Auto Parts later today and get it fumigated." We needed to take her car. If it was OK with her, "I'd like to do the hospital this morning. Let's get dressed. We'll go."

Upstairs I put on my new clothes, looked in the mirror. *Not bad. I guess this is going to be my new uniform.*

At the Financial Services of Mt. Sinai Hospital, we were told the outstanding balance of the bill for patient Stephen Brooks was $10,280.84. I handed Maria $10,300, and she gave it to the girl. I told Maria to put the change in her purse.

"I'd like a receipt for the payment. Make it out to Maria DeAngelo for Stephen Brooks." I asked where the hospital administrator was. We took the elevator to the fifth floor. Because we didn't have an appointment, the secretary tried to brush us off. I was insistent. After keeping us waiting for an hour and half, the big chief came out of his office.

"My name is John Clark. I am the hospital administrator. What is this important matter?"

"Good morning, I'd prefer to talk in your office." He paused, sighed, then led us into his office and sat behind his desk. Out of courtesy he should have invited us to be seated. He didn't. We sat in front of the desk anyway.

"My name is Paul Walker, and this is Maria DeAngelo. We would like to build a wing on the hospital, or a separate building, and establish a children's hospital. We would completely outfit and staff it. I need to know how to proceed."

He gave Maria and me a look of disbelief and scornfully said, "We do not need a separate children's hospital. In my opinion the two of you are out of your minds and have no idea in the world how much it would cost."

"I guess we're not going to get anywhere with you. May I please have the name and a phone number of the chairman of the board of the hospital?"

"I can't and won't give you that information."

"That's OK. I can get it. I just have a couple of more things. I feel everyone is entitled to their opinions. Opinions are like assholes – everyone has one. In my opinion you are an asshole!"

He stood up, and I snarled, "Sit down! I'm not done yet. You are a discourteous, arrogant, pompous ass. If you ever disrespect Miss DeAngelo again, I will cut your balls off and shove them down your throat. Have a good day, John."

In the elevator I could see Maria was really disgruntled. "Don't let that bother you. This world is full of jerks like him. We're going to get this done. I prefer to stay with Mt. Sinai because it's a Jewish hospital, and it fits what we want. If we can't, there are a bunch of other hospitals in the city that would jump on it." Maria squeezed my hand and smiled.

At home I changed my clothes then drove to Royal Auto Parts and found Luca. I asked him if his guys could fumigate my car and me. He asked if the car reeked as bad as I did? I said worse. He told me to drive my car back to the detail bay. He'd meet me there and have someone take care of the Vette and me.

While they were working on the Vette, Luca and I talked. I told him about getting two Caddies from RAS. He'd have to do the same to them as he did the others. Luca had a couple of Caddies that he was going to send to RAS in a week. He could use them. That would work, and I'd handle it with Sam. Just then some guy came up to me and sprayed me with something. When he finished, I thanked him, then asked Luca what he thought.

He sniffed, "You smell good."

I asked Luca if he knew where Sam was. He told me Beacon. I asked him to call Sam and have him wait for me. At the Beacon office Sam and Joey were talking. When Sam saw me, he gave me the usual greeting and the offer of coffee. I asked who made the coffee. "Some things in life never change. I made the coffee."

"Thanks, I'll have a cup."

I told Sam about the Caddies and Luca, and that I wanted to buy the Caddies from RAS. I figured the two of them, including Talya's commission, would be $10,000.  Sam said it would work. "Have Talya hold off on the title and registration till Fanarssi tells her who to make them out to. The work that Luca's is doing is worth $10,000, but don't make out an invoice, just work it in somewhere as cash."

I gave Sam the $10,000. "I have a new deal on parts with Hernandez. Can Joey make out an invoice for me?" I gave them the details, and, with little help from Sam, Joey made out two invoices and handed them to me. I looked them over. They were neat and perfect. Sam was right – Joey is smart.

Sam would handle it with the shed for me, and they had all the parts. I asked who replaced Mario.

"Franco, Mario's nephew. I think he knows you."

I shrugged and said, "I'll catch him some other time. I have to get going."

I drove to Muraso. *My new car's back and it smells good! I swear I'm never going to eat in it again.*

Muraso looked great. Tony must have worked these guys twenty-four hours a day. I knocked on Tony's door, and heard "Come in." As soon as I walked in I heard, "Pauly, it's good to see you."

"Same here. It's really good to see you. I need to talk to you."

Tony told me he was just about to leave to meet Hernandez at the place he was going to buy. If I wanted to, I could join him, and we could talk in the car.

# *CHAPTER 28*

We headed downtown. I told Tony about Maria's and my idea about the hospital for kids and asked what he thought. He thought it was a very good idea. I was glad to hear he felt that way, because I needed his help in a bunch of ways. I told him about our meeting with the hospital administrator, and asked Tony if he knew anyone connected with the hospital. He didn't, but my grandfather and the chairman of the board were friends. He commented that the Jews somehow make lifelong friends. They seemed to support each other always.

"I heard somewhere that rich guys set up foundations and use them as tax breaks. I want to do that. I didn't mention it to Maria because I wanted to see what you thought. I want to set up the Mateo-Donatella DeAngelo Memorial Foundation. The foundation would fund everything."

I didn't hear anything and turned to Tony. Here was the toughest guy you'd ever want to meet. This craggy mountain was sitting beside me crying. I said I was sorry, "I didn't mean to upset you."

"No, no, a memorial to my brother and wife! Oh, my God, how wonderful. Fantastico! Terrific!" I didn't say anymore. I just let it rest.

By the time we reached our destination, Tony had composed himself. The building was huge, three stories high, and it took up a whole city block. We were on the lower east side of Manhattan, a shit-neighborhood that smelled like fish. I figured the fish market wasn't far. Tony and I got out and walked around. In back there was an empty lot. The building was deserted, looked abandoned, and it seemed the whole neighborhood was.

We returned to the front. Juan pulled up. Juan used a key to open the door. The walls had graffiti everywhere; the floors were covered in trash... and shit. It looked as if people had squatted here at one time and had scavenged what they could off the walls. Our entering the building disturbed the rats. They were scurrying everywhere.

We walked to the end where Juan wanted to set up his Redirect. Tony stood in the middle of the floor, looking all around, studying it. After a while we went up a flight of stairs to the second floor, and then the third, turned around and walked down to the first. Tony asked Juan if he was sure this was the building he wanted. Yes, it was.

"How much is it gonna to cost you?"

"They're asking $12 million. I'm going to offer $10 million. The city had taken it over for taxes years ago, so I'm dealing with a realtor working for the city."

"I have a couple of things. I suggest we pave the lot and build loading docks off the back. We put the overhead doors on the back for the Redirect. Everything coming to this place comes in the back. I'd also suggest you let me buy this place for you and renovate it. It will be a top-notch facility. Do that, and I'll save you half of what you're willing to pay for the building."

"I don't know how you can do that, but if you can, we have a deal."

Tony told Juan he could have a crew of his construction engineers there tomorrow morning to look at the roof, flooring, and elevators. "The flooring is important because small forklifts will be running around on all the floors. The elevators will be replaced so they'll be able to handle forklifts with loads. In a couple of days, if you or your people could meet here with my engineers, they can spec out the place and do drawings."

"Sounds like you already own this place."

"Not yet but very soon."

We finished in the building and were standing outside. I told Juan I had the invoice on the parts for him and asked if he happened to have the sheet on the windshields and radiators. We exchanged papers. I told him I'd get back to him tomorrow and asked what he was doing for dinner tomorrow night.

"Nothing special. Come over."

"Good. You have great food. We can do business, and I have something I want to discuss with you."

As we were driving home, I asked Tony how he was going to pull off this deal with Juan. Tony knew all the big shots in the city. He could get a guy to condemn the building, take it off the market, and turn it over to him. It would cost him about $100,000 under the table. Tony figured it would cost about another $800,000 to renovate. "The city can justify it because it'd create a new large tax base. Juan would be happy 'cause he'd only be spending $5 million for everything. And I'd make $4 million on the deal!"

"You're one smart guy, boss. Since you have all this fuckin' money, how about investing $1 million in the foundation? Then the foundation will pay you for the construction."

At home I told Maria about the foundation to fund the hospital. "The foundation is going to be the Mateo-Donatella DeAngelo Memorial Foundation, for your uncle and mother. I hope it is OK with you. The foundation will pay everything for the hospital. Your dad has promised me $1 million, and the foundation would pay him for the construction.

"Hyman and the chairman of the board of Mt. Sinai are old friends. I'm going to call Hyman, find out if what we want to do is OK with him, Carl and Jacob. Then I'll see if he can get me a sit-down with his friend.

"I also want a pledge of $1 million from Amalgamated. They can use it in advertising as sponsoring a children's hospital, and for taxes. I think I can get another million from a friend of mine. He'll be able to use it for advertising for a big parts business he's setting up in the city and for taxes.

"One more thing. You're not only going to be the spokesperson for the hospital, you're also going to run the foundation. What do you think?"

"Pauly, it's terrific."

I phoned Hyman. We spoke for a long time as I explained everything. He assured me the hospital would mean as much to Carl and Jacob as it would to him. Hyman gave me the pledge from Amalgamated. After we hung up, he'd call his friend, the hospital's board chairman, then he'd get back to me.

"I have an idea that would be the icing on the cake for Hyman, Carl, and Jacob. After we're up and running and the hospital is doing well, we'll start a second hospital in Israel. They'd be sister hospitals, sharing technologies and research. Hyman, Carl, and Jacob's names would be on that hospital."

Two hours passed before the phone rang. Hyman apologized for the length of time. He had to make some arrangements. The night after next, he, Maria and I were going out to dinner with Josh Morgenstern and his wife. Josh thought the hospital was a sensational idea, and he was sure he'd have no problem with the board. He wanted to meet us to discuss it over dinner.

"I'm coming along to give you moral support, and it's a good excuse for me to visit an old friend. Joshua is not only chairman of the board of Mt. Sinai Hospital, he's also chairman of the board and CEO of Manufacturers Hanover Trust, our bank."

I asked if Josh knew about Tony.

"Only the legitimate side. This time only, Tony shouldn't come. Josh will recognize Maria's last name. It will be beneficial."

I asked Hyman to pick a suitable restaurant, make reservations, and to please let me pick up the tab. It was something I really wanted to do. Hyman said he had already made flight reservations and would be arriving at La Guardia. Vince would pick him up, and he'd stay the night at the house. He planned to spend some time the next day with Mario and Tony going over things. As far as the tab, he said we'll see. I hated that. When someone told me that, it usually meant it wasn't going to happen.

Early the next morning I drove to Muraso. I knocked on Tony's door, said, "Good morning, Sir," but didn't wait for a reply. I walked over to Mario's office, knocked, walked in. I said, "Good morning. How's my favorite guy in this place doing this morning?" I didn't wait for a reply. I just closed his door and walked into my office. My first reaction: *Fuckin' beautiful!* I sat down behind the desk and looked around. *This is my first desk, my first office.* I was feeling like I was hot shit. I picked up the phone, dialed zero. A female voice said, "Good morning, Pauly, how may I help you?"

"Good morning to you. Do you know where Sam Dawson is?"

He was at the Brooklyn yard, and then he was going to the Bruckner yard. "They're having a problem with the baler."

I asked her to get ahold of Sam and find out what time I could meet him at Bruckner.

I was sitting back thinking about a bunch of shit. There was a knock on the door. Mario walked in carrying two cups. "*Mio paisan*, how about a cup of coffee with me?"

"Definitely, any time." We sat in the chairs in front of my desk drinking the coffee and talking. I described my hospital idea. I wanted his feedback because I respected his intelligence.

Mario said the idea was great. Tony had been telling him about it. Maria being involved was a good move because I wouldn't have the time to spend on it. He added that the Vegas deal was really being run by my father and doing well. Amalgamated was at a point to run by itself, and our money situation was handled. "Hyman is kind of a free man." Mario suggested I talk to Tony about him bringing Hyman back to New York for a while to help Maria run the hospital thing, and for me to step back.

"You're probably right. It would be best. It's just that I feel so strongly about this hospital. There are kids that can't get help. I can't imagine how a parent lives if his kid dies." I told Mario I'd talk to Tony. "What's neat about this place is there's a really smart guy here."

Mario said, "*Arrivederci, mio paisan,*" and left.

I walked into Tony's office and brought him up-to-date on Hernandez and me. He already knew about dinner tomorrow night. Tony agreed with Mario's suggestion about Hyman and said he'd make it happen. I asked how things were going with the Royal Auto Parts expansion. It was about halfway done.

I brought up my thing with Hernandez and the sports cars – we could get twenty, park them in the garages, then load them in containers and ship them all at once.

"What do you think about my flying to Miami in two days? Can you ask Trafficante to get me a reservation at a hotel for a night and an airport pickup?"

Tony said to tell the receptionist to make my flight reservations and to let him know when it was done.

I headed for Bruckner. I went into the office and was told Sam wasn't there yet. I asked, "Who runs this place?"

The same guy said, "Me." I introduced myself. He said, "My name is Tony. I know who you are."

"OK. If you've got a little time, how about showing me around." We walked outside, and Tony asked if I wanted to see anything special. I told him no, how about from the beginning.

"We get cars here from everybody, our own yards, other yards, and guys dragging them in. The place is like a waterfall of cars. When cars come from our yards, they go on the line through the furnace, then through the baler, and finally on the pile. Everybody else we strip for what we want, and then through the furnace and baler. We pile the bales till we have enough to fill a barge, then we order a barge, fill it, and off it goes to a steel mill. We move a lot of shit outta here."

I told Tony thanks, he had a neat operation, and I didn't want to keep him any longer. I told him I was going to walk around a0p3 spoke to someone. He hung up, said wouldn't be a problem. We had all of it.

I asked Sam if he had a feel for how much to charge him. "I'd charge him $40 for the radiator and heater core and $30 for the windshields. As you know, the windshields are trash to us."

I asked for the phone. I wanted to get an OK. Then he could call Joey and have him make out an invoice and tell the shed. I told Juan we were OK with the parts. The radiator would cost him $45 and the heater cores $15. The windshields $60 because we'd go through a lot of windshields to get him ones that have no damage, and we were going to have to crate them special. I'd cover the containers, loading, and shipping. Juan told me two hundred windshields and four hundred radiators and heaters. Everything marked as before. We had a deal.

Juan asked if we were still going to get together tonight. "Sure, about six. OK?"

Sam heard everything. I reminded him to tell Joey the windshields can't have any damage. "Sam, there is a lot of cash moving through here. To cover your ass, you need to put in controls to prevent someone from ripping us off." He agreed.

Because I had time to kill, I headed for Muraso. In Tony's office, I sat down and asked how things were going.

"*Menza menz.* Look at this shit. Give you an office and the respect goes outta the window! What happened to my "Good afternoon, Sir?"

"The respect is still there. I'm sorry, got a lot on my mind." I asked if his deal on the Hernandez building is going OK. He said it's a done deal.

# *CHAPTER 29*

"Tony, what the fuck is bothering you?"

"There's a guy at the dock stirrin' up shit. He wants to take over the Longshoremen Union. He's holdin' meetings tryin' to get votes for president. I can't just make him disappear. I need him to walk away by himself."

I asked Tony if anyone ever approached the guy.

"No, 'cause we figured we wouldn't get anywhere. But now a lot of guys are listening to him."

I offered to handle it. "A smart guy once told me to find out everything you can about someone you're doing business with." I asked Tony to make the call for me. "I'll handle the guy tomorrow. I've got to get to Hernandez to talk about some business."

I drove to the hotel. I was early but figured I could get done with Hernandez and get home at a decent hour. At the valet parking spot, the same guy came running to my car. He opened the door and blurted out: "I don't know how I can ever thank you or Maria DeAngelo. I don't even know your name, or who you are, or who Maria is. I do know you saved my son's life! You saved my life! You saved my family! I don't know how I can ever thank you."

I told him my name, and that Maria was my fiancée. "If it wasn't for you, Maria and I would have never thought to pursue something that we now feel is the most wonderful thing in the world. We formed a foundation that Maria runs. The foundation is going to build a wing at Mt. Sinai for a children's hospital. The foundation is going to fund everything. A kid like yours will cost his parents nothing to get well. That's why I thank you – and why are you still jockeying cars around?"

He told me he gave up his day job as a teacher so he could spend time with his sons. I asked for a ticket, so I could get going. After he handed me a ticket, he said he was parking my car in the VIP area, and it wouldn't cost me.

"Last thing before you go. Mr. Walker, you and Miss DeAngelo are definitely saints."

"Maria is for sure. I'm not."

In the penthouse Juan offered me a mixed drink, Peruvian wine, or Chianti. I chose Chianti and a Cuban cigar. I lit up the cigar. "This thing is great. I've got to get Tony hooked on this instead of the smelly shit he smokes."

I told Juan that I'd be shipping the parts he wanted while he was in Peru. He could pay for everything when he got back. I mentioned that Tony was closing the deal on the building, "And it's really saving you a bunch of bucks." Then I brought up the topic of the foundation that was going to fund a hospital for kids.

"I need a favor. I need you to kick in $1 million to the foundation. Tony donated, as did Amalgamated Insurance, each $1 million. It would be good advertising for JH Parts to be associated with the hospital, and you can use it on taxes."

"OK – on one condition – the foundation consider a hospital in Peru at some point. Peru desperately needs a hospital like that. The child and infant death rate is one of the highest in the world."

We enjoyed a dinner of good food, and I was feeling great. I finished a business deal, got my mil – life was good. Juan asked if I had plans for after dinner. I didn't. He asked if I'd like to join him and four friends for a poker game.

I thought back to when I was a kid. We used to play poker for hours – penny ante, dealer's choice. I hadn't played in years. Like riding a bike, there are things you never forget.

It wasn't long before the elevator door opened, and four guys walked out. Juan introduced me. We sat around the table. Juan brought out a tray with chips, said, "$25 chips, buy in $1,000." A lot different than penny ante.

Everyone was in, and we started playing. I was doing good and having fun. After about fifteen hands I realized that the guy on my left kept winning big each time he dealt. The deal went around and got to him. Out of the corner of my eye I could see him dealing off the bottom of the deck. I folded. Before the next deal, I got up and asked Juan to cash me out. He asked what was the matter. I told him I liked playing poker, but I don't like donating. "This guy is dealing off the bottom!"

Juan asked the guy if it was true. He told Juan no.

I said, "You have been! I watched you. If you're calling me a liar, we can go outside and settle it."

The guy muttered, "I think I'm going to leave."

Juan snarled, "You're right. Get the fuck out of here, you bastard, and don't think about your money, or they'll be carrying you out. Pauly, I'm sorry. Sit down and we'll keep playing." He told one of the guys to divide the chips up evenly among us.

That was one hell of a turning point in the game for me. I couldn't lose! Two of the guys bought in for another $1,000 each. We kept playing. It was about one in the morning before everyone decided to quit. They cashed out, said their good-byes, and left. We both counted out our chips. I had won over $2,000. I asked Juan how he did. He lost. That was poker – sometimes you win, sometimes you lose. He asked if we were going to do it again. Anytime. Because Juan was leaving for Peru the next afternoon, we'd set up a game when he returned.

I got up early and went downstairs. Maria was there with a cup of coffee and a warm embrace. We sat around talking for a little bit. I reminded Maria that Hyman was coming in, and that I'd get home early so the three of us could talk about the foundation. I handed her the $25,000 to deposit into her checking. She asked where I got the money. I said it was kind of a bonus.

I drove to Muraso. All I could think about was how to handle this thing for Tony. If the guy had a family, I'd use them as a threat to get him to publicly decline his attempt to take over the union and leave town. I walked into Tony's office, didn't knock, just said, "Morning, did you get anything on the guy for me?"

"I sure as fuck did. The guy's name is Frank Malloy. He was at one time president of local 2058 United Auto Workers in Indiana. He got caught embezzling money, worked a deal to repay the money, and resigned. Then he got a union job at a GM plant in Detroit. After a few years, he was shop steward. It took him about four years to rip the union off for big bucks. He got caught, the UAW filed charges, but somehow, he got out of town. There's a warrant for his arrest in Detroit. Now he's here in New York with another scheme."

I told Tony I needed to spend a little time thinking this out. In my opinion we needed to put this guy down publicly in front of the membership. I went to my office and started to lay out my plan.

I'd have Tony ask the president of the union to write a letter to the membership, telling them that the leadership has been made aware that some of the members were unhappy with the leadership and wanted a change. The letter was notification of mandatory attendance at a meeting that would be held at the union hall. Frank Malloy would be invited to present his side, and the leadership theirs. The members would be asked to vote to retain current leadership or install Malloy as president.

Tony would get the president of UAW in Detroit and two NYPD detectives to be at the meeting. Our president would open the meeting. After some talk he'd introduce the president of the UAW from Detroit. The guy would tell the membership about Malloy and ask the detectives to arrest him on the outstanding warrant. This way, to the membership, Malloy is the bad guy, so we're not. The president could advise the membership to be careful, and not get involved with people who would try to scheme them. I went back to Tony's office and laid out my plan. He liked it and would handle the details.

Tony handed me an American Airline ticket boarding pass and seat assignment. I had never seen a ticket before – I had never flown before. The seat assignment read "First Class, Row 2, Seat 1." I didn't know what that meant, but "Seat 1" had to be good, "First Class" even better.

I'd leave La Guardia at 10:00 in the morning and return the next morning at 11:00. Vince would take me and pick me up. Trafficante would pick me up in Miami. Trafficante and Lansky made hotel reservations for me, and I was going to have dinner with them. I asked Tony to tell me about Lansky and Trafficante.

"Years ago, Santo Trafficante and I were made-men in the Luchese family. We were close. Back then the business was hardcore illegitimate. Santo and I handled contracts on guys. Santo got an opening in Miami and became boss, and I did the same in the Bronx. We were both fuckin' lost. We knew we didn't want to run our families like the Luchese family but didn't know any different."

"I lucked out with the advice from your grandmother and Hyman. Santo struggled for a while and somehow hooked up with Meyer Lansky. Like Hyman, Meyer is smart. Together Santo and Meyer got into a lot of good shit. Meyer somehow became friends with Batista, the guy runnin' Cuba. Batista is a piece of shit. He keeps his people in poverty while he lives a lifestyle fit for a king. Lansky got Batista to let him build a casino. He probably paid him a bunch of bucks.

"The understanding was the family owned and operated it. Lansky got Santo to pay for everything, and soon they had a casino. Lansky would bring people from the mainland in ships. He also chartered flights. The place started to do great. People needed a place to gamble. They built a huge fuckin' hotel and enlarged the casino three times. It was truly a fantasy land.

"Santo and I were friends. We broke the made-man code and would take our wives out to dinner together. We'd sit around for hours talkin' and enjoyin' each other's company. Santo has five kids. His family means a lot to him. He's a good family man. That's it. You shouldn't have any problems in Miami. They're good people."

"Thanks." I needed to get going. At home I got a very warm greeting from Hyman and a kiss from Maria. Maria suggested we go to the patio. We discussed what we wanted to do, and how we would accomplish things. If Hyman didn't mind, I wanted to handle tonight with both of their help. After tonight I was pretty much taking a step back.

# *CHAPTER 30*

Vince drove to Manhattan, then south to Central Park where he stopped in front of a fancy-looking restaurant. Hyman requested the Morgenstern party. The maître d' led us to a private room. The first thing I noticed was a wall of glass that overlooked the park. A man and woman seated at the table stood up and extended cordial greetings. The man hugged Hyman and said, "It's so good to see you, my old friend." Hyman introduced Maria and me to Josh and his wife, Lily.

While they were reminiscing, I studied the Morgensterns. Lily was a good-looking woman who gave off class without being snobby. Josh looked like a silver-haired movie star, fit and trim. Neither had Jewish features nor sounded Jewish. During dinner, the talk was relaxed, cordial, and down-to-earth.

Josh said, "Paul, your grandfather has told me some of what you and Maria want to do. Please tell me about it and how I can help you."

I told them about the boy in the hospital, and the need for a children's hospital that would never refuse care for a child – and would be free. I described the foundation we established to fund everything, and that we had $3 million pledged already. Before I could continue, it was as though someone turned on a light.

Josh said, "I'm sorry to interrupt you. I can't contain myself any longer. Your hospital will be a part of Mt. Sinai. I'll handle the board and remove any obstacle in your way. I'll help you anyway I can. This is the most innovative approach to medicine I've heard of in years."

Maria squeezed my hand under the table and had a smile ear-to-ear.

Lily added "I agree with Josh a hundred percent. Maria, if I can do anything for you, I will. I want to be a part of this."

"Thank you, Maria said, we'll need all the help we can get."

Josh asked Hyman where he planned on getting all the paperwork done. Hyman told him we hadn't thought that out yet. Josh pointed out that the corporate offices for the bank were ten floors of a skyscraper the bank owns. He'd make available an office complex and would staff it with two secretaries at no cost to us till the project took off. "In my opinion you're taking on a major project that's going to require a lot of hard work, and you're going to have an enormous amount of dictation and typing. Besides, this way I can see my old friend more often."

Hyman thanked him. Josh inquired in an offhand manner if we planned to have the foundation bank with Manufacturers."

"Of course, we are. We've had a very good banking relationship for years." Josh looked puzzled. I told him Maria's last name was DeAngelo.

Josh came back with, "You're Tony's daughter! I've known Tony for years. He's one of our larger customers."

I told him Tony had pledged $1 million through his different companies. Then I suggested Manufacturers use the sponsorship of a children's hospital in their promotions. He'd have a step up on the other banks.

"I agree. The bank will pledge $1 million to the foundation, and it would be our honor if you would accept a pledge of another $1 million from the Morgenstern family."

I didn't know what to say. The only thing that came out was thank you, thank you for everything. After good-byes, we were on our way home. Maria kept saying she didn't believe what happened, it had to be a dream, a wonderful dream. She had to figure a way to get Lily involved, thinking Lily was a classy, good woman.

The foundation now had $5 million, and I was going for more.

# CHAPTER 31

I was a little anxious about flying, Miami, and handling the deal. I loaded the mag for the forty-five, inserted it, set the safety, and put it in the pocket of the attaché Maria had given me. I couldn't think of anything else to put in it. To keep the handgun from bouncing around, I wrapped it in a towel. I called Tony to see if he wanted me to take anything to Santo for him. He told me no, but to have a good trip. I decided to take the coke Hernandez had given me. I wanted to get rid of that shit anyhow.

I went downstairs as usual; Maria was there. After a good-morning and a great kiss, she asked if I'd like breakfast. There was a knock on the front door. It was Vince. "Come on, Pauly, we have to get going!" I grabbed the attaché, kissed Maria and told her we'd have dinner together tomorrow night. I sat in the front with Vince. He said he'd drop me off at Departing Passengers, and that tomorrow morning I was to look for signs that read Arriving Passengers. He'd be waiting outside for me. Thankfully he also explained what to do in the airport.

At La Guardia there were people everywhere. The rushing, combined with the roar of planes taking off and landing, spiked my anxiety to a level that was out of sight.

I went through what I had to at the ticket counter, then found my gate. The door was open. I clanked down the metal steps, across the asphalt, up another flight of metal steps, into the plane. An attractive woman in a uniform welcomed me, "Good morning, Sir. May I see your boarding pass and seat assignment?"

I handed her what I had. She returned my ticket and suggested I keep it in a safe place. I'd need it for my return flight. She asked for my attaché, which she'd stow away in a compartment. I handed her my case. I had never heard of 'stow away' before. I later learned the uniformed lady was called a stewardess. She pointed to a seat. "This is yours. Please fasten your seat belt once you are seated."

People started boarding the plane. The same young lady was pointing to the back. As the passengers walked past, they stared at me. What the fuck are you looking at? I decided to sit back and close my eyes. Before I knew it, I heard the door close, the engines start up and rev, and the young lady was saying, "We are preparing for takeoff."

Only two other guys were in first class. We were advised about emergency exits, emergency oxygen, and that our seats are flotation devices – our approach to Miami will be over water. I could have driven to Miami, enjoyed the ride, and not have to put up with this emergency shit. The plane started moving, then came to stop and sat. Suddenly the engines revved and the plane was moving again, except this time the engines were screaming. The plane was moving fast and shaking. After a clunking sound I could feel the plane lifting off, and it was straining. Once we got up in the air, the pilot made a couple of turns. I figured we were headed in the wrong direction. I didn't know at the time he had to get out of the flight path as soon as possible.

We circled over Manhattan, New York City with its sky-scrapers. Central Park and the way it was laid out looked great from the air. It was easy to locate the East Side Drive by the river. I followed it up, and there was Astro. Right on, Benny.

The flight, the drinks, the food – everything was exceptional. There was no better way to travel. After we made the scheduled stop in Atlanta and were on our way to Miami, the pilot came on the intercom. He thanked everyone for flying American. We'd be landing at Miami in forty-five minutes.

The young lady was asking the other guys something, and then bringing them drinks. She came over to me last, asked if I'd care for anything. I told her I didn't. She asked if I was going to Miami on business or pleasure. Business, I said, and that I was returning to New York tomorrow. New York was her base, and she loved New York because there was so much to do. She handed me a piece of paper. "This is my name and number. If you feel like hanging out sometime, give me a call."

"Thank you, that would be really nice." I put the paper in my pocket. Even though it was never going to happen, it felt good being hit on by a nice-looking chick.

It wasn't long before the engines slowed, and the plane was in a bank turn. The pilot announced we were in our approach to Miami Airport. "Please fasten your seat belts." Before I knew it, the plane touched down. The pilot must have put it in reverse. The engines were roaring. We rumbled along on the ground then came to a stop. The door opened, I stood up, and a rush of hot air hit me. I paused on the metal steps, I felt as if someone had dropped a wet, hot blanket on me. The air was smothering. How do people live in this shit?

After I clambered down the steps, I stood on gravel looking for a terminal. The only structures were across the field – a rinky-dink building alongside two metal hangars.

I gasped my way across the gravel. *Fuckin' heat and humidity! If I had a lot of carry-on luggage, this would be a real bitch.*

I walked through a door and looked around. It was as rinky-dink on the inside as it was outside. I must be in the wrong place! I hesitated then walked out.

Cars were parked along a curb. A guy standing by a limo was holding a sign with my name on it. I walked up to him and said, "Hi, that's me."

"Good afternoon, Sir," as he opened the back door. I said, if he wouldn't mind, I'd prefer to ride up front with him.

"Not at all, Sir. I can put your case in back if you'd like, so it'll be out of the way." I handed him my attaché and got in. I asked him his name "Sir, my name is Stewart."

"Stewart, I understand your courtesy, but from now on, no more 'Sir', please."

We drove down a road for a while, then Stewart pulled onto what looked like a freeway. There was some traffic, but not bad at all. I asked Stewart how people lived in this heat.

"After a while, you get used to it, and it doesn't bother you. In fact, when you're here for a while, you have a hard time with the cold up north. Most people and businesses have air-conditioning."

Stewart drove down a ramp off the freeway, went two blocks, and made a left onto a street with palm trees and gated homes. I could see luxurious homes with manicured lawns and good-looking landscaping. To my right, behind them, was the ocean. The houses were huge and stately, and the ocean was great.

We drove for a while, then Stewart eventually pulled up to a gate. The house was modern, an impressive white marble and glass structure, framed by the ocean. What a sight! Stewart got out to speak into a box at the gate. The gate eased open and he drove to the front of the house.

"Welcome, Pauly. Tony has told me all about you. I'm so glad to meet you. I'm Santo."

As we shook hands, I said, "It's a pleasure to meet you, too, Sir."

"No, no, it's Santo to you."

We walked into the living room that was fantastically decorated – lounge chairs and sofas in luxurious white leather, all facing a wall of glass that looked out on the ocean. A suave-looking gentleman stood up, and extended his hand. "So, you're Paul Walker, my old friend's grandson. It's good to meet you."

"It's good to meet you, Mr. Lansky. Tony has told me a lot about you and Mr. Trafficante."

Santo said, "My housekeeper makes the best margarita you ever tasted, Pauly. Would you like to join Meyer and me? We'll do a pitcher."

I said I'd give it a try.

Meyer broke in. "Before we do business, I have to know how Paul Walker is my old friend Hyman's grandson." I told them the story, and ended with, "Your old friend, my grandfather, is the greatest man on the face of the earth."

Santo said, "That may be true, but I'll tell you who the greatest man on the face of the earth was. When I was a kid in Italy, we lived in a shack outside of Naples. My mother, father, two brothers, and a sister. We were all malnourished, living without plumbing, in extreme poverty. I used to sit on a corner in Naples with a cup in my hand, begging.

"One day a large horse-drawn buggy with a man sitting in the back came ripping past me, and then stopped. The man got out and asked why I was begging. I told him for food for my family. He told me to get in the buggy alongside the driver and show him where I live. He got in the back.

"When we got to the shack, this man walked right in… and my brothers and sister came racing out. The four of us were standing there, not knowing what was going on, fearing the worst. After a while my parents, with the man leading came over to us. 'Your mother and father and I are in agreement. From now on you will live in a house I will give you. From now on you will have good drinking water and indoor plumbing. From now on you will always have food on the table, and you will be clothed well. From now on you four are to get an education. From now on your father will work for me. A horse-drawn cart will be here this afternoon to take you and your belongings to your new home.'

"Everything happened like the man said. That man saved my family and gave me my start. That man, Pauly, was your grandfather, Dominic DeDomenico."

After moments of silence, Meyer said, "Let's get business out of the way so we can have some fun." I laid out everything for them, explained the network of families, and that no one was near them. After I concluded with a description of our delivery and pick up of the money, they both just sat mutely.

I thought, *Fuck, I don't know what else to say. I guess I blew this deal. Tony should have had someone smarter than me to deal with these guys. Everything I heard about both of them is true – they are sharp businessmen.*

Finally, Meyer spoke, "Santo, we can do this stuff out of the hotels, to all the coke and potheads. I can get Batista to set up dealers all over the country."

Santo agreed. "That would be good, and we can do a big job with it here. There's a lot of that shit used." Santo had a good, quick mind and added, "I see two problems. The first is we'd want more product than you'll be able to deliver. The second is getting it to Cuba."

I asked if they'd have a problem with oceangoing containers in Cuba or Miami. Meyer said there wouldn't be a problem at all in Cuba, and Santo said he could handle the port in Miami.

"I can make arrangements. I need to know when you want it and who they're going to."

Santo said, "As soon as you can." Santo wrote on a piece of paper and handed it to me. He listed "Capri Hotel, Cuba" and "Santo Distributing, Miami," with the amount of product he wanted at each location. I realized this was a lot more than Hernandez told us we'd be getting on our first load.

"If it's OK with you gentlemen, I'd like to handle this now. All I need is a good phone."

"The phone is safe," Santo assured. "Use it and let me know how much. I'll write a check on the Capri Hotel in US funds. You can take it back to New York. I own three multi-million-dollar hotels with large casinos in Cuba. They're yielding $300,000 a day in profits."

I called Tony and spelled out everything, especially two problem areas. The first was I didn't want either party to know where the containers were going or coming from. Tony told me he understood and could handle it. The second was Santo wanted to pay me with a check. I figured Hyman could get our friend at Manufacturers to handle the check and do a transfer. Tony said it shouldn't be a problem. I asked him to get me an amount and who to make the check out to, and to call me back at Santos' home.

After about fifteen minutes the phone rang. Santo picked it up and spoke to someone. If Tony tried to call, and got a busy signal, he'd call back. Meyer and I sat there kind of looking at each other. We couldn't hear what Santo was saying. Santo reached for a paper and pen, wrote something down then hung up.

Gentlemen "We have a deal. That was Tony. He said to tell you to have a good time tonight, and he'd see you when you got home tomorrow."

Meyer said he and Santo planned to take me to Cuba in their yacht. "We'll have a great time in the hotel."

"Sounds good to me. I have something for you." I took the brick out of my attaché and handed it to Meyer. "This is what you'll be getting. It's pure, not cut, and I've been told really good stuff."

Meyer said, "We can't accept this. There's way too much money here." I insisted.

Santo went into another room, after a while came back and handed me a check on the Capri Hotel made out to Anthony DeAngelo. The amount was staggering. Then Santo gave me another check from the Capri made out to the Mateo-Donatella DeAngelo Foundation – for a million dollars. When Tony told him about what Maria and I were doing, he thought it was the greatest thing he ever heard. Although he never knew Mateo, a foundation in memory of Donatella was all he had to hear. He and his wife had spent many memorable hours with Tony and Donetella. Anyone who spent time with Donatella quickly realized how great a woman she was.

Santo said half of the check was from Meyer, and Meyer interjected, "Honoring your grandfather, Carl, and Jacob."

Santo handed me a wad of cash and told me, "For tonight."

"Thank you for everything. You're both good people. Mr. Trafficante, I know why Tony considers you a good friend."

"Come on, let's get on the yacht. We can have dinner at the hotel."

Outside, Stewart was waiting with the limo. After driving for a while, and my listening to the glories of Cuba and Miami, we arrived at a marina. As we ambled down a pier, I was thinking *This must be a navy deal. These fuckers are huge.* We boarded a massive yacht with 'SANTO'S DREAM' on the back. As we sat on a deck in lounge chairs, Santo told some guy in a white uniform to get under way. Another guy came up asked if we would care for drinks, *hors d'oeuvres*, and cigars. Meyer asked what beverage I'd like.

"Whatever you're having as long as it's not a margarita. I don't think they get along with me." Meyer told the guy whiskey sours, to pass on the hors d' oeuvres, but to bring some cigars.

I was relaxing in a very comfortable lounge chair, sipping a neat drink, smoking a Cuban cigar, enjoying the ocean breeze. The only way life could be any better would be if Maria was with me. Shit, I missed her.

"How do you like my baby?" Before I could answer, Santo told me Meyer gave him the boat a couple of years ago, as a Christmas gift. "C'mon I'll take you on a tour." Santo showed me the boat. It was hard to believe. A floating mansion! The john made Hernandez's penthouse john look like an outhouse.

We arrived in Cuba, walked a short pier, to a waiting limo. After about fifteen minutes we reached an area that didn't impress me at all. It was a shanty town. A turn had us heading back toward the ocean and elegant high-rise buildings on white, beautiful, well-maintained beaches.

We rolled up to the front door of one of the high-rises, the Capri Hotel and Casino. The entrance was ultra-elegant. The structure and surroundings radiated luxury. In the lobby we were approached by a sharp-looking guy in an all-white suit, "Good evening, Meyer and Santo. It's good to see you again. Everything is as you requested and waiting for you."

Santo made the introductions, "Joe, I'd like you to meet Pauly. Pauly's a very good friend of ours. And Pauly, this is Joe

Fontana. Joe is the hotel business manager. He runs this whole damn thing."

Joe said, "Pauly, I want you to have a great time here. If there's anything you want or need, please have them get ahold of me and I'll make it happen. Gentlemen, if you don't need me for anything now, I have to leave you and take care of an urgent matter. I'll see you later. Nice meeting you, Pauly."

Santo told me we were going to eat in their private dining room, or, if I preferred, one of the four restaurants. "Or, because this guy made me do it... a Jewish deli. We bring all the food in from New York every night. When Myer first wanted to do it, I thought it was a waste and going to cost a fortune. Now the deli makes more money than any of the restaurants."

I told Santo, "I understand why it's doing well – Jewish food is terrific."

After dinner Santo was going to get some business handled – he didn't like to gamble. Meyer and I were going to spend the evening in the casino. Santo commented, "Meyer lives for it. He's a freakin' card shark!"

As we were enjoying good food and drinking Chianti, Meyer explained blackjack. "The only way you win is through money management. It's a crazy phenomenon. There are times when the dealer is getting great hands, and the table isn't. Then it switches, and the dealer can't win. If you're playing with good players, you'll see everybody laying back, and then all of a sudden big money bets come out."

"We won't have a problem because we're going to be playing at a high-stake table. The other tables could be wining like crazy, and some guy walking by puts a five-dollar chip on an empty spot, wins, leaves, and the deck changes. Everybody sitting at the table just wants to choke the bastard."

After we finished eating, Meyer and I went to the casino. We passed an aisle with rows of slot machines on both sides. People were all over the place dumping money and pulling on the machines. Every once in a while, you'd hear "ding, ding, ding" and see a little old lady waving her arms and yelling. We went beyond the roulette tables to a back corner of the casino.

Two guys were sitting at a blackjack table, and a dealer was dealing. When the hand ended, Meyer asked if they minded if we joined them. Meyer put $2,000 on the table, told the dealer eighteen black and eight green. The black chips were one hundred dollars each, and the green twenty-five. The dealer counted out the money, hollered "$2,000 incoming" to the pit boss, and put the cash in a slot in the table. He then stacked four neat rows of chips. I did the same, $2,000.

Meyer put a chip down; so did I. The dealer dealt my first card, which was up, a face card. The dealer's card was down. My second card was a three and the dealer's was a five. The guy to my right stayed with sixteen. I didn't know what to do. I was about to give the signal for a hit, but Meyer nudged me. Under the table, he motioned me to stay. I did. Everybody was in and the dealer flipped her down-card over. It was a ten. She dealt herself a three and a king and busted.

She paid everybody. Meyer left the two chips on the table as did I. I tapped Meyer and gave him a thank-you look. That's the way things were going. We won a lot, and lost some. We were about an hour into it and couldn't win a hand. I glanced at my chips and realized I was up a lot.

The dealer called for bets. Meyer put a stack down, I copied him…then I realized we were betting a thousand dollars on the turn of a card! My first card was a picture, Meyer's was a seven. My second card was an ace. The dealer took my cards, paid me

$1,500. Meyer's second card was another seven; he put another stack down and split the sevens. His first card was a four. He put another stack on the table and doubled. His first card on the second seven was a three. Again, another stack, and double. I had just won with blackjack, and Meyer was sitting there with four thousand bet, and a twenty-one and twenty.

The dealer turned over her down card. It was a picture. Her second card was a three, and third a five. She had eighteen and had to stay. Meyer must have played blackjack for a lot of years. A newcomer would have been out of his seat with joy. Meyer just sat there like he knew ahead of time what was going to happen. We played for another hour before Meyer said, "Let's cash out. We'll shoot some craps."

Meyer asked the dealer to get a pit boss. He asked for chits, so we wouldn't have to drag our chips around. M chips were counted out, and the boss handed me a fancy little piece of paper with fourteen thousand dollars written on it. I realized a chit was really an IOU. That's not bad. I just won fourteen thousand on money that wasn't even mine.

We wondered over to the craps table and watched people rolling the dice. Meyer explained the game to me. He told me the best way to win is to play the line only. Everything else is a loser.

"That's good enough for me. I'm going to follow you, partner." Meyer smiled.

We moved up to the table. Meyer put a couple of grand down and asked for all black, and I did the same. The guy used a long stick to push a pair of dice toward Meyer and hollered out "new roller".

Meyer put two chips on the line, and again I followed. The black chip was worth a hundred dollars. Suddenly everybody at the table was putting green, twenty-five-dollar chips on the line.

The thing was full.

Meyer picked up the dice, rolled them in his hand, then very neatly threw them. They hit the wall of the table and bounced back. The guy hollered out "seven." People around the table started screaming. Meyer and I just stood there. They had doubled everyone's chips. Some picked up their chips; Meyer and I left ours.

Meyer picked up the dice, threw them the same as the first time, with the same results. *How fuckin' hard can this be?* Meyer left his chips on the line; so did I. Almost everybody picked theirs up and put them all over the table.

Meyer rolled the dice. It came up six. Everybody started moving chips around. Meyer and I left what we had. Meyer turned to me and said, "It's easy. Don't worry"

He rolled the dice – it came up eight. There was a lot of action on the table. I think a lot of the green-chips were betting against Meyer. Meyer rolled the dice and up pops six. They doubled our stacks again, which by now were getting pretty good.

Meyer picked his chips up and motioned the guy to pass me the dice. We both put a chip on the line. I guess I didn't look the part because only one green chip joined us. *Fuck all of you! I'll show you.*

I picked up the dice, and, different from Meyer, my throw sucked. One die barely rolled to the wall, the other bounced off a side wall and hit the back wall. *Sure, I'm gonna show them.* Then the guy hollered out "eleven...we have a winner."

Meyer leaned over to me and said, "Don't worry about throwing them hard. Just let them flow out of your hand."

I picked up the dice and did what Meyer said. They kind of just fell out and didn't go anywhere. The guy snatched the dice with the stick and said, "Let's do it again." There was a lot of action on the table, all against me.

I picked up the dice, held them between my thumb and trigger finger, and flicked them. They went out, hit the back wall perfectly, and came up five. What happened to the sevens? Meyer used them all up.

Meyer said, "Pauly, put two more chips down behind yours." I picked up the dice flicked them out and up pops an eight. The green chips were really stacking up on the table. Meyer told me to put one more chip across both stacks. I did it, thinking *I've got five hundred on the line and don't feel all that good about myself.* I flicked the dice a good roll. The guy hollered "five…we have a winner!"

They raked in a bunch of green and started stacking chips alongside mine and Meyer's. It seems that when Meyer had me put two more down, it wasn't just two chips. Somehow, I doubled the whole thing and then the one across, tripled. I had no idea what I was doing. All I know is they gave me twelve hundred.

Meyer said, "Let's get out of here. We have a couple of more things we can do. Then, if you want, we can play some more blackjack." We walked over to a roulette table and sat down.

Meyer was explaining how to bet when this beautiful girl with a great body walked over to us. She bent over and asked if she could get us something. Not only was this girl beautiful, she was wearing a top that exposed most of her breasts. When she bent over those things were right there. I lost it.

Meyer ordered a black coffee and a cigar. The girl was very aware of my staring, but simply asked if she could bring me something. I was tongue-tied – and fuckin' horny.

Patiently she repeated, "Sir, may I get you something?" I ordered coffee, light and sweet, and a cigar.

I told Meyer I wanted to get this. I sure as hell owed it to him. "No, Pauly, it's complimentary." I asked if I could tip with chips. "Yes."

Meyer put a stack of ten black chips on the table and asked that they be greened up. I did the same. Meyer put four chips on red, then chips on four corners. For two hundred bucks, we were betting on red and sixteen numbers.

The ball started going around. It seemed like it was going a hundred miles an hour. I was thinking, *This thing is never going to stop.* Then the ball did a slight dip and landed in a pocket. It was red, and one of the numbers we bet on. Our winnings were stacked on our bets. We started to drag the chips to us as the girl brought our coffee and cigars and put them down.

Addressing Meyer, she said, "Mr. Lansky, I'm so sorry I didn't acknowledge you. I was just informed who you are." Meyer told her it was OK and not to worry about it.

"Miss, thank you for the coffee and cigars, and you are fantastic." I handed her two green chips.

"Thank you, and thank you for the compliment."

I picked up my coffee and extended it toward Meyer. He realized what I was doing, picked his cup up, and tapped it to mine. I said, "*Salute,*" and he said something I didn't understand, but I knew what he meant.

"We're doing really good, partner," he agreed.

We drank our coffee, smoked our cigars, and continued playing roulette. "Pauly, you have some choices. We can either play baccarat, which I don't care for, or we can do slots, which I also don't care for, or we can play more blackjack, or we can call it a night."

"I don't want to call it a night yet. I don't feel tired."

I told Meyer he needed to put up a few clocks in this place.

"We don't, on purpose."

I looked at my watch, "Holy crap. It's three-thirty in the morning!"

Meyer smiled, "Time flies when you're having fun." He noticed my watch, asked if it was a Rolex. I removed it and handed it to him.

He looked it over. "Very nice. Very nice watch." I asked him if he really liked it, or was he being polite. He came back with, "What's not to like about it?"

"Please, keep it. It's my gift to you." He put it on, and it seemed every time I'd look at him, he was admiring the Rolex.

No one was at our lucky blackjack table. As soon as we sat down, a dealer showed up, started shuffling decks, then handed the stack to Meyer to cut. We blackened our chips; then we took out $5,000 in cash and asked for all black. Just then the same girl walked over to us, and said, "Good morning again, gentlemen. Can I get you anything?" Meyer asked for a cigar; I told her I was OK.

I had the dealer green a black chip. I lit a Lucky and was enjoying it, amazed that I hadn't thought of having a Lucky all night. The dealer dealt a hand and we won. We left our chips on the table. Before he could deal the second hand, I put two green chips alongside my bet, for the dealer. The hand was dealt and we all won.

The girl returned. Meyer thanked her for the cigar. I said, "Miss, please take this." I handed her two green chips.

"No, Sir, I can't. We're still working on the first one."

"It doesn't work that way. The first one is history. This is now. Please, take it."

"Thank you. I get off at six. Would you like to have a cup of coffee with me?"

"That would be nice, but I can't. I have an early flight to New York, and have to get back to the States"

Meyer jumped in. "I could go for a cup of coffee with you."

"Really? That would be great."

She left, and I elbowed Meyer, "You foxy devil, you." We both laughed. We played the same as before: won a lot, lost some. At some point we decided to call it quits.

The front desk of the casino was deserted. On the back wall was a clock. Five-fifteen. I was becoming a little anxious about getting back to the airport with enough time to catch my flight. I slammed my fist on the counter. A guy raced out of a back room, apologized for keeping me waiting. I told him he didn't have to be sorry, it was kind of early. I asked if he had a message for Paul Walker. The clerk looked through a pile of messages. "I have a message from Mr. Trafficante for Pauly Walker. I guess that would be you."

Santo had left the message for me at one-o'clock, telling me we would meet in the lobby at five-thirty and have breakfast aboard ship on the way back. I no sooner sat in a chair when Santo walked into the lobby, asked how my night was.

I told him my night was great, probably one of the most enjoyable I had had. I told him I'd like to take a vacation and bring my fiancée to meet him and Meyer. "You'll really like my fiancée, Maria. She's Donatella's daughter, and, as Tony has told me, just like her mother."

I asked how his night was. Before he could answer, I said, "You look beat."

"I am. Between us, I fucked my brains out all night. Let's go."

A car was waiting, and it drove us to the pier. We boarded and collapsed into the lounge chairs. The next thing I knew was someone tapping me on the shoulder, telling me we had arrived. Santo and I had slept the whole trip.

Stewart was waiting for us. In Santo's house I got my attaché and was about to say good-bye when Santo asked if I liked the Cuban cigars. Of course, I did. He reached in a cabinet and brought out two boxes. I thanked him and put the cigars in my attaché. I told him I wanted to get Tony hooked on Cubans and off those stinky ropes. Santo said, "There are some things in life you just can't change."

"Santo, my meeting you and Meyer, the time I've spent with you and Meyer, was my pleasure and honor. It's something I'll hold close all my life."

Stewart drove me to the airport. The terminal was so different than La Guardia – no airplane noise. In fact, the place was quiet, and there were very few people around. I was thinking there had to be another airport here that was a lot more than this place. I got a boarding pass and walked out the back door. Across the field was the American Airline plane, the only plane. I started walking to it, thinking they must have enlarged the field overnight. The walk was bothering me. I was so fuckin' tired. I staggered up the metal steps, to the door of the plane. I was hoping the same young lady would be there, but she wasn't.

I handed over my boarding pass and was directed to my seat. My case was put in the overhead compartment. I sat down, buckled my seat belt, leaned back, and thought about breakfast. I was so hungry. The next thing I was aware of was being awakened and told we were in our approach to La Guardia. Shit! I missed being on the ocean, I missed flying, I missed meals, *and I'm fuckin' starving.*

The plane landed, moved on the ground for a while, and came to a stop. I got my attaché and walked out onto the steps. Down the steps, across the asphalt, and up more steps. Flying is neat but getting to and off the plane sucks. In the building I noticed a sign that read MAIN TERMINAl with an arrow. I got in with a stream of people that were going that way. People were rushing the opposite way. A lady dragging a bag hit me in my leg. She didn't say anything, just kept going. Between the noise of the planes, and all the people, I was thinking Miami wasn't all that bad.

At the main terminal, I found a large sign above a door that led to the street. The sign read ARRIVING PASSENGERS. I walked up to the door, looked at the sign, and said to myself: *I have arrived.*

# CHAPTER 32

There were a lot of cars waiting at the curb. Vince was standing by the limo, about ten cars away. Vince asked how the trip was.

"The trip was great. I'm beat, and I'm fuckin' starving."

"We'll take care of the starving part really quick; then I'll take you to Muraso and home." Vince went about three blocks and pulled into a parking lot. In front of us was a small building with a sign, Denny's. Behind it was a big building, Holiday Inn. I had never been in or heard of Denny's before. I guess they don't like the Bronx.

At the table Vince waved away the menu the waitress offered. Vince said, "Two orange juice, two coffees, and two Grand Slams."

"That's fine with me. It could be a dead horse, as long as it's food."

The girl brought out the OJ and coffee. The coffee was good and hit the spot. The waitress brought out plates of food: Pancakes with bacon, eggs, sausage, and hash browns. Vince must have been hungry, too, because we both ate like there was no tomorrow. After we finished, I lit up a cig. The waitress handed Vince the check. He gave her a ten and told her to keep the rest for herself. I saw the check. The meals cost $3.00 each. Hard to believe that much food for so little.

I gave Tony the check from Santo and said, "How about I get here early tomorrow. We can talk things over; then we can get out of here and see how some of the jobs are coming along. You need a break from this place."

Tony agreed.

I told him I had to get some sleep. "I feel like my eyes are crossing."

"Before you leave, did you figure how much we made on this deal?" I hadn't had time.

"Close to a mil."

Vince drove me home. Maria kissed and hugged me. I told her I loved and missed her and was anxious to hear how things are going. I had an idea to discuss with her later after I got some sleep and could stand without keeling over.

I don't know how long I slept. It was nine-thirty at night before I appeared downstairs. Maria greeted me with, "Hi, Sleepyhead. I have our dinner warming. We can eat when you feel like it." After I finished eating we went out to the patio. It was one of those late summer-early fall nights, perfect weather. Maria brought out a couple of iced teas. We weren't drinkers, but we were hooked on Long Island Iced Tea.

I lit up a Lucky and told Maria I had a check for her to deposit in the foundation account for $1 million from Santo Trafficante. I also had $36,000 for her to deposit into our checking account.

"There's something that I've been thinking about. Lily had mentioned she wanted to get involved. After we left, you said you wanted her to, but didn't know how. You can ask her if she wants to be co-chair with you. I heard that term somewhere, and I think it means you would both be bosses.

"Then you set up a board of directors – Hyman and Josh, and smart guys in the medical and hospital fields. To offset all these smart guys, I'd like to be on your board. If you do that, you'll be able to share the burden that's now all on your shoulders."

"You're right! I must do that. You certainly will be on the board." Maria told me her first day on the job was hectic. She spent most of the day with Josh. "The man is unbelievable. When he sets his mind on something, it happens instantly. He's a dynamo."

"During a break this afternoon Josh was telling me how everything is going to change soon. People will use checks to pay bills, and it'll be rare for people to buy something with cash. Almost everyone will have plastic credit cards. Down the road, he wants to do a HCJ Hospital, Hanover Trust card. When people use their credit card, the company would pay the hospital 1%. One percent doesn't sound like a lot, but in time, millions of dollars will transact on credit cards."

Early the next morning I told Tony and Mario about my trip to Miami and the time I spent with Santo and Meyer. I felt Tony had a true bond and friendship with Santo, but not with Lansky. "Both are good businessmen and smart. I don't think Santo would hurt us in any way, but I feel Lansky might try to cut us out and deal directly with Hernandez. I don't know if I'm right. It's just a gut-feel.

"The second thing is the network with the Caddies. Let's say the Caddy makes its drops and brings back attachés of cash. On the second trip, it makes its drops and winds up in New Orleans...and then disappears. New Orleans claims they paid the guy. What if New Orleans decided they wanted the dope and the cash? We'd be fucked.

"It goes back to what Fanarssi said about greed. There might be a better way to handle cash other than sticking a ring out there for somebody to grab. I've got two more things on my mind, then I'll shut up. I was thinking about the Dino-shit with us, and the Tito-fucking of Vito. I wonder how many guys we have that are taking a piece of the pie for themselves. It could be a little piece, but enough guys over time could be a big chunk of cash.

"We have a lot of unaccountable cash flowing in the yards. We need to get across to everyone a fear: 'If you fuck with us, you won't live to enjoy it.' And there should be a way we can account for the cash."

I asked Tony about the time he mentioned he wanted to be in the waste business, and I hadn't heard anything more about it.

Tony explained he wanted to take over the City Sanitation Department. He had a deal worked out with a lot of money going for payoffs, but the mayor stepped in and killed the deal. Tony still had a thing about making money on garbage.

"Good. That's what I want to talk to you about. When I was in Miami we passed an area where there were at least a couple of hundred trailers. I'd never seen a house trailer that people lived in before. A garbage truck was in front. Rather than dumping garbage cans, he backed up to a small container. The truck lifted the container, dumped it in the back, set it down, and pulled away. There's nothing like this in the city, with everyone putting all the trash in separate cans. This container is the way to do it, but for businesses. We could pay the city to let us dump in their barges or set up our own. We'd maintain our trucks and containers, so they looked good, not like the city's garbage trucks that look like shit."

Tony asked if I was done. I had one more thing. He said to hold on to it. "We've got too much on our plate for now." Tony said he'd handle Hernandez for as long as he could. "In time, we will be cut out." The drug business was something he never intended to be a long-term thing. "As for the Caddies, what do you think, Mario?"

"I agree with Pauly. The Caddies are the weakest part of this whole thing. We ought to park the Caddies for now. Set it up so the families bring their cash and make their own pickups in New York.

"I think Miami should stay the way you did it, except the check should be made out from his casino to ours, and from the casino to Hernandez. If you do it the way you did, and the Feds get onto you, you won't be able to explain it. You'll do a lot of time for tax evasion."

Tony said, "You're right. I still have Santo's check. I can get him to void it, and issue a new check, casino-to-casino. We'll get ahold of Fanarssi and have him tell everyone about the new arrangements.

"About us getting ripped off, it's bothered me, too. I never thought Dino would do that to me. We set up Dino to test his honesty. I want to do the same with everyone who handles cash.

"Pauly, you and Sam set it up. Use anyone in the family that's not known and is sharp. I want Royal Auto Sales with thousands involved, parts and yards with hundreds, everyone who handles cash. The only exception is Luca. I trust him with my life. When you and Sam are OK with a place, I want the two of you to get with Vincenzo and work out a system, so we don't have to do this shit again.

Tony added, "This garbage thing you brought up. Do you remember telling me how Lansky was with the dope for Cuba? That's how I feel. I haven't felt this good about something in years."

"That's great," I said. "How about hearing me out on my last thing? If we took the boom off a truck, it'd leave us with a cab, frame, and winch. We build ourselves a twelve-foot long, by six-foot wide, by six-foot high container, then figure out how to get it on and off the frame. We could drop containers at construction sites for scrap. Containers could be set at demolition sites for concrete, block and brick."

Tony came back, "We could buy a worked-out quarry and fill it with the building material. A swampland on Long Island would be perfect for the hard stuff. Down the road, we'd not only be in the waste business, we'd be in the real estate business, too. I want to form a company using the money from the dope. I was thinking of a name, 'waste something'. I'm not sure yet; it will come to me. We'll pass on looking at the construction sites together. For now, we've got a lot of shit to get done."

I went to my office and asked Cleo to get ahold of Fanarssi. I called Sam and asked him to come to Muraso. Royal Auto Sales had to be set up first because of the big bucks. While waiting for Al's call and for Sam, I called Vincenzo to my office. I told him what Sam and I were doing. When we were OK with a place, the three of us needed to develop a system that accounted for everything. Vincenzo had to make sure his people were good. We didn't want to go through another Dino deal.

As Vincenzo was leaving my office, Sam walked in, asked what happened to our parts business. I explained Hernandez was in Peru, and it'd pick up when he got back.

# CHAPTER 33

I told Sam about the concerns Tony, Mario, and I had about anyone hitting us. "We're going to test every location and then put controls in place." I wanted to start with the car lots, then the parts and yards. We'd be setting up everyone who handles cash, except Luca. I wanted him to get three guys from Beacon, Franco and two sharp guys that didn't handle cash. They needed to be clean and dressed to go shopping for a car.

"Tomorrow morning, pick them up at Beacon, take them to the lot, park out of sight. They can walk to the lot. Here's fifteen grand. Give one of them three, one five, and one seven. The three and five are to buy cars from each of the salesmen. The seven is to buy a car from Talya. They don't want an invoice. All they want is a title and paper plate. They're to say they'll handle the registration themselves. Have them meet you back at Beacon when it's done. Tell them they can either take the day off or go to work. They're not to talk to anyone about what they did."

"Why don't we do it now instead of tomorrow?"

"Better idea. Do it. I'll meet you tomorrow morning at the lot. We'll see what happened to the money."

The phone rang. It was Fanarssi, apologizing for not getting back sooner. This was the first chance he had to check in. I explained changing the way his customers were going to get their product. The decision had a lot to do with his comment at the meeting. He told me he'd get with the guys he had been to and tell them.

In Tony's office Tony said everything seemed to be falling in place. He had a deal working on the swampland, and he found a worked-out quarry that the city owned. "It's mine!" He had spoken to Santo about the garbage truck with the loading deal. "I've got a new one coming on a flatbed. When we get it, we'll copy the loading, and build our own trucks. Mario figured out how to lift a container on a flat truck."

"Sounds like you guys have been busy, and we're going to be in the waste business. It should be good. There will always be shit."

I went to my office and was trying to think. I was tired, felt brain-dead. I called Cleo, told her if anyone was looking for me, I'd be at home. I got home – no one was there. Maria and Hyman were at the foundation. I went upstairs, undressed and hit the bed. I'm not sure what time it was when I woke up, but I was hungry with one of those pizza-cravings.

At the grill I got a couple of slices of pizza, put them on a table, and walked over to the bar. A couple of guys were sitting at the bar. I didn't know them, figured they were part of somebody's crew. I asked Freddie for a bottle of Chianti and a glass. Out of the corner of my eye I could see these guys giving me a "Who the fuck is this guy?" look. I sat down, ate the pizza, drank some Chianti, smoked a Lucky, and was feeling good about things. After a while, I gave Freddie the bottle and glass and thanked him.

It was a nice night, and I felt like taking a walk. After I walked about two blocks on the curb side of the sidewalk, a figure was coming toward me fast on the building side. Somebody was in a hurry. As he came beside me, the guy did a sidestep and pulled out a knife. "Give me your fuckin' money."

"Sure. Relax. You can have all I've got. I'm gonna reach in my pocket for it." I put my right hand in my jacket, felt the grip of my forty-five in my left inside breast pocket. I pulled it out and smashed the barrel on the guy's wrist. He dropped the knife and grabbed his wrist with his other hand. Broken wrist? I hope I smashed this mother-fucker's bones.

I grabbed him and shoved the forty-five in his gut, saying, "I'm gonna give you a choice. You're gonna have to think fast, prick. I can make you a new asshole where your belly button is, or you can turn and run the way you came. Stop and I'll put a slug in your back. Which is it?"

The fuckin' lamebrain had trouble getting out "Run!"

"Good choice. Get the fuck outta here." I kicked his knife into the street, watched him for a while. Then I turned, walked back to my car, and drove home.

The next morning, I was at the lot early. Sam was there. I heard, "Pauly, Pauly." Talya came running up, asked how I was, and said it was good to see me. I asked how things were; she told me good. I told her I'd catch up with her later.

While Sam and I were drinking coffee at a table in the lunch-room, I asked if he saw the deposit slip from last night. He had, and I wasn't going to like it. There was only $5,000 deposited.

"Fuck. I was hoping that girl wouldn't do something stupid."

I told Sam to tell Meaghan we were going to use his office to meet with the sales people. Sam and I were sitting in Meaghan's office when there was a knock on the door. Sam hollered out "come in." The door opened, and there was this young guy. He looked nervous.

I stood up, walked over to him, extended my hand, and said, "Hi, my name is Pauly. Please sit down."

"Thank you. My name is Tim." I asked Tim how long he'd been working here. Two years. How did he like the job? He loved the job, thought it was the best job in the world.

"Yesterday you sold a guy a car for three grand. He didn't want an invoice or registration. Do you remember it?"

"Yes. I sold him a Ford. He was a nice guy."

"The deal was done, the guy left with the car, and you have three grand in your hand. What did you do next?"

He made out an invoice. Even though the guy didn't want one, he needed it for the company. The company requires an invoice for its bookkeeping. It reduces the inventory, and that's how the commission is calculated.

"Your commission on the deal was a hundred and fifty bucks. Three grand is a lot better."

"No, Sir, I wouldn't do anything like that. I wouldn't do anything to jeopardize my job."

"OK, you have an invoice and three grand. What's next?"

"I gave the cash and invoice to Mr. Meaghan."

Was he missing any commissions? Yes, but he figured he'd be getting them.

I asked him to write down the date, the car, and the amount of the deal on the commissions he hadn't received. The date didn't have to be exact. He was not to talk to anyone about this. I thanked him and asked him to get me the list quickly and ask the other salesman to come in.

He left. Soon after this big guy walked in, said, "Hello, gentlemen," and sat down. The guy was older, old-school Italian with slicked-back hair and a handlebar mustache.

"My name is Pauly. You know Sam. And your name is?"

"Alanzo."

"Well Alonzo, how's everything going?"

"Great. With all due respect, Mr. Dawson, I miss my cousin Al."

"Aside from that, how's the job? You making good bucks?"

"The job is a breeze – I'm making good money with the commissions."

I asked if he missed any. No, he's gotten every commission. I thanked him and told him we just wanted to make sure everyone was happy. I asked him to please ask Talya to come in.

There was a knock on the door, Tim came in, handed me a sheet of paper, then left. There was $22,000 in sales, all recent. I handed the sheet to Sam. I told him, "Something is fucked-up here. Tim gets beat out of eleven hundred in commission, and Alonzo's not missing a dime."

There was a knock on the door. I said, "Talya, come in." She apologized for keeping us waiting – she was finishing up a sale. I asked her about the $7,000 sale she made yesterday. Almost word for word she told us the same thing Tim did. I asked her if she was missing any commissions. She said she was and had been keeping track of them. She had asked Mr. Meaghan about it. He told her it had to be a screw-up in accounting, and he'd look into it.

She didn't push it because what I did for her was far more than her commissions. I told her one had nothing to do with the other. She was entitled to those commissions. I asked her if keeping track of the commissions meant writing it down. Yes she said. I asked her to get her list for me.

While she was gone, I told Sam that the two of them not going to him about the commissions was understandable, and it was nothing against him. "Tim is afraid of losing his job if he goes over Meaghan's head, and you heard Talya."

Then Talya returned with a sheet of paper. She had thirty -eight thousand in sales. I asked her if I could keep it. I'd make sure she got her commission.

Once she left. I handed Sam the sheet. "It looks like we've been beaten out of sixty grand – that we know of." I asked Sam what he thought. I knew where I was and wanted to make sure we were on the same track. Sam, like me, felt neither Talya or Tim had anything to do with the missing money. Alonzo was out of the picture altogether. Everything pointed to one person.

"We need to get him in here for a little talk. If that doesn't work, beat the living shit out of the fuck and take him for a ride."

I never figured I'd hear something like that from Sam. "Let me handle this guy, but first I want to go through his desk." The top drawer had inventory sheets, blank forms, and a bunch of shit. The top small drawer had books of pricing guides, a Blue Book, and a couple of others. The second drawer had memos from Fanarssi to Meaghan. On paper was everything Fanarssi wanted done. The bottom drawer was locked. I decided not to break it open. I didn't want to fuck up the desk and felt it could wait.

I asked Sam to get Meaghan – nicely – to join us. Meaghan came in and sat down with, "Hi Pauly, good to see you."

I told him I owed him an apology. All the time I had known him, I never got his first name. He told me his name was Tom. "Good, Tom. We have a small problem. Sam and I feel you're the man to talk to because you know everything that goes on around here. Yesterday Alonzo sold a car for $5,000, the invoice went through, and the money was deposited. Tim sold a car for $3,000, and Talya sold a car for $7,000. No invoices or deposits. Have any idea what happened?"

Meaghan sat there looking at me. I could see he was getting anxious and was trying to think fast. He blustered that he had no idea at all… he had not seen an invoice or the cash from either of them.

I asked him if it was possible he just forgot and maybe misplaced the invoices and cash. I suggested, "We could still make the deposit, turn the invoices in, and call it a day."

Tom insisted, "I never saw the cash or the invoices!"

"Both Tim and Talya said they gave them to you."

He came back with: "They're lying!"

I asked Sam if he had anything to add to this, and before he could answer, I asked him to give Tom a taste of plan B. Sam stood up, walked over to Meaghan, and, like a bolt of lightning, punched him in the face. He didn't just break Meaghan's nose. The nose was a flat piece of meat hanging on his face.

Sam Dawson is a six foot-four, two-hundred-pound guy with no fat on his body, a guy who worked junk yards all his life. Someone told me he was a badass as a young guy. I guess age changed him. To me, he was the nicest guy.

I asked Sam what he had against Meaghan's nose. "It could have been a gut shot, and we wouldn't have this fucker bleeding all over the place like a stuck pig."

Meaghan sat there clutching his face whimpering and moaning.

"Shut the fuck up. You brought this on yourself. We never had to get to plan B if you answered my questions right. Did you take the money?"

Meaghan said, "Yes, I did."

"Now we're getting somewhere. Wipe your hand off on your jacket and hand me your keys."

I found the key to his desk drawer and opened it. I was looking at a stack of invoices. I put the invoices on the desk, and there was a checkbook on the bottom. "Tom, you have to be the stupidest bastard I ever met. To do this to begin with, and then to keep the fuckin' invoices." I looked in his checkbook. The register was blank. "How much do you have in it?

"Twelve thousand dollars."

I asked how much he had in his safe deposit box. He sat there silently. "Tom, you have a key on your ring with MHT and a number on it. Answer my fuckin' question!" He admitted to $50,000.

"Tom, this is what I want you to do. Wipe your hand off and write out a check for twelve thousand to Royal Auto Sales." He did. I asked where he kept Royal's deposit slips. I found them and handed him one. "Make out the deposit slip for the check and $33,000 in cash. I want you to call the bank manager and tell him you're sending an employee to make a deposit along with your safe deposit box key. You need him to open your box, put the $33,000 with the deposit, and give the young lady the rest."

Tom made the call. It wasn't a problem. I told Sam to have Talya do it for us. Sam took the key, check, and deposit slip, and walked out. I told Tom I was going to call someone who'd drive him to the city to see Doctor Benjamin. The doc was a good man and would fix him up right. I asked Tom what he was driving.

"A Mercedes." Company car or his? "Company."

Sam returned, said everything went well and Talya would be back soon.

"You have one problem. While Tom is recovering from his accident, you're going to need someone to run this place. Tom, who do you think can run this place while you recuperate?"

"I don't know anyone who could run this place as good as I have."

"You're right, Tom, it's going to be a problem. We'll figure something out."

There was a knock on the door. Sam got up, opened the door then closed it behind him. I phoned Muraso, got ahold of Vince, and told him he was needed at Royal Auto Sales to take someone to Dr.Benjamin.

Sam came back in. I asked if everything was OK. He nodded yes. I told Sam we had some time till Vince got here. He might want to talk to everyone and tell them about Tom's accident, and they'd get the commissions they missed on their next check. I asked Sam if he knew who he was going to make manager. He said he did, and it was the same person I was thinking about.

"Good. You might want to talk to her first."

I asked Meaghan if he was married. No. Did he live with anyone? Again, no. Had he given anyone a gift of a car, like a girl-friend? He did. What kind of car? A Cadillac. What did he get in return? He told me sex, what and when he wanted. I handed him a piece of paper to write down her name, address, and phone number. Did he own a house or rent? He rented an apartment. He added that address to the girlfriends.

I thought, *You deserve everything you're going to get, you stupid, arrogant, son of a bitch.* I told him to sit back and relax. "I'm going to go for a walk and a smoke." I walked out to my car, opened the trunk, took out my twenty-two. I slid in a clip, put it in a pocket, and put the silencer in another pocket. I figured Me-aghan felt he was above it all, which gave him a sense of security. He didn't have the balls to bolt, anyway.

Vince pulled up in front. I asked him to park on the side, away from the windows. I'd be bringing someone out. Inside Sam was still talking. I interrupted him. "I need your help for a couple of minutes."

I told Meaghan his transportation was here. He should take his jacket off and cover his nose with it. Sam would help him out to the car. When I was out of everyone's sight, I took out my twenty-two, put the silencer on, and released the safety. I held it by my side.

At the limo Vince opened the back door. Meaghan was about to get in. I stopped him. "Tom, this is going be a long trip. I hate to see you in pain, so I'm going to help you." I put two rounds about two inches below his left ear. Blood shot out. I grabbed his jacket and wrapped it around his head. Meaghan was still standing because Sam was holding him. I removed everything from Meaghan's pockets. Vince and Sam threw Meaghan into the trunk. *Rest in peace, Meaghan, you fuckin' bastard.*

"Sam, hang onto the fifteen grand. We'll use it on the setups. We'll get together tomorrow morning at Muraso with Vincenzo to work on a system. Take the invoices, deposit slip, and the two papers from Talya and Tim. Have Vincenzo tie it all together and get them their commissions.

"While we're with Vincenzo, we'll make sure the money in and out for the last six months tally at Bruckner. I also want to plan a setup. When I was at Bruckner, I saw a pile of radiators and heater cores. Let's see if we can buy them for cash."

Sam left to finish talking to his people. I went through Meaghan's desk, dumped his personal shit in the trash. Next, I went to his apartment. For the most part, it was crap. The only thing that caught my eye was two new-looking pennies in sealed plastic cases, and a gold coin. The piece of paper in the penny cases read uncirculated 1909 SVDB, and 1909 VDB. The gold coin was an Indian head quarter. I took them and left for his girl's place.

The address was a high-rise on the east side of Manhattan, the 19th floor. I introduced myself as Meaghan's boss. She told me her name is Alicia Cameron.

"We need to talk about the Caddy. Meaghan's dead. Before he died, Tom told me he gave you the Caddy. He didn't have the right to do that. He stole the car, and you received stolen merchandise."

"I didn't steal anything. I worked hard for the car. That son of a bitch couldn't get enough."

"You telling me you prostituted yourself for a car?"

"Yes. That's what I am. The car was his idea"

"I didn't say you stole the car. I said you received stolen merchandise. You're gonna do time, and I'll get the Caddy back. I'm sorry you're a prostitute. I was thinking you and Meaghan were friends, and I'd pick up where he left off. I can't do a prostitute.

I've got two choices. I take the Caddy and everything you have and off you, or I call the cops. Aside from that shit, you got any ideas?"

"How about I give you five hundred a month for four months?"

"That will work. Give me a pen and paper. You'll make out the check to HCJ Hospital for Children at the address I've written. Don't pay it and I'll go back to plan A,"

# *CHAPTER 34*

I walked into Tony's office, sat down, and said, "Good afternoon, Sir." Tony said my mother had called. She received a letter for me that was forwarded from the Bronx address. The letter was from the Selective Service Administration. She was sending it airmail to Muraso.

"Don't worry about it. When we get it, I can handle it without a problem."

"Thanks. We'll see. Let's get Mario in here so I can tell you both about my day." I told them everything. When I was done, I told them when we started it, I didn't think we'd have a problem there. I felt the people were good. Meaghan was making big bucks with an easy job. I didn't think he had the balls to fuck over us, especially because Fanarssi had him scared shitless.

Tony commented, "It's a funny thing about some people. I didn't think Dino had the balls either."

I drove home thinking about this draft shit. I was struggling with what to do and hoping Maria and Hyman's opinions would help. They were on the patio. Maria jumped up and kissed me. I needed that, and it felt so good holding her against me.

Hyman told me with Tony's help, we let about fifty contracts for work on the exterior and interior of the building, and it all went well. What building? This is going a little too fast. There have to be architects and engineers and blueprints and building permits and lots of other things before contractors are hired

Maria said, "Lily came up with a fabulous idea. Every room, every piece of equipment, everything – even uniforms – is to be child-friendly. Nothing is to intimidate or give a child fear."

"Josh had the staff of Mt. Sinai develop an equipment list of everything we'll need, with suggested costs and recommendations of where to buy. It seems that the top-quality equipment we want is manufactured in Germany or Japan, or by GE here in the States. The companies will not sell directly to a hospital. We must buy it through a distributor, which I understand because the distributor handles the warranty work for them and services the equipment.

Hyman said, "The problem we have is the suggested price for what we want is at $1,250,000. We can buy it through one company only. They want $3,500,000. Maria and I have talked to this guy till we're blue in the face. We can't get anywhere! We're not going to throw away $2,000,000."

The company was Shaeffer & Associates. Hyman had spoken to Martin Shaeffer, the owner. I asked if they minded if I talk to him since they weren't getting anywhere.

"I was hoping you'd say that," Hyman said grinning.

I called Tony and asked if he could find out everything on a Martin Shaeffer, owner of Shaeffer & Associates Medical Supplies. I needed it for Maria and Hyman.

Back on the patio Maria asked how my day was. Nothing unusual, except Tony told me my mother called. "Mom received a letter for me that was forwarded from the Bronx address. It was from the Selective Service. I'm sure it's my draft notice, and I'm fighting with myself about it. I can get out of it if I want. The other side is that a lot of my friends are coming home in coffins. If I walk away, I think I'll feel like shit later on. I'm not afraid at all about fighting a war. I just don't know why we are. I never heard of this place! I don't know why we're there! I have the greatest life in the world right now, and I don't know if I could put it on hold for two years. I don't know how I can be away from everyone.

You're my life, Maria. Without you, I have no life. There's something inside me that eats at me when I feel that I've been left out of something. I'd be doing it to myself.

"A lot of guys are avoiding the draft. I think mostly because they're afraid. I'm not. When I was a little kid, I remember listening to the radio with my mother. The President was talking about the attack on Pearl Harbor. He ended his talk with: 'There is nothing to fear but fear itself.' The guy was right. I 'm not afraid of this.  I'm hard pressed to find something I am afraid of."

Maria said that whatever I decided would be the right thing. She didn't want me to go. If I decided to, she'd back me a 100% and would wait for me.

Hyman agreed with Maria, but added that if he had to bury me, he wouldn't want to live. Although there were many reasons for me not to go in, they were for everyone's benefit, not necessarily mine. He knew me, knew I had to be in the thick of things, not standing on the side looking in. The thought of my friends coming home in coffins would haunt me all my life if I chose not to be a part of it. It would only be for two years, and they'd fly by, and to always remember everyone would be with me by my side.

I thanked them and said I had to think this out. We finished dinner and were sitting in the living room. Maria and Hyman were talking hospital; I was relaxing and smoking. The phone rang. Some guy hollered out, "Pauly, it's for you."

I picked up the phone and heard, "Hey, gumba, what the fuck are you doin' to me?"

"What? What the fuck did I do?"

"The guy you gave me is one fuckin' slippery prick, and it cost me a lot of money to find it out. There are people looking for this guy to cut his balls off. Shaeffer is not his real name. This bastard was an officer in the German army, in charge of a department that procured medical equipment for the army and the concentration camps. He transferred to the SS and was described as a maniac. His mission was to acquire as much of the Jews' wealth that he could. He did and decided to keep a lot for himself. Just before the end of the war, he took the identity of a Jew he had killed in a concentration camp, and then came to this country."

I thanked Tony. How Tony did what he did was mind-boggling. Whatever it cost him, he saved the hospital a lot of millions. "Let's keep what we know to ourselves until we're done with him. Then we'll give him up or off him ourselves."

What irony this thing might be. What if Shaffer was the officer in charge of the fucks that raped and killed Hyman's wife and daughters? After all these years, I wondered how Hyman would handle the vendetta? My mind was racing. I was anxious to meet this guy and twist him for what I wanted. It was difficult to focus because of this draft shit. I was going back and forth on this draft again. And then what Hyman said made all the sense in the world to me – I wouldn't be worth anything to anybody if I didn't do it. I felt like I lifted a load off my shoulders. I kissed Maria and told them both good night. I wanted to get some sleep.

The next morning, I woke up feeling good. I hadn't had as good a sleep in a long time. I called Muraso to have Cleo make an appointment for me with Martin Shaeffer of Shaeffer & Associates to discuss a business transaction. She needed to convey in a professional way, that Muraso was an extremely large holding company with millions in assets, and that I was a senior officer. A morning appointment would be appreciated, and for her to call me at home with the details.

Wearing a suit was mandatory. I needed to look the part. Downstairs Maria told me how great I looked. She always had a way of making my day. As we were sipping coffee the phone rang. Maria got it. She came back, sat down, and said, "That was Cleo. You have an appointment at11.00 with Mr. Shaeffer, and she handled it as you asked. Pauly, I wish you luck with him. We really need that equipment."

I told her she'll have her equipment, and luck wouldn't have anything to do with it. "Your father taught me that when you do business with someone, learn everything you can about them. That way, you know their weaknesses. I know everything about Shaeffer, and I'm going to enjoy twisting the greed out of him."

Upstairs I got my .45, snapped in a clip, set the safety, and put it in my attaché. I kissed Maria good-bye and left.

I considered having Vince drive me in the limo, but I didn't want him to have to wait. I took the Vette to Manhattan. The address wasn't far from Juan's place. In front of a high-rise I lucked out – there was a parking space. Shaeffer & Associates was on the twelfth floor. If everything failed, this son of a bitch was gonna take a flying leap out of the twelfth-floor window.

The receptionist said she'd see if Mr. Shaeffer was available. I sat down and was thinking not about this guy or the deal, but about my draft and how I was going to tell Tony and Mario. I was hoping they could understand my decision and go along with me.

The door opened, and a guy walked toward me. He was trim, well-built, with blonde-gray, thinning hair and glasses. The fucker looked like Krauts we used to see on Silver tone News, in the movie theater when I was a kid.

"Mr. Walker, my office." I stood up and followed him. What happened to a greeting, prick? He sat back behind his desk and inquired, "So what is this business proposition you have?"

"Good. Right to business. Before we get into it, I feel it is only fair that I even the playing field." I told him I knew everything about him, but he knew nothing about me. "So, I will tell you. My heritage is Italian. The name Walker was given to my father at Ellis Island when he applied for citizenship. I am an executive in Muraso Distributing, which is a multi-phased company that is diversified. We are the most powerful *famiglia* in the country. The company's assets far exceed yours, and our political contacts run to the highest office of this country. If I haven't made myself clear to you...we are the Mafia."

With that Shaeffer stood up. "I would like you to leave my office. I choose not to do business with you."

"No, that's not right. First, you must listen to my proposition. It is a proposition you will not be able to refuse. So, sit your fuckin' ass down!"

He sat down and became a lot meeker, loosening the stern attitude he was trying to portray.

"I'm aware that you were having discussions with some people who are trying to buy equipment for a hospital they are starting up, a hospital for children. I don't understand why you were giving them such a hard time. The funding for the hospital is from a memorial foundation we started. You are going to donate the equipment to the hospital and take the value off your taxes. In the event you choose not to do it, these will be your alternatives.

"We are the Longshoremen's Union and the Teamsters. Equipment that you order from overseas will never leave the ship. Equipment that is shipped by truck will never be transported. You will be out of business. The next two are a little messy. I would prefer not to get involved, but if you insist, I will.

"I can turn you over to the War Crimes Commission, provide witnesses, and see to it you are executed and pay retribution to the Jews you fucked."

I reached in my attaché and put the .45 on the desk. "You will write a suicide note stating you can't live with your past any longer and choose to end your life. I will throw you out the window and watch you hit the pavement below. The choices are all yours. You can make this easy or hard. If you choose to do the right thing, it will all stay just between us. Tell me, what you would like to do? Now!"

He sat there shaking, began to hem and haw, and started stammering.

"Marty, this isn't that hard a decision. I'm getting tired of being in this shit office with you, so out with it!"

He sputtered, "I'll donate. I will donate."

"Good, I'm so glad you decided that. I 'm going to sit back and smoke while you put what you have to in motion, and then I'll leave you in peace. I want you to call those people and tell them you're going to donate the equipment. It will make you feel good."

I put the .45 back in my case and lit up. After a while I stood up, walked over, and patted him on the head. "My name is Pauly. We're going to be friends for a long, long time. I'll be in touch."

While I took the elevator down, I was wondering if the stupid prick thought he was getting off the hook that easily.

# CHAPTER 35

At Muraso, Cleo said Sam Dawson called and asked if I could call him back when I had a chance. "Al Fanarssi called and wanted to discuss something. Juan Hernandez called to tell you he's back in town. Tony wants to talk to you when you had time." I figured I'd talk to Sam and Al then bring Tony up to date on everything. Juan could stay on hold.

Sam said the setups to catch the guys were done; everything went quickly and well. The only problems they ran into were a counter guy at parts, a yard man at the Brooklyn yard, and a guy operating the scale at the metals yard. Sam got all the setup money back.

"These guys didn't have a pot to piss in, so I just fired their asses and had Vincenzo blackball them." He and Vincenzo straightened out the accounting on the setup money and put procedures in place. He'd get with all the managers, tell them what went down, and have them tell their people anyone caught fucking with us won't live to tell about it. Sam wanted to look at everyone's pay, and where it was called for, give raises.

I told him do it and keep the setup money. "We'll probably be getting together next week to go over things."

I started wondering how I was going to tell Tony and Mario about my decision to go into the service. Having to do it had me really stressed out.

The phone rang. Al Fanarssi felt we would have a problem with the southern customers having to make the trip to New York for their product. He thought they'd try to purchase it closer to home. He was probably right, and I'd think about it and get back to him.

I sat back and tried to gather my thoughts. There was so much I needed to talk to Tony and Mario about, and I wasn't sure where to fuckin' begin. I went to Tony's office and was about to walk in when I heard Tony yelling and ranting in Italian. Mario was trying to tell him to calm down, in Italian. Shit, I'm not gonna get in the middle of that. I was backing away when I heard Tony saying in Italian, "How somebody so smart can be this stupid. I can't bury another person I love!" He kept going on.

I had enough. I walked into his office and said, "Good afternoon, Sir," looking for a laugh. "I couldn't help overhearing you. In fact, I think all of Brooklyn heard you. You talkin' 'bout me'?"

"Fuckin' A right. I was talkin' 'bout you!"

"Tony, there are only two people in this world I love – you and Maria. I'd never cause either of you grief. I'd give up my life for you. This is something I need to do – for me. If I don't, I won't be worth shit. The thought of my friends coming home in coffins would haunt me for the rest of my life; if I walked away, I couldn't handle it. Tony, I need you on this. I need you to back me like you always do. I need you with me. Someone told me it would only be for two years, and the time will fly by. Then we'll be back together, the three of us, doing business forever."

Tony sat there silently. Mario was on the edge of his seat, waiting for Tony's response. Suddenly Tony grinned and said, "I still get a kick out of the fuckin' respect."

I said, "We good?"

"We're good. We always have been and will always be."

"Good, I've got a ton of shit to talk to you about." I told them about Sam finishing the setup, and Vincenzo and Sam putting procedures in place, so we don't have to fuck with it again. I told them about Al's call. "I agree with him. I have a thought about it. If the two of you don't see it as a problem, we can pass and see what happens."

Mario said, "I think it will be a problem. We need to do something."

Tony said, "Whatcha got, Pauly?"

"This is my first thought, but I haven't had time to think it out fully. We send one of the Caddies to Santo. He delivers the product to the southern families. They call their orders in to us; we prepare an invoice and send it to Santo. When he collects, he reimburses himself for the product, and we split our profit. We wouldn't make as much, but it would be worth not worrying about losing customers. That could spread everywhere."

Mario liked it. Tony agreed, and said he'd handle it with Santo.

"Al seemed really concerned, and I told him I'd get back to him. If you could call him and tell him what you've set up, I'd appreciate it."

I told Tony he never ceased to amaze me. "Someday I'll find out how you do it. There had to be people looking for Shaeffer for twenty years." I told them about my morning with Shaeffer. I didn't want to do anything till the hospital got their equipment. Then I wanted to take everything he had and give it back. "I want to make this prick hurt and hurt so bad he begs for death. Every time I think about this son of a bitch, I want to puke."

"I need your advice. If this is the guy who fucked over Hyman's world, should we tell Hyman, and open old wounds, or not tell him and handle it ourselves?"

Mario said, "Everyone is different. If I were in Hyman's shoes, I'd want to know. It would let me close it out knowing the fuck got it in the end."

Tony added, "If I remember the story right, and this is the same guy, he saved Hyman's life. We need to get him to give up the soldiers under his command, and all of them have their balls cut off."

"I need a big favor. Tony, I need you to handle this guy – any way you think is right – but not until after the equipment is in."

I asked how our waste business was doing. Tony told me it was fuckin' unbelievable. "We put out a few containers with our name and phone number, and the phone started coming off the hook. Mario has two fabricating shops building containers, and that's just the garbage side. The building material side is even better. This thing is going to be big, and one day we'll be all over this fuckin' country with it."

I asked Tony what he thought about Sam Dawson handling our car and parts business with Hernandez. He approved.

"Good. Sam's smart enough to handle it right. I thought I'd go over it with Sam and then introduce him to Hernandez."

Tony handed me the letter my mom airmailed. I opened it, and it was what we thought. "This has been floating around for a while. I have less than a week to report to Whitehall Street for a physical and induction into the Armed Forces."

Tony told me if this is what I wanted, he was OK with it, but I had better not fuck up because he was not gonna go to my funeral.

"Thanks, pal, for the vote of confidence. I'm sure as hell not gonna fuck up. I have too much good stuff to come back to and some good people – I mean Mario."

Tony and I smiled at each other.

Tony wanted me to bring in my .22. He was going to destroy it and replace it with a clean one. He handed me a check to put with my other money. In case something happened to the *famiglia* while I was gone, I'd be alright when I got back. Tony suggested I make sure Maria would be able to access it. I knew what he meant on both things and told him he was still something else. It was between us. It meant I felt he was a fuckin' great guy.

I looked at the check. It was made out to me, drawn on the casino account, and was for $830,000. I asked what this was – it's a hell of a lot of money. It was our profit on the shipment to Santo. He wanted me to have it. I thanked him.

"Thursday morning I'll get together with Sam, go over things, then meet up with Hernandez. We'll put together the high-end cars for Peru and another parts deal. If I'm right, we'd be close to a half mil."

I told Tony I wanted to spend some time with Maria. "Maybe the three of us, along with Maria, Gloria, and your wife, Mario, could have dinner together at that fancy Italian restaurant Thursday night." Tony said he'd set it up.

I spent the evening with Maria and Hyman. We talked about all kinds of things. Maria was amazed that Shaeffer changed his ways and is donating the equipment. "I never thought he was capable of this kind of generosity and kindness."

Hyman said, "He isn't. It wasn't him. He's an asshole. I don't know what you did, Paul. Whatever it was, you're good."

I didn't say anything except we must make sure he keeps his word. The evening passed. Hyman told us he was tired and was going to bed. Maria asked me if we could sleep together tonight. I smiled, kissed her, and we went to bed.

I woke up alone. I dressed and went downstairs. As usual there was Maria with a cup of coffee, a kiss, and that beautiful smile. We sat at the table and talked. She and Hyman were going to have lunch with Jacob and Carl to discuss things.

"Sounds good. How about bringing me home a corned beef on rye? And say hello to them for me." I asked Maria if she could get away tomorrow. We could spend the day hanging out, have pizza at the grill, and that night have dinner at the fancy joint." Maria said she'd really like that.

As I was walking in the front door of Muraso, Al Fanarssi was walking out. After "Morning, Pauly", he just kept on walking. That wasn't like Al. I figured something was going down.

In Tony's office, I said, "Good morning, Sir. You need to hold onto that; it's gonna to be a while till you hear it again. You doing alright?"

"Things are goin' good."

I handed him my .22 and he handed me an identical one. My old piece was going to disappear. I told him to have a good day. I was going to spend the day with Sam Dawson. On the way to my office I stuck my head in Mario's doorway. "Just wanted to say good morning." Before he could respond, I closed the door and went into my office.

Sam was waiting for me. "OK, where the fuck is my coffee?"

"In a pot in the lunch room."

"Alright, you wanna be like that."

"They make shit coffee here, so I made us a pot. Your cup is on your chair."

My response was, "Fuck you."

Over coffee I told Sam the decision was made that he was to handle the business with Juan Hernandez. Al Fanarssi would handle the shit. He was to take care of parts and cars and was not to get involved in any way with the dope.

"We feel someday Hernandez will try to get to us, but we'll get him first. For now, we're going to do as much business with him as we can. Hernandez will try to buy you. There's no sense in refusing. Take it and tell Tony as soon as you can. If Tony holds true to form, he'll tell you to keep it. And let him know if Hernandez pulls any shit."

We went over the parts deals and the cars from Royal Auto Sales. I told Sam about the high-end car deal. "Juan is gonna tell us what he wants. I was thinking we'd let him tell us how much he wanted to pay for them. My gut says he's goin' to be a lot higher than us. Once we have a deal, Luca can order the cars. They can latch them to the floor of the containers and have them transported to the pier. If you're OK with everything, I'll call Juan and try to get together today."

Juan was glad to hear from me, and he was available all day. We could come over when convenient. Sam and I grabbed some lunch before heading for the city.

A valet took the car. I explained to Sam that one of these desk guys had to unlock the private elevator for us. A woman walking to the front door caught my attention. She was out-of-this-fuckin'-world. A body you couldn't stop looking at – and I didn't. I was staring at her with my back to the desk.

Sam asked for the elevator to be unlocked so we could go to the Hernandez penthouse. I heard a familiar voice – he could not do it, that just anybody could not come and go – and on and on.

I turned around and snarled, "Listen to me closely, prick. This man is not just anybody. He's special. And if I asked him to, he'll grab you by your slimy neck and rip your head off. Now open the fuckin' elevator for us!"

Without a word, he pranced through a door, and with that faggy swagger, went to the elevator. We followed. As he unlocked the door I noticed he had pissed his pants again. I caught Sam's eye and looked down at the guy. Sam laughed out loud. I told Sam this was the second time this had happened. It's like this fag was on a power trip with this elevator.

The elevator door opened and there was Juan. We went out to the patio and sat down in the lounge chairs. Juan said his trip was terrific. He opened the two lots for the high-end cars and two new lots in Mexico. He calculated that filling the Mexico lots with our cars would be cheaper for him than buying wholesale on the West Coast. He had also doubled the size of his parts rebuilding plant in Peru and bought some parts stores. He wants to start a chain in South America.

We have a lot of work to do. He had a shopping list that would make our heads spin. I told him we could easily handle everything he wanted, and Sam would be taking care of him from now on because I was going into the service.

With sincerity and concern Juan said I was making a mistake. I explained I didn't have a choice because of the draft. We started talking business. Sam handled it well. I jumped in a few times. All in all, it went smoothly.

We said our good-byes and got into the elevator. Sam started to say something. I motioned to him with a finger and pointed to my ear. He knew what I meant. I told Sam he'll like doing business with Juan. He's a good businessman, honest, and a nice guy. I figured Juan would like hearing that bullshit.

In the car, I told Sam he did great. I had anticipated we'd do about a $100,000 in business. Actually, we did about $500,000. I told Sam to get together with Joey and make out invoices, and Franco on the shipping crates. "If Franco needs help, Mario is the best. You needed to get together with Luca and Talya, then get in touch with the pier and set up for the containers." Because everybody was going to be working their asses off on this deal, to make sure we were paying them right.

Back at the office I told Sam I probably wouldn't see him again before I left, that I enjoyed working with him and knowing him. He told me he felt the same.

# *CHAPTER 36*

When I got home, Maria and Hyman and I sat around talking. I asked Maria if she remembered my sandwich. She told me she forgot, asked if I was hungry. I was. Hyman piped in that he was ready for dinner.

Maria led us to the dining room. The dining room table had platters of meats – corned beef, roast beef, tongue, and a lot more – along with a loaf of Jewish rye bread, coleslaw, pickles, and a large bowl of antipasto.

"Maria, thanks. Payback is hell, girl."

We ate, and everything was great. I could understand how you could develop a fondness for this food. I sure as hell had. Hyman claimed you can't buy Jewish food this good outside of New York. It's like pizza: New York pizza is the best.

I told Maria we needed to go to Manufacturers tomorrow morning. "Besides making a deposit, I want to put everything in both our names, so you can access it."

"Sure, we can do that, Pauly. How much money are you talking about?"

"Do you remember when I wanted to pay for my suit and you talked me out of it because you wanted me to save my money for our future. There is now a little more than $4 million for our future."

Hyman said, "Good for you, Paul. I'm going to call it a night. I've got a hard day tomorrow without the boss lady."

The next morning, I awoke feeling terrific, turned over, and there was Maria looking at me. I pulled her close and we kissed. "Good morning, Beautiful." We enjoyed a few minutes snuggling before we forced ourselves out of the bed to start the day. After, showering together and dressing, we went downstairs for breakfast.

I returned to my room to put my attaché, the pieces, and cash on the bed. I slid $200,000 with the check in a pocket of the attaché. That left me with $40,000. I put $3,000 in the breast pocket of my suit. I decided to deposit $27,000 in Maria's checking and $10,000 in mine. The .45 and the .22, along with the clips, silencer, and ammo went into the attaché.

At the bank no one was at any of the desks, so I asked a teller for the manager. She told us to have a seat while she checked if he was available. Maria suggested she do the deposits while we waited. I handed her the $37,000.

After waiting about 20 minutes, I impatiently told the teller to interrupt the manager. "Tell Mr. Mariani the two people you just made the deposit for want to talk to him now!"

She walked away in a huff. In seconds the manager's door flew open. Mariani stood in the doorway apologizing, "Pauly! Pauly, I'm so sorry. Please come in." He repeated the I'm-so-sorry-to-keep-you-waiting. "I was on the phone with the regional director for the bank and couldn't get him off the phone. Miss DeAngelo, it's always a pleasure to see you."

I told him I wanted to open a CD. "It's to be in Paul Walker or Maria DeAngelo. The other CDs, my checking account, and the safe deposit box are all to be changed to give Maria access to everything I have. Will there be a problem with any of this?" No problem at all – he'd handle it.

In the vault he put the deposit box on the table, "Let me give you the CDs and the money for the new one. We'll meet you back in your office when we're done."

I opened my attaché case, so the pieces were not visible, removed the cash and check. I endorsed the check, and said the CD was to be for $2 million. I took the two CDs out of the box. There were still two bundles of cash I had forgotten about. I told Maria I'd leave them in the box in case she ever needed cash. I put everything from my attaché in the box, with the two bundles on top, and slid it back in place. I handed Maria the key and told her to put it in a safe place.

Back in the manager's office we wrote our signatures on our copy and on the bank's. There was a knock on the door. A young lady handed the manager our old CDs and the new ones. After we signed them, Mariani said I gave him $10,000 too much.

"I know. I want you to keep it."

"I can't, Pauly. It's against bank policy."

"That's what's wrong with banks. Any other business, the thinking is the customer is always right, but not in banking. I want you to keep it, please. If you won't mind opening our box with Maria, she can put the CDs in it. Then we can get outta here."

As we were driving to the grill for lunch, Maria asked why I did that. I told her the guy handles better than four million dollars of our money. I needed to see how honest he was. Banks don't pay their employees shit – he probably could use the bucks.

The grill was empty. A young guy came over to our table. "Good afternoon. My name is John. Can I get you something to drink, and may I take your order?"

I ordered a medium pepperoni and a couple of Cokes, "But before you put the order in, see if Tony wants to join us for lunch."

He came back and apologized for it taking so long. This was his second day on the job, and he didn't know how to get ahold of

Tony, so he had a cook do it for him. Tony was not in the building. I told him it was OK, get us the Cokes and put the order in.

He brought two glasses, two bottles of Coke, and a straw. He opened a bottle and poured it into Maria's glass. He was about to do the same for me, and I stopped him. "I'll drink it out of the bottle. If you pour it into the glass for me, I'll have to fight her for the straw, and she'll kick my ass." He looked stunned. "I'm only kidding you. That's a good touch for the lady."

"As I told you, this is my second day. I know the guys in the kitchen and Tony, who hired me. Are you friends of Tony?"

"John, I'd like to introduce you to Maria DeAngelo, Tony's daughter, and my name is Pauly. I work with Tony, and we are friends."

"Ma'am, it is a pleasure to meet you. And Sir, all they talk about here is Pauly.

"Don't believe everything you hear."

We ate our pizza, were full and wanted to get going. I asked John for our check. He went in back, returned to say it's on the house. I helped Maria up, turned to John, put a bill in his hand, and thanked him for the service. "You'll do well here."

When we got into the car Maria said she needed to buy a pair of shoes for that night. If I wanted to go home, she could shop alone. I told her we'd go together. We headed for her favorite store. On the way, Maria asked how much I tipped John. A hundred-dollar bill.

"Reminds you of another kid Tony hired some years ago?"

"Yeah, he does."

At the store Maria led the way to the shoe department. We sat down in a couple of chairs. A clerk came over to Maria, and they started talking. How long could this take? When we bought a pair of shoes for me, Maria picked them out, a clerk brought out my size, and we were out.

After more than an hour I was comatose. Maria had tried on at least twenty-five pairs of shoes and she bought two pairs. On our way home, she apologized – she was having trouble finding the right pair. I told her it was OK because I enjoyed being with her. We got home with plenty of time to kill. Hyman had left a message for Maria to phone him when she got in.

While she made her call, I sat in the living room and read over my draft notice. Typical fuckin' government – four pages of bullshit.

The notice started out Selective Service System order to report for Armed Forces physical examination and induction. I was to report to the joint examining and induction station at 39 Whitehall Street, New York City, at 7:30 a.m.

*Traffic will be bad at that hour of the morning with people going to work in the city. I'll have to leave myself an hour and a half driving. This means getting up at five-thirty. That's fuckin' crazy. People are supposed to be sleeping at that hour! The only thing running around NYC are going be the rats.*

*Hope this gets better – it really sucks starting out.* Four paragraphs down on the first page I read: "If you fail to report you will be subject to fine and imprisonment under provisions of the Universal Military Training and Service Act, as amended. Then I read: Bring necessary toilet articles. Bring enough clothes to last three days that can easily be shipped home. Bring a small amount of money to avoid loss."

The next few pages were about dependency allotment. It didn't pertain to me, so I skimmed through it. One thing caught my eye. "A dependent parent will receive $40 a month taken from the GI's salary of $78 a month." I'm not sure how anybody can live on that. It's like our government has their head up their asses. The salary and the amount of the allotment seems like regulations dating back to World War I. The high-ranking officers and the politicians are making bucks. They don't give a fuck about the guy on the bottom.

The next page was headed "Important Notice of Reemployment Rights." I didn't care about it. The next page was devoted to clothing again, and toilet articles. I think they were trying to fill space, because now they listed each item.

I finally got to a paragraph that made some sense. "After you receive your final processing, and are administered the oath, you will be transported to a US Army reception station. Most men from this area are sent to Fort Dix, NJ." With that I folded the papers, flipped them on the table. I had enough bullshit.

I sat back, smoked a Lucky, and figured I'd get Vince to drive me. I didn't want Maria in that kind of traffic. The fuckers are nuts! The cabbies don't give a shit about anybody or anything. I went upstairs and dug out my old work clothes and shoes. That's what I was going to wear for three days. I went downstairs, got a paper grocery bag, went upstairs and put all new toiletries in it, and set it on my clothes. I was all set.

Maria came up to tell me she had to run to the dry cleaner to pick up my suit. I asked if she had checked in my pockets. She hadn't. I said we'd go together. Maria asked what the matter was. I explained I had three grand in my breast pocket. "I'm so sorry. Angelo owns the place. Dad's known him for years. He knows who dad is. I think he'll be straight."

The guy greeted Maria, said the suit was ready. He brought it to the front counter. "It came out very well, and Sir, there was something in your breast pocket. I removed it and replaced it after the cleaning." We thanked him, and Maria told Angelo she'd see him soon.

At home I took the money out and counted it. It was all there. I've always been amazed how some people are so smart and some so stupid. Angelo could have beaten me out of the three grand, or part of it, but he didn't. It was a smart move.

I jumped into the shower, dressed, and went downstairs. Maria was waiting with two glasses of tea and asked if I'd like to sit on the patio; it was such a beautiful afternoon. Would I ever get used to Maria's beauty? She wasn't just beautiful, she was stunningly beautiful. As we sat in the lounge chairs, I blurted out, "Sweetheart, you are absolutely beautiful." She said thank you.

We talked about all kinds of things and time flew by. We decided to wait for the limo out front. We barely got outside when Vince pulled up. He opened the rear door for us. Maria and I sat opposite Tony and Gloria. I hated this fuckin' seat – I had a problem riding in a vehicle facing backward.

I thanked Vince and told him I needed a ride to 39 White-hall Street and had to leave the house by six. He said it wouldn't be a problem. I asked Vince to join us for dinner. He told me thanks, but he had other things he had to do.

We were on our way. *It won't be that long. I'll live with it,* I thought. I was so bothered I didn't say a word the whole trip. No one pushed it. I guess they felt I was preoccupied with what was ahead for me.

# *CHAPTER 37*

The restaurant was dark. In fact, the whole area looked deserted. I figured Tony got the place for tonight just for us. Tony opened the restaurant door and held it. We got in, and we were standing in pitch black. Suddenly the lights came on. The restaurant was packed with people, all standing and cheering, "Pauly, Pauly, Pauly." Hanging from the ceiling was a huge banner: "Be Safe Pauly."

I leaned over to Maria and asked if she had anything to do with this. She grinned, "Dad and me." I told her after the sandwich bit and this, she better be looking over her shoulder, because I'd get even. I kissed her, extended my hand to Tony and thanked him.

Tony asked that everyone please take their assigned seats. "The waiters will be coming around taking food and drink orders. Drink up, eat what you want and as much as you want. Tonight, we're all gonna have a good time."

Josh and Lily, Mario and his wife, Carla, were seated at our table. I thanked Josh and Lily for everything they had done for the hospital, and I didn't know how we could have done it without them.

"Lily, Maria was telling me about your concept to make the hospital child friendly, nothing to intimidate."

Maria interrupted, "Pauly, I didn't tell you half of it. Lily wants to have cartoon characters, flowers, rainbows, teddy bears, and rabbits painted on the walls in the rooms and on the halls. She decided on the Disney characters. She called Disney seeking permission to use them. They called her back and told her when she was ready, they would have a crew of artists at the hospital.

"One of their production people came up with the idea of making some of the equipment look like a character. If we want it, they'll do that, too. They also told Lily when she wanted, they'd fly characters to the hospital to visit the children, and they thanked her for choosing Disney. They also told Lily that Disney would donate all of that to the hospital."

I told them I wanted to say hello to everyone and introduce Maria, and that we'd be back in a little bit. As we were walking to a table, I asked if she did the seating.

"Most of it."

I asked her why she didn't seat Josh and Lily with Hyman. Although the Morgensterns would have been comfortable there, Lily would have been the only woman… and girls like to talk to other girls at a deal like this. We made our way from table to table. The introductions were repetitious and very monotonous.

I'd say: "Hi everyone. I'm glad to see you and I'd like to introduce you to my fiancée Maria. Maria, this is  – ."

Al Fanarssi introduced his wife, Connie.

Maria said, "Glad to meet both of you."

Next, I said, "This is Benito."

He said, "My wife, Lillian."

I introduced Sam Dawson, who said, "My wife, Jill."

I told Maria she made a good cup of coffee and I always enjoy it, but Sam makes the best coffee in the world. I don't know what he does to it.

"Benito, after the where's-Benny routine you put me through, don't make any comments."

Both raised eyebrows. Benito sputtered, "Me? Make a comment? I wouldn't ask what a beautiful lady like Maria is doing with a bum like you only because I know Maria is Tony's daughter."

I told Benito, non stupido Tuo come si guarda. I hoped the ladies knew we were just kidding. I told Benito he wasn't as dumb as he looked.

"Last, but not least, I know the two of you have known each other for years, my friend, Mario"

And Mario said, "My wife, Carla."

Maria had picked up on the kidding, "I don't know about you, Mario, but it's very nice to meet you, Carla." Then she bent down and kissed Mario on the check. We said we'd see them later.

We visited more tables and did the introductions. When we came to Santo, I thanked him for making the trip. "Pauly, I wouldn't have missed this and seeing you again for anything."

I explained to Maria that when her father and Santo were young, they worked for the same company. The two of them, with their wives, used to hang out together.

"I enjoyed being with your mother because of her intelligence. Maria, your mother was the most beautiful woman in the world, and you could be her twin."

We said our good-byes and went to the next table, the last one. As we were walking I felt a tap on my right shoulder and a body pressed against my back. A seductive female voice said, "Can I have a hug, big boy."

I turned around, and it was my mother. I grabbed and hugged her, saying how glad I was to see her, and how much I missed her. An arm came around us. It was my dad.

Mom said, "I'm sorry we're late. We almost didn't make it because of a problem in Vegas. At the last minute, your dad said the hell with it, we're going."

"I'm glad. I'm so happy to see both of you."

I was looking at my dad, and he looked like shit. "Pop, you feeling alright?" My mother answered it was probably from the flight.

Maria grabbed both of them. She was holding on tight to my father. I figured she also noticed he didn't look good. Hyman saw us, jumped up, and, like a kid, ran and hugged my dad. Hyman sure as hell was no kid. They stood there embracing. I thought: Something's wrong. Hyman and my father finally broke it up, and Hyman introduced everybody. He introduced my parents as his son and daughter-in-law, and Paul's parents.

"Grandfather, I'm really mad at you. You're my favorite grandfather. You could have told me about this deal."

"I'm your only grandfather."

"Mom, Dad, Carl and Jacob gave Maria and me the most fabulous wedding set you could imagine." Maria extended her hand to show them the engagement ring. "And they fed us the most fantastic lunch. Dad, I know growing up with Hyman you've had corned beef on rye. Mom, you'll love it. While you're here in New York you have to talk Hyman into taking you to a good place. You can't get it as good anywhere else.

"Maria and I appreciate what Hyman, Carl and Jacob did for us so much. We're naming a hospital we're building the HCJ Children's Hospital. The hospital will be funded by a foundation, the Mateo-Donatella DeAngelo Memorial Foundation.

"Meyer, meet Maria. And Maria, this is my friend Meyer Lansky. Meyer, how's my lucky rabbit's foot doing? I forgot, you're the brains, I'm the rabbit's foot."

"Pauly, everything is going great. Almost hard to believe how good." I knew what he meant and said good.

We talked a bit about the gambling. Then I said, "You're all great people. Enjoy each other's company and have a good time tonight. Maria and I are going to sit down and take a load off our feet. We'll see you later."

Back at our table, Maria complained, "These shoes are killing me."

Maria, Lily and Gloria started talking. Tony and Josh were putting together a business deal. All I overheard was: We would be equal shareholders and control the company. I figured it had to be one big deal. I sat back, had a Lucky, and tried to relax. I couldn't get the way my father looked out of my head. Tony said he had ordered for us. I told him thanks. To myself I thought, *I'm fuckin' starving!*

After we finished eating, Tony walked up front and onto a stage. Someone handed him a microphone, and he thanked everyone for coming. "I want to introduce someone who has had an experience with Pauly. Please welcome Carly."

She went on stage. When the applause stopped, she said, "Hello, I would not have missed this for anything in the world. I'll take a few minutes and tell everyone about the time I spent with a special friend. She cleaned up the story. When she finished, she said she wrote a song, dedicated it to Pauly, and would sing it for us.

The song was great. If it didn't make number one on whatever that fuckin' list was, those people were out of their minds. Carly finished to a tremendous ovation, walked over to our table, kissed me on the check, and said, "Hi, friend."

"Hi, Carly. I'd like you to meet Maria, my fiancée, and the lady I told you about."

Carly said, "Glad to meet you, Maria. Now I see why I couldn't get to first base with this guy."

They laughed and began talking.

Tony picked up the microphone. "We were having a meeting, and Pauly had finished talking about something. His grandfather said, "Paul, where have you gained your wisdom?" Pauly answered he didn't know. It was in him, it just comes out. I know where he gets his wisdom from – that man right there – his dad." I knew Tony didn't believe that for a second. It was something good to say.

"Pauly's wisdom is what has helped to make us the strongest, most powerful Family in the country. We are all *famiglia*." He began telling about the hospital and the foundation – he kind of choked up a little on the foundation. I was hoping he'd quit, but no, he kept going. He told about the waste concept, and how in time it would be nationwide and the biggest thing going. He told about the parts deals, how I turned scrap steel into big bucks.

He kept going. It was like someone wound him up. He finally finished with "Pauly, come up here."

*Fuck no. I'm not going.* I shook my head no.

Tony doesn't take no for an answer. He repeated himself, this time with a look I had seen before. I didn't want to piss him off, so I started for the stage. As I slowly managed my way to the stage, I heard Tony say, "I want to present my partner and my friend, Pauly." I got on the stage. Everyone was applauding and chanting, "Pauly … Pauly … Pauly." Tony grabbed and hugged me.

After a while I said, "You gotta let me go. You're wrinkling my suit, and these people are gonna begin to think there's more to it than just friends."

Tony whispered in my ear, "You better fuckin' be careful and take care of yourself. You don't need to be a hero".

We separated. I waved at everybody, thanked them, told them to have a good time, and walked off the stage. Tony followed me.

Maria came up to me, "Your dad asked if he could get a ride home. He's very tired. Hyman wants to go with him. Carl and Jacob offered to drop them off – they live close. Everyone wants to say good-bye."  Carl and Jacob were their normal caring, loving selves. Hyman told me he'd see me later. Mom and Pop asked that I wake them up when I got in.

As they left, I was watching my dad. Tired is one thing. There had to be something else going on. I sat down by Maria and whispered, "I truly love you."

Josh extended his hand. "Thank you for having us, and we agree with everyone's sentiment. You be careful." Lily hugged me good-bye.

Tony had the restaurant move the tables back and bring out four very large tables. He asked Maria and Gloria to get the ladies and sit around a table and talk. As they were doing that, I walked over to Mario and asked him to join Tony and the guys along with Santo and Meyer. I teased Santo, "You and Tony can reminisce about the old days, just like old guys do."

Waiters were taking drink orders from the ladies and brought out Chianti for us. Our waiter was a smart guy. Probably because of Meyer, he asked if anyone would care for something else. No one answered except Meyer, "Yes, top shelf Scotch, tonic water on ice, in a tall glass." The waiter nodded and left. As soon as he got back and put the drink in front of Meyer, Tony stood up. Holding his glass, he toasted, "Gentlemen, *salute*!" Everyone responded with '*salute*' then began drinking and talking.

Mario whispered, "I'm gonna miss you."

I thought to myself, *You don't know how much I'll miss you.* One of the guys came out with a zing directed at Tony. He took it well and went right back. Everybody was laughing. It was good. There was no tension, no pressures. Everyone was relaxed. Normally, the atmosphere at a meeting with the same guys would be very tense, everyone on edge – it was the nature of our business.

Talya and Carly were sitting together. Out of the corner of my eye I could see they were looking at me – I figured about the night. It wasn't long before Talya walked up. She apologized for interrupting us, greeted everyone, and then said, "Good evening, Sir" to Tony.

Tony groaned, "Jesus Christ! Another one!"

Talya said, "You deserve the respect. You made me feel good and safe at work since the first time we met." Then she asked if she could speak to me privately. We walked to an empty table. "Pauly, I'm sorry to bother you with this. I know you have a lot going on and a lot on your mind, but I don't know anyone else I can ask this of. I don't want to lose this opportunity. I've been looking at this guy all night. He's got to be the best-looking man in the room...I mean second-best. I'd like to meet him, but don't know how to do it here."

I told her to sit tight, I'd handle it. I wandered over to Luca, pulled up a chair. "You having a good night, Luca?" He had to turn with his back to the table to answer me. That's what I wanted. It gave us some privacy without appearing to be a big deal. He told me he was having the best night.

"I need a favor. See that lady sitting by herself? She wants to meet up with you but doesn't know how. She's nice, and, like you, a good friend of mine."

"No shit? I've been looking at her. She's one classy lady and good-looking. I figured she wasn't approachable."

"She is. I'm asking you to go over there, introduce yourself, have a conversation, and see if both of you click. Make sure you treat her well no matter what."

When I returned to my table, Tony asked if there was a problem. I told him no. We were all talking and joking around. Tony and Santo had a chance to relive their youth and were really getting into it. Occasionally, they'd start talking in Italian, along with the hand gestures. If you were at the other end of the room you'd swear these guys were slapping the shit out of each other.

Meyer had been belting down drinks. He didn't get into the talking much. It seemed he was getting a little tipsy, and Mario engaged him in a conversation. Meyer brought up Cuba and the night he and I spent together. After a while Mario asked how business was.

With a slur, Meyer said, "Business is good…good…yeah, it's good"

Mario wanted more. He asked, "Just good? What would make it great?"

"I need to eliminate the middle and deal with the manufacturer directly."

I knew Mario planned what just happened as soon as Meyer started drinking. He timed everything just right. Meyer soon put his head on the table and was out cold, sleeping it off. He probably wouldn't remember the talk at all. When I got back from Cuba and was telling Tony and Mario about my trip, I ended it with a gut feeling that Lansky would cut us out someday. Mario just verified it for himself. Mario's shrewdness never ceased to astonish me.

Tony happened to see Lansky out of it and told Santo he needed to get the guy back to their hotel room. If he didn't have a bad night, he sure as hell was gonna be fucked-up tomorrow morning. Tony told Santo he'd meet him tomorrow for lunch, and they could spend the day at his house. He'd have a couple of pitchers of margaritas for him.

Santo stood up. "Pauly, it's been great seeing you again. When you get back, you and Maria come to Miami. We'll show her a good time."

Santo walked over to Lansky. A couple of guys offered their assistance. Santo thanked them but declined. He picked Lansky up as if he were a little kid and walked him out.

People gradually came up to say their good-byes and to be careful. We had just about emptied out. Maria, Gloria, and Mario's wife moved over to our table. Maria sat next to me, squeezed my hand, leaned over and said she hadn't known half of what I had accomplished. I didn't say anything, thinking, *There's no way anyone can tell you the rest.*

I told Maria all I wanted was to be close to her that evening. "How about we say *arrivederci* and head home? I want to spend the rest of the night holding you … till the morning." When she reminded me I had a very early morning, I told her I didn't plan on sleeping.

We said our good-byes. First Tony hugged me; then I leaned over and hugged Mario. When we parted, Tony had a few tears sliding down his cheeks, and Mario had tears well up in his eyes. Just so only they could hear, I said, "Some tough guys."

Vince decided to take us home and then come back for everyone else. I told Vince I had been looking for him but didn't see much of him. "Tony wanted anyone that shouldn't be driving not to. A lot of these guys can't hold their booze. It was a nice night. You deserve it. You need to make sure you come back. We've got a lot of driving to do."

I thanked him, leaned back to Maria and said, "I've wanted to do something to you all night and didn't get a chance till now. May I kiss you?"

"Oh, Pauly", she sighed. We locked in a kiss neither of us wanted to break off. The next thing we knew we were parked in front of the house.

I set my alarm clock a little earlier than I originally planned, leaving enough time to say good-bye to my parents. I decided not to wake them when we got in – they were likely sound asleep. Maria and I got in bed and reached for each other. I spent the night holding her and looking at her. Maria is so beautiful; it's hard to come up with the words to describe her beauty.

My alarm woke me up. I guess I didn't spend the night awake. I eased Maria's head onto the pillow, grabbed my clothes, and dressed in the bathroom. Before I left her, I gently kissed Maria on the cheek and whispered, "Sleep tight, my love."

I picked up my brown bag with toiletries, went down the hall to the guest room. I gently tapped on the door and opened it. My parents were both sound asleep. I didn't know what to do. For as bad as my father looked, sleep would do him good. Just then the little guy on my right shoulder popped up and said, "What the hell are you debating about? You promised them you'd wake them to say good-bye."

I gently shook my mother. She woke immediately. I whispered, "Mom, it's me. I need to say good-bye."

My mother reached her arms to me. I bent down and we hugged. "Be careful and call me when you can. Wake your dad up." I said he really needs his sleep." Mom said, "Wake him, Pauly; he'll go back to sleep."

On the other side of the bed, I bent over and shook Dad gently. He opened his eyes, saw me, and reached his arms around me, pulling me to him. He said my name repeatedly. It was like he couldn't get enough of it. I had never seen him this worked up. After a while I released his grip on me and told him to lie back and relax, everything will be OK.

Dad said, "Everything will be OK as long as you are really careful and come home to visit me and your mother."

I told him I would, that I loved them, and they needed to go back to sleep. I left the room a little emotional. I had to get outside and smoke. I didn't notice it at the restaurant, but when my dad pulled me to him, he had this overpowering bad odor.

# *CHAPTER 38*

The limo pulled up to the curb. I got in the front, greeted Vince and thanked him again for the ride. Vince knew exactly where Whitehall Street was, down by South Ferry, almost at the bottom of Manhattan. I leaned back in the seat, closed my eyes, and was thinking: *We're gonna pull up in front of this place and they're gonna think a celebrity is coming. Fuck 'em if they can't take a joke.*

I must have dozed off because the next thing I knew, Vince was pushing me saying, "Pauly, we're here."

I sat up, thanked Vince again, grabbed my brown bag, and stepped out. Vince pulled away and I was standing in the street eyeballing a bunch of guys leaning up against a shit-looking building. The government probably built it for the Civil War as a military facility. The only thing I ever heard or read about Whitehall Street was guys reporting for induction into the armed services. It made news after the Korean conflict. The military was shutting it down.

The walls were large blocks of stone, probably limestone that once was white. Now it'as a greenish-grayish dirty color. The windows were fuckin' ancient. As I stepped up on the sidewalk, somebody said, "Hey, look at the rich boy."

I made eye contact with the guy, and, in the toughest voice I could muster, said, "You talkin' to me? Fuck you!" I leaned against the wall and lit up a smoke. There's nothing like getting off to a good start. Wonder why there are assholes like that. I finished smoking and closed my eyes. I heard that same voice right in front of me, "What you got in the bag? Yo money?"

My right fist clinched tight and I could feel it. I opened my eyes and was bringing my fist up to deck the fucker.

"Take it easy, take it easy. I'm only kidding. I know you. I work at Bruckner as a yard man. I've seen you and the limo many times. You look a lot better in a sports jacket. I've seen you and Tony the yard boss walking around the yard a couple of times. I figured I work for you."

"Not really. I work for the company that owns the yard."

"The word is the yard is owned by the Bronx Mafia. Is that true?"

I didn't answer him, just shrugged. He asked what was I doing here. I told him I was drafted and chose not to beat it. He said he felt the draft would catch up to him, and he sure as hell didn't want to go into the army, so he decided to enlist in the navy. He was going to be in salvage. If he liked it, he'd stay in. If he didn't, he thought about seeing if Bruckner wanted to go into marine salvage. "I got my brain up my ass. You are Bruckner. What do you think?"

"It sounds good to me. Bruckner's location would be ideal. It's on a bay that's deep and goes out to the ocean. You'd be able to salvage everything from small boats to big ships. When you decide to get out and still want to do it, get in touch with Bruckner and tell them you need to talk to Pauly."

While we were talking, the guys around us started moving, leaving us standing alone. I told him we better get going. We caught up and were following guys walking up steps to a huge front door. There was this big guy in uniform standing in front of the door. As one of us approached him, he'd ask in an authoritative voice, "Branch.?" If you answered army he'd say left side. Navy was center, marines and anything else was right.

About twelve guys were in front of us. When it was my turn, the guy asked "Branch?"

I looked at him for a few seconds, then answered, "Tree."

"Shit, always a wiseass in the crowd."

"No, not a wiseass, just figured you were bored."

The guy laughed, and I said, "Army."

The inside looked as bad as the outside. They had these 2x4s as makeshift aisles leading to pens. The place looked like a cattle barn. The front door closed, and a soldier walked into the pen. He had all of us move to a back wall and face him. He wore a tailored, starched and ironed uniform with stripes on his arms, medals and ribbons on his chest, brass that glistened. Boots that looked like mirrors. In the typical army tone, he said, "I am First Sergeant Howell. If there is a need for you to address me, you will do so by using Sergeant, not Sir. I am here to help you men take the beginning steps to becoming soldiers in the United States Army. Once you have taken the oath, you will begin the greatest adventure of your life."

This asshole was laying it on thick. "We will begin with your qualifying physical, then your qualifying mental exam, and then you will view a one-hour orientation film. After that, your urine will have been analyzed and your blood typed. If everything goes well, you will be permitted to take the oath. Are there any questions?"

Nobody said anything.

"You will line up in a single file facing the door. The corporal will hand you a container, and then ask for your name, which he will write on the container lid and hand it back to you. You will then proceed through the door to the trough affixed to the rear wall and wait. When six of you have addressed the trough, you will commence to urinate in the container. You will not overflow the container, and you will not affix urine to any portion of the container, except for the inside. When there is sufficient quantity of urine in the container, you will affix the lid to the container. You then can commence urinating in the trough. When you have finished, you will place the container on the shelf by the door on your right and proceed through the door to the next station. Does anyone have a question?"

From somewhere in the middle of us a voice said, "Sergeant, I have two questions. Is urine the same as piss, and could you repeat all of that? You lost me."

No one laughed or said anything. The sergeant looked pissed off.

The corporal motioned a container to a guy standing near him, and everyone filed in behind. Six guys got their containers and were in the room with the trough. The corporal gave them some time before starting the next six. The line moved steadily. I was in the next group. When it was my turn, he handed me a container, looked at me, and said, "You! Was that you with the mouth?"

"No. That was a true wiseass. It wasn't me." He asked my name.

I was standing by the trough waiting for the others, and I felt an elbow touch my arm. The guy asked if I could do him a favor and fill his container. He told me he was a user. They would pick it up, and he couldn't get in. He needed to get away. I nodded OK. When we finished, all of us put our containers on the shelf and walked through the door.      In the room was our sergeant. He told us to stand with our backs to the wall and face him. The sergeant pointed at a guy sitting in a corner in whites. "This is Specialist Franklin, a trained medic." Franklin stood up. He was a sloppy-looking guy – his whites were covered with blood splats. He was not a nice sight.

The sergeant said the specialist was going to draw our blood, so the army could type it. "Your blood type will be part of your permanent records and be stamped on your dog tags. It is important that you remember what your type is. At some point in your lives you will need to know it."

Standing two guys from me was this tall, skinny kid who couldn't keep his eyes off Franklin. I figured he was gay and had a thing for him. Suddenly, the kid's eyes closed, and he fell to the floor. He wasn't gay, just couldn't handle the sight of blood. If the army was anything like what we had so far, they'd probably put him in combat on the front line.

We gave our blood and walked into another room. In this room, we were told to get undressed, and to put all our clothes in a pile on the bench and our shoes under the bench. Then we were told to form a line facing the white wall. We were bare-ass naked.

A guy in whites stood in front of the first guy, looked in his ears, his throat. He told him to reach his arms up straight, as high as he could. He looked him over from head to toe, then told him to spread his legs. He stuck a gloved finger in his left nut and told him to cough. Each guy in turn got the same treatment. I thought for as in-depth as this physical was, he'd surely look in my ass. If the army really gave a shit, there would be a lot more to the physical; they really don't give a fuck what physical condition we're in, they just need bodies.

When the last guy was finished, we were told to get dressed and to be seated in the next room. We sat down at desks. When everyone was seated, they passed out pencils and a small booklet. We were told to print our names on the cover. The booklet was our mental test, or as better stated, it was a test of our intelligence. Intelligence made more sense to me; a mental test didn't make sense. We were told it was mostly true or false questions. There was no time limit. We were to take our time, be sure we answered correctly, and to begin whenever we wanted. I felt a tap on my shoulder. The guy next to me asked if I could do him a favor. He couldn't read. Could I answer the questions close to him, so he could copy? I nodded OK.

I thought to myself, *I'm going to be in Nam with a dope head on one side and an illiterate on the other side of me.*

I was running through the questions and noticed the guy copying was having trouble keeping up and getting frustrated. I leaned over and whispered, "Stop. I'll do this one, then we'll switch, and I'll do yours." I finished both, sat back, and thought: *This is bullshit.* Then it hit me: the army didn't give a shit how smart we were this go-around. They were so hard up for men that they weren't going to rule anyone out.

We were told, if we were finished, to leave the pencil and test on the table and go into the next room. There were two latrines at the back wall if we needed to use it. The smoking lamp was lit, and to relax till everyone was finished with the test. I took a piss, found an ashtray, sat down, and began to enjoy a Lucky.

My enjoyment was cut short with: "Put your butts out and pay attention. You men are about to have army chow. You are to proceed through that door, acquire your food, eat it, and report back to this room."

I went through the door, picked up a tray, and moved to the food line. It was moving fast. After having food slopped on the tray and picking up a container of milk, I sat down to eat. I wasn't sure what the meat was. It all really sucked. *This is going to take some getting used to. After the bullshit-physical and test, and now this crap, the army is making a terrible first impression.* Second thought: *They don't give a shit.*

We finished and went back to the room we came out of. There were chairs lined up in rows facing a screen. As we all got seated, some guy stood in front of the screen and called out five guy's names and asked that they follow him. As they left, another guy started calling out names and passing a card to that person. I got mine. Paul Walker, Army; second line: Blood Type B.

A sergeant who was standing off to one side hollered out, "Attention. Stand up, gentlemen."

An officer stood in front of us. "My name is Colonel James Lowell. I will administer the oath to you gentlemen. Please raise your right hand."

The sergeant moved quickly behind me somewhere, and I heard, "Your other right, dummy." The Colonel went through the oath. When he finished, we responded, and the sergeant hollered out, "Be seated." The Colonel congratulated us for becoming soldiers in the United States of America Army, the greatest fighting force on this earth.

"You men will watch an orientation film; then you will take your things and board the Port Authority bus for your two-and-a-half-hour trip to Fort Dix, New Jersey."

The movie wasn't bad. It seemed we were all getting into soldiering. We were watching lines of troops marching in cadence – it's a nice sight. Next was narrated battlefield footage of Korea and WWII. The movie was the same as the enlistment movies they showed in theaters. Guys ran up to a booth in the lobby and signed up.

After a half hour, it was obvious they had no idea of what they were supposed to do but had to fill an hour. Time began dragging. It finally ended and all of us bolted for the door and boarded the bus.

# CHAPTER 39

The driver took the bus to the Westside Drive to the George Washington Bridge, across the Hudson River to New Jersey, and headed south. It was quite in the bus, so quite you could hear a pin drop. I figured everyone was caught up in their own thoughts or sleeping. I started thinking about my friends when I was a kid. I hadn't talked to them in quite a while. I knew Ira beat the draft by being a professional student – his mother made sure of that. Some of them beat it by going to Canada, and a bunch joined.

I had seen a headline in the *Post*. "Fifteen Bronx Soldiers Come Home." Under the headline was a picture of coffins lined up on a lawn. Under the picture was a listing of the fifteen soldiers: name rank and branch of service. A second line gave their street address. Out of the fifteen, four were my friends. Rich, Joe, Frankie and Rob. It was hard reading their names. We had been good friends.

I started thinking back about Rob. Some of the guys and Rob went to Catholic parochial school. The rest of us went to public school. We were all about the same age. Parochial school started a year before public school. They spent the day at school while we did our usual, playing ball in the street or just hanging out.

One afternoon we were all sitting on the curb. Rob walked up in his parochial school uniform. He was glaring at Ira and said, "You killed my God." Ira was stunned and terrified, he could only mumble. Rob was really a good guy – this wasn't him. I asked where he got that. He told me Sister Mary Teresa told the class the Jews killed Jesus Christ.

"When you go back to school tomorrow, tell what ever her name is you heard the Romans killed Jesus, and this is a Roman Catholic school. What's with that?"

The next morning about 10:00 Rob came walking toward us. He was in his play clothes. "What you doin'? How come you're not in school?"

"I raised my hand, and Sister Mary Teresa called on me. I told her what you said. The class all began giggling. She told them to be quiet; then said I had to go with her to the office. She told the woman behind the desk to call my mother and tell her to expect me because I had been expelled from school,"

I told Rob I was sorry I opened my mouth. He told me not to be because he wanted out of there anyway. He told us Sister Mary Teresa walked around with a chair slat in her hand all day. She even switched hands when she wrote on the blackboard.

"A couple of weeks ago, I was looking at some pictures in a book, and I had a booger in my nose. I stuck my finger up my nose, and before I knew it, that stick hit my arm, and my finger went up my nose. I pushed that booger into my brain. Between my arm and my nose, I didn't know which hurt worse."

"A week ago, I ate something that gave me the farts. I farted all the way to school. When I got there, I figured there can't be any more in me. I was sitting in class and I felt a fart coming on. I tried everything to hold it back. I was thinking if it was a silent one, and someone started looking because of the stink, I'd point to the guy next to me.

"No luck. I had to have had the loudest fart you ever heard. The girls giggled, and here comes Sister Mary Teresa. She tells me to stand up and lean over my desk. She hit me across my ass with that stick so hard I had a problem sitting on it all day. I told her, 'It was only a fart; everybody farts; I couldn't hold it in any longer. You didn't have to hit me.' I wanted to bring my stickball stick to school and rap her so hard I'd send her flying out of the school. Then this happened; you did me a favor."

He turned to Ira and said, "I'm sorry about yesterday. I'm a jerk."

Rob was a good guy and didn't deserve to come home in a coffin. I fell asleep.

Suddenly there was this loudass fuckin' whistle. I sat up and thought, *What the fuck is this?* I realized we had stopped. A guy in uniform was standing in front of the bus, hollering at us to depart the bus and form up in front of the bungalow.

We piled out of the bus and stood looking at the porch of a building painted olive green; there must have been twenty of them, all in a row. Another guy in uniform was standing on the porch. He had a brass bar on his cap that fuckin' glistened. He told us he was Lieutenant John Colson, United States Army National Guard. He and his staff were assigned to ensure we completed three days of preparedness for basic training. This guy's attitude and manner made me think he watched too many news clips of Patton addressing his troops.

From somewhere in the middle of us a guy hollered out, "Lieutenant, why you flunkies instead of regular army?" There was no answer; we didn't expect one, same wise ass.

A line of sergeants marched in single file to the right of us, and on order, stooped and faced us. We were told to form lines of ten facing a sergeant. Then we heard, "Sergeants, about face, and troops forward march!" What the fuck is forward march? We walked behind the sergeant.

We went to the mess hall. The first station spooned mashed potatoes on my tray, except it was like soup. Next, on top of the potatoes, was some kind of meat, then some soggy boiled carrots and creamed corn, topped with a slice of white bread. I finished going through the line. After seeing what looked like puke on my tray, and not smelling any better, I decided to dump the tray and go outside and smoke. I was leaning against the building, and this tall guy in uniform came up to me and asked how I liked chow. I told him I didn't care for it. He asked what the problem was.

I told him the mashed potatoes was like soup, and then they piled everything on top of each other instead of using the compartments on the tray. It was all kinda floating around. He thanked me and walked to the door of the mess hall. As soon as he opened the door someone hollered out, "Attention" the guy said, "At ease, as you were" and closed the door.

We formed up after chow, and the sergeant walked us to a large Quonset hut. He told us: "You will enter this building single file. You will receive your bedding and whatever else they choose to give you. When finished you will do an about-face and proceed back to this area. I thought, *Is "you will" an army phrase or this sergeant's?*

We were told to hold our arms out belly button high. The first guy laid a duffle bag across our arms, the next guy a blanket, the next guy sheets and pillow case, the next a pillow, and last a couple of towels. We formed up in front and the sergeant walked us to a bungalow. He told us this was going to be home for three days. "Your home is Bungalow Two; don't forget it because all twenty bungalows look alike."

"You will enter the building, secure a bunk, roll down the mattress, and place everything your holding on the mattress. Then stand at the foot of your bunk." The sergeant and another guy came into the barrack. The sergeant introduced Spec.4 Morton. "The specialist will demonstrate the army way to make your bunk. The bunk is a major issue in an inspection," No one had the foggiest idea of what he was talking about and didn't give a shit.

The specialist demonstrated how to make the bunk; it didn't seem all that hard. We made our bunks.

The sergeant announced, "There is to be no smoking in the building other than the latrine. If you are caught smoking in your bunk, you are subject to disciplinary measures. Lights out will be in thirty minutes, reveille will be at 0600. We will form up at 0630 in front of the bungalow."

I got a toothbrush and toothpaste out of my bag. I figured I'd smoke a cig on the john, brush my teeth and go to bed. I walked into a room that was about ten feet by ten feet with a smaller adjacent room with shower heads. There were two rows of toilet bowls facing each other, three in each row. When you sat on a toilet and another guy sat next to you, it was so close you could rub elbows. At the same time, you'd be looking at the guy in front of you doing his business. If this was the army way and not just this building, they sure as fuck didn't believe in privacy.

I was sitting back and relaxing, smoking and thinking today was long, one of those never-ending days. Suddenly, some guy came running in, dropped his pants and sat on the first pot he could get to. As fast as he sat down, there was this huge fart and what sounded like someone dumping a bucket of water. This poor bastard must have really chowed down on the army crap. Then, like a smack in the face, this smell hit me. Son of bitch! Something crawled up his ass and died. I never smelled any-thing that bad in my life. I was plugging away on my cigarette trying to keep the smell off. It didn't work. I got up, flushed the cig and went outside. I lit up another cig hoping to get the smell out of my nose. I was getting cold. I put the cigarette out and went into the bungalow.

As I was walking to my bunk some guy lying in his bunk said, "You responsible for this stink?"

"I got the brunt of some fucker's smell, so don't even go there."

Six o'clock came around fast. Lights went on; a guy was playing reveille on a trumpet; guys were scurrying all around. I got up, went to the john. My toothbrush and paste were where I left them, both still in factory packaging. I didn't have a problem. I went over to the sink, splashed some water on my face, and brushed my teeth. I walked back to my bunk, got dressed, pulled my bunk tight and decided I 'd have a smoke outside. I didn't get much of a chance to smoke when they formed us up and marched us to the mess hall where we had to stand in another line. We were told throughout our career in the army we would always have to hurry up and wait; that's the army way. I thought, *All that's just fucked-up planning.*

The line slowly moved into the mess hall. I picked up a tray and moved to the server line. The first guy asked if I wanted toast or plain bread. I told him I didn't care. He put two slices of plain bread on the tray. The second guy ladled a white thick sauce with meat in it over the bread. I had never seen anything like it, so I asked what it was.

"Back home in Georgia we called it sausage, gravy and biscuits. The army uses bread instead of biscuits, and we call it SOS, or shit on a shingle. It's not bad. You're, going to need to get used to it because once or twice a week that's what you're going to get."

I told him thanks and moved on, got everything else, and sat a table. I began eating the SOS and thought I liked it. Different but good.  I kept on eating and began to wonder if it was going to give me the shits.

They hustled us out of the mess hall and marched us to the barber shop.  We were told to smoke if we had 'em.  I was leaning against a wall and noticed how much hair most of the guys had.  It was a time of copying celebrities' big hair – brushed back on the side to a DA (duck's ass), curled in front and high on the top.  My hair had always been short with a small curl in it.  I brushed the sides back.  That was about it.  The hair on top just lay there like it was supposed to, and I never messed with it.

They singled out five of us and told us to go into the barber shop.  We sat in the barber chairs.  A guy came up to me with a smock.  The guy next to me told the barber he didn't really need a haircut; if he could take a little bit of the back, he'd appreciate it.  He was serious.  The barber told him "Sure, I can to that for you."  He turned the chair around.

My barber asked if I had a request.  I told him to do what he had to do.  As if an order was given, the five barbers began shearing our heads like lightning.  This was the only barber shop I had ever been in that didn't have a mirror.  As I looked at the guy next to me, I realized why.  He once had a full head.  Without all the hair, he looked like a pinhead.  We finished and walked outside.  As soon as the guys saw us they stated hysterically laughing.  I figured they were laughing at the pinhead and didn't give a shit.

Next, we were to be issued our gear and uniforms.  We were told to bring our duffle bag.  We were issued winter gear: a heavy insulated coat, bibs, a hat that covered our ears and strapped under our chin, and some long johns.  We were walking single file between tables stretching the length of a huge warehouse, with guys on the other side of the tables.  A guy asked foot size, I told him, he put on the table two pairs of boots and a pair of shoes.

He told me to put them in my duffle.  On the other side of me on the table they had a pile of underwear and socks.  I put them in my bag and moved on.  Walking down the row we were told to close our duffle bag and wait outside for everyone to finish.

We carried the duffle to the bungalow and were told not to unpack.  We were issued our military ID cards.  The next morning after reveille and mess, that wasn't bad, we were told to strip our bunks, fold everything, put out belongings in the duffle, sling the duffle and carry our bedding and form up in front of the building for a bus ride to our basic training barracks.

# *CHAPTER 40*

Our barracks had a story of its own.  Each building was a white wooden, two story building.  We were told the barracks were the segregated housing during World War Two and sat vacant until now.  They hadn't been renovated, just reopened to accommodate the buildup of troops.

I had been assigned to Bravo Platoon, which was on the second floor.  When I reached the second floor, I saw a large hole in the floor about five feet in diameter on the side of a staircase.  The roof probably had leaked and rotted out the floor.  They repaired the roof, cut away the rot, and left the hole.

The building was heated with two potbelly stoves, one on each floor. A group of guys were selected and given the title of firemen. They were to stoke and feed the stove throughout the night. The first night, about two or three in the morning, the floor filled with smoke. We were all chocking and had to spend a couple of hours downstairs. For some reason a fireman closed the chimney damper.

The second night was even more eventful. Taps sounded, lights went out, and we were in our bunks, beat. Suddenly there was a loud whine. The building started shaking. Our bunks with us in them also shook. This was no Rock-a-bye, baby shake. The loud whine and the shaking lasted twenty to thirty minutes. Our barracks backed up to McGuire Air Force Base, and they fired up a fighter jet. It happened only once. Someone must have gotten the message to them. I thought, *This army is one fucked-up mess*, but then in hindsight I wondered if it was all accidental or planned. The army's thinking was to break us to the lowest we could be, then build us up the army way.

We did the warehouse bit again. This time they issued us our weapon, steel pot with liner, backpack, and a slew of gear. When we returned to the barracks we were given instruction sheets where everything went in our footlocker and standing locker. The sheets also explained how to fold everything and roll our socks. In the diagram the socks looked like a row of cannoli. Our lockers had to be exactly as the diagram showed.

We were all trying hard to get our stuff put away when we were told to stop and report downstairs. Our DI, barracks Sergeant Lloyd Moore, wanted to address both platoons. We were sitting on the footlockers and Alpha platoon was sitting on their bunks. The front door swung wide open and standing in the doorway was a guy decked out in fatigues, about six foot three. My thoughts were: *It's winter. A coat would have been right. At least get your ass in and close the fuckin' door. It's getting cold in here.*

The first words out of his mouth were, "The bunks are not chairs. They are for sleeping only. Get your dead asses off the bunks and don't let me catch you doing that again."

He marched to the center of us and said, "My name is Sergeant Lloyd Moore Junior. You will address me as Sergeant, nothing else. I am your barracks and drill sergeant. I report to Lieutenant Perz, officer in charge of the training company. From the minute you stepped into my barracks you belong to me. You will obey every order without question."

He went on to say, "So we all know where we stand. I was born and raised in a small farm town in Georgia and have maintained the Southern values instilled in me as a youngster. I dislike Yankees, especially those from big cities. I dislike niggers, spics, Jews and little guys. I don't believe any of you belong in my army. Since you're here, you had better shape up or get out.

Tomorrow at 0700 hours I will inspect your bunks and lockers; they better be right. Does anyone have a question for me?" No one said anything, he told us we were dismissed.

I was thinking, and I expect we all were, *Why would the army have this southern hillbilly, bigoted prick be in charge of and train men he disliked?* He looked young, probable joined the army when he was sixteen because he had no life except as a farmhand, too fuckin' stupid to make it in civilian life.

Most of us in both platoons were from New York City. It looked like we were going to get fucked over. Some of the other guys, even though they were Yankees, were feeling good they weren't from the big city.

I was born and raised in a low-income area of the south Bronx. It was a melting pot of races, religions, and ethnicities. We never questioned our differences. My buddies and I were just kids and friends.

To this day I have kept this mindset and I feel good that I don't have prejudices against groups. I do dislike specific individuals, most especially bigots who voice their opinions. I feel everyone is entitled to their opinion, just keep it to yourself. I don't want to fuckin' hear it. I can't understand someone like Moore who has hatred for so many people.

I've used words like spic, wop and mic. So, did most of the people around me. It was never intended to be offensive. It was a lazy habit to say something fast.

*When this guy decides to make it my turn¸ I hope I can control myself. I have never experienced any form of belittling. If I deck him or touch him in any way, I could get court martialed, and spend time in Leavenworth. If I read this loudmouth, bigfuck right, he's afraid of a little guy who looks stronger than him.*

*He's also on a power trip that the army put him on. He covers his own insecurities.*

I thought I'd use his comment about not liking spics against him if I needed to. His commanding officer was a spic.

We were told to finish our lockers, then put our civilian clothes in our duffle bag and put on our government issue. The duffle was to be folded and placed in the bottom of the standing locker. I emptied the duffle onto my bunk, got undressed, and put the fatigues on. Everything fit well.

I was finishing up putting my stuff away and this tall, skinny kid came up to me, saw my name tag, and said, "Walker, can you help me? I can't walk in these boots." He looked like a duck walking pigeon toed. I grabbed him by the arm and told him to sit on my footlocker before anyone else saw him. I was having a hard time choking back my laughter; the sight of him walking was hilarious. I told him he had his boots on the wrong feet.

I finished with a lot of time to kill so I got my rifle out of my locker and was sitting on my footlocker looking it over. The stock and wood were scuffed and nasty, aside from that everything else looked good.

I held the rifle in my lap and thought I would pick up some fine sand paper, stain, and a small can of linseed oil. "If we're going to be together for eight weeks, you're going to look good." I was sighting the rifle to the floor. It had a neat rear sight, a small knob on the side for windage, and another for elevation.

I was concentrating on the sight when I heard, "Trooper, do you know what you're doing with that rifle?"

I put the rifle across my lap, looked up and said, "Yes I do, Sergeant."

He went off. "Have you ever fired a weapon in your life?

Better yet, have you ever had a weapon other than those car-antenna, orange-crate pieces of shit you street thugs make?"

"Sergeant, I know what you're talking about. I have never owned an antenna gun and have never been a street thug. I have owned and shoot a .22 and a .45 handgun, a Savage thirty-ought-six, a Winchester, and a Remington rifle."

"Where in New York City did you do all that firing?" He made "New York" sound like shit.

"We're not having a conversation about weapons. You're just humping me, right?" He didn't answer me. I told him I shot the rifles in upstate New York in the Adirondack Mountains. I figured it was time to see how stupid the fuck was. I told him we used to hunt redneck hillbilly deer. With that, he walked away. I didn't know if he got it or not. I put the rifle back in my locker.

It was six-thirty in the morning and we were formed up in front of our barracks. I was thinking, *It's fuckin' cold, colder here than in the Bronx.* Then I realized *I don't remember ever being outside in the Bronx at six-thirty in the morning, standing with the wind blowing up my ass.* The Sergeant brought us to attention and told us we would be spending the day at the rifle range. We were to wear our winter gear. After mess, he was going to inspect the barracks.

We were marched to the mess hall with the Sergeant calling cadence and hollering out, "Your other left dummy" guys were awkwardly trying to get into step. At the mess hall, some guys were scarfing down their food, so they could get back to the barracks. I took my time. This morning was shit-on-a-shingle. My system had gotten used to it, but I felt if I didn't take my time, I'd be shitting it out all day.

Back at the barracks we were told to open our footlockers and stand at attention by the side. The door came flying open…

Moore walked in. He marched to the first bunk on my side of the room, looked at the bunk, leaned over and flipped the bunk on its side. He went to the footlocker lifted the tray out, looked at the bottom, replaced the tray, went to the standing locker and looked in it. He did an about-face and marched to the bunk on the opposite side of the room and went through the same inspection. He came back to my side did his inspection and stopped in the middle of the room and said, "Your bunks are to be made tight; your lockers are to be organized as the diagram showed, and everything is to be folded neat. 'Shouldn't that have been neatly'?"

It seemed that Moore was enjoying himself, getting his jollies off. He walked over to a bunk, flipped it over, picked up the footlocker tray and dumped it on the floor. He made his way back and forth across the room. So far, he had fucked over six guys. He walked over to the bunk that was two down from me and flipped the bunk and footlocker. He looked in the standing locker, reached in, lifted everything hanging and threw it on the floor. He walked over to the guy, got in his face and said, "What's with you, trooper? You managed to do the impossible. You screwed everything up."

I felt sorry for the guy. He was the same guy who had the problem with the boots. The kid was a fuckup! I figured he was overly nervous and Moore had him petrified. They used to say the army will make a man out of you. I don't know about that bullshit, but I felt he'd get over his nerves and be OK.

Moore continued his inspecting and finally came to me. He looked at my bunk and my lockers. It seemed to me he looked over my stuff longer than anyone else's; then he turned and walked in front of me. I stood tall flexed my chest and looked straight ahead. I felt his eyes on me; I was bracing myself for some shit. All I heard was a grunt; then he did an about-face and went to the bunk opposite mine. He finally finished the inspection and told us we had a half hour to get the barracks shipshape.

I went to the john, sat on a stool, and lit a cig. I was thinking *That poor bastard in there must be running around in circles. Not knowing what to do first, and nobody is going to help him.* I sat smoking and couldn't get the panicked look on the guy's face about the boots out of my head. I said fuck it to myself, threw the but in the toilet, flushed it, and went into the barracks.

There he was – dumbfounded – with no one helping him. I asked if he wanted some help. He came back with, "Yes, please, oh please."

I looked at his name tag. It read Warshafsky. "My name is Paul. What's yours?" He told me Abraham. I came back with, "Just like Lincoln. Glade to meet you, Abe. We don't have a lot of time to get this done. I'll make your bunk, you get the diagram and do your standing locker; then we'll do the footlocker.

 He told me that was his problem. Somehow the diagrams disappeared. I asked why he didn't ask for another one or ask to borrow mine. He said he didn't want to bother anyone. I thought, *This guy's no dummy, he knew he was getting fucked over but didn't know by whom.* I got my diagrams out of my locker, handed them to Abe, and told him "Let's get going."

He did the standup locker quickly then helped me finish the bunk. We both worked on the foot locker and finished just as we were told to form up outside.

I said, "Good timing, Buddy."

I put my diagrams away and got my winter gear out. I turned and saw Abe headed for the door with his rifle. I hollered out to Abe and held up my winter gear. We walked out together as guys were going back in. They forgot the winter gear, too.

The gear had two pieces. The legs were waist-high insulated bibs with straps that went over our shoulders and over our fatigue pants. The jackets looked just like the ones I used to see in the movies that the North Koreans wore. I guess the army learned something from that deal.

Abe was standing alongside me. I elbowed him and told him to sling his weapon. "If Moore sees the rifle on the ground, he'll get in your face about it. You're not alone in this shit. You need help on anything, I'll help you. For now, I want you to stand tall and stop taking this crap so seriously. Think before you do something; there's nothing you need to be nervous about."

We were told to form up facing left, four abreast. I went to the back of the formation, Abe to the center. We marched down the street and were ordered to halt. We were looking at three open trailers with seats built into the sides. Moore stood at the front and told us to enjoy our trip to the range. It would be our first and last. "After this we will trek to the ranges. The trailers are called cattle-haulers. Get on board."

We arrived at the range and were directed to bleachers. In front of us was a platform and the range behind it. A soldier wearing a fatigue jacket and a large brown hat, like a Calvary hat, climbed the stairs, and stood on the platform in an at-ease stance. He was a formidable sight, well built, with stripes on his jacket and a blue patch on his left side just below his name tag. I found out later the patch was combat infantry.

"Good morning, I am First Sergeant Donaldson, in charge of this range. You are seated at Alpha Rifle Range, Fort Dix, New Jersey. We maintain this range to the highest standards, and it is considered one of the finest ranges in the army.

"I am here today to convey knowledge to you about something that will become your best friend, something you may have to sleep with, something you will have to care for. And it will pay you back tenfold. I am referring to the M1 Garand you are holding. The rifle has been designated as United States rifle, M1, caliber.30, semi-automatic.

"Never refer to this or any other rifle as a gun. So you remember that, I will give you this. He reached for a rifle he had against the rail of the platform and held it out toward us. 'This is my rifle.' He placed it back against the rail and grabbed his crotch. 'This my gun.'" Pointing at the rifle he said, "This is for killing … and this is for fun."

General George S. Patton declared the M1 to be the greatest battle implement ever devised. John Garand, the designer of the weapon, was a genius. I will demonstrate the validity of that statement. He asked for a show of hands for anyone who has fired a shoulder weapon. Ten of us raised our hands. He told us we would probably appreciate the demonstration more so than those who hadn't, but everyone would learn from it.

He picked up his M1 and took a clip out of his jacket, telling us the clip and ammunition were standard issue. He turned facing the range, put the butt of the rifle against his chin and fired. "That is the genius of Garand; the rifle has no kick what-so-ever.

"The M1 was used extensively in World War II and Korea. It is an air-cooled, gas-operated, clip-fed, semi-automatic shoulder weapon. The clip is only eight rounds because of size of the round.

"Your M1 has a maximum range of 440 yards using standard amo. Using armor piercing amo, the weapon can cause a casualty at 875 yards. Men, you have in your possession a great weapon, take care of it."

He asked Sergeant Moore for a volunteer to fire his weapon at the range.

Moore hollered out, "Walker the great hunter, front and center."

I stood up, slung my rifle, and walked passed Moore to the First Sergeant. As I passed Moore, I said, "Sergeant I have never hunted in my life." I figured if he put two and two together, I was no worse off than I am now. If he didn't he'd be scratching his ass trying to figure out what was going on.

The First Sergeant and I walked to the first lane. There were three huge targets marked 200, 300and 400. He handed me a clip and told me to fire from the prone position at the 200-yard target. I inserted the clip, chambered a round, and lay on the ground. I sighted the target, when I felt good about it, I held my breath and fired.

Over the loudspeaker I heard lane one, two hundred yards, bull's-eye. All the guys in the bleachers cheered. The Sergeant said, "Good shot." We walked back to the bleachers. The Sergeant said, "Men, that's how easy it is. Sergeant Moore, the range is yours."

The five families in New York owned an estate in the Adirondack Mountains. Once a month the bosses and sub-bosses would meet and discuss business and problems. For the most part it was a way to get away and relax. After each meeting, Tony and I would target shoot in a field a good distance from the house. We would compete for money. I enjoyed the shooting and the camaraderie. I became very good and didn't mind taking Tony's money and sharing zings with him. That was my hunting in the Adirondacks.

Moore began telling us. "You will have chow in the bleachers. It will be your first taste of C rations. Trash is to go in the drum; nothing is to be left on the bleachers or ground. If you need to use a john, it is that building. Use the fountains attached to the building for water. After mess, you will man the range. The object of this session is to familiarize you with your weapon. When the cease-fire order is given, you will police your brass, take your weapon and brass to the observation tower. You will put your brass in the designated container, and a sergeant will inspect your weapon to insure the chambered live round has been removed. The smoking lamp is lit, no butts on the ground. You are free to walk around; if you do, sling your weapon."

I sat back, took out my Luckys and was enjoying the smoke and my day so far at the range. As I was relaxing I felt a tap on my shoulder. I looked up. Abe was standing over me, all excited. He was going on about how great that was, and he was cheering the loudest for me. I stopped him and asked where his weapon was. He told me he left it by his seat. In a very low voice I told him to get back to his seat fast, sling his rifle, and get back here. "We're going for a walk."

As soon as we got out of the bleachers and started to walk I put my cig out on the ground, rolled the butt in my hand, and flicked it into the trash container. I noticed Moore sitting at the bottom of the bleachers, watching us. I figured he didn't care for the fact I was chummy with Abe. I didn't give a shit.

When we reached a place where no one could hear us, I stopped and told Abe, "Don't ever leave your weapon. You need to keep it with you always. Always! You take a piss or a shit in that building, you take your rifle. The locker is different. If Moore saw you without your weapon, he'd be all over you, and he'd be right. Buddy, you need to think before you do stuff. We need to keep your fuckups to a minimum – there will always be something. The way this fucker thinks, he'll be harder on you than any of us. We don't need that."

Abe smiled and asked, "Are we buddies?"

"You bet your ass we are."

He asked why. I told him it's a long story, but when I was a kid my friends were Black, Puerto Rican, Jewish, Irish, German – everything. A Jewish family lived in the apartment next to us. Their son and I were the same age and friends. I didn't know it at the time, but my mother had asked if they could help her feed me because she was having money problems. They took me into their family. "Let's get back and eat something."

We got back to the bleachers as they were passing out small olive-green cans; they looked like one-pound coffee cans. Abe sat beside me. He looked at ease for a change. I began to read the printing on the can and came to "Packaged August 18,1943." On the top of the can were instructions to "Pull tab straight up," and a warning "Edges of the can and top may be sharp." I pulled the tab and heard a hiss.

There were four small round cans stacked in the center. Around the cans were all kinds of shit sealed in cellophane. There were plastic eating utensils, a four pack of cigarettes, toilet paper and some medical supplies.

I took the small cans out. The first was marked fruit salad, the second was ham spread, the third was a bun, the forth was vanilla pudding. Abe asked if I wanted his cigarettes – they were Luckys. I told him sure; it was going to be interesting to see what twenty-year-old Luckys tasted like. I realized there weren't filtered cigarettes when these cans were packed. My four pack was Chesterfields.

I opened and ate the fruit salad, it was very good. Next, the ham spread and bun. The bun was fresh, and the ham tasted great. Last, I had the vanilla pudding. Like everything else, it was good. I sat back and smoked one of Abe's Luckys. They were fresh and had a great taste, a lot better than the Luckys

I was smoking now. I wondered why Lucky Strike fucked up their cigarettes.

I asked the guy next to me if I could have his cigarettes. He told me sure and handed me a four-pack of Philip Morris. I asked him to ask to ask the guy next to him and down the line. He told me OK. I asked Abe to do the same. Four-packs were coming at me from both sides. The guys in front of us and behind us started passing them to us. I was stuffing my pockets and Abe was holding a pile of them on his lap.

When it stopped, I found a brown paper bag in the trash drum. Back at the bleachers I unloaded my pockets into the bag and Abe added his. I realized why I got all the cigarettes. Some guys didn't smoke, and those that did smoked filtered; these were all unfiltered.

Moore began passing out loaded clips. He told us, "When you go to the range take any lane you want. Hold your rifle pointed down range and insert the clip, make sure it is seated. Assume the prone position and wait for orders to load and fire."

Abe and I were next to each other, lying on the ground, and a command came over the intercom to load your weapons. I did and heard Abe. "Paul, Paul, what do I do?" I told him, and he was Ok. Next, we heard, "The range is clear; fire at will."

I sighted the 200-yard and fired, and then the 300-yard. Got my bull's-eye on both. Thinking, This was too fuckin' easy, I sighted the 400-yard, fired and hit about twelve inches wide at three o'clock, which pissed me off. I ran through it all again, except this time at the 400-yard I overcompensated and wound up about six inches wide at nine o'clock.

As I was debating with myself if I should do it again or relax, I heard, "Walker, eject your clip and follow me." It was the first sergeant. We walked to the far end of the range. He handed me a clip. "These are armor piercing rounds; there will be a kick. See what you can do with these targets." I looked down range. They were 500-,600-, 700- and 800- yard targets.

"Sergeant that 800-yard looks like it's in another state."

He agreed. "It's pretty far out there."

I snapped the clip in and loaded a round into the chamber, sighted the 500-yard and fired. The kick was straight back into my shoulder, not up or down. I hit the bull's-eye. The round held true without any drift at all. The 600-yard wasn't a problem; on the 700- and 800- I was off a little.

The sergeant told me to eject my clip, take the live round out of the chamber, and follow him to the observation both. He wanted to talk to me. He told me to put my weapon in the rack and pull up a stool. He told me Sergeant Moore was passing out clips to my buddies, so we had time and he would cover my not being on the range with the sergeant. He told me, "Tomorrow you'll be at the calibration range. Calibrating the weapon and the rear sight, after that you'll shoot even better."

He told me the army had a marksman ship unit, "Part of the unit is a competition rifle team. After basic you could get into that unit. I know you'll make the team. You would spend your tour firing at targets rather ducking rounds coming at you."

I thanked him and said I appreciated what he told me, but I was in the army for a reason. "I need to stay on the path I'm on." He told me he understood, but if I changed my mind, to get in touch with him. We were watching the firing on the range. Moore walked up and told the sergeant we were done. Then he saw me. With an outraged voice, he said, "Walker, what are you doing here?"

The first sergeant replied, "My order, sergeant."

Moore steamed away in a huff. Sure, as shit that didn't do me any good.

The sergeant got on the intercom, "Cease fire, cease fire. Eject your clip, remove the live round from the chamber, and police your brass. Proceed single file to the observation booth."

I thanked him and told him I had to get back to the range. Abe was standing by my lane and told me how glad he was to see me. He couldn't get the clip out. I showed him how to eject the clip and remove the round. After he policed both of our brass I told him to sling his rifle, so we could get in line. Abe thanked me and asked where I'd been. I said, "I'll tell you later."

After the sergeant looked in each chamber to insure the round had been removed, we were told to move to the bleachers. When everybody got there, Moore started, "On my order, you men will form up in front of the bleachers. You will march in formation to the road, at which point, on order, you will form a single file and walk to the barracks. When you arrive at the barracks, you will immediately begin to clean your weapon until the order is given to form up; then you will march to the mess hall. After you have eaten, you will return to the barracks, finish cleaning your weapon if needed, and clean and polish your boots till taps."

The week went fast. We were doing calisthenics, running, marching, and shooting at different ranges. Moore didn't hassle me, but he got in a lot of guys' faces. He was hard on the Puerto Rican and Jewish guys.

Saturday morning at formation Moore told us we would be cleaning the interior of the barracks. He wanted ceiling, walls, windows, and floors washed and shining. We were to do the shower room, the latrine, the sleeping area, and the stove room. He would inspect the barracks at 0400 hours."

He told us he was going to assign three squad leaders to assign jobs and insure it was done right. He also needed a volunteer to go to the PX for cleaning supplies.

I said, "Sergeant I'll volunteer."

"I don't know if you can carry it."

"It depends what you have on the list. If you can carry it, I won't have a problem." The only reason I volunteered was it gave me a chance to pick up what I needed for my rifle.

He told us after chow tonight we were free men till formation Monday morning. We could sleep in tomorrow, but once we were out of the bunk, it had to be made. "For those of you that attend church, there are several on the post. Form up your marching to mess."

Moore handed me the list and five dollars. I ate, went to the PX, and got back to the barracks. I was making my bunk when some guy came up to me and told me I was doing the stove room. He asked if anyone wanted to do the stove room with Walker. He needed two. Abe said, "I will," and the Puerto Rican kid next to him nodded, yes.

I picked up a stepladder, Abe grabbed a bucket and cleaner, and the kid got a mop and rags. We walked into the stove room. "Holy shit. This place is fuckin' black." I asked the kid to get another bucket and more rags. I set the ladder where I wanted to start and put a bucket on it. I told Abe I was going to do the ceiling and down the walls some.

"You and the kid need to work the walls in the opposite direction."

We're going to have to go over everything more than once to get it right. "If we fuck up, Moore will take the opportunity to nail us hard. He's got a thing for us." The kid got back with the bucket and rags. I extended my hand and told him my name is Paul. "This is Abe and you are?"

"Pablo the same as you, only in Spanish."

The three of us began to hump it. Fifteen or twenty minutes into it I was covered in black from the drippings off the ceiling. Abe and Pablo were black also. A guy stuck his head in the door and asked how everything was going. I gave him one of those "fuck you" looks. He left, we didn't see him again.

Time flew by. We kept changing water, washing out rags in clean water, and changing it again when they hollered out, "Chow, C rations at your station." We wiped our hands off with a rag, and Abe told us to take it easy, he'd get them. He came back, flipped each of us a can, and told me he put my bag on my foot locker, told everyone that didn't want the four pack to put it in the bag. He asked a squad leader to ask downstairs. I thanked him and realized that sometimes Abe was quick on his feet, sometimes not. But he'd get through it because he 'as a smart guy.

By late afternoon we finally finished, after mopping the floor three times and making sure nothing was missed. I told them I was going to polish my boots, take a shower, and tomorrow I was going to take all my shit to the laundromat.

Abe said, "Sounds good. We'll do it together."

I was in the shower when Abe walked in. "My God, Paul, you've got some muscles on you, and how come you've got a circumcised dick?"

"Abe, you're not a fag, are you?"

He told me no, he has a wife back home. I told him my mom was a free thinker she wanted my brother and me to be circumcised. She thought it was cleaner. "I don't know if it is or isn't, but I probably could have had two more inches on my dick."

Sunday came I did the laundromat thing and then spent the rest of the day working on my rifle. Monday at formation we were told we'd be marching to the range, and we were to wear our steel pots.

As we formed up for the march, our company's first sergeant joined us. He started us off; when we got out of the populated area, he began a chant cadence. For most of the march he chanted. He must have had thousands of them from all the years he was in the infantry. It took away our agony of marching with the helmet. The pot has its purpose, and it's good, but sure as fuck not wearing it while marching. The day went well. Tuesday and Wednesday were the same old shit.

# CHAPTER 41

Thursday morning, we were waiting outside for formation. A guy came up to say something to Moore. Moore hollered out, "Walker, report to the lieutenant's office. You have a phone call from a Father DeAnglo."

In the office I saluted, "Private Walker reporting as ordered." The lieutenant saluted me back and told me to be at ease, and to take as much time as I needed. Then he hollered out, "First Sergeant, let Walker use your phone in private."

I got on the phone, "Good morning. Sir. Bet you didn't plan on hearing that for a while. How you doin'?"

I'm doin' good. How about you?"

"Putting up with a lot of shit. I never expected this crap, but I'll get through it."

"Pauly I need to tell you something. Your father had been diagnosed with cancer. They treated him with chemotherapy. It didn't work. They told your parents he had a month or two to live. They advised him not to make the trip to your party. Your father felt it would be the last chance he would have to see you and decided to come. Your parents didn't want you to know because you had enough on your shoulders with the army. Everyone else knew. Your father passed away at three o'clock our time. Your mother was with him and relieved that he was finally out of pain. Hyman and Maria are going to Vegas to attend the funeral and be with your mother for as long as it takes. I'm sorry to have to give you this shit."

"It's OK. Thanks. I've got to get off. I'll talk to you later." I hung up and walked out of the sergeants' office.

The lieutenant said, "I'm sorry for your loss; take the day off."

"Thank you, sir, but I'd rather not sit around feeling sorry for myself."

After the call I was feeling like shit. I headed back and saw everyone was in formation, I joined them. I heard, "Walker front and center." I walked up to the sergeant and stood at attention.

"What was the phone call from the priest about?"

"It was personal, sergeant"

Red in the face, he started. "There is nothing personal in the army. You are government issue and you belong to me. Now, what was the call about?"

I repeated, "Personal, sergeant."

He was furious and told me to give him twenty. I did the twenty push-ups easily and stood up.

"For the last time what was the call about?"

"Sergeant, for the last time it was personal. Lieutenant Perez told me to take the day off. I'm doing it now."

He stammered, "That pansy lieutenant can't do that. You work for me."

I came back with, "That may be true, but you work for him, and he outranks you."

I started to walk away and heard, "Walker I didn't dismiss you."

I turned and said, "No you didn't but the lieutenant did." I kept walking.

"Walker! Get back here. I'm putting you on report."

I turned and walked back to him. He told me to report to the lieutenant's office first thing in the morning.

"How about the three of us go to the lieutenant's CO's office. You can file your report, and I can have my say. Sergeant, someone in this man's army needs to set your act straight."

Moore said he'd meet me in front of the barracks tomorrow morning after mess and we'd do it. "Now get back in formation."

After chow, back in the barracks, Abe asked me what was that all about. I told him my father passed away this morning. I didn't feel it was anyone's business. The lieutenant and first sergeant knew; that was enough. Abe told me he was sorry for my loss. I thanked him and asked what we were doing today.

"We have hand grenade range in the morning and flame thrower in the afternoon." Abe told me I had better not get kicked out because he'd be lost.

I told him, "Don't worry about it; if it comes to that you won't be lost."

The two ranges were fun. At the grenade range we were told to stand by a concrete wall and proceed one at a time to the range. I was in the last row of the formation. When we got to the range, I was last in the line; this was going to be a typical army hurry up and wait.

After Abe's turn he came over to me I asked him, "How was it?"

He told me terrible. "I got into a concrete box that didn't have a top, with a hole in the bottom. The DI showed me how to hold and throw the grenade. Then he told me he was going to pull the pin. If I accidently dropped it, he would kick it in the hole and push me against the opposite wall. When he handed me that live grenade I was so nervous, I couldn't get rid of it fast enough. I'm on the floor of the bunker, and the explosion is loud, the earth starts shaking. You can feel it in the bunker."

I told him. "It's done; take it easy and relax." To make my wait even longer, they took breaks, probable for the DI's benefit. It had to be nerve-racking for him to hand a live grenade to a nervous guy and worry about him dropping it in the bunker or not throwing it far enough away, like Abe.

Finally, it was my turn. I got in the bunker and told the sergeant I was the last. Down range they had a target against some logs. He told me not to worry about the target. "This an exercise to familiarize you with the grenade, that's all." He went through his routine; I threw the grenade and dropped to the bottom of the bunker.

After it went off, I asked, "Sergeant, I know it's been a long day for you, but how about one more? I want to see if I can get a little more elevation and hit the target."

"Sure, and I'll show you how to pull the pin." I don't know if I hit the target. I thanked him and went back to the wall.

Moore formed us up and marched us back to the barracks. After chow we marched to the flamethrower range. We were seated in bleachers. In front of us was a field with six, rusted out, blackened vehicles, and a concrete bunker with the opening facing us.

A sergeant was standing on a platform on our right side and began telling us we may have the opportunity to fire a weapon designed to emit a controllable stream of fire. "The weapon was introduced in 1943 to aid troops advancing on Japanese strongholds.

You cannot fire this weapon flatfooted. One foot must be behind the other as a brace. The pressurized gas leaving the wand will exert pressure against you, taking you off your feet."

"The flamethrower can incinerate a target 165 to 270 feet from you. It is a formidable weapon." He finally ended and asked

Moore for seven volunteers to demonstrate the weapon. Moore singled out six big guys telling them they volunteered. Then he called my name. *This asshole wants to see me get knocked on my ass.* We were ordered to proceed to the range, take a lane in front of a target.

The sergeant instructed us in the proper method to put the backpack on, secure the straps across our chest, and how to grip the wand. He told us, "It is important you grip the wand tightly with your non-trigger hand to insure it doesn't get away from you, and be sure to brace with the back foot. Hold the wand low, aimed at the target." Once we had the feel we could move it any way we wanted.

"Gunners man your weapon. Fire" The kick wasn't as bad as they made it out to be. The feeling of power firing it was great, and the sight of the seven streams of fire was awesome. I had a jeep in my lane. I moved my wand up and set the stream in the jeep's side window and held it. Some of the other guys were moving back and forth over their vehicles.

The order came to cease fire, engage the safety, remove the backpack, and report to the bleachers. The sergeant gave a short gave a short critique on our demonstration; then Moore formed us up for our march to the barracks.

In formation, and when we are marching, the army has the tall GIs in front, graduating to the smallest in the rear. I was standing in my usual position in the rear. Moore walked up behind me, said, "Walker."

I turned. He told me he was going to forget about today and not put me on report, then walked away. This guy is dumb, but he must have given it a lot of thought. I guess he realized when they heard everything he said, the least being calling his lieutenant a pansy, he'd be up shit's creek.

*This isn't dead. I might need to use the pansy and spic thing someday.*

On Friday morning we ran, did push-ups, squats, and a lot of jumping around. It was good exercise. After lunch, we went to a different rifle range, a pop-up range. I had fun. Friday was a good day.

We needed to prepare the barracks for an inspection Saturday morning at 1100 hours. Then we were free till Monday morning formation. That would be great. I'd call Tony and ask if Vince could pick me up at the Port Authority bus terminal. We could go to Muraso, I could say hello to everybody, then out to dinner and some good food. I was feeling great about it all.

Saturday after mess we were all scurrying around cleaning the barracks, polishing our brass and boots, squaring up everything. Just before 1100 hours we were ordered to open our footlocker and stand at attention by the locker. A major in full dress uniform came up the stairs, followed by Moore. He stood at attention in front of the first guy, looked him over and his area, and moved to the next. He did the same to all of us, looked in the latrine, and went downstairs. We had to stand at attention till they finished downstairs.

# *CHAPTER 42*

Moore came up told everyone at ease. "Close your lockers, you are dismissed … all but Walker. Walker, you are confined to the post this weekend. You will clean the barracks."

I thought to myself, *You motherfucker.*

He told me I was to clean the latrine – around the bowls and scrub the grout in the tiles on the walls and floor with my tooth brush.

We closed our lockers and leisurely walked to the mess hall. Abe and I were sitting at the same table. He said he was going to stay and help me. I thanked him, but told him no. He needed to go home and see his wife. I could handle it.

I got back, grabbed my toothbrush, and started cleaning. The bowls weren't much of a problem, but the grout was another story. The latrine had tile three-quarters the ways up the walls, and the floor was tile. It was about four o'clock. I had finished, and Moore showed up. He asked if I was finished. I told him I was. He said, "This floor isn't clean" Moore unzipped his pants, took out his dick, and pissed on the floor by a bowl, and told me to clean it up. I stood there debating with myself whether to tell him to fuck himself or clean it.

"I'll clean it, but know this. After I finish basic, I'm going to AIT, and then Vietnam. When I get out of the service, I'm gona look you up. You'll regret the day you met me"

"Are you threatening me?"

"No, not a threat. A promise!"

After he left, I cleaned up with toilet paper and redid the grout with my toothbrush. When finished, I threw the toothbrush in the trash, washed my hands, and sat on my footlocker. This fucker wasn't going to give up, and there was nothing I could do about it. He's dead set on breaking me. Out of the blue it came to me. When I was at the PX I saw a public phone at the entrance. I needed to call Tony.

Cleo accepted the collect call all excited to hear from me and connected me to Tony. After greeting both ways he asked what was wrong. I explained everything and asked for a favor, for him to come to Dix early Monday morning in a priest getup. He was to tell the gate he had an urgent message for Sergeant Moore of C Training Company. "I need you to give this guy the talk like you gave the priest with my mom's deal. Not as bad as that – I just want Moore off my back."

"No problem. For my Pauly, anything."

Monday morning was the same as any other morning. We got back to the barracks after mess. Moore was beating guys up over the gigs they got from the inspection. A spec-four came upstairs and told Moore the lieutenant wanted him at his office.

After a while we heard, "Form up." The first sergeant told us he would be escorting us to the range that morning. Sergeant Moore was not feeling well.

We did the range and got back for lunch, and the order came down to form up. Standing by our formation was Moore. He looked like shit, like a guy suffering a major hangover.

Tuesday came and went easily. Wednesday, I had KP duty. There were five of us. My assignment was to clean trays with a scrub brush and feed a specialized washer, then scrub pots and pans. After lunch it was the same thing over again till the mess sergeant handed out peelers and took us to a corner of the kitchen. He told us to peel the potatoes that were in six crates and pile the peeled potatoes on the floor in the corner. We could sit on the floor to do it.

When we finished there was a good-size pile of peeled potatoes on the floor. The sergeant told us to take a break, but don't sit on anything in the mess hall.

They called us back in to get ready for the dinner meal. When I got in they were putting boiled potatoes in a huge mixer. The sergeant came out of the freezer with a big block of butter. As he was unwrapping the butter, it slipped out of his hand, hit the floor. He picked it up and put it in the mixer. He could have cleaned it off at least. These fuckers handle the food we eat with their bare hands. I wondered if they wash them after they piss. Probably not.

The dinner meal went the same as the others. After we finished our jobs, the sergeant told us to get on our hands and knees and scrub the floor. We scrubbed a greasy, dirty floor with the same brush we cleaned trays we ate off. After KP I had a queasy feeling every time I went to mess.

I was hoping Moore would say something about his talk with Tony, but he didn't. In fact, he ignored me all week till Thursday about midnight. We were sleeping. The lights went on. We were ordered to stand at attention by our foot lockers the way we were – standing there, fuckin' freezing in our tee shirts and bloomers. I hated the army issued boxer shorts.

Moore stood in front of each guy, getting in their faces. The first had a dirty tee shirt, and probably dirty shorts. The second had legs like a little girl. And then there was, "Suck that gut in. We're going to have to put you on a diet." He went down the line brutally criticizing ever one and spraying us with his spit. When it came to my turn, he stood in front of me looking straight ahead. He bellowed, "Walker, where are you?"

"Here, Sergeant." He looked down. I thought, *That was really funny, prick.*

He looked me over then commented, "I thought you were this little fat guy running around. Hell. You're all muscle." He had me remove my tee shirt; he looked me over, then told me to put my tee back on. Turning he left the barracks.

Someone caught the light and we jumped in our bunks. I bet he had me take off my shirt was to see if I had tattoos. We were not allowed to have them. *The fuck is up to his old shit again.* I was wrong. If anything, he went the other way with me.

When I got home on leave, I tried to get Tony to tell me about his talk with Moore. He didn't want to, so I didn't push it. Moore wasn't going to tell me about it. I didn't hear anything until a sergeant in AIT brought it up to me. Moore was at the NCO club after the talk crying on everyone's shoulder.

Basic wasn't all that bad. After four weeks, I had a five-day leave and then weekends. I spent a lot of time with Maria and visited with everyone. It gave me the opportunity to spend time with Tony, reinforcing how much he meant to me and how much I loved him.

When I was a kid, and we were all sitting on the curb, an older guy came out of the building. He told me he was Donny and he lived on the fifth floor. If I ever needed him for anything, all I had to do was ask. I didn't find out till years later he worked for Tony. We used to see a guy standing on the corner in an overcoat and fedora, smoking a cigar, but didn't pay attention to him. In the spring and summer, a guy would be on the corner smoking a cigarette. We just figured they were up to no good. In hindsight Tony had guys watching out for me. I can never fully express the gratitude I have for him, not just for the life he has given me, but for always looking out for me. I enjoyed the time we spent together, no business, just us.

After my first leave, Tony insisted on Vince taking me back to Dix. It was Sunday about six when Vince picked me up in the limo. I was going to get in front with him, but Vince said to get in back and take a snooze. Good. I needed some sleep. I didn't wake up till Vince was pulling through the gate. Because it was Sunday evening, there were no MP's and the gate was wide open. Vince drove to the lieutenant's office. I told him to go down the street further. We pulled up in front of the barracks.

I walked into the barracks. Moore was standing by the entrance. I walked past him and didn't say a word. I hope he shit his pants when he saw the limo.

# CHAPTER 43

The weeks flew. On Monday morning of the sixth week we were told we would be qualifying with weapons. There were three categories of qualification: Marksman, Sharpshooter, and Expert. Expert was the highest you could attain. Moore announced, "Everyone must qualify with M1. It will take three ranges to qualify. You must meet the standard at each range or remain at the range till you do."

We were ordered to man the range. I took lane five, and Abe took six. This range was different from what we were used to. The targets were smaller and scattered rather than being in a line. Over the intercom we were told the standard for this range was to hit at least five of the eight targets. After the cease-fire is ordered you will be given by lane a "yes" or "no." The "yes" meant standard was met, and we could remain at the range or clear our rifle and go to the bleachers.

The order to fire came, and everybody began firing. When everyone stopped, the order came to cease-fire. We were all lying there, waiting for results, and it started: "lane one yes, lane two yes, lane three no, lane four no, lane five yes, lane six no, lane six you hit only one target." And he continued down the line.

I looked over at Abe. The poor guy was so nervous to begin with. This didn't do him any good. Abe was a certified public account on the outside. Surely the army would utilize his skill. He'd never have to fire a weapon. I motioned to Abe to aim at the targets. I'd fire at them. We did it. He got a 'yes.' Back at the bleachers, Abe couldn't thank me enough. I guess he had been worrying about that day for a while and got himself all worked up. The six guys on the range kept getting "no's." I was really bored to shit.

I got up, told Abe I was going to fire some rounds, for him to relax. During the cease-fire I manned lane two. When the order was given to fire, I sighted on the targets beyond the qualification targets and fired on 300, 350, and 400. After the cease fire I heard a familiar voice call out: "lane two, 300 bull's-eye, 350 bull's-eye, 400 six inches three o'clock."

I got up cleared my rifle, nodded a thank you to the observation tower, and went to the bleachers. In the bleachers Abe was sleeping. I sat down and elbowed him. "Relax, not sleep. If Moore saw, you he'd be all over you like shit on a stick. Considering all of us, he doesn't like your probably number one. Must fucked-up southern hicks hate Jews. You have to be especially careful."

After lunch we marched to the second rifle qualifying range, an easy range. No one had a problem with it. We marched back to the barracks. After dinner, we had to clean and oil our weapons and polish our boots. I had plenty of time till lights out, so I stretched out on my bunk, relaxed, and started thinking. I could never get Maria, Tony, Mario, everybody and the business – off my mind. In so many ways it was good. I was back home and away from this army shit.

Tony was so smart – taking the advice and setting up the family in legitimate and illegitimate businesses. For the most part made-men ran the businesses; there were exceptions. The exceptions were men who Tony had a history with and were loyal to him.

Graft was a way of doing business in the city. Every contractor doing business with the city did it, and most of the construction companies did it. We paid off cops, city inspectors, heads of departments, the Mayor, the Governor, and a Senator. It all came down to a cost of doing business.

We used the money laundering through the casino for illegitimate bucks and the legitimate bucks we didn't want to pay taxes on. If the feds picked up on it, we could be nailed and do time.

We were making more money legitimately than the other families were making illegitimately. We had so much money floating around, it was mind-boggling. I remembered Tony talking to the other bosses about going into legitimate ventures. They were old school, and after the dope took off, they didn't want any part of legit. For us, if it wasn't for the dope money, I don't think we'd have gotten into the waste business as big as we did.

Taps sounded, the lights went out, I got undressed and under the covers. I began thinking about the time my mother and I spent, her explaining her spirituality to me. One thing stood out. It is still with me all these years. My mother believed there was no heaven or hell. When we passed, our souls moved on to someone else. I believe I received the soul of a brilliant person, and my brain developed the ability to connect with my soul.

My rationale for this is I never had a formal education. I absorbed basics early on, but that was it. Once I began working, I never paid attention, never studied, never did homework. I graduated high school, and it wasn't a thing of pushing us through in those days. I wasn't worldly, never traveled. I knew the city, especially the Bronx. Yet no matter where, I was comfortable and could always adapt.

So many times, I've been told, "That was brilliant; you're a genius. Where did you get that from?"

I'd answer, "I don't know. It's in me and just comes out." There were times I'd say to myself, *That was just logical*, and other times *Where the fuck did that come from? Or, What the fuck are you talking about?*

I got tired thinking about that stuff, fantasized about Maria, and fell asleep.

The next morning at formation we were told we'd be transported to the range. Because it was too far, they didn't want the time loss for us to trek there. The drive seemed like hours but wasn't. I couldn't get over how big Dix is. At this range, as was all the others, we were seated in bleachers.

The difference of this range was there were no targets. It was woods. A range DI began instructing us by picking up a white board that was a silhouette of a person and telling us this was our target. The targets will pop up all over the woods, one at a time. We should move our weapon constantly, catch a target in our sight, and fire. There wouldn't be time to do anything else. Each target has an electronic sensor that is transmitted to the observation booth to determine hit or miss. We had to engage every target.

One of us was to man the range while four others where to line up in single file. Five eager beavers hustled down. I figured I'd observe these guys to see how I could cover Abe. Most everybody who didn't want to fire anyhow just sat back. When the first group finished, there was no intercom, no scoring, no standard. Everyone got excited.

I got into the second group and, as usual, Abe was right behind me. While we were waiting our turn, I told Abe all he had to do was relax and point his rifle at a target and fire. He'd do well. We finished the range, and the cattle-haulers took us back to the barracks.

The next morning at formation Moore told six guys they would be assigned to another company to redo range one. He singled out ten of us and told us we would be marching to the M1 carbine range for qualification. The others were confined to the barracks on cleaning detail. The morning went well and fast; I was back in formation for lunch.

Moore singled out five of us, to be joined by troops from another company, and be taken to the BAR range for qualification. BAR stood for Browning Automatic Rifle. The only experience I had with the BAR was at a familiarization range. I fired the weapon from the prone position with a bipod holding the barrel up. All I had to do was aim and fire. Because I enjoyed firing the weapon qualification was very easy.

The next qualification was a machine gun and then .45 hand gun. I was told I had to qualify with two more after the .45. I was getting pissed off that I had to do all this qualifying when I felt I'd never fire half of them. Then I realized this was for Moore's benefit. It made him look good having so many troops qualifying in his command. The army only saw the number of qualifications, not the number of GIs qualifying.

Qualifying came and went. We were into our last week of basic, a week of bullshit. First a major barracks inspection, then a field inspection, followed by a dress uniform inspection, followed by a dress parade. Everything was being done to prepare us for our graduation from basic. Our qualification badges were issued, and we had to wear them on our dress uniform.

We were also given our new assignments. Most of us stayed at Dix for advanced infantry training. Some were going to Fort Sam Houston for medic training. Abe was assigned to the Army Accounting and Finance Center in Indianapolis, Indiana. I was happy for him. The army wasn't so stupid after all.

The preparation for the barracks inspection was the same old shit. For the field inspection we were supposed to set up our pup tents and lay our gear in front of it. The problem was we couldn't get the stakes in the frozen round. The tent was placed on the ground.

The preparation for the dress uniform inspection was the worst. Our shirts had to be starched and ironed, our brass had to glisten, and our dress boots had to shine like patent leather. Hours and hours of boring, tedious bullshit. I vowed when I got out I'd never polish brass or shoes again in my lifetime.

Graduation finally came. At 1000 hours we were formed up in the street in front of the barracks, two companies in front of us and two behind us. We were ordered to close ranks, stand at attention, arm's length apart. The order sounded to "forward march." It had to be a great sight: that many men with weapons slung, in dress uniform, marching. The column marched to the parade grounds. The bleachers were full. In front, was a podium, and to the left was an honor guard holding flags. In the center was our country's flag and the army flag; on their flanks were flags commemorating the different conflicts.

The order was given for "eyes left and salute." We marched past the flags and the bleachers. We were then ordered to form up by company in front of the bleachers. It all had to be a terrific sight. An officer went to the podium and began the Pledge of Allegiance. We were ordered to join him, and the bleachers did as well. Next a minister took the podium and gave us a religious talk. He ended his talk with, "We should always keep Jesus Christ in our hearts and minds and a two-minute silent prayer for our comrades in battle."

Next an old guy in dress uniform with a chest full of ribbons and badges, took the podium. He introduced himself, telling us he was the Commandant of Fort Dix. He gave us a speech that he had probably given a thousand times before. It wasn't very enthusiastic till the end, when he told us, "For those of you who will see combat, come back to us with sound body and mind. Congratulations. You are dismissed."

# *CHAPTER 44*

We had ten days off between graduation and our next assignment. I had made arrangements for Vince to pick me up. I didn't want to make the bus trip to the city with my duffle on my lap. As I was at the barracks getting my duffel, Abe cane in. I asked him if he wanted a ride home. He told me his wife drove to be at the graduation, and he was in a hurry to get back to her. He left without even a good-bye.

"Fuck you prick." I never saw him again,

"Where to, Pauly?"

"Home…to see Maria and get out of this uniform. How's the business going?"

"Everything is doing unbelievable. The price for scrap metals and steel has skyrocketed because of the war. Sam worked out a deal to sell all the tires to a wholesale guy, and he bumped up the parts prices. The guy from Peru understood. He's also buying used cars like they're going out of style."

"Astro just got a $20 million contract to take the retaining wall all the way to the Battery. By the time it's done, Benny is gonna be an old man. Fanarassi has the shit going well, and Tony is a rejuvenated man with the waste business. On the way home, you'll see containers everywhere. This thing is getting so big, I don't understand why no one else is in it."

"That's great to hear." I didn't say anything about the waste. I knew why we were the only one. The city issued permits to haul trash. Tony made payoffs, so no other permits are issued.

Vince told me Maria came back from Vegas and had been putting in a lot of hours at the hospital thing. "She might not be home. All she can talk about is you coming home and the two of you spending time together."

I asked Vince how he was doing. He told me good but busy, running Tony all over, from Albany to Trenton, to talk to the governors. "He wants to take over two abandoned quarries. When he's finished with them, he's telling these guys, he'll create a state recreational park. Today been visiting all the businesses. He keeps telling me all the time how much he misses you."

Once home I grabbed the duffle from the trunk, slung it and headed for the door. Nobody was home. In my room I hung up some stuff, put some things in drawer, and left a bunch in the duffel which I put in a corner.

The pair of slacks I put on fit like shit. I had lost my gut. After dressing in my fatigues, I grabbed all the slacks and the suit and headed to the tailor who had made my suit. As soon as the guy saw me, he excitedly welcomed me in Italian and English, like I was his long-lost brother. What had given this guy an attitude adjustment? He measured me and said he'd take the pants in, and I could pick up the clothes first thing in the morning. I said *mille grazie* as we shook hands.

Next on my agenda was Muraso to visit with Tony and Mario. I had an idea I wanted to pass by them. I walked in to find a guy standing in a booth that had a bulletproof window. He asked if he could help me. When I told this new guy I wanted to go into the offices, he said I had to be on the authorized list and asked my name. He checked, said he was sorry, "Paul Walker is not on the list."

Because he told me neither Mr.D nor Mario was there, I asked him to get ahold of Cleo and explain the situation. After a short time, he hung up and told me he was sorry, he was only trying to do his job. He buzzed the door open.

I told him he was doing a great job. "We're going to have to make some changes to the way you're doing it. If I told you my name was Al Fanrassi you'd let me in, but that wasn't my name, and I could blow this place away."

At my desk I phoned Maria and we talked for a while. It was good to hear her voice. She would be home late because she had to attend a dinner conference for hospital administrators.

Next, I called Cleo to thank her for getting me in and asked if she heard from Tony, to ask if he and Mario had some time to spare tomorrow. I also asked her to call Sam to make sure he was at Beacon and had a pot of coffee on.

I sat back enjoying my office. I missed this life so badly – the people and the hustle. After a while Cleo notified me that Sam said he always has a pot for Pauly. She had spoken to Tony, and "It's lunch at Muraso tomorrow."

I got up and walked into the hallway. A deep voice commanded, "You stop! What the fuck are you doing here?"

I told him I needed to make a couple of phone calls and was just leaving. "Your leaving alright. How'd you get in here? What the fuck do you think this is? A public phone both. You better start giving me some good answers or I'm going to tear you a new asshole."

Looking him over I felt I could take him, except it was obvious he was packing, and I didn't want any part of it. I told him, "Let's go back into the office. I'll call Cleo the receptionist. She can tell you who I am instead of us tangling. It's easier."

"OK, get in there."

I dialed Cleo and told her I needed her help again and explained the situation. I handed the phone to the guy. After a few minutes he hung up the phone. "Sir, I'm sorry, I'm so very fuckin' sorry."

"Nothing to be sorry about. You did good. What's your name and what do you do here?"

"My name is Pietro Fettuccini. I run the waste business for Tony, Mario and … and you."

"That's good Pietro. If you weren't packing that piece, I would have taken you. Have a good day. I'll see you around."

Beacon was humming with activity. I'd never seen this many guys working the yard. As I was looking around, a guy called out, "Soldier boy, you lost?"

"No, I'm looking for Sam" He said Sam was in his office. I remarked, "I'm not sure where the boy-shit came from." He looked rattled but didn't say anything.

In the office Joey was sitting at a desk, yelled, "Pauly! It's good to see you."

As he said that, Sam's huge body came rocketing out of the back room. He lifted me off my feet. "How's my soldier? I missed you so much. It's so good to see you."

"Sam, it's great to see you, and I missed you. But if you don't put me down you're gonna break my ribs." He did, and we stood there looking at each other.

I'm home, and so lucky to know people like this. There's none better in the world!

I followed Sam to the back where he had a pot on for us. Sam's coffee was as usual out-of-this-world. I told him he needed to set up some little stores around the city to sell just his coffee. People will come from all over to have some good java.

"When you get back, Pauly we'll do it together."

Sam filled me in on everything that was going on and added that Juan had given him a satchel of money. "I told him thanks, but I can't take it. He insisted. I told Tony about it and tried to give him the money. Tony told me to keep it, so I opened a bank account. When you get out, we'll use it for the coffee shops."

I said, "I'll match it; we'll be partners."

After talking for a while I told Sam I was going to head out and let him get back to work. I was on my way home feeling hungry. I knew Maria wouldn't be home till later, so I drove to the bar.

At the table a young guy asked if he could take my order. I told him a small pizza and whatever is on draft. He told me no problem, but he needed to see something that showed I was old enough to drink. "You're kidding me."

After I handed him my driver's license, he said, "I'm sorry, Sir, you don't look your age."

He brought a large glass of beer and said the pizza would be out soon. The beer hit the spot. I always preferred draft over the bottled stuff. Soon the guy put a pizza box on the table. I dug right in, thinking, *This is still the best fuckin' pizza anywhere.* I was enjoying it, but I got full. I wasn't used to eating this much.

When I asked for a check, the waiter said Tito, the man who runs this place, told him it was on the house. "We don't charge GIs here." I asked to thank Tito personally.

The kid came out with Tito following him. "Thank you, Tito. That's a great attitude. Most people don't feel that way these days."

"I know, and it's a shame."

"Tito, look at me closely. You don't recognize me?" He stood there looking me over, and finally said he didn't know me. "Tito, either you need glasses, or I've changed a lot. It's me, Pauly."

He stared a few more seconds then grabbed and hugged me. "It is you! Pauly, I missed you."

Tito had been running the kitchen for Tony for years. When I started working for Tony he told me to tell my mother I'd be having dinner at the grill, so she wouldn't worry. Tony must have told Tito to take care of me. We developed a good friendship.

"Tito, my friend, I've missed you, too. It's good to see you again. Thanks for the great pizza. I'm gonna get going. Take care of yourself." I picked up the box and took a $100 bill out of my pocket and handed it to the waiter and told him to have a good day.

At home Maria was sound asleep. I went to bed thinking tomorrow would be a good day. I'd see her in the morning. I woke after a great night's sleep. In a bed instead of a fuckin' bunk! Downstairs I found a note. "Sorry I missed you. I'll be home early tonight. We'll spend the night together. Love you."

I glanced at the time. It was ten o'clock. *What the fuck? I didn't intend to sleep in.*

I drove to the tailor. In the shop I heard, "Good morning, Sir."

"*Buon giorno*, and no 'Sir', please."

The tailor put my slacks on the counter and asked me to go in back and try them on. I said I didn't need to and asked how much I owed him. "For you, there is no charge."

I told him he did fine work and he was in business. "In business there is no such thing as no charge."

"Sir, I cannot charge you for the alterations."

I said OK, Sir, I won't pay you for the alterations. I took out a $100 bill and handed it to him. "This is a Christmas gift. *Bene, grazie.*"

As I was leaving he called, "*Grazie.*"

After putting on my civvies, I looked in the mirror. Not bad. And then it hit me. There was one advantage to being in the fuckin' army – I didn't have to brush my hair.

At Muraso the same guard asked if he could help me. *Not again. I don't want to go through this again.* I told him, "My name is Pauly Walker."

He looked closely. "Holy shit! I didn't recognize you. Please go right in."

Mario's office was empty, so I walked down to Tony's office. Tony and Mario where talking. Suddenly I heard a loud booming voice. "Pauly, you look great, and it's so good to see you!"

I paused for a second before replying. "You're lookin' pretty good for an old guy."

Tony came out with, "I oughtta slap the shit out of you. What happened to respect?"

"Your right." I looked at Mario and said. "Good morning, Sir, it's good to see you." Tony looked frustrated. I finally came out with. "All bullshit aside, good morning, Sir. It is so very good to see you. I've missed you more than you'll ever know."

Tony walked around the desk, hugged me, whispering, "I missed you, too,"

In the dining room Tony and Mario were filling me in on everything as a waiter started to bring out lunch and Chianti. Lunch was not a sandwich or a snack – but was a full-blown Italian meal. I ate only small portions. We finished and were sitting around smoking – me with my Lucky. Tony and Mario with the fuckin' stinky ropes.

"Pauly, you really had me there for a while."

"I knew it, but you're not an old guy."

I'm not sure what came over us probably the Chianti. The three of us couldn't stop laughing.

Back in the office I told them I had three things to talk to them about. "The first is I want to fly to Vegas and spend some time with my mother and Hyman. I was hoping Maria, you and Gloria could join me. I know Mom and Hyman would be happy to see you." Tony wished he could, but right now there was so much going on, he was running around like a chicken without a head. I told him I understood.

"My second thing. Most nights, after lights out, I lay in my bunking thinking about shit. One night I got on a kick thinking about our waste business. On the way home Vince was telling me you're trying to take over two abandoned quarries. That fits in with what I was thinking. You construct a two-story concrete building. The ground level has two openings that trailers can back into. The second story has two smaller openings. You do some ground fill and set a concrete pad in front of the second story openings.

Build a 40-foot container with high sides on a dump trailer and back it into the lower level. If there is a stone crusher at the quarry good, if not you buy one and set in one of the openings on the second story. The small containers with block, brick, asphalt and rock dump their loads on the pad, then a dozer pushes it into the crusher. The crusher fills the trailer in the lower level. My thoughts are you'd have a better fill in the swamps than solid. You'd save money with one large haul than a bunch of small hauls. You may be able to sell a container load for fill."

"In the other door you buy a crusher, have them modify it so it doesn't crush, it shreds. You dump the light building waste along with the garbage. It all gets pushed into the shredder. The containers dump their loads in the quarry. In time this would all pay for itself. What do you think?"

"Sounds good. Something to think about."

Mario added, "It doesn't sound good – it sounds fantastic! It's what we should be doing. I don't know how you came up with it, but it's great. We need to get on this right away."

"The last thing I want to talk to you about is coffee. Yesterday I stopped by; no one was here so I went to Beacon." Tony interrupted me, telling me he heard about my visit here yesterday from a bunch of people, and I really know how to stir up shit.

"Sorry 'bout that. Can I get back to what I was saying before we start throwing punches? I don't know if either of you have had Sam's coffee. I drink a lot of coffee and have never had as good as Sam's. Yesterday, over a cup of coffee, I told Sam he needed to open a couple of little places and serve coffee and donuts or something. Word of mouth about his coffee would spread; people would come from all over. Sam told me when I got back, we'd do it together.

"I don't want to wait till I get out. Maria should be at a point she could turn over the hospital stuff to the hospital and just concentrate on the foundation. This would give her time to work with Sam and set up a business. The more I think about this thing, the more I like it. It could become very big, with locations all over. I want to see Sam become very wealthy from it. And I'd like to see the family be partners with Sam instead of me. I'm done. What do you think?"

Tony, said, "I like it; we'll do it. I've had Sam's coffee."

For the next hour, we sat around talking. Mario was excited about my suggestion for handling the waste. He explained that the city elected a new mayor, and he was on a rejuvenation kick. "They're tearing down the abandoned projects and a lot of the old buildings. We're moving as much building-material shit as we are garbage, and we do a big business in garbage."

Tony came out with, "We could park a forty-footer at each of the big sites. We'd charge the city more and make one haul instead of four."

Tony said, "Pauly presented a good plan. Mario, you thought it was great, and something we should move on quickly. I agree with both of you. If it's as good as I think, we'll build a second station. I'm fucking glad we're partners"

I came back with, "Me too. More than you could imagine." With that we said our good-byes and I headed home.

Maria hadn't gotten home yet, so I grabbed a Cuban and went out to the patio. I was in a lounge chair smoking, thinking about the day, and feeling great. Suddenly I got pissed off. I started ranting to myself. What the fuck was I doing in the army, treated like a maggot, shit on, missing my life and everyone? Then a voice inside of me said, "You made the decision for the right reason. Stop beating yourself up about it and stay the course." I was right. I never thought that way again.

I was sitting there reflecting on my wisdom about the army and the day, when Maria walked onto the patio. I got up and we kissed. I embraced her tightly in my arms and didn't want to let her go. After a while she asked how I was. I told her great, now, and asked how she was. She answered the same.

"How about I get us a tea, we relax for a while, then have dinner."

"Sounds good to me. I haven't had one of your Long Island teas in a while. I might get drunk." We were sitting back enjoying the tea, talking, and I was smoking my cigar which didn't bother her – she liked the aroma.

Maria told me the hospital was up and running. She had been busy in meetings with the administrator, and chiefs of staff for each department. She wanted to make sure everyone was on the same track. Everything and everyone must adhere to the hospital's philosophy of loving child care, and always the children and the parents must be treated with respect.

I sat listening intently. I couldn't take my eyes off Maria. *My fiancée is the most beautiful, radiant, intelligent woman in the world.* After eating dinner, we returned to the patio. I told Maria I was hoping we could get away together for two or three days and go to Vegas. "I want to see my mother and Hyman, but I completely understand if you can't do it on such short notice" She told me she was sorry, it wasn't a good time.

Maria said she needed a favor from me – a loan. She had not taken any money from the foundation or the hospital but spent a lot on things for the hospital. She didn't want to ask Tony for money or touch our savings. Our checking account was empty, and she owed about two thousand on the credit card.

"No problem. Tomorrow I had planned on stopping at the bank before Vegas. While I'm there I'll deposit money into the checking account. With everything you have going on you shouldn't have to worry about money". It was something I never wanted her to do. "As far as the loan is concerned, you know there is a healthy interest on that money. If you don't repay it, well, you know what happens. I'm going to have to change the rules and take repayment in trade for the rest of your life." She smiled.

I told Maria about the talk with Tony and Mario about the coffee shops. She was in favor of working on the coffee project.

It was getting late. We went upstairs to the bedroom. While we were embracing Maria said she wanted us to get married and start a family. I told her I wanted that more than anything, except, I wanted to be with her when she had our child. "This is wrong timing, and we need to stick to our plan."

I woke up the next morning feeling better than I had ever felt in my life. I must have slept in, because Maria was gone. She left me a large paper taped to the refrigerator with I LOVE YOU scrolled across it. I added a second line, I LOVE YOU TOO. At the bottom, I wrote, "Please don't throw this away. I want to keep it."

# CHAPTER 45

I called Cleo and asked her to book me a three-day roundtrip flight to Vegas, book a room, and have the hotel pick me up. She asked when I wanted to leave. "Either late this morning or early this afternoon." I was sitting around drinking coffee when the phone rang. Cleo scheduled a United flight leaving La Guardia at 1:30. All I had to do was go to their counter for my tickets and boarding pass. Everything was paid for. Someone from the hotel would be waiting for me at Vegas International.

I went into the kitchen for a paper bag then went upstairs. I took my attaché out of the back of the closet. I tossed in thirty grand, a clean piece, and two loaded clips. I put fifty grand in the paper bag. I took my luggage out of the closet. It felt heavy. What the fuck was in it? I put it on the bed and opened it. Maria had packed my suitcase, left a note on top reminding me to take my suit carrier. I took everything to the Vette and headed for the bank.

I took the bag, locked the car, and went in the bank. I told a teller my name and that I needed to deposit money into my checking account. I didn't have a deposit slip or my account number. Could she help me with it? She started to go on and on about how she couldn't do it. I stopped her and told her I was in a hurry to catch a plane. Would she mind getting the manager for me, telling him who I am, and that I was in a hurry. She went to his office, stood in the doorway talking to him. It almost seemed that he pushed her aside as he came rushing out. After I explained what the problem was, he said he'd take care of it. I handed him the bag with the $50,000 and thanked him.

At LaGuardia I checked in and boarded the plane. The stewardess directed me to a seat in first class. After I put my attaché case in the overhead compartment, I sat down, and put my seat belt on. People kept boarding and going back to coach. No one joined me in first class. *This is going to be a boring flight.*

The plane was moving, and they were still giving instructions over the intercom. When they got to the life preserver under the seat and the flotation cushion we were sitting on, I wondered what water were we flying over from New York to Vegas. I mentally turned them off, sat back, and closed my eyes.

When we leveled off, the captain came on, introduced himself, and told us the weather in Vegas was 80 and sunny. We would be arriving on time. "For those of you who are gamblers, good luck."

A stewardess leaned over to me and asked if I would like something to drink or eat. I declined. It wasn't long before I felt a light tap on my shoulder. A good-looking young woman asked if I minded if she sat up front with me.

She explained that she was seated between two guys. One was looking out the window. The other guy wasn't big, but was crowding; he kept elbowing and touching her.

I told her I didn't mind at all, and if the stewardess would have a problem with it, I'd handle it. First class had these roomy seats in a row, with a separating console. She sat next to me. I told her I was to visit my mother and grandfather, would gamble a little, and check in on a business I have an interest in.

She introduced herself as Kathy. Her fiancé was a dealer at a casino. "He's been trying to persuade me to move to Vegas, so we can get married and start a family. I'd like to see what Vegas is like and if I can line up a job in the casino or hotel. My fiancé told me that if I was approached by the manager, to be polite, but not to tell him I was looking for a job or for her fiancé. "If possible, avoid the guy."

I asked her fiancé's name. "Andrew. We got together in Brooklyn, and he loves blackjack. We played it together all the time. One day he told me he was moving to Vegas to get a job as a blackjack dealer. When the time was right, I'd join him. I guess the time is right."

"That sounds great. The only problem I have is Brooklyn, I'm from the Bronx." We laughed.

Time flew by as we talked about New York and blackjack. A voice over the intercom told us to fasten our seat belts for the approach to Las Vegas International Airport.

I asked Kathy if she was going directly to the casino when we landed. Yes, the Royal Palms. I offered her a ride. Kathy asked me if I would wait with her till the plane emptied out. She had a carry-on in the overhead compartment and couldn't fight the crowd to get it. The door opened, and coach started pouring out of the plane.

A runty guy leaned over to Kathy and said, "Girl, I wondered where you disappeared to."

I stood up, leaned over to him, and softly warned, "Get the fuck out of here before I tear off that arm of yours and beat you over the head with it." I must have scared the weasel good, because he took off.

We got Kathy's carry on and my attaché then made our way to the baggage pickup. I handed our tags to a guy in a red hat wheeling a cart and told him we'd be out front. On the street in front of us was a limo, with the driver holding a sign, "Mr. Walker."

I nudged Kathy and said, "This is our ride."

She looked at me startled, "You're Paul Walker! Oh, my god, I've heard of you. I've got a big mouth. I'm sorry. I'm so sorry if I said anything inappropriate"

"Everything is fine, and I can get you a good job at the casino."

We pulled in front of this large building standing alone on the main drag. The huge neon sign on the front read Royal Palms Hotel and Casino. It was impressive. As a bellhop went to the limo for the luggage, I walked in. The impressive front of the building didn't come close to the grandeur of the upscale, plush, very dignified lobby. At the counter, a young lady said, "Welcome to Royal Palms. May I help you?"

I told her I had a reservation. Paul Walker. She hesitated, then said, "It is very nice to meet you, Sir. Mr. Salassi asked to be informed the minute you arrived."

She got on a phone.

In a matter of seconds this distinguished-looking guy in an expensive suit came toward me, with outstretched hand. "Mr. Walker, I'm Joe Salassi. It's my pleasure to meet you."

I told him to call me Paul.

Joe asked if he could escort me to my suite.

"It's not necessary. I don't want to take any more of your valuable time. I just want to get settled in, contact my mother, then do some gambling."

"When you're free, I'd like to take you on a guided tour of the facility."

The bellhop took my luggage and I followed him to the penthouse. Luxurious! The suite had a patio and a private pool. When the bellhop offered to put my things away, I told him I could handle it. I asked how long had he worked for the hotel. He said three years. I was curious if the change in managers affected him in any way. The bellhop revealed the old manager would alternate bellhops to the penthouse. "The new one doesn't, and to top it off we must give him a share of the tip."

He added that when he gets a penthouse call, the tips are good. "But more often we get Midwesterners who don't believe in tipping." I told him I understood and handed him a hundred-dollar bill. He thanked me and said if I needed anything to please get ahold of him, and he'd make sure I was satisfied.

After I put my stuff away I called the front desk to page Mrs. Walker. The girl replied Mrs. Walker was supervising the stage rehearsal, and had asked not to be disturbed, but she was sure she'd take my page.

Mom got on the phone. Before I could say hello, she blurted, "Pauly, are you OK? What's wrong?" She kept going on. I finally stopped her and told her nothing was wrong. I was at the hotel and wanted to know if she was free to have dinner with me.

"Of course, I'd love to have dinner," but why didn't I let her know I was coming. I told her I wanted to surprise her. She said she'd find me in a couple of hours, and we'd go to dinner. She was eager to see me and loved me.

"Love you, too, Mom."

I took a couple of bundles of cash out of my attaché, put them in the breast pocket of my blazer, and took the elevator down. In the lobby I looked around but didn't see an entrance to the casino. At the front desk the clerk was reading something. After a while I said, "Excuse me. Can you tell me where the casino entrance is?"

She looked up, apologized for being so distracted in reading an important memo about a visiting owner and how to treat him. Pointing at double doors, she said, "The casino is through those doors."

My thought was to take the doors off and enlarge the opening. *What the fuck are we hiding the casino for?*

As I was walked toward the doors, I heard my name called. It was Salassi. He asked how I liked the room. I told him it was good. I didn't want to get into a discussion with him now.

Salassi said, "While you're our guest, I want you to have a great time. Mr. Walker, please accept this, and good luck in the casino."

Salassi handed me an envelope. I could feel a bundle of cash. I told him thanks, but it wasn't necessary. After he insisted that I please accept it, I asked him if it was house money. No, it was from him.

"Thank you. And Joe, between us, it's Pauly."

In the casino, I told the cashier I wanted to bank money. I took the money out of my pocket, peeled off $2,000, and handed the rest to him. He counted out the money and told me I had $18,000, then he asked to see my driver's license. After examining it, he said, "It's an honor to meet you. I'm truly sorry about the loss of your father – he was a great man."

I thanked him, and told him I didn't need a receipt. Then I asked to set up another account. "Call it Royal Palms Special; put whatever is in this envelope in it."

I began looking for Kathy and the table Andrew was dealing. The casino had many tables but very few slots. People were waiting around to play the machines. When I was in Cuba with Meyer, he told me slots were the best moneymaker of all. They had row after row of slot machines.

I found Andrew's table. There were two guys playing, and an empty seat next to Kathy. I asked if they minded if I joined them.

Kathy was facing away from me. I asked her if she was gambling or just a lucky charm for these gentlemen. She turned to me and screamed "Paul!" Then she said, "Andrew, this is Paul Walker." He got visibly shook up.

I told him to relax – this isn't the time to lose your cool. "If I lose, then it is." I told Andrew it was nice to meet him, and he was a lucky guy to have a fiancée like this non-gambler here.

Putting a thousand on the table, I asked for five black, and the rest in green. I handed Kathy the other thousand and told her we were going to take the house broke. We started playing, the table was doing well. The guy next to me said he was glad I joined them.

Andrew called for bets. I put a black chip down, and everyone upped their betting. He dealt all of us good cards, himself a five. Everyone at the table handled it well by staying, and Andrew flipped his down card revealing a king of hearts.

The two guys next to me started chanting bust. Kathy and I joined. It became loud. Andrew dealt himself a ten and busted. As he was paying everyone off and clearing the table, a guy in a suit walked up behind him.

"Gentlemen, and lady, we want you to win and have a good time in our casino, but you need to do it quietly."

I told him he was right. We just got caught up in the moment and were sorry about the noise. He was obviously a pit boss tracking our gambling. He had a name tag on his chest.

"Sal, it's nice to meet you. My name is Paul Walker."

He blanched. He told Andrew to take care of me and walked away.

We were all doing well when Andrew broke it off. They were going to fill in his chips. The two guys beside me started grumbling, "Not now, not now."

I told them not to worry because we had a lucky charm, meaning Kathy. I asked Kathy if she'd be there tomorrow. I had a job interview set up for her, a very good job.

Andrew called for bets. We had another good hand. Sal walked over to the table, "I'm sorry to disturb you gentlemen. Mr. Walker, Mrs. Walker asked if you would like to have a before-dinner drink with her at the bar." I thanked him, told everyone it was my pleasure playing with them. I thanked Andrew with a black chip as a tip, slid all my chips in front of Kathy, and left.

Mom was sitting at a table. She jumped up and hugged me. "Pauly, it's so good to see you. I missed you so much."

"Me, too, Mom. We need to sit down. These guys at the bar are getting all excited." She had taken the liberty of having them serve us her reserve Chianti. We picked up our glasses and toasted. The wine was great. When I told her, I couldn't remember her looking so ravishingly beautiful, she blushed and thanked me. I asked how she was.

"Good. Your father had been sick and hurting for so long. When he passed, it was the best thing for him. For the last years, he had been a great husband. We loved each other so much. He was a good man. He talked about you all the time. When he heard about the going away party, he consulted with his doctor and was told not to make the trip – it could be fatal. When we left the doctor's office he insisted I make round-trip reservations. Nothing in this world was going to stop him from seeing you and saying good-bye."

I stood up, told Mom I'd be right back, asked where the rest room was. She pointed it out. I walked in, took a handkerchief out of my pocket, and sat down on a john; tears started flowing. Uncontrollable crying. I was brought up that big boys don't cry.

I had never cried before. I guess this was something I had to get out of my system.

I washed my face off and walked out. As I was passing the bar, a guy tapped me on the arm and asked what I had that he didn't, to be with that hot chick. If I didn't feel as bad as I did, I would have decked the fuck. Instead I told him, "She's my mother." As I sat down I could see a guy in a suit talking to the guy. They left the bar together.

Mom told me it's OK. She knew I had been crying. She ordered us a second round of Chianti. I asked if there were eyes and ears in the bar. She said eyes, but no ears.

"Mom, what's going on here with this guy Salassi?"

"When your father ran this place, it was great. No drugs, no prostitution, everything was legit. The employees liked and respected your father. He treated everyone as if they were family. It was a good job, and everyone was happy. Now people work here because they need the job. No one is happy. Nobody gets respect. Nobody puts out the extra 10% as they did for your father.

"This guy acts as if he's king. He doesn't ask, he orders. He has a string of hookers for the high-rollers and pushes dope to them. It's a circus here."

I asked my mother if there were eyes and ears in the dining room. She said no, but she was sure someone would be there keeping an eye on you. I suggested we talk more as we ate.

We took the elevator to the second floor, walked into a lobby that was rimmed with restaurants, all with simple signs above their doors. The first one had elegant double doors. The sign read "Steak and Seafood." The second had a single door – the sign read "24 Hour Buffet." Next Chinese, followed by Mexican, and then a Jewish Deli. Finally, two double doors for "Fine Italian Cuisine."

I let my mother lead the way – no surprise into the Italian restaurant. There was a line of people waiting to be seated. The large room was elegantly done. If my mother had anything to do with the food, it'd be great.

The maître d' noticed my mother. "Mrs. Walker! Your table is ready. Please follow me."

We sat down. "Louis, thank you, I would like to introduce my son to you. This is Paul Walker."

"It is my pleasure to meet you, and our honor to serve you in our restaurant."

A waiter came over, introduced himself, and asked if we would care for a before-dinner drink. My mother ordered a drink, but I declined. I asked Mom what her responsibilities were. She supervised everything except the gambling and money transfer. "Your father and I spent a lot of time and effort to hire the best people to manage everything, so my job is easy."

I told my mother I had some problems with the place. "It seems to be run old-school Mafia – that's not what the Family is about. When I went down earlier to gamble, Salassi stopped me and handed me a bundle of cash. I told him it wasn't necessary, but he insisted. I asked if it was house or his. It was his. Salassi is making good money, but not enough to hand out $10,000."

I asked my mother if she could run this place. She told me my father had been sick for a while, and she had run it. Did she want to do it again? She answered yes.

I told Mom about Kathy. "She has a great personality and is smart. She came to Vegas to be with her fiancé. He's a dealer here, and she needs a job. Her fiancé Andrew warned her not to go near Salassi. I'd like you to interview her tomorrow to become your assistant. If you hire her, you could do on-the-job training."

Mom said she would interview Kathy mainly because she wanted to meet someone I thought was smart. Nine tomorrow morning. I told my mom I still hadn't met a girl as smart as she is.

While we were eating dinner, I praised the food: great, almost as good as her cooking, reminded me of home.

"It should. The restaurant uses many of my recipes."

Mom encouraged me to see Hyman while I was there "He's not doing well. Although he knew it was coming for a while, when your father passed, Hyman crumbled. He hasn't overcome it." I told her I had planned on it.

For dessert, my mother ordered amaretto coffee and cannoli for both of us. "Mom, you keep feeding me like this, I'll never get into my uniform."

After we finished, I was trying to get the waiter's attention to pay the check. My mother told me there was no check. All our meals in the hotel were comped. I handed the waiter a hundred-dollar bill, saying it was for him for superior service.

Outside the restaurant, I hugged my mother, said I really enjoyed being with her. "I love you, *buona notte*." As I took the stairs down, I realized why Mom walked away so abruptly – she teared up and didn't want me to see it.

Andrew and Kathy weren't in the casino. I asked a clerk at the front desk for Andrew's home phone number, and a phone. She got Andrew on the line and handed me the phone. After saying hello to Andrew, I asked to speak to Kathy. I told her I set up an interview for a job in the hotel at nine the next morning. I advised her not to get over-dressed but to look sharp, and not to be nervous. It was a done deal if she handled herself right, and I knew she would. "The interview is with my mother."

Kathy was excited and couldn't thank me enough. She told me she deposited three thousand in my draw account. One was what I gave her to start, one was what I started with, and she split our winnings in half. I told her that was very nice, and I didn't think most people would have done that.

"Your last name is Gibbs, right?"

"Yes."

"Ms. Gibbs, I didn't slide my chips to you for safekeeping. I gave them to you. I'm going to have the cashier withdraw three thousand out of my account and start a Kathy Gibbs account."

I was standing in the lobby debating with myself whether I should get some shut-eye or gamble. I needed the sleep, but with everything I had running around in my head, I didn't think I could. I walked into the casino, handled the Kathy thing with the cashier, then sat down at a blackjack table.

I stacked the ten black chips I had in my pocket in front of me on the table, asked the dealer to green five black chips. I was playing heads up with the dealer; nobody was at the table. The dealer shuffled, and I cut the cards. We began to play. I was playing two hands with a green chip on each. Before I knew it, I had lost three hands. The dealer was hot. I told him it was not good customer relations for the house to win. He told me he was sorry, it runs in streaks. He asked if I was a regular. No, this was the first time. I told him home was New York City. He was from Cleveland and had only been working here less than a week. That's why the graveyard shift.

I put a black chip in a square and slid a green chip toward him. "Your bet. We're going to change this deck." He dealt the cards, and I lost again. I put a black chip in two squares and slid two green chips toward him. He dealt the cards, I got two blackjacks. He paid off the bets, putting his winning in the tip box. I left mine on the table. I was betting $250 on each hand.

I asked how he liked the job. He said the job was great but didn't pay well. "We pool our tips. For the most part players don't tip."

I told him it didn't seem right to me. "They ask you to handle big bucks, and not pay you right."

I won the next two hands, then went back to a green in each square. After a while I was winning but getting tired. I told the dealer to cash me out, change the green to black. Ten chips went in my pocket, leaving five on the table. I asked the dealer to have his pit boss to come here.

The pit boss arrived and said, "Sir?"

I asked him if he knew who I was. He knew exactly who I was. I asked him to bend the rules a little for me. "I want to give this gentleman these chips, not in the tip box."

"For you, Sir, that's not a problem." I thanked the boss, and he walked away. I told the kid this should make up for the shit pay, and to have a good night. Before he could say anything, I left.

I took the elevator to my room. I was tired but didn't want to go to bed yet. Grabbing a Cuban, I went out on the patio, sat in a lounge chair, and began thinking about the day. It was great to be with my mother – *She looks terrific. I need to get this army thing over, so I can get back to my life.* I was thinking about the changes I wanted to recommend about the casino. I was thinking about Hyman. My mind was bouncing everywhere.

# *CHAPTER 46*

My thoughts were interrupted by a knock on the door. *Who the fuck could be knocking on the door at this hour?* I sure as shit didn't want to get up, but I did. A stunning-looking woman said she was sorry to bother me at this hour, but could she come in and speak to me? I motioned her in and couldn't help but notice a great body, terrific ass, and nice tits.

She said her name was Terri, and Mr. Salassi thought I would like company. Suppressing sarcasm, I said that was nice of him… she was hard to turn down. She refused my offer of a drink or a cigarette, so I suggested we go out to the balcony. "I'd like to get to know a person who is keeping me company." We sat down in the lounge chairs, and I asked her to tell me about Terri.

She told me she was born and raised in a small town in Ohio, graduated with a degree in education. After returning home, she got a job as a teacher. Ever since she was a little girl she wanted to be either a Vegas showgirl or a Rockette in New York City. "One day I decided I wasn't getting any younger, now was the time. New York City scared me, so I came to Vegas."

She tried all over, but every place that had showgirls had stacks of applications. "I was running out of money, so I came to the hotel to apply for a position. I met with Mr. Salassi who told me he was the General Manager. He told me there were no positions open in the hotel, but he wanted to make me a proposition...and here I am."

"That sucks. How long have you been working for Salassi?" She just started. I was her first. When I asked why she didn't apply for a showgirl job here, she was surprised. She didn't know there were showgirls here.

"Tell me what his proposition was."

If she spent the night with a high-roller and showed him a good time, "Salassi would give me a thousand dollars, and the gentleman would probably give me a good tip."

I asked if Salassi went into detail what a good time was. A good time meant sex. I asked her if Salassi told her anything about me. "Only your name, room number, and that you were a high-roller."

I told Terri to sit back and relax while I thought this deal out. *Here I am with a young lady who is probably a virgin, who is being paid to prostitute herself. The temptation to screw her was almost overwhelming. Cheating on Maria aside, Salassi knows who and what I am. He's very aware that my sleeping with a prostitute is against the Code. This whole fuckin' thing, the $10,000 and Terri, is a setup.* Salassi would have something to hold over me as an insurance policy for himself.

"Terri, I have a new proposition for you. You'll spend the night with me, and I'll match Salassi's money for a tip. If Salassi asks how the night went, you will lie, tell him it was wonderful; the sex was great.

"We won't have sex. It has nothing to do with you. Hell, you're a fantasy come true for any guy, and I'm not a fag, so don't get that in your head. Do we have a deal?"      "Yes and thank you so much."

"Good. We're business partners, and as partners we level with each other, no BS.

My gut tells me you're a virgin. You were afraid to eat and drink because you would get sick and lose everything."

She looked at me, then at the carpet, and mumbled that I was right.

"Good. Let's go down to the buffet. I'll buy you something to eat and drink; then I need to go to the casino and conduct some business. Are you a gambler or drinker?" She answered no, neither.

We took the elevator down to the 24-hour buffet and sat at a table. I asked Terri if she minded eating alone. She didn't. I told her to go to the buffet, take whatever she wanted, but eat and drink very slowly or she would get sick. I went to the cashier, told him my name, and her tab was on me.

"OK. You going to wait here till she's done at the buffet?"

I told him no. That fuckin' pissed me off. "Here's a hundred-dollar bill. When I get back from the casino cashier, I'll get my change"

I went to the casino thinking that sucked no matter who it was. I asked the casino cashier to transfer ten grand from my bank to a different account, PW Royal Palms. Back at the buffet, I told Terri to continue taking her time eating. We were not in a hurry. At the cashier, I asked for my change. As he handed me $12, he said the buffet was $8.

"Wrong. I gave you $100."

He insisted I gave him a twenty. I told him I was tired and didn't need this crap. How long had he been a cashier here? Two weeks. Who hired him? Mr. Salassi. I told him get on the phone and get Salassi down here. He refused, saying he couldn't do that at this hour.

I thought to myself, *Fuck this shit.* I went back to Terri and told her I had a problem that I wanted to get handled. Did she want to go to the room and get some sleep or wait here?

"I'll wait for you. I'm curious how you're going to handle this."

I stormed back to the cashier and asked him to get the front desk on the phone for me. He handed me the phone. I told the clerk good morning, explained who I was, and that I wanted her to get ahold of Mr. Salassi, and have him come to the buffet now! Immediately!

I got a cup of coffee, sat with Terri, and asked her if what she told me was legit or bullshit. She told me it was true, all she had left off was that she had to get away from her parents and have a life. I asked why prostitute herself? She was out of money, and it was the only way she could survive. She didn't want to go home a failure. I said I understood, and later today I'd get her an audition for a showgirl here. If that didn't work out, another job in the hotel.

"You can do that?" I answered yes.

Salassi came at a run to the table. I told him to get someone to give the cashier a break and bring him here.

"Joe, since you hired this guy, and since you are the General Manager of the Palms, you needed to resolve the issue." I asked the guy to tell Joe his side; he did.

"Sound like a problem to you, Joe?"

"No, not really, except he shouldn't have charged you."

Joe, "He left one thing out. It wasn't $20, it was $100. That's the problem. How many other people has this shithead fucked?" I asked the guy if he knew who owned the Palms. Certainly – a Family from the Bronx.

"The problem is you fucked over the wrong guy. I'm one of the owners. Under different circumstances you'd be pushing up daisies in the desert with your dick up your ass. You're a penny ante fuckin' scumbag! No asshole ever shits on me! Give me back the $100 now!" He did, and I passed it to Terri.

"Joe, this fuck bothers me, but what bothers me more is your hiring this shit. Whatever you're gonna do is your business, but this guy never works here. Terri, let's go upstairs and get some sleep."

In the elevator, Terri asked if that was legit. I told her yes. I was going to sleep in this morning. She could sleep in the other bedroom or with me. She would prefer sleeping with me.

I got up early. Terri was still sleeping. I went into the head, took a crap, a shower, and shave. As I was walking into the room, Terri said, "Good morning. Wow! Look at you!" I replied good morning and asked if she slept well. Yes.

As I dressed Terri said, "Mr. Walker, I have a lot of questions, but one is really bugging me."

I stopped her and said, "I'm Paul. My friends, and I consider you a friend, call me Pauly. Now what's bugging you?"

"Please, don't misunderstand this because the best thing that has ever happened to me was meeting you, but what am I doing here?"

"Fair question. I'll answer it. After I do, you can't mention to anyone what you heard at the buffet, and my answer. You're smart enough to put two and two together. You heard who owns this place, and that I am one of the owners, which makes me one of those kinds of guys. We live by a strict code. A part of it is we do not sleep with prostitutes. And Salassi knows it. He figures you're an insurance policy for him to have something on me."

I told her, "Salassi is not going to be here any more, and there isn't going to be prostitution in this hotel." I gave her the grand tip, told her to get dressed, find Salassi, and get her money. "If he asks, tell him the sex was great. If he welches on you, just walk away and I'll get your money. Then, if you want to eat something, go for it, but I need you back here, so I can get in touch with you."

Downstairs I asked the clerk to page Mr. Salassi and inform him I was waiting at the front desk. Then I asked her to page Mrs. Walker.

My mother answered the page. "Good morning. I need another favor. I need you to audition a young lady for a showgirl job. If you give her the job, spend a little time with her and help her out, but don't tell her your last name."

"Now would be good. We're in the theater." I called the room and told Terri they were waiting for her in the theater.

I hung up and noticed there was a big guy standing at the counter. Looked like a wop. He walked toward me, said, "Good morning, Mr. Walker. My name is Vincent. Mr. Salassi asked me to show you the security we have in the hotel and the casino."

"OK. How about you call me Pauly and I call you Vinny when we're alone?" He nodded yes. I thought to myself: "Where the fuck is Salassi? Out of respect for me, he should be here."

Vinny pointed out all the security we had; it was a good tour. I thanked him and asked if he'd have a cup of coffee with me, so we could talk. I realized how important security was. Aside from protecting us from having partners, in our business the casino was our way to wash big bucks. We didn't need to have any kind of incident that would raise the attention of local law or the feds.

We were sitting at a table in the deli. I asked Vinny how long he had been running security. Twelve years. I commented that I thought Salassi would have put his own man in charge. "How many of his guys did he put in?"

"A few. I don't think it's going to be long before he dumps me for one of them."

I told him, "Don't worry about that. It's not going to happen. I'm going to need your help later today."

I told Salassi I wanted him to take me to accounting and introduce me to the person who runs it. After I met John Catore, I told Salassi I was going to be there for a while and didn't want to keep him from his work. He took the hint and left.

John took me to every department, introduced me, and explained each job. He told me he'd been there from the beginning, since Hyman hired him. Pointing out a glass-enclosed office away from the others. John said the gentleman in that office didn't work for him, he worked for Hyman. John introduced me to Howard. Of everyone I met at the casino, this guy was the coldest fish. I told Howard I'd see him later.

I told John I'd require a private office or conference room and someone to go over the books with me. "I don't know a lot about accounting. What I want to see is how much we make, how much we spend, and our accounts receivable."

After John set it up, I spent three hours going over everything with the head accountant and two department managers. There were some eye-opening numbers in our expenses. In accounts receivable, there was a bunch of little shit that was handled well. Then there were these big-dollar hits that were just sitting there. I asked and was told these were high-roller markers. Mr. Salassi was handling them.

I asked John to have Howard come in. My thought was he'd open up in private rather than in the glass office. Howard walked in and sat down. He was fidgety. I told him to relax and asked if I made him nervous. Yes.

"I don't understand that. You work for my grandfather and worked for my father. Why would I make you nervous?"

"That's the way things are, and I have nothing to say to you."

Without losing my cool I stood up, looked down at him, in a calm voice, I said, "That's fuckin' bullshit. I'm going to give you two choices. Either you tell me everything that's going on, or you leave here in a coffin. It's up to you."

He started whimpering, then turned on the waterworks.

"Stop this crap! I don't have time for it. Make a choice."

He stopped crying and looked up, at me, "Just before you came into my office, Mr. Salassi called and told me if I talk to you I'm a dead man."

I told him no matter what he told me, Salassi was going to be gone. "I assure you he will never come near you or harm you in any way. What are we going to do?" He said he'd tell me everything.

"Good. Out of respect for my grandfather, I couldn't do choice two. I was bluffing."

"After your father died, Hyman lost it, couldn't get it together. He's been out of the picture. Salassi took over. Salassi receives the cases from the couriers, signs for them, takes 20%, then gives me the money and the manifest. I am instructed to alter the manifest, log it, deposit company money offshore, and his money into his personal account."

I asked if he took any for himself. No, he never would. I asked how much is in Salassi's account. Seven hundred thousand now. How much had he deposited?

One million. I asked how much is in the company account. Howard explained there are six accounts. Together there is enough money to buy a small country.

I told Howard to transfer Salassi's account into an account we'll call Royal Palms Special. I was going to get Hyman involved.

I picked up the phone and asked the desk to connect me with Vincent, head of security. I asked Vinny if his phone was tapped or his office bugged. He replied no on both accounts. I told him I was going to use his phone, and I needed him to have a good guy shadow and safeguard Howard in accounting till this was over with.

I got Tony on the phone, told him we had a problem in Vegas. I explained everything. The reason for the call was that he put Salassi here on the recommendation of Gino. "Out of respect for both of you, I didn't want to off him without your knowledge." Tony asked what extension I was on, then said he'd call me back.

I looked at Vinny who seemed to be glowing and told him I'll need him and a couple of his men to pull this off. I also wanted him to make out a list of guys in security loyal to Salassi that need to go with him.

Tony called back. Salassi was a cousin of Gino's wife. I could put Salassi on a plane to the city instead of offing him, and Gino would deal with him. I told Tony I would.

"I intend to get back everything he has, and I'll make my mother manager. While Dad was sick, Mom ran this place well." Tony agreed.

I told Vinny, "We are going to have a meeting with Salassi." I called Howard and asked him if he could transfer Salassi's personal accounts. He said he'd find out. "While you're at it, see if he has a safe deposit box."

Vinny rounded up a couple of his men, and Howard called to tell me Salassi had three personal accounts and a safe deposit box. He couldn't transfer the accounts without Salassi being there. The four of us went to Salassi's office. Salassi jumped up. I told him to sit down. We just wanted to have a meeting with him. I sat across from him. I decided not to get into any bullshit and get right to it. I told him, "Before I say what I have to say, put your hands on the desk. I'll feel better.

"Joe, after our meeting, you're gonna take a plane to New York. You no longer run this place."

He got red-faced and blurted out, "Fuck you! You can't do that! This is my place. I'm the boss here. You don't have the right to do it."

I got pissed and told him, "You're nothing! You're a fucking nothing! Out of respect for Gino's wishes, I'm sending you back to him instead of blowing your fuckin' brains out. Do you know what respect means, you stupid prick? How could you disrespect the Family by skimming a million dollars, and bringing drugs and prostitution to the hotel? You are the dumbest son of a bitch I have ever met!

"You are going to the bank, transfer all of your accounts, empty your deposit box, and bring it here."

Salassi shouted out, "Fuck, no!"

I said, "*Gesu Christo*! I'm tired of fucking with this prick."

I reached in my breast pocket, took out my forty-five by the barrel and slammed the butt on his wrist. He jumped up, screaming. I told one of the guys to take Salasssi jacket off, empty the pockets, and wrap it around his wrist. I asked him if it was still "fuck, no" or was he going to work with me. He mumbled he'd work with me.

"Vinny, have someone bring a lot of bandages in here. Get ahold of the limo driver and Howard. All of you take this prick to the bank." I asked him if the key to the box was on his key ring. He nodded yes. "Hand me the keys." I removed the safe deposit box key off the ring and kept the rest. I called the front desk, "Make a reservation on a one-way flight to New York for Mr. Salassi, anytime today, even red-eye. Then page Mrs. Walker."

When my mother picked up the call, I told her she was now the manager of the hotel, and I'd explain everything over dinner.

"Please call Hyman. Invite him to dine with us, stressing I won't take no for an answer. I want to say hello, get him to stop mourning and get back to work. It would be good for him, and this place needs Hyman."

I unlocked Salassi's desk. Aside from all kinds of shit, I found a book with his string of hookers and their phone numbers. There was also a file with pictures of guys fucking, guys giving other guys blow jobs, guys getting fucked in the ass, and groups having an orgy. On the back of pictures, were names and phone numbers. The prick was blackmailing! Hard to tell how many lives he fucked up.

I found a small note with numbers and the word "safe." I located the safe and opened it. There was cash and bricks of coke. I took the cash out and closed the safe. There was $100,000 in cash. I put it in the desk.

The phone rang, and a young lady told me she booked Mr. Salassi's flight. It leaves in two hours. All the particulars would be at the front desk. I thanked her, lit up a cigarette, sat back, and relaxed. It wasn't long before they all came back. I told Salassi to sit at the desk.

Howard said, "It went well. The box had cash and jewelry. "I asked Howard what he did with the cash, thinking he might have put it into the account. Howard brought it all there. I told him to put it on a table for now.

I had Salassi write down the name and a phone number of who he was buying the shit from. Then I asked him if the guy was connected or a middle man. Middle man. I placed the photos on the desk, face down, and told Joe to put a figure on them of how much he got from each one.

I told Vinny to have two guys escort Salassi directly to the airport. "At no time are they to take an eye off Salassi. They are to stay with him until he boards and remain until the plane takes off."

"Joe, back in the city, if we ever bump into each other, you better run the other way, or I'll blow your fuckin' brains out."

The five of us remained in the office. I told Howard to take the money from the box, along with $50,000 from the desk, and deposit it into the casino account.

"Hyman is coming back. Ask him to convert the jewelry into cash and deposit it." I reached into the desk drawer, took out a thousand dollars, and handed it to Howard. I told him thanks, this was a bonus for him. After Howard left, I told the other two guys, "Today was a good day's work," and gave each of them the same bonus.

After they left I told Vinny I had three jobs for him. I handed him the book with the hookers' names and numbers. "Make the calls. Tell them Salassi is no longer here, and they are never to set foot in this hotel as a hooker."

"Next, check with accounting to see if any of these have outstanding markers. Call them, say Salassi is no longer here, and we regret this happened. For those with markers, tell them we're applying what Salassi told us they paid him against the marker. And for those that don't have markers, have Howard send them a check.

"Last, this is the name and number of the guy Salassi was buying the dope from. Call him. Say what you want, and how you want, but basically, if he ever sets foot in this hotel, he's dead.

"Get ahold of Howard. Have him tell you when the courier from New York arrives. Load the courier up with the shit in the safe. He'll take it back to New York. Vinny, thank you for everything. I won't forget it. This is for you." I handed him $10,000.

I called the front desk, got Salassi's info, and asked her to get me on an early morning flight to New York. I called Tony, told him about Salassi's arrival time, about the coke coming with the courier, and my coming home the next morning.

With time to kill, I went to the casino. My mother paged me, said Hyman and she were in the deli waiting for me. Hyman warmly embraced me. I always knew why Tony liked Hyman. Hyman is the most caring, gentlest man I know. We sat, and I told them about everything that went down, and about the account we set up. I suggested Hyman ask Tony to get in touch with Trafficante, and the two of them fly to Miami.

"They'll take you to Cuba. Meyer will show you their casino and give you a lot of good tips. Take what you want and put it in here. Look over their security system. It's new, and good. Ours is old, and outdated. Use the special account money, and if you need more, use the courier money. We need the hotel and casino to be a profitable venture. More important, we need everything to be legit for it to serve our purpose."

I suggested, "Mom or someone she appoints, needs to review the employees Salassi hired." I described my incident in the buffet. I told her, "Vincent, head of security, is a good man, and he'll handle the security guys." I told Hyman, "Howard is a good employee. He did everything great in your absence, but you need to check with John in accounting for any of Salassi's hires."

The dinner went well. Hyman seemed uplifted about being involved, and my mother was excited about everything.

I finally got to New York, drove home, and slept until 1 p.m.

At Muraso I told Tony about Vegas, and he told me what was going on. It wasn't long before Mario popped in. He hugged me and joined the conversation. Mario described the waste business, how it was growing so fast it was almost hard to keep up with. They were planning on expanding all along the East Coast.

*This is so great – my being a part of everything with these two guys. The three of us truly like and respect each other.* There isn't anything we wouldn't do for each other. We talked some more, then I said my good-byes and went home, anxious to see Maria.

Maria hadn't returned yet, so I grabbed a beer and a Cuban, and went out on the patio. There I was, smoking, drinking, and thinking life is good.

I put the cigar in the ashtray, the beer on the table, and dozed off. When I opened my eyes, Maria was standing over me. I reached up to her, and gently pulled her on top of me. We were kissing and holding each other and kissing some more. This beautiful lady is my breath of fresh air. I love her more than anything. We spent that night, and the next two days and nights together. We couldn't get enough of each other. Carefree, we did whatever we wanted and spent hours just talking.

# *CHAPTER 47*

Time flew by. Before I knew it, I was back at Dix to check in. At the door, a sergeant told me to put my duffle bag against the wall and report to the first sergeant in the next barracks.

"Private Walker reporting as ordered, Sergeant."

"When I was in the NCO club having a beer, Sergeant Moore came in and told us a story about you. I won't have any outside interference with military matters. I don't care if it's a friend, priest, or whatever he was. There will be no interfering because a whiny baby cried. If things don't go right for you, bite the bullet and take it. Do you understand?"

"Yes, Sergeant. I understand. If I can, I'd like to tell you my side, and what really happened."

He said, "Shoot."

"From the beginning, Sergeant Moore told us who he didn't like, which was almost all of us. He especially didn't like little guys from the big city who thought their shit didn't stink. In formation, he would stand in front of me and holler out, 'Walker. Where are you?' He'd look down then say, 'There you are. How do they let midgets in this man's army?' I knew what he was doing. He was trying to get me to Section Eight out.

"The company had a weekend pass. He told me I was confined to the post. He didn't have a reason to do it. I had to clean the grout on the walls, floor, and around the bowls in the latrine with my toothbrush. I spent the entire Saturday doing it. At 1600 hours, I was done, and it looked great.

"Moore walked in, looked around, went over to a bowl, took out his dick, and pissed on the floor. He ordered me to clean it up and walked out. I did. He came back in and told me I was dismissed. As I was walking out I told him, 'I'm going to AIT after this, then Vietnam. When I get out, I'll find you, and when I do, you'll regret the day you met me.'

He came back with. 'You threatening me?' I said, 'No, it's a promise.'

"I walked around for an hour. I knew he wasn't going to stop. I went to the PX and called my priest for advice. I told him my circumstance, and he told me to be patient and put my faith in the Lord, everything will be all right. The rest you know. I never heard what happened."

The Sergeant evaluated what I said, "I can't believe anyone in their right mind would do something like that. I'm sorry about what I said to you … dismissed." I went back to my barracks and checked in. I never heard anything about that again.

Advanced Infantry Training was good training. We soldiered rather than put up with the bullshit of basic. The ranges were intense; the maneuvers were designed to prepare us. Time flew by. The last week of AIT was a free week. We cleaned our gear, turned in most of it, and prepared for graduation. We were told graduation would be at 1100 hours. After chow, we would board a commercial jet for Oakland, California, then a ship to Hawaii.

The sergeant came over to say Top wanted to talk to me. In his office he told me a memo went out from the office of General Westmoreland, commandant of the Twenty-Fifth Infantry Division. "They are forming an elite company with a specific mission and are looking for troops that meet certain specs. You fit those specs. We put your name in."

I asked what the mission was. "They'll fill you in. I just wanted to give you a heads-up. You'll like it and be good at it."

Graduation came and went. The only good thing was all of us were promoted to corporal. We were crammed like sardines into a jet. If they could have sat one of us on top of the other, they would have. After finally reaching Oakland we were bused to temporary quarters. In four days we were to board a ship but for now we were confined to the base. There were fourteen hundred troops boarding a reconditioned WWII transport that would be making stops at Hawaii, the Philippines, Okinawa, and Korea, dropping off troops.

When I first saw the ship, I was shocked. It was a rust bucket! They took it out of mothballs. Most likely they didn't have enough time to recondition it because of the troop buildup in the Pacific. I could tell this trip was going to be a lot of fun from the get-go. Because they boarded us alphabetically, I was in the back of the line. Typical army: after three and a half hours I boarded the ship.

A sergeant came up to me and said, "Troop, follow me. We're going to have to find you a bunk. This ship is overcapacity." The bunks were metal, stacked four-high, row after row. The bunks were all full. We went from one area to another. At last the sergeant pointed to an empty bunk on the bottom – it was mine. The only way I could get in was to lie on the floor and roll in. I figured it was only five days, I could live with it. I was wrong.

It wasn't long after I got settled in they called chow. The ship was still in the bay, moving slowly. It was easy to get to the mess hall. There were four long, skinny tables with chairs on one side. I'd swear the tables were a mile long. There were four-inch-high boards on both sides. I figured that was if the ship rolled, the food would stay on the table.

They began to slide trays at one end, and sailors were carrying trays to the other. It wasn't long before everyone had a tray.

I don't know what happened next. I assume the ship left the bay and was headed for open sea, and they turned the screws up all the way. The ship lurched. I grabbed my tray and held it on the boards. Trays were moving back and forth beneath mine. Everything settled down, but you could feel the ship rolling. The food wasn't bad; it was better than the army's.

Making my way to my bunk, was a little hard because of the rolling and pitching. I lit up a cigarette, and was thinking this isn't all that bad, at least I can get rocked to sleep. The guy in the top bunk leaned over and puked his guts out. It hit the floor and splattered. Although I got some, the guy across from me got most of it. He was pissed, started yelling, "Fuck, puke head, get down here and clean this shit up."

Just then a navy officer came over to see what the commotion was about. He ordered a sailor who was with him to get a mop, bucket, and towels here now! The kid that puked came down as the sailor was mopping. I asked the officer if I could switch with the pucker, just in case it happens again. He told me no. Under my breath, so he couldn't hear me, I said, "Thanks, prick."

The trip sucked. It was boring. There was nothing to do. The only enjoyment I got was going out on the poop deck and watching the flying fish. They'd come out of the water, go for about twenty feet, then dive back in. At night, the screws turned up jellyfish that glowed as they came to the surface.

Finally, it was over, and we were off-loading at Pearl Harbor. The ship we had been on looked like a pitiful rowboat next to the carriers and battleships at the pier. They loaded us onto buses. We were told it would be about an hour and a half ride. After passing through Pearl City we caught a three-lane highway that turned into a two-lane road. As we began climbing a mountain, a Spec4 stood up in front of the bus and welcomed us to Hawaii. "On either side of the road for miles all you will see would be sugarcane fields. Further up the mountain, for as far as the eye can see, are pineapple fields. By army law any GI taking a pineapple from the field will be court-marshaled."

The elevation kept increasing. The bus was straining. Suddenly, the road leveled out, and we rode for about a half hour on flat ground. On our left was the huge, sprawling Schofield Barracks Military Reserve. The Spec4 stood up again and told us we would be coming to the main gate shortly. "On our right, will be a small town called Wahiawa. It's wide-open. We can get anything we want." We pulled through the gate and an MP saluted us as we passed. They off-loaded us into a huge Quonset that had guys who arrived before us, waiting. Our duffle bags arrived in a deuce-and-a-half. We put them on the floor and sat on them.

This was typical army – hurry up and wait. There was nobody to ask where the latrines were. There were no signs. Everybody's eyeballs were turning yellow. We hadn't had any food or water. We just sat in this fucking hot hut, waiting. And sweating.

Finally, a row of sergeants marched to the front of the hut. The first one hollered out twenty names and told them to form by twos behind him, then marched them off. The second sergeant did the same. As the third sergeant was about to start, a first sergeant came running out of the building across the street. When he got to the hut he called out my name.

I shouldered my duffle and went up to him. He told me to follow him. At a good pace, we went to the second floor of the building. The sergeant told me, "You will proceed down the hall to room B4. You will leave your duffle in the hall with the others." He said he should have been waiting at the bus when they dropped me off but missed my name on the roster. "If anything is said, don't bitch about waiting." I told him I wouldn't, I'd cover for him.

About forty guys were sitting at tables facing a podium. A major standing at the podium said, "My name is Major Allan Malone. You men have been recommended and selected to form an elite unit to be deployed in Vietnam. You will undergo extensive physical and mental training. You will be prepared for your mission. The Vietnamese, having to combat struggles for decades with the French and Japanese, have devised extensive tunnel systems.

"GIs have been ordered or volunteered to enter tunnels. They are not specifically trained for that mission. Loss of life is extensive. Entry to the tunnel is generally a long narrow shaft, usually booby-trapped. If you enter a tunnel, and can avoid a trap, you will proceed down the shaft headfirst. If for some reason, they become aware of you, they'll kill you in the shaft. If you can enter the tunnel, you will eliminate the enemy at close range or be eliminated."

The room was silent. I was thinking, *This fuck is preaching doom and gloom.*

He broke the silence with, "If any of you feel you are not up to the mission for any reason, you are free to decline this unit and be reassigned to the division. There will be no mention of this assignment in your records. The mission we have accepted is the most dangerous mission in the army. Those of you who feel this is not for you, please stand."

About a dozen guys stood up. The major asked the first sergeant to escort the troops out of the room and draw the paperwork for their transfer to division. The major told us their goal during training will be to wash GIs out. "The unit will be twenty-strong. As I mentioned earlier, once you enter the tunnel, you will encounter the enemy and eliminate him at close range, more often than not by holding him and slicing his throat. Not everyone has the capacity to do that and live with it. Based on a self-analysis of your endurance to withstand very harsh training, and what I just told you, if you feel you do not want to be in this unit, stand."

Five stood up. The major asked them to join the others. He went on. "Gentlemen, you have been assigned to Zebra Company, United States Army Special Forces, the elite fighting force of the world. When you have finished training, you will be reassigned to the Twenty-Fifth Special Operations Unit. Once in the Twenty-Fifth you will be designated 'Tunnel Rats.' History will tell of the great significance, dedication, and sacrifice of the Tunnel Rats.

"When I dismiss you, you will form up in front of the building. Buses will take you to your barracks. The barracks are secluded, as are the ranges. You will have no contact with anyone outside of Zebra Company. No TVs, no radios, no phones. The only thing you will have is training. You will train sixteen hours a day. You will attend classes. The balance of the time will be for chow and sleep. The training will be seven days a week. Dismissed."

We went downstairs and stood in a line. In the middle of the street were six soldiers: three sergeants and three corporals. One of the sergeants hollered out, "Attention, face forward." These guys were all decked out, and sure as fuck looked like badasses; not anyone you would want to mess with. The sergeant spoke to us in a very authoritative voice. He told us we would be divided into three platoons: Alpha, Bravo and Charlie.

"We are your platoon leaders; we will also be your DI. When I call your name, I will inform you of the platoon you're in, and you will board the bus."

When we got to the barracks the sergeant told us if we needed to use the latrine, "Do it now. We will form up in front to get your bedding and gear, and then chow. You will be able to get squared away after chow." The food was good, a lot better than what we had been getting. Back in the barracks the Sergeant told us to get squared away and then relax. "The smoking lamp is lit. Reveille is 0500 hours. The company will do a five-mile slow run before chow."

Our training was intense and accelerated. They needed us in combat. The focus of our physical training was on endurance and leg-and-arm strength. I'm sure they felt they would be able to wash out some guys and bring the unit to twenty men. We went from one training exercise to another – no breaks, no rest. On one range, we had to climb a fifty-foot tower, and come off it by rope. We were told once we had it down, we would be dropping out of choppers and dealing with the chopper turbulence. After that range, we'd run to a gym, engage in hand-to-hand combat, then we'd run to a firing range.

That's the way it was, day in and day out. We never marched, we never walked – we ran everywhere. The two-hour class we were told about came after the evening chow. They were teaching us Vietnamese. After the second week, all that would be spoken while we were in training was Vietnamese.

During the second week, we were in a room where they were teaching us how to eliminate the enemy at close range. I was listening for about ten minutes, then I turned it off. The speaker had read a manual someone wrote and was repeating the words to us. It was not going to work.

Suddenly, the first sergeant hollered out my name, and wanted me in his office. He sat at his desk, I stood in front. He told me he was watching me during the class. He got the strong impression I was squeamish and couldn't kill at close range. I told him I was not squeamish. (I didn't know what it meant. Didn't matter.)

"I have no problem killing at close range. What Sargent was reading I felt was wrong. We were issued a bayonet. We should have been issued a knife that we can wear strapped to a leg, in our boot. A knife, razor-sharp on one side, serrated on the other. A bayonet is not going to slice the enemy's throat. Its purpose is to plunge.

"He told us how to hold the enemy and shoot him in the head. We were issued a forty-five. Anyone who shoots a forty-five in a tunnel will never hear again. Having a forty-five is good, but we should have been issued a twenty-two with a short silencer for the tunnels.

"How about killing at close range?"

I told him I needed his word, that what I was about tell him stayed just between us, never told to anyone. He gave it to me.

"My heritage on my mother's side is Italian. When I was a kid, I went to work for a pizzeria and found out it was the home of the largest Mafia family in the country. I worked for them for many years. When I got older, I had to eliminate people. Sarge, I need to hold you to your word."

He stood up, told me to follow him. We went back to class; I took my seat. He spoke to the sergeant. Next, we heard, "You are dismissed. The class will be redone in a few days."

One night before taps our platoon sergeant told us that tomorrow at 0500 we will move through a jungle to a range that was the largest on the reservation. We would spend four days and three nights in the jungle. "Pack your gear and get some rest. You're going to need it."

The three platoons moved through a jungle. No paths, slow moving mostly because of the bulging backpacks we were carrying. Branches would snap back, cutting our neck and face. Stabbing thorns. My body was a pincushion. Every bug in the world was crawling on me, and some had sharp teeth. We finally got through the jungle to a clearing beside what looked like a good-size lake. We were told to take off our backpacks and sit on them. If anyone needed to piss, do it in the jungle. A range corporal handed out cans of C rations. We were told, "Smoking lamp is lit, take your time. Do not litter. Your trash will be picked up. Do not leave your position."

The rations weren't bad. The only problem was the C rations they had were all the same. Breakfast, lunch, and dinner. I'm not sure what they meant about taking our time. Before we knew it, a DI told us to stand behind our packs, leave about four feet between us.

"In front of you is Kalona Reservoir. Your mission will be to cross the reservoir with your gear, then climb the mountain and transverse to the shore on the other side. Remove your poncho from the pack. Spread it out on the ground. Put your pack in the center of the poncho. Remove your boots and socks, pack them tight against the pack. Remove your blouse and pants and fold them on top of your pack."

They then told us how to close everything with the poncho, making it watertight. We were told to wear our pots, hold our weapons on top of the poncho, and float it across. It was easy. I don't know what anyone else thought, but for me the water felt great.

When we got to the other side we were told to unpack the poncho, get dressed, roll the poncho and strap it back on the pack, and get ready for the next phase. You would think after crossing the reservoir we'd be soaking wet. The minute we stepped onshore we were dried off by the intense heat from the sun.

They formed us up at the foot of the mountain. It wasn't steep or rocky; it was a reddish-coppery fine lava and dirt. We had to get a foothold, grab a shrub, and work ourselves up. It sounded easy, but it took forever…it was still a mountain.

At the top, were heavy wooden beams anchored with a steel cable that ran across the reservoir to the shore on the other side. They instructed us on how to use a slingshot piece of wood with rawhide loops on each leg to go down the cable. We were told to secure our weapon on our shoulders, with our head through the sling. Place the slingshot over the cable, put the loops around each wrist, and hold on to each leg.

The ride down was fun. They didn't tell us at the bottom we had to get out of the loops and let go before we slammed into the beam. We were instructed to put our pack and weapon on the ground and sit on large palm trunks arranged in rows. They passed out C rations again. It was early afternoon; time went by quickly.

After chow and another good cigarette, we were formed up at the foot of another mountain like the other one. I wondered how these guys came up with these fuckin' mountains. Then I realized this must have been a volcano at one time, with the reservoir, the crater, and these mountains the rim.

We worked our way up the mountain to a level area with bleachers. When everyone was seated, a DI began instructing us in rappelling. When he was finished, we set ourselves at the top, and in two bounces, went down the sheer lava wall. We formed up and were waiting for everyone to catch up before moving on.

I realized why early on the focus was on endurance, leg, arm, and upper body strength. Every fuckin' muscle in my body was sore. I was hoping that was it for the day.

When everyone was in formation, our platoon sergeants told us we would be moving through the jungle to a clearing to set up a base camp. When we got there, he paired us. We were to dig a foxhole. He told us when we finished digging, to set our bayonets on either end of the wide side, secure a poncho to the top, and slope it to the ground. It would be a cover from the rain.

We dug the hole, set the poncho, got in, and collapsed. After a while we started talking. The guy's name was Mickey. His family had a farm in Illinois. He talked about his life on the farm, his girlfriend, his family. He was really fuckin' homesick. I told him about growing up in the Bronx, not going into any detail. I told him, "It sounds like you've had a great life. When I get out of this shit, back home, and retire, I'd like to become a farmer." I told him I was going to slide out of the hole and take a piss. While I was pissing, it started raining. I cut it short and hustled back to the hole. Mickey was asleep.

No matter what I tried, I couldn't get to sleep. I lit a cigarette and sat watching the rain. I don't know how long I sat there. The poncho started pressing on my head. I couldn't get away from it. I kicked Mickey and told him I needed help. He could see the poncho pushing down on me. He took his weapon, butt first, and shoved it into the sag. We could hear the water gushing out the back of the poncho. When we had set up the hole, we forgot to tuck the hood in, and it had filled with water. We both went to sleep.

The next morning, we were seated on the palm logs listening to surviving in the jungle. What to eat and what not to eat. How to trap and butcher. How to acquire coconuts and shuck them. How to purify drinking water. How to gather rainwater. Then we were told one of the more abundant food sources in Nam is not available here. Decades ago ships brought rats to Hawaii. Snakes with an abundant food source flourished. To minimize the snake population, they introduced the mongoose to the island. Today there are no snakes in Hawaii.

The DI reached in a burlap sack and took out a snake, another DI held its body. He told us this guy is from Nam, we will come across many of them. They described poisonous and non-poisonous, and showed us how to butcher and fillet.

Next a DI stood in front of us and told us if we were in combat, we would be dead. As he said that, six weapons came out of the jungle, pointed at us. He gave an order to lower weapons and step forward. If we didn't know better, we'd think it was still jungle. He told us this was the latest in jungle-warfare camouflage and would be issued to us in Nam as needed.

In the next session, a DI told us if we did not have the right mind-set and wherewithal, we would not make it in Nam. "They have been fighting for decades and have developed a full arsenal of booby traps and mines. In country, tunnel entrances and shafts are booby-trapped. We will teach you how to identify a booby-trap. We will teach you how to locate a mine and disarm it. You will need to pay close attention to this session – it means life or death."

Afterward the platoons went on a seek-and-destroy mission. A point man was designated, and the platoon sergeant and DI accompanied each platoon. Every man was killed. They made their point. Back at camp we settled in, and it started raining. An order came down to leave our weapon, pot, and any gear we were carrying in the hole. After emptying our pockets into our pot, we formed up.

We went back to the palm-log area. We were instructed to group in fours, lift a log over our heads, and run through the mud to a grassy area two hundred feet away. The logs were heavy.

Holding a log above our heads and running was a strain. Some guys bailed out. Special Forces accomplished what it wanted. We were now a twenty-man unit.

Back at camp we spent the night in our holes, wet. At reveille, our sergeant formed us up, and asked if anyone was not chafed. No one answered. He told us, "Crotch rot and foot rot are major distractions – you will avoid it."

After chow each platoon went on a seek-and-destroy mission in designated areas in the jungle. We moved through the jungle for a while then got caught in an ambush. We heard "Surrender!" in Vietnamese. About ten guys dressed in Vietnamese uniforms, looking very much the part, took our weapons and began pushing and shoving. We were herded through the jungle to a POW compound that looked very real.

When the other platoons arrived, we were ordered to get on our knees, with our hands on our heads, in a row in front of a platform. On both ends of the compound they had two guys with their legs and arms tied around poles. They were naked, bleeding, extremely sunburned. They looked like shit. Whoever the training unit had doing makeup was good.

A Vietnamese officer got on the platform, started ranting in Vietnamese, and ordered two guards to shoot the animals on the poles. They did, then walked behind us. They pulled the pot off two guys, grabbed them by the hair, and began yelling. They put their weapons against their heads. All we could hear were two clicks.

With that a DI got up on the platform. He told us that was a small part of what to expect as a POW. "No matter what is done, the only thing you are to reveal is name, rank and serial number. Anything else could mean the loss of lives. When you are dismissed, you will proceed to the open hut behind you and be seated. You will be taught all aspects of POW internment."

Next, we went to chow. Everyone looked forward to it, not so much for the food as for the half-hour break – we needed it. They marched us off to a range, and we were seated on bleachers. In front of us was a large area of grass about a foot high. On one side was a dirt ridge with visible tunnel holes, then the same ridge without visible holes, and a hill with no visible tunnels. A DI was telling us the range had been designed to incorporate every tunnel they knew about in Nam. We would be taught how to negotiate the tunnel, inspect it, disarm if needed, and exit. We would be taught how to destroy the tunnel if ordered to. All of it would be repeated over and over till we had it down pat.

On a signal, the grass stood up in four places. The DI told us this would be the second camouflage suit we would be issued. "Under certain circumstances you will use the suit to approach the tunnel shaft without being a target in the open field."

A platoon was assigned the tunnels in the ridge and hill, the other two were assigned the vertical shaft tunnels scattered throughout the field. The horizontal shafts were narrow till they opened into the tunnels. The vertical shafts required arm and leg strength to enter and exit. Doing several tunnels with different configurations took its toll on our bodies. The rest of the day was spent at the tunnel range.

There was, as was at most of the exercises, a small group of officers and a couple of sergeant majors viewing what was going on. I assumed they were critiquing our progress and the training. It appeared we were a top priority to the army. At camp, we were told that in the morning after reveille and chow, we would break camp, fill in our holes, and be transported to the barracks.

Something was missing: our rifles. We were told all along our weapon was our best friend. We had to clean and maintain it, never be without it. We figured the army knew what they were doing. Nobody questioned it. At the barracks the sergeant told us we had two hours to get cleaned up and squared away, and then to form up in front.  At formation, he told us we would be going to the warehouse and be issued new gear; then we would return to the barracks. The balance of the day was free. He suggested we get some rest.

At the warehouse, we were issued a brand new M16 rifle replacing our Ml, a new carbine, a forty-five, a twenty-two with a silencer, and a knife with a serrated edge and a razor edge. They also issued two specially designed ammo belts with clips and live rounds, and a duffle bag to hold it all. When we got back to our barracks, I doubt anyone did anything but go to sleep.

Reveille came around quickly at 0500. We went through the exercise routine for an hour, chow, then off to a firing range. The day was spent at different ranges. After night chow, we resumed our two-hour Vietnamese class. The day wasn't bad after what we had been through. The rest of the week was made up of classes and exercise.

On Friday night, we were waiting for the Vietnamese instructor. The door opened. A Colonel, Major, Sergeant Major, and Staff Sergeant walked in. The sergeant hollered out, "Attention" as soon as he hit the door.

We stood, and the Colonel said, "As you were." He introduced himself and his staff and told us we have completed our training course. "You are now corporals in the Special Forces." The sergeant passed out berets with Special Forces insignias. "The beret is to be worn with dress uniform only, and to be worn proudly. You will be moving on to the mission you have been trained for. There is no doubt in our minds that you will make a significant impact on this war. May God be with you and come home to us."

The Major told us at 0800 Monday we would be boarding a transport at Hickam for Nam. The unit would then be assigned back to the division. We were to form up tomorrow morning in our dress uniforms. "After chow, you will board a bus that will take you on a tour of the island. For lunch, you will be treated to a traditional Hawaiian luau. After, you will return to the barracks, and be free till formation Monday. If you have them, you can wear civilian clothes on your free time."

The Sergeant Major began telling us how to handle our gear, what we needed to turn in, what we needed to take, and what we needed to leave. "You will put what gear you are leaving in your footlocker. You will be given a stencil with your serial number that you will paint on your locker. When you are done, you will lock it. The footlocker will be stored in the warehouse. You are dismissed."

I got back to the barracks and felt I had a lot of time to get it done. For now, I just wanted my bunk. I was lying there thinking the training we just went through was good. I was glad it was all over and I could move on. Get the next shit done and go home. I was tired of the fuckin' army. The tour was good. Hawaii was beautiful. The luau was neat. The food was out-of-this-world.

Back at the barracks the platoon decided we'd go to the post beer garden. Everyone was in civvies. We were seated at a table joking around, talking about the training, and drinking 2% Corona beer from Mexico. We had enough of that crap and decided to take the bus to Honolulu. We hit a couple of bars and were all feeling good. The next bar we went to was crowded, packed with sailors in their whites. We were in our civvies and stood out. Someone made the comment to a sailor, "Yankee, go home." A punch was thrown. Before it got to an all-out brawl, we got out of there.

We wandered around Honolulu for a while, then made our way to Waikiki. We hit a bar that wasn't crowded and sat at the bar. My buddy Mickey was sitting beside me. A local came over and asked if we wanted a joint. Mickey told him yes, and we'd go outside and share it. Here I was standing next to this huge fuckin' tree in the middle of the international market place sharing a joint.

When we got back to the bar, I was feeling no pain. I noticed there were five local girls sitting at a table laughing and having fun. I caught the eye of the one closest to us. I thought she was beautiful. How great it would be to get some and go to Nam with a smile on my face. I was planning it out, getting excited. I turned to Mickey and asked if he wanted to go over and pick up a couple of them. I wanted the beautiful one on the end. He told me no, and neither should I. They're not girls.

"No fuckin' way. That one's beautiful."

"I'll bet you $5.00 they're not girls." I told him he was on.

I walked over to the table, said, "Hi."

She came back with a very sexy, "Hi."

Hearing that, and as horny as I was, I almost came in my pants. I told her I needed her to win a $5 bet for me. "I bet you were a beautiful girl. He bet you weren't a girl."

She looked at me for a little bit, then said, "You lose."

I sat back down at the bar and said out loud, "This is fuckin' bullshit."

The whole platoon was at the bar. We were all drunk. I got everyone together and suggested we go back to Honolulu and find a tattoo place. We weren't allowed to have tattoos in the army. What the fuck were they going to do to us in Nam? We drunkenly staggered through the streets but couldn't find a place even though there had to be twenty of them because of the navy. We went back to the barracks.

I spent Sunday getting over a hangover. Almost everybody else went to church services. Monday came, and we boarded the bus for a long ride to Hickam. When we passed through the front gate, it seemed almost as long a ride to get to our plane – the place was huge. Standing on a tarmac alongside the plane, and looking up at it, I wondered how something this fuckin' big and heavy could get off the ground let alone fly.

"The flight is nineteen hours. Midway, we will refuel, giving you a chance to stretch your legs, use the latrine, and eat on land. If anyone needs to use the latrine now, there's one in the hangar. You will board the plane in twenty minutes." I didn't need to use the john, so I leaned up against a building and had a couple of cigarettes.

In the plane, we sat in cargo nets on either side. Stretching from where we were to the back was a row of large shipping containers. Our gear had to be in one. Urinals were distributed – there was no head on the plane – along with earplugs.

The plane began to move slowly, came to a stop, then the jets started to scream. Even with the earplugs the noise was hard to take. The plane moved faster and built up speed. We heard the clunk as it lifted off. As the plane moved out of Hickam airspace and began a low trajectory climb, it became very comfortable, and then it got cold. An officer came out of the cockpit, to explain there was no climate control in this cargo bay. Heaters would be turned on and off, so we would be somewhat comfortable.

After that, the flight was uneventful. Everyone fell asleep. I was awakened by a thud. Engines screamed; then we were moving on the ground. We debarked to see a large airstrip with several military craft parked: jets, choppers, and everything else. The odd thing about this place was there was nothing on the buildings or freestanding signs to tell us where we were. We chowed down in a mess hall that was not army – the food was too good. Back on the plane, we settled in for the rest of the flight.

# *CHAPTER 48*

We landed in Saigon, debarked, and boarded a bus; the side glass windows had been replaced with steel sheets painted army green. The ride took a half hour. We arrived at an army base. A GI standing at an open door motioned us into a room that had rows of chairs and a large chalkboard across the front. On the board were six names. Mine was one of them.

An officer introduced himself and welcomed us to Alpha staging in Vietnam. "Our mission is to receive equipment, logistics, and troops that are flown in then coordinate the distribution.

For those of you who care, it is now 0400 the morning you left Hawaii. You passed through seven time zones. From here you will be transported to your commands for field assignments. The six of you that are on the board are to exit the building and be transported to Long Binh, one hour north, for assignment."

As I walked past Mickey, I shook his hand and told him to be careful. We'd hook up when this was over. The six of us boarded a deuce-and-a-half. They had loaded our gear on the front. This was the first time I felt the army was efficient. A sergeant got in alongside the driver, and we were off. The countryside was lush and beautiful. We passed a village. People walking on the road waved to us. Everything seemed peaceful.

After forty minutes of bouncing our asses around in the truck, we came upon hell. The land was scorched black; equipment in the field was burnt-out hulks of scrap. We were passing a war zone. At Long Binh. It looked as though they were feverishly building a base. Of the concrete buildings the largest looked like command and operations, the other barracks. Most of the base was field tents. We drove past them, turned down a street then drove behind the line of buildings to a single-story concrete building that looked like a motel.

The sergeant told us to off-load with our gear. "These are your quarters. Each unit is set up for two troops. The units are marked on the front. You will occupy Alpha, Bravo and Charlie. You will square away your weapons. You will use the duffle for the rest of the gear you will get from the quartermaster. Dismissed."

I made a dash for B unit. I had to piss. When I came out of the john, standing in the middle of the room was this Black guy. In a, nervous uncertain voice, he said, "My name is Duwayne Hawkins. Do you have a problem?" I knew what he meant and didn't have a problem.

"Duwayne is your problem, not mine. My name is Paul Walker. Grab a bunk." This place didn't seem to be army. Our bunks were already made, and the head had a shower, toilet, sink, and a door. A door!

We got our gear and went back to our quarters. We had been told we had two hours to get squared away, relax, and then chow. After chow, we'd go through orientation and a briefing.

Hawkins and I had a chance to talk. He was from Chicago. He had gotten into some trouble, and a judge gave him a choice: jail or army. I didn't get into much about myself except I was from the Bronx.

The mess hall was new, had good food – hard to ask for more in the army. At the Command Center we were shown to a briefing room. An older, very fit troop in fatigues, no stripes, no bars, was standing behind the podium. "I am Colonel James Bolton. Standing behind you are Sergeant Major Carter, First Sergeant

Baker, Staff Sergeants Jones, Carrera and Brown. We are Special Forces. My orders are to have in place a long-range Special Operations Company. You are the initial troops. Twenty-four more troops with different missions will fill out the company. We are attached to the Twenty-Fifth. The company's declaration came from the Twenty-Fifth Command.

"You will be in constant radio communications. We have developed a new radio, small and light. The operator will have ear and mouthpiece. The radio is equipped with a tracking beacon to be used only in an emergency. If the radio is down, the beacon will still work. You will be physically located. You will operate in pairs. You have already paired yourselves.

"When I dismiss you, you will join a sergeant in his office for an extensive, detailed briefing on your mission. The sergeant conducting the briefing will be your contact at Command. After the briefing, you are free till 0400 when you will begin your mission. You are dismissed."

A sergeant hollered out, "Hawkins, Walker." We followed him to his office. He had cleared off his desk except for two small pads of paper and two pens in front of us, a file in front of him. An easel and board were behind him. He told us his name and that the briefing would be three hours. If we needed the latrine or water, it was in the hallway. Smoking lamp was lit.

"I have a team of techs manning the radio 24/7. They will plot your location continuously. The call sign here is Bravo. If you need to talk to me, you use Big Bravo. Your call sign will be Hawk Walk." He handed us a laminated map, about eight by twelve, with coordinates covering the map. He put a larger version on the easel. "The map is the area of your mission. It is 80 klicks wide by 90 klicks long. A klick is short for a kilometer. One kilometer is equal to 0.62 miles.

"The red dot at 74632 is your base camp; the green dot at 74187 is the LZ. LZ means landing zone. The line zigzagging from top to bottom, right center, is the trail."    I asked for a break. I needed to use the head. Hawkins followed me. When we returned, I lit a cigarette and was ready for more. Hawkins was taking notes. I figured if he was doing it, I wouldn't. We didn't need two of it.

The sergeant continued: "At 0400 two choppers will leave. They will take a roundabout route to the LZ. The chopper's crews will help haul the gear to your base camp. It's situated in a jungle area. Our military has reconnoitered the area and found no mines. This was understandable because of the isolation." He continued for two hours and two breaks. When he finished, the three of us went to chow. The mess hall was empty. We went through the line and sat at a table. Brown told us mess was open twelve hours straight. We could chow at any time. Regular troop mess was located elsewhere.

We sat eating and mulling over everything. Brown told us the sector we've been assigned is the most active and dangerous of the three sectors. The trail is heavily used; everything travels south. The tunnels are used for storage and camping. Nothing is visible during daylight hours, everything is done in darkness.

We went back to our quarters to pack what we were told to. We had four duffle bags, bulging at the seams. I decided to put on the fatigues they issued us and put mine in the locker. The blouse was lighter, and ventilated, with no name tag or army tag. There was nothing on it. The pants were also lighter, and ventilated, with pockets running down both legs. The boots had soles twice as thick as normal, with a padded leather half-cup to protect the heel, and another for our toes, while the rest of the boot was a mesh.

We got dressed, took a walk, then went back to the quarters. We agreed it was all good. The boots would take getting used to but not a problem. We lay on our bunks talking, I was smoking. What I was doing is considered taboo and punishable in the army. Hawkins suggested we refer to each other by the call names rather than our full name. It was OK with me. I was getting antsy and suggested we look the base over, go to the club Brown told us about, and use Bolton's tab.

The base was big. We passed two rows of field tents with red crosses painted on the top. Farther down we came upon a parade field. Troops were marching to cadence. In another section troops were doing exercises. We kept walking, found more field tents, turned around and went to the club.

No one was in the place except a bartender standing behind the bar. We sat at the bar. I asked if he had Bud. He asked can or bottle. I answered bottle. Hawk asked if he had Miller. He said only in cans. After bringing us beer, he started the conversation. He had been in the army eight years and was going for twenty. This was his third assignment; all he did was work clubs. I told him we just arrived. We wanted to do our tour and get back home. He asked where home was. Hawk answered Chicago and I the Bronx.

"No shit. I'm from the Bronx. My name is Frankie, you?"

I told him Pauly. He looked Italian. We talked about different places and things we did, and high school. We both went to DeWitt Clinton, the all-boys, fucked-up school.

Out of the blue he asked if I ever ran across the Family.

"What family?"

"The Bronx Mafia Family. They're huge. I've heard they're the largest Family in the country."

I said no, I never came across them. He told me his father worked for them as a laborer, pouring concrete on Manhattan's eastside. That ended our conversation. The bar started getting busy. I commented to Hawk it was a small world we lived in and ordered another round. We were talking and kicking back, not thinking what was ahead of us.

A big guy walked up behind Hawk and growled, "You're in my seat, boy. Get up."

I said, "I don't think I heard you right. What was that?"

He came back with, "I wasn't talking to you. I don't talk to fags. I was talking to this here boy."

I told him we didn't want any trouble. "How about I buy you a beer, and we'll leave."

It caught him off guard. I reached for the neck of my bottle, told Hawk to duck, came across him, and caught the guy in the face. I broke his nose. He went down on his knees, clutching his nose with both hands, blood pouring out of them. Hawk got up and walked around him.

I walked straight at the guy. "Boy? Fag? Fuck you, prick!" I hit him in the balls with the sole of my boot. He curled into a fetal position, screaming. Frankie was standing at the bar. He heard and saw everything. I looked at him.

Frankie said, "Get outta here," he'd cover for me.

On the way back to our quarters Hawk asked if it was true I never heard of the Family. I didn't say anything. We were lying on our bunks. We had three hours to get some sleep. I told Hawk, "Don't let what happened bother you. There's a lot of stupid shits in this world. If he has any kind of brains, he learned a lesson."

Hawk snickered, "He may be skipping to a new beat after what happened at the end."

We fell asleep. It seemed I just closed my eyes, and I was getting pushed, "Up, up. The mess has a pot of coffee on for you. Get some. It's going to be a long day." After two cups of good coffee and a cigarette, we went back to our quarters, shouldered our duffle bags, and went out to two waiting jeeps.

In about fifteen minutes, the jeeps came alongside two choppers. As soon as we pulled up, three GIs jumped out of the second chopper, loaded in our gear, and got back in. Two GIs were with us in the first chopper. They passed out earplugs. The motor started, the chopper lifted off the ground, dipped forward, and up it went. Once we cleared the base it was total darkness. I don't know what happened to the moon. Hour and a half later we landed at the LZ with a major thud.

Everyone off-loaded. The crew of the second chopper was forming a line shouldering the duffle bags. The first troop shouldered one bag, behind him the troops shouldered two bags. When it was our turn, they handed down one bag each, and motioned us to move on. The two pilots drew one bag each, and the rest of the crew two bags each.

Our base was five klicks east on the same latitude as the LZ. Five klicks didn't seem like a lot, but through the jungle it was slow and torturous. No machetes. It was side-stepping, moving vines and vegetation aside. I don't know how long we had walked when the point man raised a fist. He put his bag down, walked over to an outgrowth of vegetation, and moved it aside. There was a rock formation with a two-foot wide opening. He got his bag, went for the opening, and motioned the guys behind him to follow. The bags were moved down the line into the opening. When the bags were in, Hawk and I walked to the opening. Three troops were coming out. The point man stopped. The other two joined the line.

"This is home. One suggestion: when you get squared away, use three or four of those bags under the sleeping bags. We're out of here." The line moved the same way they came, except two guys in the rear were eliminating any sign anyone had been there.

Hawk and I walked in. The cave was big, not high but deep, giving us a lot of room. I told Hawk to get the radio out of his backpack and call in. He stood by the opening, saying, "Bravo, this is Hawk Walk." Through his earpiece, they acknowledged the call. "The hawk has landed." They told him to check in after squaring away. It took two hours to get it the way we wanted. We decided to break out some rations and water, and kick back before checking in.

Picking up the radio I said, "This is Hawk Walk checking in." I was told to proceed to 76518. There are six hatches running north and south. I showed Hawk where we had to go, a little more than 15 klicks through jungle. 76518 was in a clearing close to the trail.

We geared up, put our camouflage suits on, and headed out. Moving through the jungle was easy but slow; we didn't encounter any major obstacles. Three hours later we were at the clearing. I broke out the binoculars and located the shafts easily – bamboo hatches about half a football field apart. Handing Hawk the binoculars, I told him I was taking the first three, and he needed to set his radio on our frequency. I took off my suit and draped it over my weapon alongside Hawk. My head and hands were covered in camo paint.

I started a belly-crawl across the field. I reached the hatch, opened it slightly, and slid in headfirst. I wasn't concerned about the hatch being trapped. The ground around it looked well worn. Moving down the shaft just as they taught us, I came to the tunnel. About twenty feet in was a single lightbulb. Five VC were sleeping on bamboo mats on the ground. I walked around them, popped the one furthest in, leaned over, and the one next to him. No movement, not a sound. So, I stepped over them and standing above the remaining three. I popped them. I went back to the shaft, changed my clip, and went up and out.

The second shaft was the same as the first. When I got to the tunnel, the same lightbulb. There were six VC on mats, the closest one to me was a woman. I always had a problem doing a woman – I wasn't the only one. In training, they showed us a clip of three GIs with their weapons shouldered approaching a VC woman. From under her black skirt she took out an AK47. From the hip, she blew them away.

I went about the task at hand. When I got to the woman, I needed a new clip. The sound of the clip seated in the weapon woke her. She sat up. I put one in her face, a second in her throat. She fell back. I put a third in the side of her head.

The third was different. I could see the first two guys sitting playing cards with six behind them sleeping. I made my way behind one of the cardplayers and slit his throat. The other guy was in shock. I leaned over and slit his throat then plunged my knife in their hearts. The sleeping six were easy.

I made my way back to Hawk, shouldered my M16 barrel down, put on my suit, and motioned him to follow me. We walked along the jungle till we were midway between the three shafts. Stepping into the jungle, I filled Hawk in, and told him if these were the same, he won't have a problem. He took his suit off, and his weapon, turned to me, brought a clenched fist to his heart. I did the same. He was off.

I had lumbered across the field. Hawk was like a snake. With a blink of an eye he was at the hatch, and down. After a bit,

I started worrying, and hoping he was OK. If he wasn't, he'd sure as fuck get me on – . Before I could finish the thought, the hatch opened, and he was going for the next, then the next. In a short time, he came across the field right at me.

We stepped back into the jungle. Hawk changed the frequency on the radio and called in. I heard him say, "Thirty-eight VC down. Destroy?" The response was, "Negative, proceed to base." We found our way back to camp. It took us a lot longer getting there than we expected. As we walked into the cave, it was dusk. After we stowed our gear and cleaned our weapons, I went to the back of the cave and smoked a cig.

Hawk dug out chow and filled our canteens. He was sitting on his sleeping bag with a black pouch and canteen in front of him. He had put a similar pouch and my canteen on my bag.

I sat down. Hawk clenched his fingers, bent over the pouch, and said a prayer. I told him to say it for both of us – it wasn't my thing. Either the army ran out of WWII C rations or we were something special. The food was good. I'm not sure what the meat was. Aside from that, no complaints.

I mentioned to Hawk we ought to check in. I did and was told to proceed to a coordinate at first light. There were six hatches half-mooning a large hatch in the center, engage as you see fit. I was told to hold for Big Bravo. Brown asked how the day went, were there any problems?

"No problems. The crew that made the delivery was outstanding. The job was a cakewalk. We had good training. I don't know if the VC were out of it, on something, or just exhausted. We had no resistance. One thing we need are larger clips. Ten rounds aren't good enough."

He came back with, "10-4. Get some rest. Tomorrow's another big day. Out."

Hawk and I set a camouflaged aluminum mesh over the opening. We were told it would keep out everything except for mosquitoes. This place was overridden with the bastards. We were issued a salve to keep them off, and the sleeping bags had a mosquito netting hood. We went to the back of the cave to look over the map. The coordinate was about fifteen klicks northeast, all jungle, and east of the trail. It looked like a strip of the jungle had been cleared. The VC didn't bother to camouflage the hatches, so air recon picked them up easily.

We were wondering if the shafts were for easy access and ventilation for one long tunnel, and why the larger hatch? We decided how we were going to handle it and determined the six first, each of us taking one on each end. If it was one tunnel we'd meet in the center. If there were individuals, we would each take three. While we were mulling it over, the radio went off.

"Hawk Walk, this is Bravo. Hawk Walk, this is Bravo. Come in" Hawk answered and was told to proceed to the LZ for a drop at 0100 hours We put our suits on, shouldered our weapons, and headed for the LZ. We were early and stood in the jungle waiting.

It wasn't long before we could hear the chopper. Then there was a spotlight and a rope with a netted bag hanging over the LZ. We took the bag off the rope and yanked on it. As fast as the rope had come down, it went up, and the chopper was gone. We carried the bag into the jungle. Through the netting we could see what was in it: a bunch of different-sized magazines, a small case of ammo, two new weapons, and two large magazines.

The new weapon accepted the magazine in a slot midway instead of in the grip. We pocketed all the mags and opened the big magazines. One had cigars in it, and one had cherry licorice. During our briefing, we had a break, and Brown asked what we missed most from home, not meaning friends, family or pets. I answered a Cuban cigar, and Hawk said he was addicted to red licorice. I shouldered the bag with the ammo. Hawk carried the two weapons and magazines. We made our way to camp.

We settled in. I looked over the new .22. It was lighter and had a grip in front of the clip slot. The grip was good thinking. It would enable us to steady the weapon for a long shot. Then I noticed the grip folded down. We could use this fucker like a machine gun! We began loading the mags. For the most part, they were thirty rounds and there were some fifty rounds.

I got on the radio, made contact. I told him to tell Big he's a good man. Hawk and I agreed that tonight we'd both catch ZZZ's instead of the four on, four off. Today had been a long one. We probably should have sacked out but were too riled up to sleep. I broke out a Cuban, Hawk started munching licorice.

Sunup broke. We were geared up in our suits, moving through the jungle. It became a long, hard trek. We had to zigzag to move around obstacles. In some instances, backtrack and take a different route. We finally reached the trail, crossed it, located the strip, and took a break in the jungle.

Once we got our wind back, we headed for the shaft hatches. When I got into the tunnel, I realized we were right. One long tunnel with a string as far as I could see of these shits sleeping on their fuckin' mats. I didn't know if they were sleeping off something, but they sure as fuck were out of it. I started with the first one, then one after another. Some moved and got it. A couple sat up and seemed to be in a daze. I reached over and slit their throats. The whole thing was like shooting clay pigeons in an arcade.

At one point, I turned my back on them, buried the weapon in my gut, to load a fifty-round mag. I turned and kept going. I was like a robot, doing the deed without thought or care. After a while I could see Hawk coming towards me. We met up, I asked if he got a count. He said no. We went back to where we began and counted. When we met up again, we totaled eighty VC killed.

We went up the shaft and headed for the big hatch. We opened it. Instead of a shaft, it had rock steps leading down to the tunnel. When we reached the tunnel, I motioned Hawk to wait, while I went in. To my right were cases of weapons and ammo from the ground to the ceiling. Looked like it was going far in. To my left there were five VC sleeping, and five were playing cards further in under a light. Beyond them a bamboo enclosure.

I gave Hawk a hand signal to follow me. We did the five sleeping. I motioned Hawk to move down one side of the tunnel, I took the other. They never saw us. I slit the first one's throat and put a twenty-two in the second. Hawk hit the three with the twenty-two. I motioned Hawk to stay. I opened the enclosure door, saw a bed with a naked guy on his back and a woman beside him on her side. Seeing the woman, and as horny as I was, I thought I'd pop the guy and fuck the woman. Then I realized that was my dick thinking, not me.

I moved to Hawk and told him what we had. I suggested we wake them, find out who he is, then contact Bravo for instructions. We did. I held them at gunpoint. The woman was crying. On the steps leading out Hawk checked in. We were ordered to eliminate them and destroy the ammunition tunnel only.

Out of our leg pocket we took the pouch that had the C4 and leads. I set mine as far as I could reach on the ammo. Hawk had his about six feet away against the wall. We set our leads and brought the wires as far into the jungle as we could. We were on our stomachs and detonated the C4. The ground imploded.

Then, as you would picture a volcano going off, dirt and rocks were flying, smoke and flames were shooting out of the ground. We could smell the phosphorus smoke, and the barrage of explosions seemed like it was never-ending. I gathered up the leads, threw them as far as I could. We suited up and got out of there. We were trying to re-step the way we came but fast. That thing was going to create a lot of attention. We wanted to be as far away as we could.

After about three klicks it started to rain, not a gentle rain. It was a fuckin' downpour. Even with the jungle canopy we were soaked. It was good because it covered our tracks, but it slowed us down. After about another klick we had had it and decided to sit down. I looked at Hawk. He looked like a clump of vegetation. Anyone following us would just walk on by. We were rested then continued to camp. When we got there, it was dark. Home never looked so good.

After stripping, we put out our wet clothes up to dry. We had been issued a shaker with a powder that went every place on our body that could be irritated or chafed. We cleaned and oiled our weapons, then I checked in. I was told to stay at home tomorrow and not to play in the street but keep an eye and ear open. We did the four-on, four-off all night.

The day gave us a chance to square away base and relax. It went by slowly. We stayed off the radio. When night came Big Bravo checked in. Intelligence informed them there was a company of VC searching south. The VC believed a large contingent of South Vietnamese and US Army moved north from the south and caused the problem.    "They have a reward out and a name, *ma guy*. It means ghost devil. You have a new name!" He signed off, told us to hold for the tech. The tech gave us 69176, two shafts could be boobed.

The map indicated 69176 was about twenty klicks southwest of base, all through jungle. Hawk and I knew we were going to need to keep an eye out for wires down there. Home was smart: they were keeping the VC's attention south of us. Before sunup we headed out. I don't know why but moving south was easier than east-west. Twenty klicks was a good trek. Midway we began to feel it and took a break. When we reached 69176, we found a small clearing with two visible hatches on either end. I motioned to Hawk I was going to take one, for him to wait.

I made it to the hatch, took out the bayonet from my left boot, and slowly began lifting the hatch. I could look into the shaft. Nothing. As I lifted a little more, a bamboo arm with bamboo daggers swung across the opening and into the dirt. I slid under the arm. Using my bayonet, I poked all the way down the shaft. When I reached the tunnel, there was no bulb. It was pitch-black except for the light from the shaft. I took out my flashlight. There was nothing in the tunnel.

I checked in and was told to use two mines. If the second was the same, mine it and depart. I dug two small holes in the ground, got a couple of mines out, pulled the pins, put them in the holes and covered them. The fuckers would do some major damage even though they were the size of a billiard ball. I got back to Hawk, told him everything, and he took off. It wasn't long before Hawk was back. On the way out, I was thinking this was a waste of time and energy, a letdown.

At check-in, we were told to stay at home. Staying at home was OK, but the day dragged by. I took the time to set a trap using the net bag from the last drop and a rainwater-gathering array. For the most part we just kicked back. The cave was comfortable in comparison to the fuckin' heat outside. Late afternoon I became curious and checked on my trap. I had caught a big snake.

The trap snapped shut just behind its head. It couldn't get out. From its color and marking, I could tell it wasn't venomous. We were told nonvenomous snake meat tastes better. I gutted and filleted the body on a fallen palm trunk, buried the waste, and took the meat into the cave.

In our gear was a can about the size of a twenty-five-gallon paint can, with a hinged door on the side. It was a grill. I opened the door. On top of the grate was a small can. I took it out and screwed it on the top of the big can. Through the grate, I could see a burner and a propane tank. To one side on the bottom was a metal container. I opened it poured a little on my finger and tasted it. We were going to have barbecued snake tonight!

I lit the grill, put on four pieces, coated each with sauce. While I watched it cook, I realized the small can I had screwed on the top was a smoke filter. Small bubbles appeared on the side of the meat. I cut a small bit off to sample it. The meat was cooked and tasted great. I shut down the grill and put the meat on the two open-rations containers. I carried one container to Hawk, kicked him on his sole, told him to wake up. "We're having chow." I got the other ration container and sat opposite him. He skeptically stared at it.

"What the fuck is this?"

"Try it, you'll like it."

He tried it, and he liked it. I told him it was snake.

Bravo checked in and gave us a new coordinate. "Four hatches. If the same as yesterday, do the same." We located it on our map, east of the two the other day. Another long-ass trek through the jungle. We were about a klick in when Hawk stopped. Over the radio, he whispered, "Walk…help." I looked toward him. A snake was hanging off a vine about head high. Hawk was frozen.

I took out my bayonet and knife. I slashed its head with the bayonet, which knocked it to ground, then I shoved my knife in its open mouth, pinning it to the ground. For good measure, I plunged the bayonet in it. I cleaned my knife and bayonet with a banana leaf, and we were off. I broke our normal radio silence and told Hawk I didn't know he was afraid of snakes.

"They scare the shit out of me, nightmares and all."

I told him, "This is a good place to overcome the fear, there're all over the place. When we get back, you can bury your drawers."

He came back with "ha, ha."

We were on the move. After about three klicks we stopped for a break, took a piss, sat down, drank some water, and rested. Before long we were up and moving. It wasn't the jungle that was getting to us as much as the heat and the gear we were carrying. After what seemed forever we reached our site, a strip cut out of the jungle, with the four hatches in a row. We decided each of us would take an end one. If it was one tunnel, we'd meet in the center.

Down the shaft the tunnel was black. I had my flashlight on and saw a flash light blink at me from the other end. We met in the center, set our mines back to the shafts we came in. We shouldered our weapons, suited up, and headed back to base.

After we squared our gear, I checked in with Bravo and was given a new coordinate with eight hatches. I told Bravo this seemed to be a waste of time.

"Negative. The tunnels are used by North Vietnamese regulars as base camps on their way south for offenses." I told Hawk what the guy said, and it made it all worthwhile.

The next four or five days were the same except at one site when Hawk approached a hatch. Against the inside of the hatch he could see a snake. He plunged his bayonet into it. As he did, the head whipped around as the snake tried to get through the bamboo slats. Hawk sliced it open with his knife. Later, he told me, "That son of a bitch ain't gonna bother me no more."

One night, instead of talking work, we talked about ourselves. Hawk told me he got caught for possession and selling drugs. The cops were on a campaign to clean up Chicago, concentrating on the Black community. He had a clean record so was given a choice of either prison or the army. He figured once training was over, and he was in a permanent duty station, he'd make a contact and peddle dope.

"My luck. I wind up here with you." He told me something was fishy with me. "You don't look Italian. When the bartender asked if you heard of the Mafia Family, you hesitated before you said no."

"Think you're a smart shit? Have it all figured out? Well, you're right. My mother's side is Italian. My grandfather and uncles were big-time Mafia in Italy. They were all killed along with the man who was my mother's fiancé. My mother, her mother, and sister came to America. After a long courtship, my mother and father got married. He was Polish. I went to work for the Family at an early age. Found out later the boss, Tony, and my mother had a history. My mother's fiancé in Italy was Tony's younger brother. Tony vowed to protect my mother and her children till the day he died. He kind of took me under his wing and brought me up in the Family.

"One day I saw a headline that read 'Our Boys Come Home.' Under it was a picture of coffins in rows, with American flags draped over them. The article listed names; many of these guys where my childhood friends. I was drafted. Could have beat it easily. I didn't want to. I had a vendetta. Nothing could change my mind. My luck! I wind up here with you." We both stood up and hugged and pounded each other on the back.

After a couple of more days on the east side, we were given a site on the trail. We did our thing, got back to base, checked in and were told to stay home tomorrow. The next check-in gave us two sites on the east side and a message that the VC were really pissed at us. The next four days were all east side. On check in for the fifth day we were told to square away base, proceed to LZ the next a.m. at 0200 for pickup home.

# *CHAPTER 49*

In the jeep, the driver told us we were going to our quarters. After morning chow, there would be a briefing with Sergeant Brown. The driver followed us in. On our bunks were two new pairs of fatigues. These had been tailored and would replace our old ones. We were told to put everything we were wearing, except for the boots, in the sac hanging on the door. We hung up the fatigues in our lockers.

Hawk claimed, "First in the shower!"

"OK, but when do you get old enough to have facial hair covering that thing you call a face?"

He came back with, "Listen here, honky, some of us have outgrown the animal stage and don't get facial hair."

I told him he didn't know what he's missing. He stripped and went into the head.

While I was waiting my turn, I was thinking *I wish I didn't have to shave.* I didn't for the time we were out. I sat on my bunk enjoying a cigarette thinking about my life in the world.

I had finished my second cigarette when Hawk came out saying, "I's clean, and you isn't." He got in his bunk.

I was stripping when Hawk said, "You got to use the john? You wouldn't believe how good paper feels compared to leaves."

I told him I hoped he used some of his perfume or that place was going to stink. I was standing in front of the mirror looking at my beard. I decided to trim it. If anyone says anything, I'll shave. I used the john. Hawk was right: paper felt great. In the shower, I couldn't believe the brown water I was creating.

I shampooed then noticed a wash cloth. I wet it and rubbed a bar of soap on it. As I scrubbed my face, the cloth became filthy. I rinsed it out and repeated, washing three more times. I walked out feeling great.

Hawk asked, "You run out of water?" and fell back to sleep.

Reveille came too soon. We dressed in our new fatigues and went to chow. The food was great. I told Hawk I was going to hit that line three or four more times and pass on the briefing. After a cigarette, we went to Brown's office, stood at attention in front of his desk. "Hawkins and Walker reporting as ordered."

Brown looked at us for a second. Cutting to the quick, he said, "Sit your asses down," with a smile. "You're looking good. As for the chin hair, no one will say anything. The colonel and command are amazed at your accomplishments. We have been told your headcount is the largest of any troops so far. You have been promoted to sergeant. I have something for you."

He handed us a pack of playing cards and watched the look on our faces. He told us to open it. The cards were all the ace of spades with a skull and cross bones, and the words *ma guy* across it.

"The Vietnamese are very superstitious. The ace of spades is bad luck to them. They named you '*ma guy*', ghost devil. Use the cards as calling cards whatever way you want."

Brown advised, "Command has intelligence that the north is preparing for a major offensive. Their intent is to overrun and destroy the forward base camps of the Twenty-Fifth and the First. They'll bring tanks, artillery, equipment, and all form of logistics south on the trail. Two divisions will move south by land. They'll be using the tunnels you mined on their way south."

After a lot more, input of what was going on, he told us that our unit assigned to the field platoons lost some men. I didn't ask but was hoping Mickey wasn't one of them. He told us the guy we met in the bar before we left had been ordered to take a dishonorable discharge or face a court martial. He took the discharge. "You need to thank Frankie for that."

Unless we had something to say, that's all he had. Transportation had been arranged. We were to spend our time-off at the Rex Hotel in Saigon. "You'll stay in two rooms assigned to Colonel Bolton. The place is a top-notch hotel with all kinds of luxuries: restaurants, clubs, spas, pools – all kinds of shit. Whatever you do or buy in the hotel, charge it to the room courtesy of the Colonel."

I asked Brown what we were doing in this fucked-up country on the other side of the world. He explained that we are fighting the Communist takeover of the south.

"Cuba, very close to home, went Communist. We didn't do shit."

"Like you, I follow orders. Other than that, I don't have an answer for you." He stood up, extended his hand. We shook hands and left.

I looked at Hawk and joked, "You're a big shot now. They'll probably make you a general before you get out."

His rebuttal was: "When they do, you better watch your scrawny ass."

Once we left the burnt-out area, the countryside was beautiful all the way to Saigon. We pulled up in front of the Rex Hotel, a five-story building that looked like it had been renovated a couple of times. The driver told us to notify base when we were ready to go back. He'd pick us up.

At the front desk a Vietnamese gentleman asked if he could help us. "We have two rooms reserved under Colonel Bolton."

He replied, "Yes, Sir, your rooms are ready for you," and passed us keys. I asked if I could get a trim (pointing to my head), a shave, and a massage in my room. "Certainly, Sir, I'll arrange it. And you Sir?" Hawk told him he would like just the massage.

My room looked great. There was a small refrigerator in a corner. I opened it to find beer, soda, bottled mineral water, a bucket with ice, and a lot more. The cabinet above it had all kinds of booze. I lay on the bed with my boots hanging off. It had been quite a while since I slept on a mattress this good. Someone knocked on the door. I opened it to see a good-looking Vietnamese girl holding a satchel. I stood there staring at her.

She chirped, "Haircut, shave." I motioned her in. She put her satchel down, moved a chair from the carpet to the hardwood. She motioned me to sit in the chair. "Before you begin, how about having a drink of anything you'd like with me?"

She said. "Thank you, but I'm not."

"If that's I'm not supposed to, it's only the two of us in this room. I'm not telling anybody. There's soda, water, beer, booze. I'm thirsty and I know you are. I'm getting something to drink."

She took a folded apron and an electric hair trimmer out of her satchel. When she was finished, she asked if I would like to get up look in the mirror to see if it was OK. I told her no, I was sure it was OK. She began trimming my beard down to whiskers with a scissors. Then she went into the head. I could hear water running. She came out juggling a small white towel, waved it in the air a couple of times before putting it over my face. She asked if it was too warm. No. She had a shaving mug and brush in her hand. On my lap was an old-time, single-blade razor, folded in half. She brushed lather on my face, picked up the blade, and began shaving. I had never had a beard or had anyone shave me before. This is nice – I'll have to do it again. She got a wet washcloth, patted my face, saying she was going to use aftershave lotion, but I was too broken out. I thanked her for everything and asked if she would join me this evening for dinner in the hotel. Before she could answer, I handed her five ones. She refused, saying the haircut and shave are billed to the room. I told her I knew that; this was for her.

She said, "Too much."

I told her no, it's a bribe for her to have dinner with me. She smiled and took the money, "I didn't need a bribe. I was going to before it."

There was another knock on the door. This time there was a good-looking girl, not fat but big-boned, with nice tits, who said, "Massage." I motioned her in. I walked over to my barber, whispered would it be OK if I offered her a drink?

She whispered "yes" I backed away and told her to get a glass and ice from the fridge, sit down, and take a break. Both ladies were drinking and talking.

The masseuse told me to strip to the waist, take off my boots, and lie on my stomach on the bed. When I got my tee shirt off, I could hear what sounded like two deep breaths. I was always muscular, and the army had built the shit out of me. I was on the bed with my head on the pillow.

The two of them started talking in Vietnamese. The barber said I was the nicest GI she ever met and was hoping to see a lot more of me than just today. The other girl said, "The first guy told me, 'He's my buddy. Take good care of him.' That was about all he said. He was quiet and shy."

I was thinking to myself, she can't be talking about Hawk. They continued talking while I was getting this great massage. My body needed it. My barber told the masseuse we were going to have dinner together and she should join us. The masseuse thanked her but said she wanted me to invite her. While she was kneeling over my butt, massaging my neck, her tits rubbed my back. Accidental or intentional? Didn't matter. I loved the whole thing.

When she finished, I got up and dressed. Looking at my barber, I said, "I apologize. I should have done this much sooner. My name is Paul."

She smiled and told me her name is Chua and introduced Hoai Mi.

"Nice to meet you. My buddy's name is Duwayne."

Hoai Mi commented it is a beautiful name.

"Chua and I made dinner plans for a restaurant in the hotel. Would you like to join us with Duwayne?"

She said she'd love to.

I asked if they drank wine, beer or any kind of alcohol. They did. I said, "Good. We'll meet you in the bar downstairs at 6:00 o'clock, if that's OK."

I walked to Hawk's room. Shirtless, he opened the door. "This army hasn't done shit for you, Hawk. You're still a skinny fuck."

I told him about Hoai Mi saying his first name was beautiful, and she thought he was quiet and shy.

"Me? Quiet and shy? Fuck, no! I was lying on the bed with a hard-on, trying to control myself. She kept rubbing her tits on my back. When she finished, I came and couldn't move."

He asked how mine was. I told him the same, except I had full control. I told him I didn't think the rubbing was intentional. I said my shave and haircut were great, and Chua was a beautiful girl.

We ordered room service – a sandwich and beer. While we were munching, Hawk asked if these girls spent the night with us, was I going to fuck mine? I told him I was horny enough to. I don't know, we'll see." We decided to take a walk, and see what Saigon looked like.

The street was busy, Vietnamese running all over the place, and GIs walking leisurely. A couple of sailors in whites drunkenly bumped into Hawk and kept walking. We let it pass. In the window of a butcher shop something was hanging from hooks. We didn't know what it was.

At a jewelry store we stopped and looked in the window. Something caught my eye. There was a heart with a zigzag cut down the center, with two fine chains, one on each piece. I told Hawk I wanted to go in, he followed me. I asked how much that heart in the window was. Three dollars American, engraved. I asked if that was the whole heart or half. He said whole, and it was silver. I thanked him and walked out, turned around, and went back in. I asked him to engrave one with the Vietnamese word – "friends." I paid him and told him I'd get it later. He told me he closed at ten.

We were at the bar having a beer and decided to go for a swim. At the front desk the clerk said we could get bathing suits in the gift shop around the corner. I found out where the pool was but was told changing had to be done in our rooms. The pool was big. Four GIs were in it. It would have been nice if they had been broads. I always wanted a blow job in a pool.

I swam up to Hawk, "I'm never leaving this pool. I'll die of old age in it." He splashed me in the face.

A voice came over my shoulder: "There will be none of that in the pool."

"Really? I missed the sign that says no splashing."

He came back with, "That's the rules."

I asked whose rules?

He answered, "The hotel."

"You know what? You need to stick the rules where the sun doesn't shine."

He asked if we were guests in the hotel, and what room? I said "Our rooms are under Colonel Bolton, Special Forces. You?"

He said, "Lieutenant Sizemore, First Infantry."

"Troop, if you plan on making the army your career, move to the other end of the pool, and keep your mouth shut." He did, very quickly. Hawk gave me one of his I-don't- believe-what-you-just-did looks.

We swam around for a little bit, dried off, and headed back to our rooms. We passed two maids in the hallway. We got a couple of wide-eyed looks. I asked Hawk if he was up again; he said no. We had our wet towels in our hands and were bare-chested.

As we stepped into the elevator, a voice called out to hold the doors. Two girls in dress army uniform walked in. They stared at us, looking us up and down. I was taking it all in and liked it. The one looking at Hawk made a noise like she was having an orgasm. I glanced at Hawk. He said, "I can't help it." We got out of the elevator; I told Hawk we could get laid by a different girl every day here.

We sacked out for a while, then went to the bar and sat in a booth. Six o'clock on the nose, the two girls were standing by the booth. They looked stunning and smelled great. After ordering drinks, I asked which of the three restaurants would they like to dine at. They started to talk in Vietnamese. Chua was saying "I don't want them to take us to (I can't remember the name) – it's too expensive. We can go to Chang's. The food's not bad, and it's a lot cheaper." Chua told me they would like to dine at Chang's. I told her that since this was our first date, and one I wish to remember for a long time, we can eat at Chang's tomorrow night. Tonight, we'll eat at (the place I couldn't remember).

The restaurant was busy, and very classy. A waiter came to the table, introduced himself, and described the house specialties. He passed out the menus and asked if we would like wine with dinner. I looked at Chua and got a look like yes. I told her to tell the waiter the name of a wine she really liked, and the cost didn't matter. She told him. I told them I would have ordered, but the wine I like none of them would – Chianti.

I thought I needed to shut up and give Hawk or the girls a chance to talk. I turned to Chua and was staring at her. I guess I got a little intense. She turned and seemed to be a little flustered. I backed off and sat back. The waiter came back with the bottle and four glasses. He pulled the cork and handed it to me. I motioned him to Chua. He handed her the cork. She smelled it and handed it back. He poured a little into her glass, she smelled the wine, tasted it, told him "very good". He poured our glasses.

"Hawk, how about one of your famous toasts."

Without batting an eye, he lifted his glass, and said, "I wish for us peace, joy, and happiness, and most of all, love. Cheers." We all sipped our wine. Hoai Mi was staring at Hawk. I guess she got a different perspective of the guy.

The girls ordered. I selected a steak with a funny name and a baked potato. Hawk wanted the same. The girls started talking in Vietnamese. Chua was saying after she showered, she sat with her mother, and was telling her all about this wonderful GI she met. She told her about the day and went on and on about me. She told her about the $5 bribe, and her response. She told her mother she never met a man like me and was going to marry me if I'd have her. Hoai Mi said she felt the same about Duwayne but didn't know if he even liked her.

Hawk looked at me, and I nodded yes. In Vietnamese, he told her he liked her very much, enjoyed being with her, and I was the shy one of the two of us.

Chua asked, "You, too? All this time?" I nodded yes.

She bit her lip and looked worried. I held her face in my hands and told her she was the wonderful one. The waiter brought the food. We broke it off while the waiter was placing the food. Chua held my hand under the table and squeezed it. She looked very happy. The girls were saying their food was good. I told everyone my steak was great, I never had a steak this good.

We told the girls we wanted to go for a walk and see what Saigon looked like. While we were walking and holding hands, I asked Chua what kind of steak I just had.

She told me it comes from Japan. The cows are massaged for a long time before they are butchered. It is very expensive. The steak I just had cost more than she makes in three months. I hugged her, and we just happened to be in front of my jewelry store.

I took her hand and we went in, followed by Hoai Mi and Hawk. The guy saw me and put the heart on a piece of velvet on the counter. I turned over the engraved half and Chua hugged me. I could see a tear she was trying to hide from me. She wiped it away with a finger, and told me it was beautiful, but she couldn't. It was too much. I had spent too much money on her already.

The old guy walked down to help Hawk. I told Chua in Vietnamese she had to. I bought it for her and paid for it earlier today. She gave me her cute little smile. I put the chain on her, then took my dog tag chain off, and added the heart to my tag. I handed Chua the silver chain and told her in case she broke hers.

Stepping outside we began to kiss. Hoai Mi and Hawk walked out. They showed us two very sharp rings he had bought. Hawk's was on his dog tag chain.

After walking for a bit, I asked Chua if she would come back to my room. We could talk, and then if she wanted, I would walk her home. She said yes. I told Hawk what we were doing. They talked, then joined us going back to the hotel.

Chua and I were in bed with our underwear on. She rested her head on my chest, and I had my arms around her. "I'd like you to tell me all about Chua."

"My father's family was wealthy. He was a doctor, had a practice, and was head of a department in the hospital. My mother worked as an administrative secretary in the hospital. Our home was a big, beautiful house in the countryside."

"I had a very good childhood. I attended the college of nursing. My older brother made the army his career. My father got into politics. He was a fervent believer in democracy and was pushing for socialized medicine so everyone who needed it could be treated." While she was talking, I realized there was a lot more to Chua than barbering.        "Three years ago, the VC invaded our home. We were all there. They killed everyone except my mother, me, and a maid. We were forced to flee. The VC burned our house. My mother and I came to Saigon, and the maid went to her home. My mother bought a shanty in a poor neighborhood with the money she had. My mother couldn't work, not even at a menial job. She went into a deep depression. I realized I couldn't support both of us on my nurse's pay, so I got the barbering job at the hotel. It was good timing because the US military had just taken it over for officer's quarters,"

I interrupted her by telling her I was not an officer. Hawk and I were here for five days R and R in rooms assigned to our colonel.

"I didn't think you were an officer. Here only for five days? Then what?"

I told her back to work. She gave me a questioning look. I didn't want to go into any details except Hawk and I were partners. She asked why I refer to Duwayne as Hawk. I told her his last name is Hawkins, mine is Walker. We chose to use our nicknames, Hawk and Walk.

She kissed me, not one of those little pecks. This was a loving, passionate kiss. My hand moved gently to her breast. She turned around and snuggled up to me, wiggled her butt on me. I'm thinking: here I am with my arms around this doll puncturing her back.

"Your turn. I want to hear all about Walk." There's not much to tell, I started working when I was twelve to support my family. I worked for the same boss till the army drafted me. Here I am.

Then she got up, turned off the light, and took her panties off. She slowly undressed me. On her hands and knees, she began sucking my dick. I'm laying back enjoying it, thinking if her head wasn't in the way, my dick would hit the ceiling. I had to move her off me.

Chua fell on her back, and asked, "It was no good? I could do better. I'm sorry."

I leaned over and kissed her, saying it was wonderful, but I didn't want to come in her mouth. She told me she had read it was nice, and sweet. I moved over, got on top of her, and penetrated her. She moaned. I began fucking. She was tight and moist. It was fantastic. I don't think I lasted a minute before I came. I lay back relishing the moment.

She said, "Thank you. It was wonderful." She went into the bathroom. After a bit, I could hear water running. She came out with a washcloth and washed my dick. We were on our backs letting it all hang out. I asked if she was a virgin.

"Yes, but it's alright because I want to have your child."

In the morning, as I was getting dressed, I told Chua we could have breakfast in the room and plan our day. She told me yes, but she had to go home, check on her mother, and spend a little time with her. I understood.

After Chua left, I called Hawk's room. He told me he hadn't been to sleep – I would never believe the night he had. It was great "How was yours?" I told him it was good.

"Hoai Mi had to work. I'm going to sleep. When she returns, we're going to pick up where we left off." I said I'd catch him later. We can all have dinner again.

After dinner Hawk announced that on our next five days off Hoai Mi and he were getting married, and it would be nice if it was a double wedding. Chua and I didn't say anything.

Chua couldn't spend the night with me. She needed to go home to be with her mother. She was going to ask Hoai Mi to join her.

I thought, *Fuck, I really wanted some tonight.* I waited awhile before I called Hawk.

Before I could say anything, he told me he didn't know if he'd ever forgive me for this. "Fuck you! What are we doing to-night?"

"I'm going to sleep my frustration away."

I told him good night and hung up. Even though I knew Hawk was kidding with me, I was thinking how horny I was. He's frustrated, but at least he got something. What about my frustration?

I said *fuck this* and went to the bar. I figured I could talk to the bartender, have a couple of drinks, and pass time. I ordered a drink and was enjoying it when I smelled perfume. A woman sat down next to me. I looked over at her. It was the girl from the elevator, now in civilian clothes. I couldn't help but notice how much her uniform had hidden her tits – she had a great pair. We struck up a conversation and I bought her a drink. She asked what I did here. I told her I was on R and R. when she asked what room I was in. I gave her the number.

"That floor is reserved for high-ranking officers!"

I didn't clarify anything. After a while she asked if she could see my room. I said, "Let's do it some other time. I'm beat and going to sleep."

I got up early, went downstairs, and was sitting at a table drinking coffee. Hawk walked in. He asked how my night went. I shoveled the shit about the bar and hooking up with the girl from the elevator. "We had great sex. She has nicer tits than Hoai Mi. You still horny?"

"More so than ever."

"I could keep going on about it, but you'll get a hard-on and embarrass the both of us. The truth is I met her in the bar, bought her a drink; she wanted some. I passed and went to bed alone"

When I finished, he held up a hand. "Give me five."

I never heard that before but held my hand up. He kind of slapped my hand saying, "You the man."

"You know I was only kidding you last night on the phone." I told him I thought he was dead serious, and I was a little pissed off.

He came back with, "No, no, I was only kidding."

I realized Hawk must have spent the night worrying about it. He told me he tried to call me after and I wasn't in. I told him I knew he was only kidding, and he can't let shit like this bother him – we're too close. I asked Hawk if he decided on a best man yet. He told me he hadn't. He was looking for someone better-looking than me.

Hawk and I decided we would have a leisurely lunch, then go for a swim. After, I was going to sit on the balcony, smoke a cigar, and get a suntan. He was going to get some sleep, so he'd be able to go all night.

When I woke up the cigar was on the concrete, and I was beet-red. I went inside, looked in the mirror. I sure as shit got too much sun. I called downstairs and asked if they could get me something for a bad sunburn. He told me, yes, it would be right up. I added, "A loose-fitting shirt and a nice pair of shorts, twenty-nine-inch waist."

I was sitting in a chair thinking that was stupid. A dumbass mistake. But I was glad I had on a bathing suit. The little guy didn't get sunburned. *All is not lost.*

A guy arrived with clothing over one arm, balancing a tray with a jar and bottle on it. He explained the jar contained sunburn cream, and the bottle is aloe Vera lotion. I asked if he had any idea how to use them. "Don't shower. Apply the cream wherever you've been burnt, and the lotion on top of the cream." I thanked him and handed him two bucks which he accepted very appreciatively.

I slipped out of my bathing suit, and very gently put the cream on every part of me that was red. In the john, I looked in the mirror, and added the cream to some spots I missed. I placed the new shirt and shorts on the floor, got in bed on my back, and fell asleep.

A knock on the door woke me. I opened the door a little. It was Chua. I opened the door all the way. She gasped and asked what happened. "Sunburn… on the balcony."

I realized I didn't have on underwear, turned, and slowly moved into the room. Chau closed the door and told me to stand there for a minute. She came out of the bathroom with a washcloth, gently patted my lips, and then kissed me. Kissing was good, and I needed it. She walked me to the bed and helped me lie on my back.

She said, "Walk – "

I stopped her. "Call me Pauly."

She continued, "Pauly, there are times when you are amazing, wonderful, and all-knowing. Then you do something like this to yourself!"

She took my dick in her hand and began to suck on it. I lay back and felt this was like no blow job I ever had. This was more like caressing my dick in her mouth. I came.

She lifted her head up "It is sweet, and nice." She swallowed it and went into the bathroom. I fell back to sleep. I don't know why I woke up or what time it was. Chua was beside me, naked. I wanted to take her in my arms, but I couldn't, so I lay there looking at her. She was so beautiful. I was never into Oriental women. There, I had yet to see an ugly woman. Even the older women have a beauty about them. When I lifted her head to kiss her, she woke up.

I asked if she could put the aloe lotion on me. She got the bottle, straddled my waist and was rubbing the lotion on with her fingertips. She told me the cream is to keep my skin moist, so it doesn't crack and get infected. The aloe will penetrate the cream and has healing properties.

"It's good to have a nurse in the family." I fell asleep. The sun was coming up when I woke and had to piss. When I got back to the bed I asked Chua if she had a good night.

"Yes. I was watching you. I wanted to make sure you didn't turn over on your sunburn." She asked for my arm, pressed down with a finger, asking if it bothered me.

Not at all. She tested other areas. As before, it didn't hurt!

"My love, you sleep differently from anyone I have ever known. When I was nursing, I checked on adults and kids. While I was lying beside you, I could feel what you were going through in your sleep. It wasn't me. I knew it was coming from you."

She asked that I not laugh at her. I told her I wouldn't. "At first I felt as though I was on a train. Then I was content for a while, then this overwhelming feeling of love, next great joy, and then the feeling of relaxation. I never closed my eyes all night."

"We never talked about religion. What you went through last night is my spirituality. My mother and I used to spend hours together, she telling me about her spirituality. I liked it and took it all in. I do not believe in heaven or hell, or that God is in heaven. I believe God is within me. God is my soul and is infinite. When I die, God moves on. Only my shell remains.

When I fell asleep last night, I was in severe pain. I sought my God. I worked hard at it, because this was a first for me. When I felt I was there, I was on my back in the sky. Bright colored clouds passed me and went through me. My mother walked up to me. She was wearing an Indian dress, a leather robe with beads, and she touched me. In the distance, I could see a wolf running toward me. As it got closer, all I could see was an enormous head, moving fast. When it reached me, it stopped, licked me, then ran off. After that I felt good." I told Chua the wolf in my spirituality is the healer.

Chua suggested I shower. She didn't think it would bother me. I should try an arm first. If it bothers me, stop. I did the arm – nothing. I got in ran a bar of soap over my head, washed my body, and got out. I was standing there with my dick hanging down. Chua asked if I felt well enough to have sex. "Yes, but not now. I'm very tired and need to get some sleep." When I woke, she was not in bed. I checked the john, then saw a note on the table.

She started with "I love you," and wrote she was going home to spend some time with her mother. She also wanted to pick up a gift for me. She was spending a lot of time with her mother. I realized this was all bullshit, I felt I was being played. I'd play along as long as I could get some.

Dressed in shirt and shorts, I took the elevator down to the gift shop. I bought a cheap pair of sandals then went to the small breakfast-and-lunch restaurant. I had to have coffee and ordered pancakes and eggs. As I was sipping my coffee, Hawk and Hoai Mi came over to the table. She sat down, and Hawk stood beside me.

"What happened to you?"

"Nothing. I just wanted to get a shade closer to my main man."

Hawk sat down. After they ordered, I told them all about what happened. Hawk said they were going to do a little browsing in the gift shop. I asked if they minded if I tagged along. Hawk needed shorts and shirts. I wandered around and noticed this beautiful jewelry box that was four-drawers high. It was very inexpensive. I picked it up, took it to the register, and told them it was with theirs.

I kept walking and glanced into a mirror. If it wasn't for the short hair, I'd look like a local. I asked Hoai Mi, to pick out two bathing suits, one for Chua. At the register the clerk told Hawk that the jewelry box was mine.

In a falsetto voice, I said, "Oh yes, it's mine and, you're going to pay for it, Daddy."

Everyone looked at me. Hawk signed the ticket in a hurry, and we left. In the elevator, he said, "You sure know how to embarrass a guy."

In my fag voice, I told him to get over it.

As I was putting the jewelry box in the closet, the desk called. Brown had phoned and had asked I call him back. Brown told me he was sorry, but he had to shorten our R and R. "A jeep will pick you up in front at 0300. We'll have a briefing, then you and Hawk will be choppered to the LZ. Walker, there's a big push going on. Both of you are needed."

I said 10-4, and hung up, and went to Hawk's room. He had changed into his civvies. I told him about Brown's call. Hoai Mi started crying. Hawk took her in his arms and told her it would be alright. "Time will pass quickly, and I'll be back for our wedding." I told them I'd see them later.

Hoai Mi followed me out. She had wiped the tears away." She leaned over to me and kissed me on the cheek and whispered, "Please, take care of him, and both of you come back to us."

Chua arrived. The first words out of her mouth was a local greeting. She couldn't wait to show me the gift she got me. She handed me a narrow gift-wrapped box. It contained a single-edged knife with a wrapped grip, about half the size of mine. She told me she hoped it would keep me safe. I told her thank you, I would use it well. I never mentioned my knife. I told her I had a gift for her. I took the jewelry box out of the closet and put it on the table. She leaned over it and started crying.

"If you don't like it, I'll return it."

She lifted her head. With her hand waving she said, "No, no, no. It's so beautiful."

I asked her to sit on the bed with me. I told her about Brown's call. The tears started flowing. I took her in my arms, and we fell back on the bed. I wouldn't have broken it off if it wasn't for my arm falling asleep. I told her, "I had Hoai Mi pick out two bathing suits. We can have lunch, and then jump in the pool. You'll have fun."

As we walked through the door to the pool area, I heard, "Attention!"

I hollered at Sizemore, "What did I tell you yesterday?" He didn't say anything. We put our towels on chairs. Holding Chua's hand, I led her to the steps.

In an authoritative voice, Sizemore sounded off again. "You are not permitted to have civilians in the pool."

I hollered back that these are not civilians, they're probably more military than he is. I yelled, "I want you out of this pool post haste! I don't want to see you again till tomorrow."

He turned and was walking to the ladder to get out when Hawk shouted "Trooper." He turned. Hawk asked if his size was more. Sizemore jumped out of the pool and ran for the door. Hawk gave me a look. It was a look telling me I had big brass balls.

I asked Chua if I could show her how to swim. She hesitantly nodded yes. I had her to lie on her stomach, while I held her up with my hand. I explained how to breathe and showed her how do the crawl. She swam across the pool and back. A fast learner, and a great teacher! I demonstrated the sidestroke, and the backstroke. She went across the pool, turned, came back, and gently tapped me on my head. "You were just playing with me, right?"

"Yes. I was on the swim team in college." I splashed her; she splashed me back. We were splashing each other and laughing until I dunked her. She went down and grabbed my crotch on the way up.

When she surfaced, I told her, "You win." We played around, swam, then got out.

Hawk and Hoai Mi were sitting on the chairs watching us. While Hoai Mi kidded Chua in Vietnamese, Hawk said, "You have some pair."

I said, "Me? You broke him with the more-size bit. I don't think he'll ever get over it. Hawk, I wonder if he is an infantry second louie or a desk clerk. If he's infantry, and sees combat, he'll be a changed man."

Back in my room we decided to shower together. Chua wrapped her hair in a towel, got in facing the showerhead. I stood in front of her, washing her with a soapy washcloth. I especially enjoyed washing her nipples. Rinsing off the cloth, I washed her back with just water. Then it was her turn.

The washcloth was slowly moving over my muscles, and from the look on her face, Chua was enjoying it. After we finished, we cuddled on the bed. She started talking about the future – she was really into it. I bent over and started kissing her neck. She let me do it for a little bit, then nicely told me to stop. This was important to her.

I listened, and when she finished, I told her that's good. Something inside me was saying we didn't have a future.

Later the four of us were in the restaurant. Before the waiter came, I told everyone to order whatever they wanted, and not to worry about cost. This was going to be a celebration of the upcoming marriage. The waiter came over and asked if we would like wine with our dinners, I told Chua to choose, for the others and requested Chianti for myself. If he had Italian, it would be great. Everyone makes Chianti, but the Italian is more robust. Hawk raised his glass and said, "A toast to us."

After we sipped our wine, I offered Chua a taste of Chianti. She took a small taste, then handed the glass back without a word. I asked Hawk if ever had Chianti. No. I handed him my glass. He drank, his face contorted, his arms started flapping around.

"I'll take that as you didn't like it." Hoai Mi, after seeing Hawk, declined a taste. "I tried to give you a taste of one of the finer wines in the world. I guess you're not mature enough to enjoy it."

"That sucks. Even Red-eye is better."

Back in my room, I put my civvies on the table, the bathing suits, along with the knife. Moving them to the far end, I asked Chua if I missed anything, or was there anything she wanted. She answered no. I wrapped everything except the jewelry box in a large bath towel and asked if she would take my clothing home and hang on to it for me.

I kissed her and suggested we get undressed and get in bed. I wanted to hold her in my arms. Nothing was said. We were at peace with everything and were as one. We stayed that way until I fell asleep.

After we got dressed I put the knife in my pocket and picked up the jewelry box. Chua carried the bundle. I told her to put the bundle in her car while I signed the bill. I woke the clerk who was sleeping in a chair, gave him my room number, and told him I needed to check out. He looked through a stack of bills, removed mine, and I signed it.

I put the jewelry box on the floor of the back seat of the car and took Chua in my arms. "We're going to kiss, and then you'll get in your car and go home. I don't handle good-byes well." We kissed. I handed her a bunch of money, turned, and walked away. She got in her car and drove off.

Hawk and Hoai Mi were quickly walking toward me, both looking a little panicky. Hawk said, "I'm sorry we're late."

I told him he wasn't; we still had some time. I walked down the sidewalk, lit up a cigarette, and leaned against a post, trying to give them privacy. After I finished smoking, I walked back to Hawk and asked, "Where's your shit?" He hesitated, then said it was in the room.

"Get up there and bring it down. Hoai Mi can take it home."

She and I were standing in a poorly lit part of the sidewalk. Out of the corner of my eye I was looking at Hoai Mi's big tits. Her top was cut to show her cleavage. If it wasn't for Hawk, I'd be in there squeezing.

# *CHAPTER 50*

The jeep drove up. I said good-bye to Hoai Mi, and told her, "When I get back, I expect one of your massages."

She said, "Good-bye. You can have two. Just bring Hawk home to me."

Hawk came out of the hotel. I got in the jeep, told the driver he'd only be a minute. When Hawk came to the jeep, I told him, "You're late. In the back."

We were on our way to base. I felt Hawk was having a hard time dealing with leaving Hoai Mi, more so than I was with leaving Chua. I was already looking forward to the action.

At base, we went to Brown's office., "Sarge, before we start, I need to get something off my mind. Hawk and I spent a lot of money at the hotel. We charged everything to the room. I'm not comfortable getting freebies at the Colonel's expense."

Negative, Brown told me. "It's not the Colonel's expense. The rooms and all the charges are on the Army. He gets it as a perk for being a Colonel."

After the briefing, we did our twenty, then two more. We couldn't hook up with the girls. Hawk was devastated that the wedding was on hold. He was all fucked up.

During the third briefing Hawk and I were promoted. Brown told us *ma guy* was all over, almost like the Kilroy graffiti during WWII. The VC had a reward out and were searching for two platoons in the field.

He told us we were taking a short detour for twelve hours before moving to base.

"The 25th Command has been getting rumors about Alpha Base, and they're concerned that when the major offensive happens, the base will be overrun. They asked the Colonel to verify the rumors. You will be choppered to the base at 1600 hours tomorrow. Then a chopper with your gear will pick you up at 0400 and take you to your LZ."

We were dropped off at Alpha with supplies for the base. The only thing we had were our weapons. A lieutenant told us HQ informed them of our arrival, and that we were under HQ authority only. He'd introduce us to Major Strum, the base commander, and then we would spend the night in his hooch. The HQ, was a dugout with sandbags covering the roof and piled everywhere. The minute we got in, it was obvious this was all fucked up. Guys wearing only shorts were lying around drinking, and others were face down on tables. A drunk in fatigues staggered over to us, mumbled something, and told us he was Major St – . He couldn't finish his name.

I told the lieutenant, "Let's go to your hooch. Is it like this all the time?" He replied most of the time, and that he and three sergeants were in charge. I asked how long had he been in country. One month. He was ROTC. Stateside he spent two months training, was assigned to the 25th and ordered to Alpha.

Hawk and I were going to walk around so I asked if he wanted to join us. He preferred to stay in his hooch. Outdoors was a little too hot for him. Hawk and I wandered around. Most of the GIs were smoking joints and out of uniform.

We walked into a hooch. A GI in fatigues saw us and came over, introduced himself as Sergeant Coleman. I asked if he was the NCO in charge. He told me he was. I asked, "How can you let this go on?"

He had no choice. "The lieutenant is inexperienced and afraid of his own shadow, overrides me on everything. If this base takes a frontal attack, they'll overrun us."

I asked if the base had tunnel rats. They had two assigned, but both had been killed. While we were talking, a GI started screaming. "Incoming." He ran to the wall and started shooting a .50 cal everywhere. The sergeant pulled him off, threw him on the ground, and then came back to us. He was angry, saying if it wasn't pot, it was the fucking cocaine. I asked why he didn't go over the lieutenant.

"To whom? They're all fucking drunk, and don't know what's going on. I tried getting a chopper pilot to get help from 25th Command but heard nothing."

Coleman asked what we were. I said we were Special Forces on our way to an assignment.

It got dark. We were in the lieutenant's hooch, had just finished rations, when the base was bombarded. I told the lieutenant to call for an air strike. He asked who he should call. I told him to show me where the radio was. He said he couldn't go out there.

I made my way to the Command Center. Everyone was under a table or bunk. I got their radio and adjusted the frequency. When Bravo answered, I told them it was Hawk Walk. I needed to talk to Big now! Brown got on.

"The base is under attack. Call for an air strike, the tree line, half a klick north of the base. Burn the motherfuckers!" I got back to the hooch and asked Hawk his opinion of this place.

"It's a fucking death trap. I'm glad we are where we are and have each other's backs. If this place gets overrun, Coleman is going to be the only one fighting for his life." I motioned toward the lieutenant who was cowering in a corner.

"It's sad. The whole thing is sad, but it's typical army – all fucked up."

"Yeah, it's sad. This poor bastard leading troops in the field, not knowing what to do, not able to make a decision – that will get everyone killed. A guy taking ROTC in college, graduating and joining the army, sure as shit doesn't want to do a tour in Nam. Those that get forced into it are fucked. The statistics say a new lieutenant has about two minutes to live in the field. That's why the army takes what they can and shoves them in."

We could hear the roar of jets. On the first pass, they strafed the tree line. The second was a combination of frag bombs and napalm. The sky lit up. A chopper picked us up, and we were out of there.

Back at our base I radioed Bravo and told Brown what went on. I suggested he replace the command and have someone contact Sergeant Coleman and let him tell them who was worth keeping and replace the rest. "They'll probably retaliate because of the air strike. There's nobody able to man a post. You're going to lose the base and a lot of lives."

# *CHAPTER 51*

Our mission this twenty was to seek and destroy in the jungle the men and their camps. They were North Vietnamese Army regulars on the move south. We would pick a group, usually twelve to fifteen, and move among them. They never knew we were there.

When one of them moved alongside of us, we'd yank his head around with our left arm, slice his throat open, and then plunge the knife into his throat. The only thing that bothered me, and it did for years after I got out, was their fuckin' eyes looking at me as I killed them. For the most part it was easy for us. When one of them gave us a hard time, we'd use our .22 then move off to a safe location. They were so intent on moving through the jungle that they never realized anyone was missing.

We used our cards for headcounts but knew sooner or later we'd have a problem. We heard yelling in the distance, then orders given to halt and not retreat. They must have come upon bodies with our calling cards. The group we were following broke rank and headed for the commotion. They tripped over bodies and panicked. As more bodies were discovered, the whole jungle was in a turmoil. Officers yelling orders and firing weapons. Troops running in circles. A fuckin' mess. We moved off, away from the columns, and cooled it for a while.

Hawk and I climbed a couple of palms. On the top, the fronds and our camouflage suits made us invisible. We started picking them off with the modified carbine we had been issued. It had a built-in silencer and a modified gas chamber. When the trigger was pulled, there was nothing: no sound, no smoke, and no flash. The spent ammo was our headcount. We spent the day in the palms or on the ground.

For the next two days, we stayed in the jungle doing our thing. They never saw us or came after us. On the night of the third day we went back to our base camp. We were running low on ammo and needed to get some rest and cleaned up. I checked in, gave our headcount and our plan for the day. I was told to hold for Big B.

Brown told me division replaced everyone at Alpha Base except for Sergeant Coleman, a spec4, and two privates. The officers and enlisted men were stripped of rank and given dishonorable discharges. He also said intelligence has informed them the NVA we were tracking were to join the VC. "Their plan is to overrun Alpha Base on their way to Cam Ranh Bay."

At sunup, we were on our way. Refreshed, we moved through the jungle easily. Our camouflage was amazing. If the guy who came up with it was military, he should get a medal. If he was a civilian, they should give him some kind of award.

We caught up with the column and started doing our thing. By late afternoon we realized we were in the back of the column. There was no one north of us. We decided to follow them. They would camp because night was coming on quickly.

The NVA were on a fast pace. Suddenly, they stopped. Guys broke formation, ran about fifty yards, picked up bamboo – one on each end of two shoots. They lifted what looked like a garage door covered with growth. Troops started filing in.

This was a major tunnel complex, not like the VC's sleeping tunnels. There had to be at least fifteen companies of NVA, along with radio center, command center, storage areas, sleeping areas, and kitchens. This large underground complex was used as a staging area. When the last moved in, the doors were closed, and guards were posted.

Hawk and I moved away. We crouched down behind a fallen palm trunk. I asked him if he had any ideas on how we should take them. Hawk said he didn't have a fucking clue. "No matter what we do, we'll have to take care of the guards first."

I suggested we call for an air strike. Hawk asked how would they know where to hit?

I told him my first thought was to build a pile of the remote bombs we just got, add the phosphorus from our flares, set it off, and run like hell.

Then I had a brainstorm. "You, my noble friend, will sacrifice your radio for the good of mankind. We'll set the radio in the center of the complex, pull the homing beacon and walk away."

"Good idea. But why my radio? You don't know how to use yours."

I told him he was right. "As I said, you are the noble one, concerned about mankind. I am not noble and don't give a shit about mankind."

He said he never met anyone who had more bullshit than me, then said, "OK, we'll use your radio"

"No, it was my idea." He said I was acting like a little baby. I countered, "Better than a dickhead." I waited for it … It came …

"Fuck you!"

I got on the radio and told Brown what we came upon. I explained we couldn't figure a way to get them all except for planting a radio dead center. After pulling the homing beacon, we could be far enough away when the air strike hits.

"They have to be down there in tunnels, spread out. The strike should take a wide path east and west. I'm going to use my radio because I'd hate to see a grown man cry."

Brown told me 10-4 to the cry. "I'll set up the air strike for 0200. A squadron of jets will drop enough shit on them to blow them from here to New York City."

"Negative. Make that enough shit to reach Chicago. I don't want that crud dropping on my hometown."

We had plenty of time. We settled in, ate our gourmet dog food, drank some water, and talked. I told Hawk at 0100 hours we should take out the guards, then find the center, pull the plug on the beacon, and head home. Tomorrow we'd cool it. Hawk told me it sounded good, but under no circumstance did he want to hear me mention the radio. Not once. Never.

We talked about all kinds of stuff. I told Hawk the two small hatches that were not camouflaged were punji-stake traps. He said I was probably right. They would make good decoys for the big one. We took out the guards. It was easy. Most of them were dozing off. We set the radio and headed home. We were a good distance away when the ground started shaking. It felt like a tornado was above us. Palms were bending. Things blew past us. The sky lit up. If we were closer, we'd think we were moving through the jungle in daylight. We finally reached base and fell on our sleeping bags.

The next day I spoke to Bravo, told them we had 72 walking, no count on the other. I was told Big would handle it. Air recon had given them pictures. It looked like a huge coal strip-mining operation. On the last pass, they had spread two decks of cards over the area.

We finished our 20, enjoyed our R and R, and were back at a briefing. Brown told us the operation was a total success. Intelligence informed them the NVA canceled the offensive. The troops that were positioned elsewhere were ordered north. Hawk and I were promoted to staff sergeants for our heroism.

Brown said, "This mission is going to be out of your element. At 0400 a chopper will take you and your gear to an LZ one-hundred miles southwest of your base. You will join two GIs from the unit. The four of you will proceed ten klicks northwest to a prisoner camp. Two jeeps with heavy armament will be dispatched from Zebra Base, their ETA 0600 hours. The other two GIs from the unit will ride shotgun on the jeeps.

Air recon has told us the camp is surrounded by fields of brown grass. You will wear your grass camo and set up a perimeter close to the fence.

"At 0600 hours, a chopper will take out the towers, then move off to an LZ nearby. The two choppers will wait for orders to return for a POW pickup. The jeeps will destroy the gate and take out fence. We know of one building where guards are quartered. The jeeps will destroy that building and the guards. You will provide cover for the jeeps, and then move into the camp to secure it.

"While the POWs are being evacuated by the choppers, the two of you will proceed to their HQ and search for dog tags. The jeeps will return to Zebra Base with the other two GIs. You will mine the area in front of their HQ, then move off to a safe position. When the attack starts, they will radio for help, more than likely tanks and troops. When you observe them, radio for an air strike. You will proceed to the LZ for transport here."

The mission went off as planned. Hawk and I took out twelve from the HQ. We went outside. The other two GIs were in a confrontation with guards coming at them. We picked off the ones coming at their backs. The jeeps moved into position and blew the rest away. The camp was secure; the choppers came in. All of us searched for POWs. Hawk and I found six in cages in a stream behind the camp, and a pile of bodies in a ditch. A call went out for two more choppers. Hawk and I searched the HQ and found an ammo can in the bottom drawer of a desk. It contained tags, gold-filled teeth, and jewelry.

As soon as the camp was evacuated, we set our mines then moved off about a klick away. We could observe the camp. We sat back and waited. I don't know where they came from, but as predicted, tanks and trucks began moving across the field for the camp. I radioed for the air strike, then we moved to the LZ. Back at command I gave Brown the ammo can and advised him someone's going to need a strong stomach to go through it. He told us to go to our quarters, get cleaned up, and rest. The next morning after chow we would go through a debriefing. He and two shrinks that would debrief us.

In our quarters, I told Hawk, "This is good. It's not about the killing It's about helping us deal with the ammo box and the sight of the POWs." I asked Hawk if the killing bothered him. He said it did. Despite all the training we had, and his knowing what to expect, it still bothered him.

"Maybe they can help both of us. I sure as shit don't mind the killing. In fact, I like it. That's probably wrong. I'm having a hard time dealing with the pile of corpses."

After the debriefing, Brown told us we would be transported to Saigon for three days R&R. "The second day you will be taken to the Twenty-Fifth Division Command Center. They're going to have a ceremony and present the six of you with commendations and medals. If the next mission is like the one you were just on, I'm going on it, too. I could use a promotion. It's hard to believe this fast-track promotion thing the two of you are on. If they promote you to officers, I'm not saluting you. When you go to Saigon wear your fatigues. Take your dress uniforms and berets for the ceremony."

We arrived in Saigon, and still couldn't hook up with the girls. Hawk took it hard. I had suspected this would happen. It confirmed my belief: it was all bullshit.

The ceremony was neat. Six of us were standing shoulder to shoulder alongside a bleacher. There were more officers in the bleachers than I have ever seen in my life. A company of troops in dress uniform, shouldering weapons on their left side, marched in front of us, saluting. We saluted back. They did an about-face and lined up in front of the bleachers.

A colonel took the podium and told everyone in attendance of our accomplishment at the POW camp and that we are now able to account for twenty-one MIAs. The general took the podium, presented us with our medals and commendations, and shook our hands.

Back at the hotel we decided to eat at the best restaurant. I ordered Chianti and a steak dinner. The waiter boasted that the steak was the finest cut of beef I would ever have. He was right. The only problem I had was I ate too much and just wanted to go to sleep. We relaxed the next day, then caught our ride to the base. We were with Brown at our usual briefing. He had heard how it went at Division.

For the next six 20s, it was business as usual. We were never able to get together with the girls. Hawk was devastated. I was hurt but somehow knew it was coming. The first two R and R's were shit. For our third I requested a seven-day R and R in Tokyo. It was granted after Brown pulled some strings. We were in a hotel rather than at an army base, and a female lieutenant was assigned to us. She planned an itinerary, and we toured Japan.

For the next R and R, we went to Hong Kong. After that, a seaside resort in South Korea. We hooked up with two local girls and spent the whole R and R with them. Hawk finally came out of it. Hawk and I were partners, buddies, and good friends. It bothered me to see him the way he was before. When we were in the field he was as good as ever. It was the R and R that had him fucked up.

# CHAPTER 52

At our briefing, Brown told us there was very heavy movement south on the trail. "They're moving tanks, artillery, logistics, and troops. The three teams have concentrated on disrupting the troop movement through the jungle. You will now concentrate on the trail. At 0500 hours tomorrow, you will proceed to 70163. There are six hatches. You will kill all and move to 68412 and do the same, and then back to 70163. If it's not dark, remain in the jungle till it is."

"A truck or trucks should move to the site and off-load troops. Give them enough time to find the dead VC and load the bodies on the truck. While the truck is gone, rig the other with C4 on the throttle. When truck one returns, do the same. Give them enough time to get to sleep, then drop a couple of grenades down the shaft. Proceed to 68412 and do it all over again. When you have finished, proceed south along the trail twenty klicks to this site." He pointed to the map behind him. (The site was off our map.)

"You will find a good-size hill at this site. Climb the hill and set up a recon point where you can observe the trail. Command wants to know everything moving south. Check in every fifteen minutes with your recon. You can give us your count then." He asked if we understood. Together we said 10-4. Brown stopped us in the hall and said he forgot one thing. "This will be your last field mission. The colonel wants to establish a training facility here, and he wants you to run it."

We were standing on the LZ with the biggest backpacks I'd ever seen. At base, we took out of the packs what we needed for the mission, geared up, and were on our way. It was still dark. The site we were going to was twenty klicks south of our last hit. This was going to be a long trek through the jungle.

Daylight broke. It started getting hot and we felt it. We moved faster in the daylight. I came to a stop, and asked Hawk what was the water pouring out of him. He told me he pissed his pants. "Great, now we'll have every animal following us, wanting to mate with you."

He had only two words for me, "Fuck you."

We got on our way. After a lot of breaks, we were finally at the southern site. We could see the hatches spread out in a line. We didn't know if it was long tunnel. As we were about to leave, Hawk hugged me. We stood there. He had the same feeling I did; this mission wasn't going to be good.

I went in a tunnel, did them, and went up the shaft and down the next. Seven more sleeping – I shot them. Went up the shaft, down the other. There were six sleeping. I did five. The sixth sat up. It was a girl, and I hesitated for a moment. The thought of not hurting her and just leaving crossed my mind, till I saw her reaching for a sack near her.

I caught her arm with the sole of my boot. She pulled it to her and grabbed it with her other hand. I kicked the sack to the side – an AK-47 was under it. I put the 22 to her forehead. Her arm was broken. I was still having a problem with killing her. I looked at the weapon and thought: she'd have no hesitation at all blowing my brains out. I pulled the trigger.

We finished the site and headed north to the first site. We did it, moved to the jungle, drank some water, broke out dried beef and chewed on it. We could hear the trucks coming. When they came to a stop, there was a lot of laughter and joking. Our thoughts were, *Get out of the fuckin' truck.* They finally did and began to go down the shaft. There was a great commotion by the shaft, screaming and cursing. We had left our calling cards on the bodies.

They loaded the bodies on the trucks, along with their belongings. The trucks went north. We sat back and waited, thinking *The same is going on south, and at least we won't have to wait around.*

The trucks came back; the drivers went down the shaft. I guess they figured lightning doesn't strike twice, so they didn't post guards. We rigged the trucks with the C4, went back to the jungle, and waited. When we felt the time was right, we headed for the shafts. When I got to the tunnel, they looked like sardines in black. I dropped the front grip and sprayed their heads. I emptied the clip and shoved in a 50-clip.

The next tunnel was the same, except I sprayed forward and back. I emptied the clip. The last tunnel I did was a 30-clip. We were tossing our calling cards on each body, so we'd have our head count. When we finished, we dropped grenades down the shafts, destroying the tunnel then moved south.

We got to the site – it was so quiet you could hear a pin drop. *These fucks are stupid. If they were Americans, there'd be guards posted.* We went down the shafts, did our thing, and headed south for the hill. The only problem was that I had run out of cards, with some bodies left.

We got to the base of the hill as it was getting light. I looked up thinking it wasn't a hill, it was a fuckin' mountain. We climbed to the top, set up our post and began the recon. There was a lot of movement going south. Hawk told me he would do the first fifteen. I told him when he checked in with our count, I had sixty, and I was going to do some recon across the top of the hill. I started crawling and heard a tank moving with me at the bottom of the hill. I crawled over a small ventilation shaft and kept crawling.

I moved to the south edge and watched the tank do a ninety-degree turn, then move into the hill. Another tank did the same thing, and then another. I decided to crawl to the far end of the hill. I passed over five more ventilation shafts. I looked for another opening. There was none. On the way back, Hawk got me on the radio to see if I was OK. "I'm on my way back. Hawk, you won't believe what we have here"

I crawled back to the opening. They must have fueled the tanks. They moved them and the artillery outside, covered them with camouflage netting. Trucks with large fuel tanks and munitions were going in. And then trucks carrying troops unloaded at the entrance. The trucks turned back for the trail. I counted twenty heads on each truck.

I crawled to Hawk as he finished checking in. I told him I'd take over and told him what I saw. I told him to crawl across the top. "You'll go over a vent shaft. About a hundred feet further you'll see a large opening on the south side."

By the time he got back, there was a long procession of troop-trucks moving south and empties going north. It seemed forever. These fuckers just kept coming. After seven hours we logged four hundred troop-carriers had moved past us. After a few more trucks with logistics, the trail got quiet. I checked in, told them all was quiet, and I'd call when we had something. It got quiet because the sun was up.

Hawk and I hunkered down. I told him what I wanted to do. I drew the hill on a piece of paper, pinpointed the six vent shafts and the opening. I wanted to get ahold of Big Bravo. "We'll find an LZ close by, have him get us six bundles of C4 with fifty feet of cable for each, a good-sized detonator, and seven hundred and fifty feet of leads for each. I'm going to ask for a crew of four in the chopper. The six of us could each take a shaft.

"Before we detonate the C4, we'll get the crew out of here. What do you think about it? Did I miss anything?"

As Hawk was thinking, we heard explosions north of us. We gave each other high-fives. Hawk said, "I like it, but the hill is going to implode bringing down everything inside. We ought to ask B for an air strike to hit the tanks and artillery outside."

"Good idea. I knew there was a reason I kept you around.""

I was expecting "fuck you" – instead he gave me the birdie.

I got on the radio, told Bravo, "Everything is quiet; we are leaving our post and will check in later, and will need to talk to Big. Out".

We went down the hill into the jungle and started walking north. After a while we came upon an area that looked like it got hit with napalm at one time. It would make a good LZ.

We moved back into the jungle, got on our knees. I called Bravo and told Brown everything. I told him this was why there was little movement further south on the trail, and I didn't think this would end it all, but we'd make big dent. It would give us time to build our offensive instead of waiting for theirs. Hawk was on his radio listening. I asked if he had anything. He replied no, I had hit it all.

Brown came on, "At 1100 hours a chopper will be on the LZ with what you want. At 1200 jets will take out their target. Out."

We sat down, leaned against a trunk, broke out water and the beef. We had about three hours till 1100. I knew Hawk fucked his brains out before we left, and he probably hadn't slept in thirty-six hours. I don't know how long it's been for me. We were feeling it. We had a long day ahead of us till we were back at base. I told Hawk to take some ZZZs while I stayed awake. He nodded yes. I leaned against the trunk, took out a cigarette, cupped the glow in my hand, and exhaled on the ground. I was thinking, This cigarette tastes so good after the fine dinner I just had. In my opinion Hawk and I were lucky. We had encountered only twelve tunnels out of all the ones we did that required hand-to-hand. Between our 22s and our knives, they were easy. In a weird kind of way hand-to-hand hyped me up.

I started thinking about Chua, wondering how much of it was bullshit. It was still worth it to me. That slant-eyed bitch is probably sucking some other GI right now, looking for another score. I was thinking about the girl in the tunnel: if she hadn't gone for the weapon and pissed me off, she'd be alive. I'm sorry I offed her. I could have fucked that slant up. Then I thought about Hoai Mi's tits, her shoving them in your face whenever she could. The only good thing in thinking about all that shit was it passed time.

The chopper was overhead. I got Hawk up. The chopper set down, four troops came out, shouldering bags. One was carrying the detonator. Two of them had our bags.

We got our bags and set off for the hill. We climbed the hill, opened the bags, and dropped the sacks of C4 down the vent shafts. After securing the cable, we ran the leads down the hill. The six of us were at the detonator. I told the crew to get out of here, and they took off for the chopper.

We attached the leads. Hawk waited till the chopper had time to get out of the area, then he did it. Like before, at first there was silence. After everything fell inward, fuel and munitions exploded. It felt like we were on a fault line of a major earthquake. The ground shook violently, and then the volcano erupted, twice as high as before. Shit was coming down all around us.

We started running through the jungle as the jets made their pass. I don't know if it was because we were tired, or the running, but we separated. We had always moved through the jungle side by side. I heard Hawk yell "wire!" I was going over a good-sized trunk. I heard the click. Hawk must have gone down on it.

A piece of him flew over me as the shrapnel opened my leg like a book with pages flapping, from my knee to my ankle. I pulled myself up using the good leg and the trunk. Hawk was all over...in the palms...on the shrubbery. I began cursing and fell back down, pounding the ground, and I kept doing it. I began cursing in Italian. Then I went off on a tirade.

I screamed. "You fuckin' prick!" ... "You son of a bitch!" ... "Why'd you fuck up?"... "We were going to have a great life together!" ... "We were going to conquer the world, and you had to do this!" I calmed down and thought, It should've been me, not you. I hollered out, "Hawk, I love you."

At that point I realized my leg was hurting bad, and shrapnel had to have severed arteries – I was lying in a puddle of blood. I took off my belt and drew it tight above my knee. Then I tried to close my leg and wrap a strap around it. That didn't work out too well. I fell back, probably from exhaustion, and reached the beacon knob on the radio.

I went into myself to bring my god to me, and suddenly I was out of it. I was on my back moving through the clouds, feeling good. I was enjoying the different cloud colors. Hawk walked up to me and hugged me. We gave each other a high-five; then he walked off. Later my mother walked over, kissed me on the forehead, and stood by my side for a long time. I waited for the wolf. I kept waiting. He never came.

I don't know how long I was out. A day? A week? I had no idea. I heard voices. They seemed to be far off, but they weren't.

One said, "We'll have to get a team out here to get all the pieces. I'm going to look for a dog tag."

The other said, "This one's had it. We'll bag him."

I was in blackness. Wherever it was, it was hot as hell and smelled like shit. I was going in and out. I don't know how long it was before I heard a chopper, and then it stopped. I felt like I was lying in something on the ground. A hand reached in and yanked my dog tag off the chain. The chain, other tag, and my half-heart went down my blouse. A guy hollered out, "We have to get rid of this one. Hard to take the stink."

I had no idea how long I lay there. I felt the bag being lifted, and I started pounding on the bag with my arm. The bag unzipped, and I shoved my arm through the opening. I heard, "He's alive!"

Another voice said, "We have to get him out of that bag and to the medvac."

I was on a gurney. A guy hit me in the leg with a needle. My leg went to sleep. Another guy was running alongside, trying to wrap my leg in a big bandage. The needle guy hit me again in my body, and I was out.

I opened my eyes. I was on a gurney staring at a tent top. My wrist felt funny, and looking at it, I could tell they stuck me again. This time I had a tube sticking out of it going to three bags hanging on a rack. Two were clear and one was blood. I was thinking, *These fucks like needles.* I wondered if I now had pierced ears. I felt like I was drunk – even my thoughts were slurred.

There was a guy in med whites standing by the side of my bed. He said, "Good, you're up. I found this when I cut your clothes off." He was holding the half-heart and dog tag chain. He seemed excited to show me the heart.

I motioned toward the trash can. I didn't realize I had just my tee and shorts on. "You didn't happen to slip? My dick feels funny."

I don't know how long I was out. When I woke up, my eyes were closed, but I was alert. I said to myself, "Motherfucking cocksucker. I pissed the bed!" And I got mad, thinking, *What the fuck is happening to me?* Then I realized the bed wasn't wet. I smiled to myself – I just invented dry piss. I could package it and make a bundle.

I fell off. I was on a ride, in and out without any concept of time. I could have been there weeks, even years. I woke up and a guy in whites was standing by the bed. My leg was hurting. I asked him what was going on with my leg. He told me I had been in OR for three hours. "They were concerned the tendons that were intact would dry out. They packed them and closed your leg temporarily."

"What do you mean by temporarily?"

"You're going to have a lot more OR time before it's permanent."

I asked how long had I had been here. "Almost a month. It took a long time to pump you with enough antibiotics to kill the infection."

"Time flies when you're having fun." I told him I had one more question, a little personal. "I had the feeling that I pissed, but the bed's not wet" I told him I didn't want him to look or touch my dick, just to tell me. He smiled and walked to the other side of the bed, picked up a plastic bag, stepped back and showed me the bag. He said that when I arrived a catheter was inserted in my penis to my bladder, and my urine is collected in this bag.

I asked if he was saving it, didn't get an answer. I thought to myself, "So much for worrying about it." I fell off. I woke. The same guy in whites was talking to the guy in the next bed, saw my eyes were open, and came over. He asked if I was OK, did I need something?

"If you're collecting my piss, which you can keep by the way, what's going on with my shit?"

He smiled again and told me, "We're getting that, too."

I fell off. When I woke up, my leg hurt and felt different. He told me I just had another visit with the OR. "If you're collecting my shit and piss, what have I been eating and drinking?" He told me they were feeding me intravenously, and it'd been sustaining me well.

"I hope it's Italian. Whatever it is, I don't taste anything." I fell off. Three more times I'd wake, feel my leg hurting, and fall off. I decided I had a new way of life. I woke, and looked around, feeling alert. A guy in whites walked up to me and asked how I felt. "I feel good. Where's my guy?"

"My name's Robert. I'll be taking care of you. James did ten and is on two days R and R. He told me you were a good patient, and funny."

I told him I didn't know about either of that. He asked if I would like to be washed and shaved. I told him only by a female nurse. He told me there were no females in the unit. So, I said no, I don't.

He told me I was to be transported to Tripler Medical Center in Hawaii at 1000 hours tomorrow. "You are being transferred there because it's a large military medical center. They have teams of medical specialists to treat your leg, and we don't. Also, they have a concern of you reacquiring an infection here."

I asked if everything was going with me; he answered yes. I told him to be sure to empty the piss bag because James was collecting it.  I fell off. Robert woke me up and said he had to clean me up. A Captain Johnson was on his way to see me.

"We've been through this. Forget it unless you've grown a pair of tits."

"Word on the base is they're going to make you the most decorated GI in this campaign. Is it true what everyone is talking about? What you've done?"

I told him probably not.

Johnson walked into the tent. Robert saw him and hollered out, "Attention."     Johnson immediately said, "As you were" He was a young guy in dress uniform. He stood at attention by my bed. He started talking, and it was like it had been scripted. He rattled on, and then he stated he wished to express the gratitude of the army and our country for valor and heroism. He wished to bestow…

I stopped him and said, "I'll accept the gratitude, but that's it. I don't feel that good about our country or the army. I just lost my best friend, my brother. For what? Nothing! It's the politicians' and the army's fault. Can you tell me if Sergeant Duwayne Hawkins' remains have been gathered?"

 He said he didn't know but would check on it.

"If they haven't, you order a team out there. His remains are to be placed in a coffin, never to be opened by anyone, and shipped home to Arlington National Cemetery.

He's to be buried in a prominent plot. I want the army to bring his family and anyone from his hometown that wants to attend his funeral to Washington. I want officers and enlisted men at his funeral. I want the President there. I was going to tell you, you could bestow the medals up your ass. Instead, have them bestowed on him. I want Hawkins declared posthumously the most decorated soldier of the Vietnam War. Can you do that?"

He didn't answer. I demanded, "I asked you a question!"

He answered, "Yes I can do that."

I told him, "Good. Dismissed."

He turned and walked out. Robert walked over, extended his hand, and asked if he could shake my hand. After he left the tent, I lay back thinking I was glad it went down the way it did. I didn't have to use plan B. I didn't have a Plan B.

Robert pulled up a chair. He had a clipboard in his hand. He had to do the paperwork for my transfer. He read off a form: "Sergeant Paul B. Walker, US 51484707. I need your MOS (military occupation specialty) and description." I told him my MOS. He told me he never heard of that one. I explained: Special Forces, Long Range Special Operations. He filled in line after line. He concluded by saying he was going to need help on something but would handle it later. I asked what.

He said, "Your records show you're deceased. I guess no one knew how to correct it."

I pictured going to Hawaii in a cushy, open coffin, with my bags hanging out.

# *CHAPTER 53*

Two guys rolled in a gurney. It took all three of us to get me on it. Robert walked next to me holding the rack of bags. They put me in the transport. The rack was attached to the roof. A guy ran to the transport and got in. I said to myself, *The needle guy.* Sure enough, he hit me with a needle. Had to be good stuff – I began feeling it right away.

He got out, and Robert was standing at the backdoor, at attention, saluting me. They closed the door.

The transport moved out of the med area to the base main street. Out the window I saw troops lining the street, saluting the transport as it passed them. The transport stopped. The back door opened, and Brown was standing at attention, saluting me.

I said, "Hi Sarge," and out I went again. I opened my eyes. I was in an air transport, strapped on a gurney. There were a bunch of other guys, some on gurneys, others in wheelchairs. A guy in whites was hanging another bag on my rack. "Don't overload it, they're liable to come down and hurt me."

He said he'd try to make sure that didn't happen. I asked if it was chow. He told me no, it would be a very long flight, and this would let me relax.

The engines started. An officer came out of the cockpit and was moving through the plane, checking to make sure everyone was secured. When he reached me, he asked if he could shake my hand. Brown saying good-bye was right and good, but I didn't understand the rest of the shit. I was out.

They must have hung a lot of that good stuff. The next time I opened my eyes, I was in a hospital bed against a window, in a ward with eleven other guys in beds. I was at Tripler in Hawaii.

A guy in whites came over ask how I felt. He then said Saigon had sent a duffle bag which he took the liberty of unpacking for me. He listed what they sent. Two pairs of sharp fatigues with first sergeant stripes, a Special Forces badge, and Twenty-Fifth patch on it. Two pairs of boots – one pair was a jungle boot, a pair of dress shoes and a uniform. They also sent new tees, briefs and socks. Two knives, one big and one smaller. A carton of cigarettes and a box of cigars. There was also a deck of playing cards with a note that read: "So you don't forget us."

I asked if he had opened the deck. He hadn't. I told him to trash the small knife, get the deck and open it. He took out a card and studied it.

"That was my partner's and my calling card in country. The words on it are in Vietnamese. Ma guy means ghost devil."

The guy lying in the bed next to me had bandages covering most of the right side: face, neck, shoulder, and down to his knee. He leaned over on his left side and asked, "You were *ma guy*?" I said yes. He asked if he could have a card. I said sure. The medic handed him one.

The medic told me they were going to take me to the OR soon. He would see me when I got back to the ward. There must have been a lot of GIs from the First and the Twenty-Fifth in the room because I heard *ma guy* go around the room. Guys sitting up looked at me, and those who could, waved.

A guy in a dark blue med suit asked if I was Sergeant Paul Walker. He said his name was Bryant and was taking me to the OR. I asked first or last – he said first.

He unlocked the wheels and started to push me out of the room. Somebody called out, "Sarge, can I have a card?" Another asked if he could also have one. I told the medic to give the cards to whoever wanted one.

Bryant asked, "What's with the card?"

I asked the medic to give Bryant a card first, so we could get out of there. Bryant was looking at the card while pushing me. I told him look at it in the elevator – I wanted to get to the OR in one piece. The elevator took us to the basement. Bryant pushed me through a double door into a room outside of the OR. On my left, it looked like a row of curtained cubbyholes. On my right were four double doors that looked substantial, with an illuminated sign above each door. The sign had two words, "In Use."

Bryant pushed me down the row till we came to an open curtain. I looked in. It was a cubbyhole. He pushed me in, head first, closed the curtain, and flipped a light switch on the wall. I asked what the switch was for. It was to tell the nurse's station we were here. I told him I hoped a naked nurse would come through the curtain. He laughed. If it did happen, I wouldn't know what to do. And with my luck, I'd fall off the gurney and break my dick.

Bryant asked about the card. He knew the Vietnamese feared the ace of spades. "The skeleton is a good touch, but what is '*ma guy*' and why the card?"

I explained *ma guy* meant ghost devil. "My partner and I were long-range ops. We used the cards as calling cards. It also made it easy to keep track of the head count."

"I was told you and your partner have eliminated more of the enemy than any two GIs in any war. True?" I told him I didn't know about that.

He said he had to leave. Someone would push me into the OR when they finished with me there.

"You mean you're not going to? Thank God! I was worried about that. You pushing me, I wouldn't make it there and miss the surgery." He smiled and left.

I was lying there, looking at the curtain, twiddling my thumbs. I was bored. Normally I could get wrapped up in something or think about the operation. Now I was a blank. The curtain opened, and a female walked in wearing a hat, mask, full-length operating suit, and plastic gloves. Cheerfully she said, "Hi, my name is Lisa. I'm your prep nurse." She explained she was going to take my vitals and get some information from me. She would help me strip and then wash my body with an anti-bacterial solution.

"After I wash you, I'll set an IV in your wrist and another in your right arm, and I'll hang a bag. When I've finished, they should be ready for you. Do you have any questions or problems with what I have told you?"

I told her I had a problem. "For my well-being, could you do all of that with your mask off, so I can look at a beautiful, sexy woman?" She brushed my arm and told me when I got out.

"With my luck, you'll be off duty and I'll have to look at a guy." She promised she'd be there.

She began, went through it quickly, and got to the strip. She asked if I could lift myself up without putting any pressure on my leg. I put my hand flat on the bed and lifted easily, and she removed the gown. She had me sit up, so she could remove my tee shirt. I did, and she took it off. She realized she was staring at my body and hurriedly told me she was going to cut the right leg of my shorts and slip it off my left leg.

"OK. If you cut down the middle, and slip, don't worry about it. I haven't used it for a while. Not sure if it still works."

She laughed and told me she was going to cut my shorts on the side. She put the scissors on the bed, put her hand on the wall and leaned against the wall, still laughing. She stopped, picked up the scissors, cut the shorts, slid them off, and asked if I could lie on my left side, again not putting any pressure on my leg. She began washing my back, swabbed down to my butt, even my asshole. Next came the legs, the injured one washed very gently. She told me to turn over on my back. She washed my body slowly, seemed like she was enjoying it. She got to my belly button, washed it, and moved down to my crotch, washed my balls and dick. After she threw the last pad in the trash she told me it was going to be a long operation.

"When you're back and over the anesthesia, I'll remove the catheter. You won't be seeing us for a month." With a chuckle, she said, "You will be able to use that thing again," and covered it with a towel. As she opened the curtain to leave, I asked her to lift her mask, so I could peek. She said, "Later."

I opened my eyes. I felt good except for my throat. By the side of the bed was this beautiful blonde. My preppy had kept her promise and taken off her hat, mask and gloves. "You're very much worth the wait. You are beautiful." I held her hand and asked, "No ring? Because of the job, or you're not married?"

"Job. My husband is a surgeon. He was one of the team that operated on you." She bent over, cupped my dick with the catheter between two fingers, and told me to take a deep breath. And it was out.

I yelled, "Thank you. I'm free, I'm free."

She covered me with a towel and told me, "When they pick you up, they will help you dress. A new gown, tee shirt and shorts are on the shelf. You might want to wait till tomorrow to put your shorts on." I was so into her looks, and the way she moved her mouth when she talked, that I didn't realize I had a cast from above my knee to the bottom of my foot. She bent over kissed me on the cheek, "If I wasn't married, I'd be all over you in a split second."

Bryant helped me get dressed. Not much was said. He asked if I was alright, I nodded yes. I told him I wouldn't be seeing him for a while because the next operation was in thirty days. He asked if that was bothering me. "The way you drove? Hell no."

I asked if he had some time. He answered all the time in the world as he sat by the bed. I asked if he was a Holy Roller. He said no, that he tried to get as much as he can.

I told him about what happened with my prep nurse.

When I finished, Bryant told me Lisa is two things. "She's the best piece of ass in this hospital. From top to bottom, she's all woman. Just looking at her dressed, at her great features, could make you come in your pants. The second thing is she's intelligent, classy, a loving wife, and mother."

"Bryant, ever since I got hurt, I hadn't thought about a woman or sex. Today after the catheter came out, and she said that stuff, if she meant it or was being nice, it didn't matter. I felt a twinge in my dick. I need to ask a favor. If you have a problem with it, I understand. I need to get some."

He asked if I wanted a kind of loving, long-term deal or a blow job, fuck when you wanted it.

"When I want it."

He told me he'd see what he could do. I raised a hand and told him give me five.

Before I could finish, I dropped my hand. My chin dropped to my chest, and I was cringing. He asked, "Hawkins?" I didn't answer. He said, "It's OK. Let it out." I don't know how long I was like that. When I lifted my head, Bryant was sitting there. He looked sad.

I snapped, "You still here?" We started laughing. He asked if I wanted to talk about Hawkins.

"Fuck, no. I tried hard to bury Saigon, the war, the whole fuckin' stupid thing. No, I don't want to talk about anything that has to do with it."

"Down the road, we'll talk about it. You need to, so you can put it behind you and move on."

"Bryant, you're not a bed jockey.  Exactly what are you?"

"I'm a counselor assigned to the hospital to counsel GIs from Nam. I'm in the Twenty-Second."

I said, "Easy duty," with a smile.

"Not really. I'd rather be in action than go through the grief I hear." He asked if I minded if he popped in on me. I told him no, he was good company.

When I woke up. A medic asked how I felt. I told him good. I had gotten a restful sleep, something I hadn't had in a while.

"Great. You're going back to the OR this morning. They're going to put you out, pull the bowel hose, stitch you up inside and out, and send you back here. You will still have the feed bag for another day. When I sit you on the bedpan, all you'll have is water running out."

I asked who wipes me. "If you can, be my guest. If not, I will."

Joking, I told him, "You gotta be gentle with me."

He was taking my vitals when Bryant walked in. He asked if I was ready for our little trip.

"Hell no. Banging into walls? Almost running over a guy coming out of the elevator? I have to tell them you don't have a driver's license. My heart can't take it!"

"Yeah, yeah. It's fun. Let's go." All the time we were razzing each other, the medic was laughing. I told Bryant, "At least somebody's having fun." He laughed.

In the elevator, I asked, "What do you think? Lisa?" He answered maybe.

At the OR Bryant pushed me into the cubbyhole, closed the curtain, flicked the switch and stayed with me. The two of us were waiting for the curtain to open. The expectation of seeing Lisa was getting to us.

The curtain opened and in waddles this heavy-set guy in the prep uniform. Bryant told him hello and was walking out when I said, "My luck. If I didn't have bad, I'd have none."

From the other side of the curtain I heard "Hi, Bryant," and "Hi, Lisa."

I thought, *That fuck! He sees Lisa and look what I get.* Actually, the guy was great.

I woke up in the ward. No Bryant. I felt a rumble in my gut. I thought, Not yet, I need some rest. I had that feeling it was on its way, not immediately, but it was coming.

In walks Bryant with this beautiful woman in civilian clothes, great looking body, nice tits, and terrific legs. I was thinking, *Is this what we talked about? Not now! Your timing sucks.* I was concentrating on my bottom so hard, I didn't get a hard-on looking at her.

She walked over to me, said, "Hi, Paul," and kissed me on the cheek. She stood upright and said, "Lisa."

"Lisa! Wow. It's great to see you. You're beautiful and absolutely perfect!" While we were talking, I was in agony, not because of her.

"I stopped by to say hello and good-bye. We're transferring to Bethesda."

"No chance of him going and leaving you with me?"

"That would be nice, but no chance. Good-bye, Paul."

"Good-bye, it's been my pleasure meeting you."

I told Bryant to run over to that medic, tell him I need a bedpan right now. While he was gone, I dropped my drawers, lifted my gown up and was sitting in bed bare-assed. The medic ran over with a towel and bedpan. I lifted, he spread the towel on the bed, and set the pan on it under me.

"These are moist wipes. They're best for you right now. When you're finished with one, put it in this plastic bag." I nodded OK.

He was standing by the side, and Bryant was at the foot. "If you two don't mind, get out of here. And Bryant, next time I see you, I'll tell you about what I just went through."

"That will be good. I've got an idea of what you're going to tell me." They left.

I figured the guys in the beds had their own problems and wouldn't care about a guy in bed shitting. Then it sounded like a fire hose hitting a tin bucket. It splattered, caught me everywhere. My balls felt like they were dripping. With all that, I had a sense of relief. I cleaned myself as best I could and then it started again. After two stop-and-goes, I felt like I was done. Then it hit me again. I was almost out of wipes. The bag was getting full.

I reached inside of me and said, *You're punishing me for the bad things I've done. Fine! Enough is enough.* I know it wasn't that, but it seemed to have stopped. When I was in the world and didn't have facts to back up what I was saying, I'd say "I had a gut feeling." *After this I'll never use that expression again.*

I called the medic and told him I was on a break and the pan was going to overflow. I lifted. He took the pan, dumped it in the toilet, and put it on the floor. After he washed his hands, he put gloves on. He walked over to me and put a new pan and more wipes on the bed.

He said he was a ten-year corpsman. He had a wife and two kids, and he had absolutely no interest in me or my body, other than medically. He needed to wash me – it wasn't healthy for me to be the way I was.

He washed me everywhere, then told me to lift up. He pulled the towel out, spread a dry one on the bed, and told me to sit on it. Handing me a towel he told me to dry myself. After he cleaned up everything, he left the pan, wipes, and disposal bag on the bed.

My night went great, no problems at all. A medic told me he needed to take my vitals. I was going to radiology to have a sonogram. They want to look at the internal stitches, and a doctor would check the ones on the outside.

"From what I can tell, they look fine. After radiology, you'll come back here for your first chow, if you want it. It will be very light." He went over to one of the other beds.

Bryant walked in and asked if I was ready for radiology. I asked if he was going to jockey me there. "I figured you gave up on it because of your lack of skill." He said he was having too much fun pushing me around.

In radiology, there were a bunch of GIs, mostly in wheel-chairs, waiting. Bryant took my order to the desk and returned. I told him about my problem while Lisa was there. He told me he knew it. He didn't know how bad it was till I told him to tell the medic, "I need a bed pan now!"

There was a bunch of female techs scurrying back and forth. When we got a good looker, we'd look at each other and nod our approval. I saw a couple that I really wanted to fuck. Looks like I'm getting it back! A neat looking one passed close by the bed, stopped and was staring at Bryant before leaving. I commented, "Looks like you have a sharp-looking admirer."

A GI in a wheelchair came over to the gurney. He was missing a left leg and arm. He extended his right hand to me. "Twenty-Fifth. Can I shake your hand?" We shook hands.

One of the techs that I had fantasized about came over to take me back for my sonogram. Up close she was cute and carried herself well. On the way, I asked why I was going ahead of all these guys. She told me ninety percent of the GIs seen are here for X-rays. She pushed me into a room and told me she was going to remove my gown and tee shirt. I needed to move onto my left side. She took the gown and tee off and seemed to be transfixed on my body. I turned on my side.

She played with a screen on a stand. There were a couple of clicks. She spread a cold gel on my right side, leaned over and began rubbing what looked like a microphone over the gel. What was nice was I could look at her face and watch her expressions as she worked, pressing the microphone down and moving it back and forth. Each time she moved the microphone, her tits rubbed me. They felt good. The little guy perked up.

She reached the screen with her left hand, steadied her right, pushed a button, and told me, "We're done." She cleaned the gel off. I put my tee on. She put my gown on. She told me if I cleaned up, I would look fantastic. I told her she didn't need to clean up – she looked beautiful.

I told her under different circumstances, I'd ask her for a date. "We would have a great dinner and then do whatever we wanted and have fun. Instead, when you're off, if you have nothing else to do, I can get us a room. We can talk, and I can look at your beautiful face." She said she'd love to.

She started to push me out. She stopped, bent down and kissed me on the cheek, then asked if she could bring her girlfriend. Bryant was talking to his admirer. He broke it off and started pushing me. I asked if he hooked up.

"Yes, I think this is the one."

"Good for you. Home, James."

In the room, I told Bryant I needed him to do some things for me. I wanted a wheelchair – not an enlisted-man's piece of shit, an officer's. I wanted a pair of crutches that fit me.

"I heard they don't make them that small."

I asked if he said something.

He said he didn't hear anything.

"Make sure the rubber on the bottom is small enough to fit. After we go on a tour, I need you to have somebody shave me. I don't care if they don't have tits – but not you. You probably shave as well as you drive."

I lay back thinking, *I enjoy the banter we have.* A medic put a portable pot by the bed. He seemed proud of himself. I told him, "For most of my tour I had to shit with an audience – I didn't care. But now I want to have a private moment and enjoy a cigarette." He picked up the porta pot and walked out. I guess I hurt his feelings by refusing the pot. Otherwise he would have asked how I planned to get to the latrine.

Bryant came into the room with a wheelchair with a pair of crutches across it.

"Maintenance cut them down." And in case I got any ideas, he had them put an extra-large rubber tip on them. I didn't come back with anything. He told me he lined up the shave, "And she has tits, nice ones." He turned the chair around. Stenciled on the back was FOR OFFICER USE ONLY. He was going to have it blocked out, but changed his mind, because I was the best officer he had ever known. He locked the wheels and put the arm down. "Slide over, stand up with the good foot, hold onto the standing arm." He would handle getting the cast into the rack. It all went smoothly, although I was a little wobbly standing.

Bryant put the arm up, unlocked the wheels, got behind the chair complaining, "How come I always get the hard job?" We were off. Bryant told me, "This floor has wards like yours." On the floor below we passed different departments: cardiology, neurology, audiology, and everything you could think of. We took the elevator down to another floor. This one had room after room of physical therapy. One was marked aqua therapy.

The next floor was the best. All kinds of different rooms. On the opposite side, offices. Bryant pushed me by a reading room, a lounge, a room that had ping pong tables, and a room with card tables. As we passed the various rooms, Bryant hit the brakes so hard I slid up in the chair. He said, "We're going in here!"

I told him I wanted to go outside and get some fresh air.

# *CHAPTER 54*

"Later. Now we're going in here." I looked over. There was a good-sized color television. On the screen was a coffin with a flag draped over it. I told Bryant I didn't want to go to a funeral. We had gotten close – that gave him the liberty to tell me to shut up and watch the screen. The camera panned up. There were two rows of civilians, three white guys, and the rest Black. The camera moved. There was row after row of GIs in dress, standing at attention. The camera then moved left to a row of officers standing shoulder to shoulder at attention.

The next focus was on the civilians. Most of the men and women were holding handkerchiefs to their eyes. Those that didn't had their heads bowed. The camera moved to the right to a small podium, and more officers standing shoulder to shoulder at attention. I could have sworn I saw gold stars on several of them. My first thought was the president died and this was his funeral. The camera moved further right. Standing by himself was the president.

A bugler began to play. The music sounded sad, mournful. There was a twenty-one-gun salute. A squadron of jets in formation passed overhead. The one in the rear dropped a wing – it was a salute. Taps sounded, and an officer took the podium and asked everyone to join him in a prayer.

An officer who had three gold stars on his epaulets took the podium. He introduced himself as General Westmoreland. He started by saying he felt humbled to be here in the presence of this man. He went on to say, "It is important we do this. It is important that those of you watching, and the world, know that First Sergeant Duwayne Hawkins is, and will always be, the most decorated hero of the Vietnam War."

Then he said, "Without further delay, I present to you the President of the United States of America."

Without fanfare, the President took the podium and gave a short speech. He ended with, "It is hard to express the magnitude of the gratitude the country and the military have for Sergeant Hawkins." I thought his speech wasn't written for him, it came from his heart.

He walked to Mrs. Hawkins, took her hand and helped her stand. He presented her with the Congressional Medal of Honor, saying he would give anything to be placing the medal on Duwayne rather than this way. Kissing her on the forehead, he asked that she remain standing while the officers expressed their condolences and presented her with Duwayne's medals.

A general took the podium to say, "Before I present the many medals I am holding to Mrs. Hawkins, it is equally important the country, the military, and especially the army, express its gratitude to First Sergeant Paul Walker, Sergeant Hawkins's partner who is recovering from wounds and could not be here." I was sorry the guy mentioned my name.

I looked at Bryant and told him I needed to make a phone call. "What time is it in Nam?" He looked at his watch, thought for minute and said 0900. I told him I needed to call a Sergeant Brown in Long Binh – it was very important. He told me to drive my own wheels and follow him. I made a U-turn and followed him into an office.

There was a lieutenant behind a desk looking at a screen. Bryant said, "Lieutenant, you will place a call to Sergeant Brown, Special Forces, in Long Binh this instant for Sergeant Walker?"

The lieutenant was on the phone. We heard, "No. Right now. Force the call." He handed me the phone. All I heard was a humming noise.

I looked up at Bryant and said, "They at least could have had music on here." He shoved my shoulder. I looked at him and said, "Invalid abuse."

At last Brown picked up the phone. After greeting each other I asked if I outranked him. He told me no, we're the same. I said, "OK. Instead of giving you an order, I need to ask a favor."

I told him I needed him to get ahold of Captain Johnson and tell him thank you, and I apologize. After a hesitation, he came back, "Negative. There isn't enough rice in this screwed-up country to get me to do that. If I ever see the shit-head, I'll stick him in a toilet and flush.

"Let me tell you what happened. I got a call that Captain Johnson wanted to meet with Colonel Bolton. I asked him to hold and told the Colonel. The Colonel told me to tell him to come over and for me to join them. I walked into the Colonel's office with Johnson. I stood off to the side as Johnson stood at attention in front of the Colonel's desk. He saluted. The Colonel told him we do not do that here, at ease. Johnson remained standing at attention.

"He told the colonel he wanted to bring up court-martial charges against Sergeant Walker. That uptight dipstick ran through everything that went down between the two of you. Johnson specifically emphasized the 'up his ass' and 'dismissed.'

When he finished, Bolton looked at him with a stern, impassive face and asked if he omitted anything. He said no. Johnson was beaming, figuring he nailed it.

"Colonel Bolton is a brilliant strategist. He evaluated what Johnson said. With the same stern expression on his face, he said, 'Captain, you are a fucking idiot. Dismissed – that means get the hell out of my office, asswipe.' Johnson slinked out.

"The colonel got on the phone and said, 'Let me talk to Westy. This is Bolt'. He was told the General was in a meeting with his staff. The Colonel got angry and told whoever he was talking to, to interrupt. He must have gotten an objection. He exploded and yelled into the phone, 'Do it, goddamn it! This is important!'

"He began with, 'This is the situation.' When he finished telling him everything that went down, he hung up. Later we heard Westmoreland gave his staff orders. They got on phones. He did, too.

"Brown told me Colonel Bolton was fuming. He wanted me to investigate every aspect of what happened to you and Hawkins after the beacon went off. He wanted to know who brought you in. Did they follow-up on Hawkins' remains? What took them so long to get to you?

"I did and gave him a complete report. The simple version is the Vietnaese brought people in from everywhere to scour the surrounding area looking for whoever did it. When they came upon the area you and Hawkins were in, they gave it a wide berth. The sight must have been horrific, that's why they missed you.

"During an interrogation, I was told when our team reached the beacon, they were trying to do everything by the book. Everything went out the window when you came to life in the bag. They were so concerned about getting you out of there they dropped the ball on Hawkins. That was corrected immediately."

"Sarg, please convey my heartfelt thanks to the colonel for making everything happen, and I thank you for being you. Out."

The lieutenant got up and asked to shake my hand. He turned to Bryant and told him, "Sir, if I can ever be of service, don't hesitate to ask."

Outside the office, I said, "Bryant, I didn't know you were an officer. I should have known by the way you drive."

He smiled, "I'm not, but I sure as hell sounded like one."

Then I asked how he knew I was Special Forces. "We've got a good-size file on you. We should get back to the room. You have an appointment for a shave. We'll go outside after."

He took me to the room and left. There was a spec4 leaning against the bed. She stood up as I rolled in front of her. She took off her blouse, laid it on the bed and folded it. She was wearing a tee shirt but no bra. I could see the outline of nice, perky tits, and her nipples poked against the tee.

I looked down said to myself, "Exercise, exercise." A little later I realized I had a tent in my lap. I nonchalantly put my hand under my gown and moved my dick between my legs. All during the shave her tits were close to me. At one point a nipple brushed my cheek. That was it! I came! I thought to myself, *Fuck this shit. What a waste of good cum. My legs are gonna stick together. I'll never walk again.*

I was glad she finished. The room was getting dark. No one had turned the lights on. She leaned over me, kissed me, and said, "Sarg, I'd do anything for you." I gently nudged her up, introduced myself, and asked her name. It was Jennifer.

I told her it had been a long day. "How about I make arrangements for an officer's room? We could spend the night together."

She said, "Outstanding." I told her I'd get in touch with her. She put on her top, got her things together, and left.

I looked at the crutches and thought, *Next time.* I did a half-turn and shot into the john. With the help of a disabled railing, I sat down, lifted my gown up, and pulled my shorts down. Like a bullet, it shot out of me. This is great – *I'm not loose.* I sat there in case there was more, thinking, *Oh, what a relief it is.* There wasn't any more. I cleaned myself, got back in the chair, and rolled into the room.

I sat by the window thinking. *This fucking army has taken my brother from me, has made me half of what I was, and has made me into a sexual nutcase. What happened to respect for a woman? What happened to me? I'm one fucked-up guy.*

Either Bryant was getting his brains fucked out or he fell asleep. I decided to get something to eat and go outside. I opened my locker to get a pack of cigarettes and a cigar and noticed my fatigues. I took the gown off and put on the top. It felt good. They had put on my sergeant stripes. My 25th patch was on one shoulder and the Special Forces patch on the other. It had the army band and my name band.

I had finished eating and was drinking when a mess hall guy in whites walked over. He offered me a slice of apple pie he had in back. He returned and put it on the table. He nodded when I thanked him. My first thought was: The army's not so bad. Second thought: *Bullshit. It's not the army – it's some people who happen to be in the army.*

I went to the main entrance. A corporal standing in front said, "Sergeant, this door is locked. My orders are not to let anyone pass." I told him I understood and asked if there was any other door I could use to get out. He said, "All doors are locked."

"Get me your NCO on the horn." He handed me the phone. I identified myself and told him I had not had a breath of fresh air in a long time, or a smoke. I asked him to override the corporal's order and let me pass. The sergeant spoke to the corporal. He listened for a minute, hung up the phone, unlocked the door, opened it, and held it. As I was rolling through, he said, "I'm sorry, Sarg. I was only following orders."

I sat near a huge palm tree, looking at the moon. I bit the tip of my cigar off and lit it. There is nothing as good as a Cuban cigar. I was sitting there thinking, *This is the good life,* and then I thought, *Life would be better if I was getting a blow job.*

I opened my eyes, looked out the window. It was a great sunny morning. Bryant appeared at the foot of my bed. "Seeing you has ruined my mood. What happened to you last night?" He said he fell asleep.

"Sure. You fell asleep. You must have been fucking hard, without a care for your invalid buddy, who was starving, dying for a smoke."

"I really fell asleep, and I'm sorry."

I wasn't going to let it go, and told him, "While you were fucking and making little Bryants – who will also be selfish – I had a great dinner with a piece of apple pie for dessert and a fantastic Cuban under the moonlight. I didn't miss you at all"

"Hungry?"

I told him I wasn't. "But you must be after all the work you did."

"If we're not going to chow, what do you feel like doing this morning?" I told him if he had the time I needed to talk to him about something that had bothered me for a long time.

He asked if I wanted to talk lying down or sitting. With that I sat up on the edge of the bed. I was in my tee and shorts. I asked Bryant to get my fatigue blouse out of my locker. I slid into the wheelchair and asked if he could get me a towel – I didn't want to sit here half-naked.

Bryant pulled up a chair saying, "I really did fall asleep." I told him I knew it and was kidding, having fun doing it.

I began: "The speech the president gave. I thought it came from his heart and wasn't prepared. I was wrong. The American people have no gratitude toward Hawkins. They saw it as a funeral for a killer of women and children. They didn't know what the military knew, that this soldier had saved thousands of GI lives. The only one that made any sense was the officer who added the army's gratitude.

"I am fuckin' angry with the army. I can't wait to get out. When I was in Long Binh a sergeant and I were talking. I was confused as to why we were killing in this fucked-up country on the other side of the world. He gave me the standard line about stopping communism. I brought up Cuba. He told me that, like myself, he follows orders.

"That's the point. The army, without questioning, takes orders from fat-assed politicians who are only concerned about getting reelected and filling their pockets. They don't give a shit about the GI laying in a field with something blown off, bleeding to death. All they care about is us maximizing the kills and minimizing ours, so they look good. The orders are accepted from the top and passed all the way to the bottom. We follow them without question and die. It would be great if this army changed and had some balls, and up-top questioned orders from the know-nothing politicians who are killing men."

Bryant never interrupted me. He just let me get it out. He asked if I was angry with the army over the loss of Hawkins.

I told him, "Fuck, yes. I'm even angrier with the slants. It doesn't matter – man or woman, if they're slant-eyed, they're fuckin' dead. For me, that's a vendetta I bear, for my brother. Hawk and I hooked up with two Vietnamese girls. Now I couldn't look at them with the rage I have in me. Don't start telling me how wrong I am. I know it, but I can't help it."

We went into the mess hall. GIs sitting around tables sat up straight and saluted. I thanked them and told them they didn't need to do that. We got our coffee and sat down.

Bryant told me I had to get used to it. I was probably the only GI my fellow GIs respect. "The salute is meant to honor you, not like the mandatory salute to officers."

"Where's your salute?"

"I know you better."

I let it pass and moved on. I asked him if all the action I seemed to be getting is because of my good looks or because they know about this shit. He said I was not good looking. It was my turn:

 "Fuck you!"

I told him we oughtta go outside to get some fresh air, and I can smoke. I thought, The Bronx English is coming back "oughtta."

We were outside. I told Bryant I was getting more pleasure out of his being uncomfortable because of this fuckin' heat than my cigarette. I suggested we go in and view the beauties. First floor, second floor, nothing. I asked if he had them stashed somewhere, waiting for him to fuck them all night. "That was wrong. I know you sleep all night. Sure."

We were in the hallway trying to figure out what to do next, when Bryant asked me if I knew how to play chess and checkers. I told him I knew how. "Great. Let's go to the game room. I'm actually good at both." At a table, he asked which one I wanted to play first, and was I up for it?

Either one. He set up the checkers and told me I could go first. (In checkers the first move establishes an aggressive posture, the second player a defensive stance.) I made a move; he moved. After eight moves he couldn't move – the game was over.

I said, "Beginner's luck."

He said, "How about another one, Mister Beginner." We set up the board. He claimed, "My turn to go first."

After two moves, I switched things around, and I became the aggressor. Three jumps, a king, ten moves and it was over.

"I used to think I was a good checker player," Bryant complained. "I don't even come close to you. What were you? A checker champion?"

I told him I wasn't. I used to sit in an office and talk to a guy who was shrewd. While we talked, he taught me checkers. We talked about our business and planned the best way to convince the boss to do something we wanted to get done.

Bryant said, "He was a good teacher. What was the business?"

I told him, "Some other time."

He asked, "Chess?"

I told him, "Yes, but you're going to have to set up the board. I'm not sure what to do with all those soldiers and horses."

"OK, you mean all those pawns and knights."

I just looked blankly at him.

He set up the board and said, "Whites go first. Go."

I remembered a very aggressive strategy Mario taught me, named after some guy. I made my first two moves to set up my attack, and then in six moves it was over. Bryant sat there, glaring at me with a "you bastard" look.

"Bryant, the same guy that taught me how to play checkers also taught me chess. I told you he was brilliant, not in a book way but an everyday way. His logical mind was beyond all of us."

I described how I first met Mario in the yard. "I knew we would become good friends. He amazed me."

Bryant glanced at his watch, and said he was sorry, but he was late for another GI. We would talk later. He wanted to hear more about my life in the world.

# *CHAPTER 55*

Moving slowly in the hallway, I decided to hit the sack to kill time, but wasn't in a hurry to do it. I heard a woman walking toward me. When she reached ,me she gave me one of those hi-yahs. I said hello. She was a major, older, and looked military-butch.

I asked where she was going in such a hurry. "To my office. I want to get out of these shoes." She told me her assignment was to supervise the nursing staff. She'd been all over the hospital. I suggested I join her, offering to give her a foot massage while I got some medical answers. She said that would be very nice.

In her office, she asked if I was kidding about the foot massage. "No, I even have a towel on my lap for your feet. Bring your chair around. We'll cross. You can relax while I do my magic."

She put her feet on my lap. *I'm a bull-shitter,* I thought. *I never did this in my life.* I started rubbing. She uttered these little moans and moved slowly side to side. As she moved, her heel rubbed my dick. Her chair was lower than my lap and her legs were apart. Her skirt moved up. No underwear. I could see this fantastic camel-toe cunt. She sat up, took her feet off me, said she should not have had me do this.

"You didn't have me do it. I offered. We both are enjoying ourselves. What is the problem?"

She told me her younger brother had been killed in Nam. She has a great deal of respect for me, and just felt this was beneath me. She feels a deep gratitude toward me for all the GIs that one of these days can go home.

"Thank you. That's the nicest thing anyone has said to me, and rubbing your feet was certainly not beneath me. My name is Paul. What's yours? And don't start it with major."

She smiled and said, "Grace."

"Fits you. A beautiful name for a beautiful woman. Are you quartered close by?" She was in this building on the first floor. When I suggested we go there to talk while I finished my massage, she agreed. She put on her shoes, moved her chair behind the desk, bent down and kissed me. It wasn't one of those swap-spit kisses, but a soft graze of her lips. Her quarters resembled a motel room rather than military. As soon as we got in, she told me it was against military protocol for an officer and an enlisted man to fraternize. We could both be court-martialed.

I told her I didn't plan on telling anyone. If she didn't, we could have a good time. She took off her shoes, her cover, and let her hair down. Next, she removed her blouse, bra and skirt.

I stared at her. She had big tits and big nipples. I was thinking, *This isn't real … it's a dream. I'm in a room with a broad with big tits and a camel-toe cunt.* She knelt in front of me, slid the towel off my lap, and went down on me. She didn't have to take my dick out of my underwear. The little guy was standing at attention. He had opened my fly. I've had better blow jobs. I was rubbing her big nipples in my palms, then I moved my hands to hold her tits. That did the trick – I came in her mouth. She swallowed it. We stretched out on the bed facing each other. I don't know where the other tit went, but I had this big nipple pointing at me. I wanted to suck the shit out of it.

"I don't mean to hurt your ego and hope you won't get angry. I enjoy sex with a woman more than with a man."

I felt her nervousness. It sounded like a plea for understanding more than an out-and-out statement.

"I'm not hurt or angry. I feel life is too short. We need to enjoy it. If having sex with a woman gives you enjoyment, more power to you." I sat up and was going to leave.

She stopped me by saying, "I can call a friend of mine to the room. The three of us can play around. You'll like her; she's very nice."

I was watching this little nervous twitch she had and got aroused, and that tit hanging out helped. I put my arm around her and told her she was a fuckin' doll, and that she probably didn't know it, but two women making out with a guy watching is making my fantasy come into reality.

She went to the phone. I couldn't help gawking at her tits bouncing, her tight ass. She had a good figure and great legs. She made her call, got back in bed. I moved over to her and began sucking on a nipple and playing with it with my tongue. There was a knock on the door. I thought, *Why the fuck couldn't you be in Honolulu rather than next door.*

Grace opened the door to a lieutenant. She was shorter than Grace. The girl said, "Hi, love," and they kissed. I was lying on my back in bed with a hard-on. The kiss made him grow another inch.

Grace introduced me to Julie. The two of them were standing there eyeballing my cock. Grace got in bed. We both moved over and watched Julie undress. She took off her cover – blond hair came cascading down to her shoulders. With her high cheekbones, terrific definition to her face, and great neck, she was fuckin' beautiful. Her stand-up, perky tits had protruding nipples. Julie got in bed and they started making out. Grace was on her side with her back to me. I slid my hand under her and found the tit she was resting on. I moved my cock between her legs, my cock was rubbing her cunt as I gently squeezed her tit.

The two of them got up and knelt on either side of me and began taking turns sucking my cock. Grace would suck, lift off, then Julie would do it. Julie didn't seem experienced, but she put more into it and stayed on me longer. She lifted her head, and Grace began. When Grace got off, Julie went down. This time she started licking alternating with sucking. I lifted her head off and came.

Grace fell back on the pillow and Julie started licking my cum off me. She would glance at me. I was staring, not at her licking, but at her. She finished licking, swallowed, and kissed the head of my dick. I gently pulled her face to mine. We kissed slowly. I wanted to take her in my arms, but Grace seemed to be getting upset, so I didn't. Grace got up went into a drawer and took out two skinny little dildos. They sixty-nined and started going at each other's pussy. I could see Julie; it didn't seem like she was into it.

After a while they broke it off. I told them I had an idea. "What if we fucked? If one of you gets pregnant, you could raise a kid together." Julie was for it; Grace wasn't too keen about it. I told Grace I'd let her be on top. She still didn't care for the idea.

The three of us were lying there with our own thoughts. They got up and went into the john. Julie came out first. I told her I didn't mean to offend her, but was her thing with Grace the real thing or career?

She looked at me and said, "Career." I asked if I could see her again.

She said, "Yes, soon."

When Grace came out of the john, I kissed her and told her thank you, I had a good time. I got dressed, got in my chair and rolled toward the door. I heard Julie ask Grace, "Is that him?"

Back in my bed I was thinking, *It's still early; I've got the whole day.* My thoughts went to Julie. I couldn't get the way she looked out of my mind. And that she didn't know who I was made the loving and sex real, not put-on.

I decided I wanted to find a therapy room, so I could get a workout. All I had been doing was lying on my ass. The only part of me that exercised was my cock, and it boned-up. I found a room that had all kinds of equipment. A spec4 cleaning equipment saw me and walked over.

"Morning Sarg, what can I do for you?" I told him I'd been lying around for a while, felt I was losing muscle, and wanted to work out. He said I looked as if I knew my way around a gym, and he probably didn't have to tell me to take it easy and build up.

I rolled over to a piece of equipment, slid onto a chair and grasped an overhead bar with both hands. Slowly I brought it to my chest, then released it. After three I asked the specialist if he could see how much weight I had. Eighty pounds. I asked him to set it at 150. I wanted to do ten progressions, and then twenty at 200. After I finished he brought me water and asked if I was done. I told him no. He asked if he could get me a headband and towel. He suggested I take off the tee, put on the headband and work out like that. "Use the towel to dry yourself, but more important, your hands, so you don't slip." I finished, put my stuff in my lap, and rolled to a mirror. My muscles had definition.

I went to my room and asked the medic if he could have someone wash me. He was staring at me and told me he'd do it. I thought, fuck it. It doesn't matter anymore. My wash was uneventful. I was sitting with a new tee, shorts, and my fatigues.

Bryant walked in and said, "Where have you been? I was worried you fell in a hole or something."

"Forget the or something. I happened to be in a hole. I, my wholesome, sleepy friend, had two broads." Under different circumstances, and with someone different, I would have gotten a high-five and you're-the-man. Instead, nothing.

I asked Bryant if we could talk before chow. "What we're going to talk about, you can put in my file. Your superiors will think you're doing your job. There are times at night I'll sit up in my bunk. I'm not sweating, hollering 'in-coming,' or disoriented about battlefield conditions. My adrenaline is pumping away. I'm killing VC in the tunnels. I'd do a tunnel, look back at the shits lying on their mats on the ground, dead. I had no remorse, no regret. In fact, I was elated. There had been times that required hand-to-hand. I would twist their head to the side and slice their throat open. The only thing that gives me nightmares is their fucking eyes looking at me as I did it."

"You have anything to say, Bryant?"

"Let's have chow."

While we were eating, I told Bryant about Julie. I left Grace and the other shit out. I told him I needed his help to get in touch with her and see her again.

"Julie. A blonde. Second Louie. Not a lot to go on, but I'll get it done."

We talked for a while. I asked Bryant his rank; he replied sergeant. "I outrank you! Bryant, from now on you better start following orders."

"What have I been doing all this time? All you do is order me around."

I told him I was only kidding, and hoped he was also. "I never meant to order you. I'm sorry if you took it that way."

"You're sorry – really sorry?"

I nodded. He laughed, "Good, I was only kidding."

Without even thinking the old expression came out. "Fuck you."

Bryant stood up and told me he had to see another GI and would catch up with me later. I finished, got a Cuban from my locker and was headed outside. As I passed men and women in the hall, they came to attention and saluted. While I was relaxing outside two guys walked past and saluted. I decided I would get rid of this billboard for now and just wear my tee. If there was a problem, I'd get Bryant to hustle me an operating room blouse. I couldn't get Julie out of my mind. I decided to cruise and look for her. No luck.

I was in bed with my eyes closed, thinking about Julie – her hair, her face. I couldn't stop picturing her face. Then my mind went to the tunnels, the killings and the girl. If she hadn't gone for the weapon, I wouldn't have killed her. My mind was all over the place, and Bryant was pushing me, telling me to wake up. He handed me a slip of paper and told me it was Julie's number.

"She told me to tell you she was off duty at 1900 and would be waiting for your call."

I told him he was a good buddy and I owed him.

He said, "Let's hit the mess hall. I'll let you spring for chow."

I slid out of bed into my chair. Bryant asked, "You're not going to chow with just your tee on?"

"I am. I understand the saluting, but it's starting to make me uncomfortable."

He told me to sit tight, he'd be right back. After a while he came bouncing through the door with a green operating-room blouse. Bryant told me I needed to wear it because as we went down a hallway, we'd have girls fainting or coming in their underwear from the excitement of seeing those muscles.

"If I was pushing you down the hall, the girls, looking at you, would react in the same way, only this time they would see a dickhead."

At chow I was so preoccupied with seeing Julie and having sex, I wasn't good company. The only thing that was said was I told Bryant he was a good buddy. He told me I was also. After we finished eating, he took off. I went to the room and sat by the window. I couldn't get Julie out of my mind. At 1900 I called, we talked. I was on my way.

I opened the door to her room. She was standing naked, posing. I looked at her thinking it's the same as I visualized. I got undressed, got into bed. I was holding her in my arms, kissing her, looking at her, and kissing again. She got up, knelt over me and started sucking. The sight of this beautiful face with my dick in it, her lips around my dick, moving up and down, excited me more than the blow job.

She stopped sucking, held my dick in her mouth. She slid her hand under me and had my balls in her hand. Her face contorted as she squeezed my nuts. I told her to stop – she was hurting me. She squeezed harder.

I grabbed her hair and pulled her off my cock and squeezed her tit. She screamed, dropped my balls, and was trying to get my hand off her. I got to a kneeling position still holding her tit and told her this is for the second ball squeeze. I squeezed harder, and she screamed louder. I yanked her head back, she was crying. I got in her face and hollered: "Shut the fuck up." She did. I yelled *vaffanculo zoccola* (fuck you, bitch). I had her by the hair and told her she was a fuckin' sick bitch.

Scowling at her, I moved closer and added, "Nothin' but a fuckin' waste." I got dressed and slid onto the chair. Sitting on my nuts sent a lightning bolt of pain through my body. I had been stabbed, shot, blown to shit. Nothing had ever hurt as bad as this. I lifted off the chair a little by pressing my forearm against the arms of the chair. I went into the hall using my left leg to move the chair. In the hall, I started taking deep breaths, hoping that would ease the pain. A fitting ending to this shit would be her getting up to close the door and getting her good tit caught in it.

I finally made it to my room. A medic was checking on the guys. I asked if he had a donut that guys with hemorrhoids use. He answered yes and asked if I had them. I told him no, something worse.

I spent the night in agony. The sun came up and I was still hurting bad. I thought, *Fuck chow, and this means the end of my workouts.* For the week, I ate, shit, pissed in a urinal and spent my days in bed. While lying in bed, no matter what I thought about, I couldn't get a hard-on. It's dead and will never rise again. My balls must have slapped my cock around and told it not to get hard. They didn't want to go through this again.

After another week, I still had a twinge there, but no pain. I was back to my normal life except still no hard-on. One night while I was in bunk, my mind was going over the different women I fucked. I looked at my dick and thought, *Soldier, it's time you stood at attention and be proud.* Nothing. I fell asleep.

# *CHAPTER 56*

Time seemed to fly by. I was told I would be transported to the OR at 0500 for an operation. I was up and ready to get on with it. In walks Bryant. I greeted him with, "Hi sleepy. What are you doing up at this hour?"

"No one else wanted to get this close to you. The only other choice would have been Lieutenant Julie. I thought she might try to get even."

I extended my hand to him; he took it in his. I told him he was a great buddy and a very smart fella. Then I said, "I goofed. I didn't mean smart fella. I meant to say fart smella."

Still holding my hand, he said, "Listen up, troop. I intend to bring you back to this room. In no way, shape, or form are you to fuck up."

I hadn't heard "in no way, shape, or form" since basic. The sergeants would use it constantly. They'd have us lined up in front them and get worked up over something, yelling and spraying us with spit while saying it. Every time I heard it I would think: *You're a stupid fuck. You could get your message across without the yelling and the "no way" bullshit.*

I was in my cubbyhole. Bryant did his thing, told me good luck, and left. A nurse came through the curtain wearing her camouflage. She introduced herself as Darlene, my prep nurse. She started to go through the script of what she was going to do. I stopped her, told her I've heard it before. She pulled over a stool and sat by my bed.

"OK. You've heard the speech I'm supposed to give you, but you never heard what I'm about to tell you. The staff doctors and surgeons agree you are strong enough, and your leg is healthy enough, to combine the rest of your surgeries into this one. This means unless something goes wrong, you won't be back here again.

"A team of surgeons will remove your left side lat muscle, another team will prepare your leg. The most time-consuming will be attaching everything to your leg. They must keep the muscle alive. I don't want to scare you, but in case something goes wrong,  you could lose the leg."

I told her I understood, and if she would be kind enough, to grant a possibly dying man his last wish. "Take off your mask and leave it off, so I can see if your face matches your beautiful name." She did. "It does. While you're doing what you have to, I can have your face etched in my brain. It will make things easier for me." I thought she was good- looking in an impish way.

She started the prep and was conscious of my stares. When she bent over, I tried to make out the outline of her tits. I couldn't. The little guy started to stir, not hard yet, only movement. I thought he was something else, reading my thoughts. She got to the part where she needed me naked. She undressed me and put a small towel over my guy. She washed my back, turned me over, and couldn't take her eyes off my muscles. I could have sworn I saw a quick glance at the towel over my little guy. Before she finished she said she was curious about two things. "The first is, in our file you're listed as deceased."

I told her army bookkeeping. "I can assure you I'm not dead anywhere."

She smiled and said, "The second one is you are listed as Paul B. Walker. What is your middle name?"

I told her my mother wanted my middle name after her father Barnardino, who was an aristocrat in Naples, Italy. My father didn't like it. They settled on Barnard.

"You don't look Italian."

I told her I take after my father's side. If I took after my mother's side, I'd be some stud.

"I don't know about that. You look good the way you are. In fact, you look great." She washed me, got to the towel, and lifted it off. I was limp. She looked at it. I could have had her. Something inside of me said, *Fuck, no, not again.*

I opened my eyes. It was night. Bryant was there; he said he was glad to see me. How did I feel? I told him good except I had to piss. He told me do it – I had a bag hanging. I realized the cast was gone. My leg had this huge bandage. I couldn't feel my dick and worried it was wrapped in the bandage. I thought, *That's stupid.*

Bryant told me they briefed him before the operation because if it didn't go well, I'd need counseling.

"What were you supposed to do? Find a good counselor?" I fell off.

I opened my eyes. The sun was shining. Bryant was standing on the other side of the bed. He asked how I felt. I told him I felt good, but I was fuckin' starving. I asked if the mess hall we eat at is for everyone, or was there an officer's mess. He told me there's an officer's mess. "We could go there. I'll be in my wheelchair. I'll go in backwards. No one will question us."

"Taking you to the officer's mess is stepping over the line. If I get caught, I'll be demoted and have to clean your bedpan."

"You have to be demoted to do that? I thought you've been doing it all along?"

I got "fuck you." He added, "You might run into someone with a knife, looking to cut your dick off."

"If I run into the knife lady, she might have a cast hanging from her chest."

We went to the mess. Everything worked as planned. We were eating and agreed this is fine dining compared to the crap we usually get. In walks this good-looking captain. Her facial features were American Indian. She was stunning.

Bryant said, "That's Beth." He caught my look and clarified: "The admirer."

I told him he had that wrong. "She wasn't the admirer; you were the drooler. The only reason you two hooked up was she felt sorry for you being mentally incapacitated."

She walked over, shook Bryant's hand, and very quietly asked how he was.

He replied, "Terrific."

"Me, too, I can't wait till later to get it on again."

"It sounds like this is serious."

"More than serious, my love."

I felt like a third wheel. I was going to get out of there and smoke a cigarette when she extended her hand to me. "You must be Paul. I'm Beth. You are all he talks about – constantly. There are times I'll plant a big kiss on him to try to shut him up – it doesn't work. We get done kissing, back to you." She admitted she exaggerated a little. "I will tell you he feels like you're the best buddy he's ever had. You're smart and very sharp. I feel as though I know you from what he's told me."

I told her if I met her before Bryant and we connected, I'd be walking on clouds now.

She kissed me on the cheek, thanked me, and told me that was very nice. Then she snapped to attention, saluted me, and walked away. I told Bryant "I hope the two of you have a great life together – she's a fine lady."

We finished eating. I told Bryant, "We have to do this again." I asked Bryant if there was someplace we could relax outside other than the front. He told me there are a lot of terraces around the hospital for GIs to smoke and relax. He thought I'd liked the front because I could size up prospects, plan my attack, and make my move.

"Bryant, you disappoint me to think I am like that and would stoop that low. You're fuckin' right! Let's hit a terrace – different hunting grounds."

On a terrace, GIs were smoking and soaking up rays. When I finished a cigarette, I told Bryant I wanted to get in bed and cry – there hadn't been a female here all this time. I also wanted to take a shit. As we headed for the room, a medic stopped me and said they wanted me to have a sonogram of my leg. Then to the OR, where a doctor would check the condition of my leg and the stitches. I told him I'll do that after using the latrine.

I told Bryant I could handle this. He should try to counsel the person we spoke to at mess, or whatever he needed to do. I did my thing and felt good. I wasn't loose, and I thought I might hook up with an old friend in the sonogram.

I made it to the sonogram, checked in, and was told they'd be with me shortly. A guy called out my name. I rolled over to him. He told me he'd be doing my sonogram. In the hall on the way to the OR I told the little guy we've had a minor setback – I still will need him to rise to the occasion.

In the OR a Black nurse asked if I was Sergeant Walker. I told her yes. She pulled a curtain aside and told me to lie on my back on the gurney. "If you need help, I'll help you."

I told her yes – I was thinking I could at least get a cheap feel. She helped me slide over. Her tits were pressing against me. It felt like two pillows pressing against me. While she was taking off the bandages, she commented, "You have the most beautiful blue eyes."

"Since we're getting personal, my name is Paul. What's yours?" She told me Barbara. "Barb, thank you for your help getting me on the gurney, which I truly appreciate, not for the help but for the cheap feel. I have determined you have outstanding tits."

She said, "Thank you." The little guy moved.

The curtain opened, and Darlene walked in. Barb looked at her. Darlene walked over to Barb and they began kissing. I crumbled. Darlene asked, "How about we do a threesome one night in one of our quarters?"

"That sounds great! I'll get in touch with you when I can handle it."

"It looks good," Barb said, "No infection. A little swelling, which is expected. There's a hell of a lot of stitches in the leg. Aside from some soreness in your leg, and the pain from the stitches, how is it?"

"You missed my left armpit, which hurts."

We were interrupted when the curtain separated, and a doctor in OR garb walked in and asked how I was. I told him good.

"The sonogram showed nothing separated, muscle is doing well." He examined the stitches and told me this looks good, too. "If everything stays the same, in three weeks I'll remove the stitches, give you a week for the site to heal, then begin physical therapy."

2I asked if I could shower. He was concerned about infecting the site, so I should wait till the therapy. After he left Barb asked if she'd ever see me again. I told her I've got to be back here. When she opened the curtain, Bryant was talking to a nurse. I looked more closely – it was Beth. I asked Bryant to ask Beth if she had a friend as nice as her that she could hook me up with. For as long as I was going to be here, it would be nice to have someone to care about, hold in my arms, have good conversation with instead of the crap I've had.

Bryant told me he was surprised. While he had been waiting on the other side of the curtain, it sounded like Barb and I were hitting it off. I told him we were, but it's the same as the knife-carrying blond.

"No shit. You mean her and Darlene?" I nodded yes.

We were in the room and Bryant asked about chow. I replied "officer" and we were off. We went through the line. We had a great breakfast – lunch made it seem penny ante. While we were sitting at a table, I noticed three female officers at a table talking. One had her back to me; the other two kept looking at me, smiling and flirting. They didn't look bad, but most women in their dress uniforms look good.

Bryant had his back to them. I asked if he'd go to the line and get something. "On your way, back, look at the three girls sitting behind you and tell me what you think."

Back at the table he told me, "Those three are the same as the blonde with the knife and the OR pair."

"What the fuck! Is this army a haven for lesbians?" He told me a lot of women join the army for that reason. We finished and went out to a terrace. As I was smoking I asked Bryant how many GIs he counsels.

"You. You're my assignment. I'll help out another counselor occasionally."

The "I-have-to-go-and-see-another-GI wasn't legit, was it?"

He told me for the most part, no. I asked "Beth?" He nodded yes.

I was going to tell him "good for you," but changed my mind. I realized he was getting laid on my time. "Since I'm your only mental case, when are you going to start counseling?" He said he had from the very beginning, when he developed the close relationship we have. He had gone over my file looking for a crack he could explore to have me open up about Nam.

"Once I opened up, what I said might have sounded unpatriotic, but I feel it's absolutely true."

He was hoping he could get me to talk about Hawkins, but I seemed to have shut that down. He also was hoping we could talk about my life before the army, and why was I in the army, especially feeling the way I do.

"We do have a close relationship, one I thoroughly enjoy. You're a terrific counselor. Your approach to it is outstanding. Had you sat me down and began probing, I would have said to myself 'fuck this shit' and clammed up. Bryant, you're a good listener, and easy for me to talk to. You're right – I need to talk to you and let out what I buried."

I told Bryant I am a little surprised, with the relationship we have, with his mealy-mouthed way to try to open me up.

"I probably could have gotten you to open up. I didn't want to jeopardize our relationship. I felt it was better to send you home the basket case you are."

"What relationship, basket case?"

"What relationship, mealy mouth?" He bent down and hugged me. I hugged back and told him he was a good friend.

We stopped hugging. "All of this hinges on you getting me hooked up with Beth's friend, or all bets are off. We'll talk, but now I need to hit the sack."

I opened my eyes. It was dark. Bryant was standing by my bed. He asked, "Chow?"

On the way, I told Bryant. "To me this really sucks. The GIs, all busted up, who have been through all kinds of shit, eat reconstituted rations. Everyone should be served the same food in a hospital, no officer-grunt difference. Our mess: all you see is wheelchairs. Officers, none, except mine. This army needs to get their heads out of their collective asses."

Bryant told me almost everyone in the officer's mess is hospital staff. We went through the line and sat at a table. While we were eating, one of the girls from lunch came to our table and said, "I'm sorry to disturb you."

I told her, "You wouldn't. Please sit down. I like to look at the person I'm talking to, especially one as beautiful as you."

She asked if we were a pair. "The only reason I asked is the three of us are lesbians. We thought the five of us could get together. You guys could do your thing, the three of us our thing; then we can all have fun."

I said, "Lieutenant, are you the moxie one of the three, or did you lose a bet to talk to us?" She was the outgoing one.

"We are not like that," I explained. "He cross-dresses in the privacy of his quarters. Aside from that, he fucks his brains out with any broad that walks."

"I have gone around and around with the general. I feel a person's sexuality is his or her business, as long as it does not interfere with their mission and is not flaunted. The general is without a doubt homophobic, old-school army. He starts ranting and quoting the Bible – how it's against God's will, and he will have none of it in his command. He's the general, and I follow orders.

"If I were you, outgoing one, I'd play it down. Keep it just between the three of you. You never know who you're talking to.

Mustered out of the service dishonorably for being a lesbian will ruin your life and be with you forever."

She was tearing up, saying, "Yes, Sir. Are we OK now?"

"Lieutenant, we have never had this conversation."

She stood up and walked away in a hurry. Bryant kicked my chair, muttering "cross-dresser!"

I told him I was trying to involve him in the conversation, instead of him sitting there like a bump on a log.

"There are a lot of other ways you could have done it. 'I go around and around with the general.' You are hot shit!"

"I was tempted to tell the three of them if any or all decided to take the other road, I would be more than happy to guide her. I didn't." I told Bryant I was going to get some sleep. "For as much of it that's here, you or someone in your unit should be counseling these girls in private and try to get them turned around before they get hurt by the army."

# *CHAPTER 57*

One day melted into another. Bryant and I talked a lot. I began working out, had physical therapy, and showers. Bryant hadn't mentioned girls, probably because of what I told him. I didn't care. All I wanted was to stand and walk. One day Bryant told me he and a group of his superiors were discussing my file, specifically my notes.

"We are all in agreement that your feelings and thoughts about Nam will disappear when you're home, in a different environment, no military. Your grief for Sergeant Hawkins will subside in time, will turn to the fun times the two of you had. I'm not saying you won't grieve, but it will be deep in your subconscious. The hurting of a woman because you see her as an Oriental is wrong. You know it's wrong. I don't have a way for you to overcome it. I am confident, if you think it out, you will overcome it yourself."

We were looking at each other and I said, "That's it? I sure as fuck thought you'd have a lot more. After all my talking, the sore throats I've overcome, that's all you have?" I told him thanks. "You are not only wise, but also levelheaded and practical."

"One more thing," he said, "Then I can close the file and trash it, or file it away somewhere."

I asked what it was. He wanted to know everything about me, from as far back as I could remember to Nam, everything, every detail.

I warned him he needed to mark off four or five days. I didn't have what his people call a normal life. I needed him to keep most of what I tell him to himself. No notes. No one is to ever be told. If he could do that, we'd talk. If he couldn't, we wouldn't. He promised me he would keep what I tell him in strict confidence.

"There's a lot of bad shit. Still want to hear it?"

"Yes. For now, I will let you buy me chow."

While we were eating, I told Bryant, "This will be good for me. The Special Forces training at Schofield required me to set my life aside. In Nam, I abandoned it and lived for the moment. Here I'm just fucked-up. I want to tell you about my life. For me, I want to relive it and bring it into focus. My life was fantastic. I have told you I thought Beth is one of the most beautiful women I have ever seen. My fiancé is as beautiful. By the way, are you still together?"

"Yes, and it's wonderful. The only problem we have is an officer cannot fraternize with an enlisted man. So, we have to stay in the shadows. We want to get married and we can't because of the same reason. If we could get married, there is no one in this world I would want for my best man other than you."

"I want to visit our phone louie or anyone else that can place a call to Nam." He told me the louie was it. "When I get the call through, I want you to tell him to leave the room because the call contains sensitive material. Actually, I don't want him to hear you're an enlisted man."

We were in the lieutenant's office. Bryant told him we needed another call to Long Binh. "Yes, sir. Who shall I have them connect to?" I told him Colonel Bolton, Special Forces. He said I could get to Special Forces Command; they won't let him get to Colonel Bolton. I told him if he gets through, tell them First Sergeant Walker needs to talk to Colonel Bolton – they'll let him through.

He got on the phone. After the usual, he handed me the phone and told me the Colonel was on. Bryant did his thing. I sat at the desk.

"Hi, Sir. How are you?" He replied he was fine, they were busy as all breakout. He wished I were there.

"I wish I could be. I hope Sgt. Brown conveyed my appreciation for the rooms. I also hope he told you how much I appreciate what you did for Hawkins."

"Let me tell you something. I have commanded thousands of GIs in my career in the army. I have never met anyone of your caliber. I salute you. I know you won't let me, but if you would, I would tell the story of First Sergeant Paul Walker."

"Thank you, Sir. Your telling me how you feel is all that matters. When they hand you that gold star, I am hopeful I can be there. If I'm permitted to say something, I'd tell them the star is given for your achievements, and rightfully so. It is being given to the greatest warrior and finest gentleman this army has seen."

"Thank you, Paul."

"Sir, I need a favor. I have a very close friend at Tripler. He and a captain are very much in love and want to get married. They can't because he's enlisted. I thought perhaps you could pull some strings and get him a field promotion to captain."

"I can do that. What is his name, serial number, and present duty assignment?"

I asked him to hold on for a second. I told Bryant I needed his ID quickly. I got back on the phone and gave Bolton all the information. He told me it would be handled today.

"One more for me – a dress uniform with all the goodies, dress shoes, beret."

"It will all be transported to you. I've got an important briefing. Get well and stay in touch."

I told Bryant to get the lieutenant back here and tell him job well done. In the hall, I told Bryant, "Get ahold of Beth, tell her whatever you want, have fun, and enjoy the moment. This is serious! When you are officially a captain, if you give me an order, I will put you in the trash."

I decided to work out – find a therapy room with a big-titted tech, talk her into helping me take a shower, get a blow job. Then, after a shave and massage, I'd be in good shape. I worked out, cruised the therapy rooms – all guys. There had to be a broad in the aqua therapy. At this point I didn't care if she was flat-chested. My luck – a guy in a Speedo bouncing around in the pool. I have often said it: If I didn't have bad luck, I'd have no luck at all.

I was out front smoking, getting some rays, and viewing the sights. Probably the time of day...I had nothing. I lifted a cigarette to my mouth, caught a whiff of my armpit, and thought, You stink. It brought me back to Nam with the fuckin' heat and all the clothes and gear I had on. I went to the room, showered and shaved. I came out of the shower. Standing by the bed was Bryant. I barked, "I thought I got rid of you."

"Shut up. We're eating chow with Beth. She wants to talk to you."

"OK, but maybe tomorrow or the next day you can tell me to shut up and give me orders. Today I outrank you."

He told me shut up, we had to get going.

"Once a dickhead, always a dickhead" was my response.

While we were eating, Beth said, "I will never forget what you've done for us. Saying thank you isn't good enough. Our children will know about Paul Walker, their children and their children. When I know as much as I need to about you, I'm going to write a book and title it *Paul Walker: A Great Man*."

"Thank you. I've never had anything like that said to me before. But your title, A Great Man … no. Beth, there are and have been great men. I'm not one."

"To me, you are a great man, and I love you. I would like you to meet my maid of honor, Pam. Maybe we can go on a double date." She told me she spoke to Pam about it. "She's excited and looking forward to it. She's good-looking, smart, personable and funny."

I told her that sounded great. "Is she as good looking as you?"

"Better. We're related."

I asked Beth if they had set a wedding date. She told me she has a lot to work out, so it wouldn't be for a while. They would be married in a military ceremony. I asked if she had someone to walk her beneath the raised sabers. "No, there is only one man I would want to do it. I haven't asked him."

"Ask the guy. If he says no, it's his loss, and you move on to someone else."

She asked if I would do her the honor of walking her down the aisle. I told her yes, it would be my privilege to escort her.

Bryant explained, "Beth has been so worried about asking you. She didn't want to offend you. I've been trying to tell her walking down the aisle is an expression, and it wouldn't bother you being in a chair."

"Bryant, you didn't hear me. I told Beth it would be my honor to walk beside her, and I will stand proudly by your side as your best man."

The next day Bryant was summoned to the Twenty-Second Operations and was given the orders promoting him to captain. Bryant enthusiastically described how it went.

A medic carrying a cardboard box walked in and said, "Sergeant, this is for you." I knew what it was, but it made me feel good to see the shipping label: urgent, sensitive material, for the eyes of First Sergeant Paul Walker only. The shipper was Colonel James Bolton, Command Special Forces, Long Binh, Vietnam.

My focus became walking. Before, I felt it would happen in time. Now I was going to make it happen quickly. During the morning workouts, the tech helped me strengthen the muscles in my legs. Physical therapy worked on my leg. In aqua therapy, I worked on my leg. When Speedo asked if he could help me, I told him I could handle it myself.

All this exercise was followed by showers and talks with Bryant. That's how my days passed, and they flew by. During one of our talks Bryant asked when I wanted to do the double date. I told him anytime everybody else wants to.

"I'm free, so it doesn't matter when. And it would be great, for a change, to talk to someone intelligent and personable."

I was expecting "Fuck You." It didn't come and that started to worry me that he took me seriously. Bryant was good at what he did – getting me to talk, taking me back through my life.

One day I told Bryant, "I need to use the john. After, I'm going to make a call. How about we pick this up tomorrow?"

I went into the john, sat on a stool, got all emotional, and began beating myself up for pushing aside the people that have meant the most to me. I agonized over Maria. My Maria. No one could ever compare to Maria. I kept wondering why. Where did I ever lose myself? I answered myself: "Why? Because you're the fuckin' stupidest shit that has ever walked this earth. You're a fuckin' stupid asshole!"

Eventually I composed myself and went in search of a public phone. I told the operator I needed to make a long distance collect call to the Bronx, New York. I got Tony on the phone. After a long greeting, he began talking. I could have sworn he was crying. I couldn't picture this tough guy, the ultimate boss, blubbering like a baby.

"When your mother called and said she had been notified you were killed in action, I started calling the army to find out where your coffin was. After the third call I was ready to go through the phone and put a hit on the son of a bitch. On my fourth call I was told there was no coffin, that you were severely wounded, not dead.

"I asked, 'How can I get in touch with him?' I was told I couldn't. You wouldn't believe what this place was like when I told everyone you weren't dead. Maria started screaming. Then she got on her knees, crossing herself, and cried,"

I told him I was sorry I didn't call. I explained I had been out of it for a long time. We yacked awhile, and I asked him to have someone wire Tripler Medical Center Credit Union ten large for me. No questions asked, he told me done.

"Thank you. When I walk into your office in thirty days, I won't mind a hug, but no kisses. It makes me feel like a frocio (fag). I can't wait till the day we can be together, plan things, and fuckin' enjoy life." I asked if he knew how I could get ahold of Maria. He told me he built a large warehouse and office on the back lot for Dawson Coffee. You won't believe what she's done with Dawson. Tony was having Cleo connect me.

Maria spoke passionately, releasing all the words and feelings she had restrained for months. Hearing her voice made my heart pound. At one point, I interrupted and said, "We need to get married quickly – I desperately want to make love."

"We will," Maria said, "And then we'll work hard at it. I want five Paulys running around the house."

Our conversation was long and ended with my telling her I loved her and would see her in thirty days. Next, I called my mother. Her overwhelming joy hearing my voice was great to hear. As we spoke she mentioned she put into effect all my suggestions. She told me, "Hyman is a new man, better than he was before." When she started telling me about the Palms, I interrupted and told her I'd be seeing her soon, we could talk about it then.

"Not today, but soon, you and Maria have to get together and plan our Vegas wedding." I sat back feeling better than I had in a long time.

I told the physical therapy tech I wanted to focus my therapy on walking. He told me OK but we had to take it slowly or I could hurt myself. I told him negative, we're going to push it. He said he couldn't do it. I asked if I outranked him. He told me yes, but not in physical therapy. I thought, *Fuck him – I'll push myself.*

Standing, holding onto two parallel bars, I could feel my arm muscles flexing. I was standing, something I hadn't done in a long time except in the pool. That's not really standing. *Once I get it down, I will never sit again, I'll do everything standing.*

I started off with my left leg, and then slid my right on the floor. I got to the end, turned around. This time I was going to walk on my right leg.

With the first step, I had this horrible pain shoot through my whole body. I kept on walking, without an outward sign of what I was going through. I got to the end. The tech told me that was enough for today. I needed to lie on the table, so he could massage my leg. I told him the leg felt good. I wanted one more turn. He walked away.

I didn't sleep at all that night. The pain in my leg was fuckin' killing me. My morning routine stayed the same. After a shower, Bryant and I would talk.

I told Bryant about my calls and how terrific they made me feel. I asked if he remembered his promise to me. He said he did. "That promise starts now."

I began talking. I told him about my childhood, about everyone in my life. I told him about my father and Hyman, about my mother's life. About my mother and father's church experience, and my mother's spirituality. I told him about the business, but never mentioned anything that I felt breached my oath of *omerta*. I told Bryant about Carl and Jacob, the children's hospital, the foundation. I spent hours talking about Maria.

When I told him about the fat cop I planned to hit in the nuts and then run down the subway, I got a chuckle out of him, as happened when I told him about Tony telling me to burn the rags I was wearing, and my thinking they weren't that bad. All the time I talked, he never interrupted, but he had an endless variety of expressions on his face. We spent many days and nights together – my talking and he listening. He told me, at night after we finish, that's all he thinks about, and he can't wait to hear more.

One night after we finished he told me when he retires, he and Beth are going to write a novel about my life. He would make some changes, but, for the most part, it would be as I told it.

I got to the army part, told him my reason for being in it. That nothing, nobody, could talk me out of having my vendetta. I told him about Abe and Moore. How I could never understand why the army would have this ignorant, bigoted, hillbilly asshole training men they needed. How he did everything he could to get me to Section Eight out, pushing me to hit him. When I told Bryant about the latrine, he cringed in disgust as I described the pissing on the floor. He laughed when I told him about the priest's visit.

One morning Bryant came to my room. Before I began my morning routine he had something to tell me, and later wanted to have chow with me. He had called Long Binh to thank Colonel Bolton for what he had done for him. Colonel Bolton was killed in action leading the unit on a major offensive. I remembered that was the briefing when he cut our conversation short.

Some years later I found out what happened. Westmoreland and Bolton were buddies. When Westmoreland's strategy to go on the offensive was rejected, he released Bolton from the Twenty-fifth Command. Bolton gathered all the Special Forces troops to Long Binh and began offensive maneuvers. The first three missions in country were very successful. Nothing was ever reported. The fourth mission was in Cambodia. Intelligence was faulty, and the mission was a disaster. I told Bryant, "This fucking war has taken too many good men. It needs to end."

I asked Bryant to go to the door and look out, not to turn around till I told him to. I got my cane and started walking toward him. I told him to turn around. His jaw dropped open. "Let's walk to mess. I want to give you and Beth something. You're going to have to loan me your bars or paint a sign on my back."

"Negative. You don't think these guys know who you are? It's their honor that you choose to eat with them."

When Beth saw me walk in she stood, walked over, and grabbed my arms. She said she was glad to see me walking, how fantastic I looked standing.

Walking through the line, Bryant asked if he could hold my tray for me. I said I could one-hand it easily. At the table, Bryant told me he was, with an emphasis on was, going to get me a cup of coffee.

I said, "Yes, Sir."

Bryant explained the reason for this breakfast together. It was to tell me they had set a wedding date. I congratulated them. I know Bryant was expecting a crack. He didn't get one.

"I have a wedding gift for you. I want to give it to you now instead of at the ceremony. I hope my gift will give you joy and a head start on a long, happy, and great marriage."

I handed them a check for five thousand dollars. Beth sat there with her mouths wide open; Bryant looked stunned.

I felt Bryant knew all about me. He could figure out this is something I wanted to do, and five K didn't mean that much to me. Beth overcame her shock, couldn't thank me enough, then excused herself and left. Bryant told me she didn't want me to see her crying tears of joy. He said he was at a loss for words. He didn't know how to adequately express his feelings toward me.

"No shit? Mr. Quiet, silent listener, is at a loss for words?"

That's when I got my "fuck you" and we left.

We went on the double date. Pam was just as Beth described her, and everyone had a great time. Pam was funny. She'd nail Beth with something, turn around, and sock it to Bryant; then we all jumped in. Everyone was laughing. Laughing was great: it had been a long time since I laughed out loud.

Pam and I decided to see each other again; we dated twice before the ceremony. We talked and laughed a lot together. We both declared we enjoyed each other's company. We would kiss good night, and that was all.

I felt I could have gotten a lot more, but she was too much a lady to push herself on me. On one of our dates she asked if it was true what everyone was saying about me. I told her that people have a way of embellishing, so the listener is impressed with their importance.

"I agree with that, except a high-ranking officer told me what you did for Sergeant Hawkins, and the other things you've done. He had no reason to impress me."

"I don't know what he told you. Whatever it was, Duwayne Hawkins deserved all the credit. He was a true hero."

She told me from the short time she knew me, she expected me to say what I did. To her I was also a hero and one of the greatest men she ever heard of. We kissed. And that was the last date we were on.

I was in the sack, thinking how good Bryant was at his job, and how much I had changed. Before I would have hit on Pam and fucked my brains out. Now I didn't want to. Mostly because of Maria, I have regained my respect for a woman like her.

The day of the ceremony I was up early. I showered then looked in the mirror. I shaved yesterday and had a haircut. I thought I looked sharp. I had seen the dress uniform Bolton had sent me. This time I examined it closely. It was tailored. My stripes were on it. On the left were my qualification medals, then three rows of ribbons, Purple Heart, my Combat Infantry badge and Special Forces insignia. On the right were two badges, one an army badge, the other a Twenty-fifth. I stood at attention looking in the mirror.

I walked to the ceremony hall. As soon as I entered, everyone stood at attention and saluted. I walked in, thinking they're saluting the uniform, and accepted their salutes. I walked over to Bryant and asked where Beth was. He pointed to a room. I told him he looked sharp, and today was his day – enjoy it. I knocked on the door and heard, "Come in." Beth and Pam were talking.

I said, "Look at these two beautiful women! Beth, you're radiant."

"Look at you! If I wasn't getting married, I don't think I could control myself."

I told her not to let a little thing like getting married stop her. Pam left to tell everyone we were ready and to position the honor guard. After a knock on the door, we began walking beneath the raised sabers. I held Beth's hand. As we were walking I told her she was very beautiful. And, as I told Bryant, "This is your day – enjoy it." The ceremony went smoothly and nicely.

At the dais, Bryant and Beth sat close to each other, and Pam next to me. The table looked great: a wedding cake, champagne glasses, napkins and utensils, and the typical wedding knife to cut the cake. Bryant and Beth did the traditional cake-in-your-face bit. Pam removed the top of the cake and asked a waiter to put it in a container for the newlyweds. We ate, drank, and had a lot of fun.

I don't know if it was the champagne, the moment, or something that had been brewing. Pam squeezed my hand under the table and whispered in my ear, "Let's get out of here. I want to go somewhere private and have sex with you."

"That would be wonderful," I said, "But you deserve more than a one-night stand. You deserve a loving husband, a family and a great life."

She squeezed my hand tighter and told me she loved me. I told her I loved her, too. "If I didn't, I wouldn't have said what I did."

Beth took Bryant's hand, stood, and announced they wanted to go around the room to thank everyone for coming and then leave for their honeymoon. I asked her to sit for a minute. "I've got something I need to tell the three of you. I have received orders to proceed to Oakland, California at 0600 tomorrow to be mustered out of the service."

Beth said, "No-o, we need you here longer. Please, don't do it. "I told her it was time. She kissed me, took Bryant's hand and left, sobbing.

I looked at Pam and told her, "Have a great life, beautiful." She kissed me a long, passionate kiss, then she left the room crying. I sure know how to put a damper on a great night.

I was in bed when Bryant walked in.

"No matter what I do, I can't get rid of you. The only reason you want me here is, so you won't be out of work."

He grabbed my arm and was going on about how much he would miss me. I told him, "I'm going to miss and will never forget you. I owe you so much for making me whole again."

Bryant said we have to stay in touch. "You know my life... that isn't going to happen. Hey, best buddy, you need to be with Beth instead of slobbering over me. Get outta here."

He headed for the door. Without turning around, he said, "Fuck you," and left.

# CHAPTER 58

I packed all my stuff, put the five grand Tony sent me in my pocket, laid back and relaxed. At 0500 a GI walked into the room and told me he had orders to transport me to the airport. I shouldered my duffle, followed him through the front door, got into the jeep and left. I never looked back.

As I walked through the airport, I got some shitass looks. I thought they felt sorry for me because of the cane. At the ticket counter I showed the lady my orders and asked if I could upgrade to first class – coach would be too hard on my leg. She had a seat in first class, but she couldn't upgrade a military ticket. I bought a first-class ticket and forgot about the military.

The concourse was wide. People on my side moved quickly, people on the other side moved slower. Maybe I wasn't moving fast enough – I kept getting hit in my left shoulder as guys passed me. Just like city people – in their own world, not giving a fuck what they do. Then I realized the concourse is wide enough. These fuckers are doing it on purpose. The next time it happened I planted an elbow in the guy's ribs. I became more aware of the looks I was getting. A woman passed with the shittiest look. I smiled at her as she hurried off.

A skinny guy, dressed like a hippie, walked past me, turned, and spit a glam on the floor in my direction. I stopped him with "Sir" and walked over to him with my hand extended. He took it. I was holding a perspiring, limp hand. "Was that for me or were you clearing your throat? It doesn't matter. You are going to get on your hands and knees and lick that up, or I'll crush this thing you call a hand." I slowly increased the pressure of the handclasp.

"OK. OK. I'll do it," he groaned. "Please...you're hurting me bad."

People gathered around. Perhaps they thought he was sick and vomiting.

As I continued toward the gate. I was thinking: "Our country's gratitude, my ass. Those cocksuckers say what they think sounds good."

We arrived in Oakland – same fuckin' concourses. A couple of GIs in fatigues were in front of me. The looks they got didn't seem to be as bad as the ones I was getting. I figured it was because of my dress uniform, beret, and all the shit on my chest.

Once I got my bag, I made my way outside to the street. A jeep was waiting. The driver called out my name; he took me to the Oakland base.

I was standing in a short line waiting to be mustered out of the service. When it was my turn at the booth I handed the paymaster my orders. He searched out my file. As he verified the information on the form he came to an abrupt stop. "Your records show you're deceased!" I shrugged my shoulders. "If that's the way the army wants it, leave it." He printed out a form and handed me cash. I asked if I was entitled to financial compensation for being dead. He laughed ... and I was out of the army.

I got a ride to the airport. At the entrance an older woman was sitting at a table with USO banners and signs. I walked over to her and got a smile. "It's nice to see a smile. I've been getting only nasty looks."

"I know," she said, "and it's so wrong. Our country is warped. I have been sitting here for hours, and not one contribution. They have no idea how much good we do for the GIs."

"I'm here for the smile ... and to give you this. I don't know how much is there. It's my mustering-out pay. I do know the good the USO does for GIs." She stood up, leaned over, and kissed me on the cheek. I thanked her for the smile and the kiss and wished her a good day.

There was a lot of time before the flight, so I called Muraso and asked Cleo to connect me to Tony or Maria. She said both were out of the office. I left Tony a message: I would be arriving LaGuardia at three this afternoon, flight 256, United, and I'd appreciate it if someone would pick me up.

At a bar, I grabbed a bite to eat, drank a beer, and smoked a couple of cigarettes. I had just ordered a second beer when an attractive Black girl sat next to me. She had big tits and was showing them off. "Hi, how'd you like a date?"

"No, thanks. If you want a beer, have this one."

On my way to the gate I decided to look straight ahead and not pay attention to the fuckers. On the plane I sat with my eyes closed. I was working myself into a frenzy. I was squeezing the arms of my seat so hard, I passed the cushioning and was down to the metal frame. I was angry with the politicians, the army, and the slants, I was furious at the fuckin' war. All the lives that had been lost, us and them: civilians, old women, young children, babies, the innocent farmer working rice paddies. All dead. What got me so fuckin' angry was, it was all for nothing. I have no problem killing someone if there's a reason for it, but all those deaths were for nothing, not a fuckin' thing.

I gradually calmed down after I remembered a talk Bryant and I had. He told me everyone has mood swings. The problem is mine are so severe that my thinking becomes irrational. He felt with my intelligence, I should be able to curtail the swing at both ends of the spectrum and think things out rationally. He told me the army was done. History. In my line of work, being irrational would get me killed.

The stewardess interrupted my thoughts and asked if I cared for something to eat and drink. I told her a bottle of vodka, no glass, just the bottle. To eat, anything, I didn't care.

My thoughts went to Hawk and Bolton. Had the wire been twenty feet over, I would have tripped it. When everything went off, we were close to it. Our only thoughts were to get out of there fast. Hawk and I had always moved through the jungle close to each other, very cautiously. This time we veered away from each other on a run. My grief over Hawk's death is not only because we were so close, but because he gave his life for me. He could have tried to get away from it and might have been killed anyway. But he chose to cover the mine with his body.

Colonel Bolton never liked being a desk jockey. Achieving the rank of colonel in the Special Forces is a major accomplishment. He was the ultimate warrior and died doing what he loved. Rest in peace, my friend, rest in peace.

I opened my eyes. There was a tray of food with the small bottle of vodka on it. The stewardess was standing nearby. "I apologize for the way I was, and what I said. I was reliving something and in a very bad mood." She accepted my apology and told me she understood. I told her I was not going to drink the vodka, do what she wanted with it. I wasn't going to eat either and asked if she could, pass the tray back to a GI who might appreciate it. I leaned back, closed my eyes and thought I was so glad Bryant was a true friend. His knowledge and his skill at what he did has often come into play.

The plane made its approach and landed at LaGuardia. As it emptied out I waited till almost everyone exited. I walked to the door with my trusty cane. My stewardess was standing at the door. I switched hands on the cane and extended my right hand to her. Not shaking hands, just holding her hand, I told her thank you and left.

I made my way to the baggage area. Standing by the carousel was Vince, holding my duffle. He dropped the bag, ran over and hugged me. It probably has to do with being Italian – we do a lot of hugging. Vince said he was glad to see me, and the limo was outside.

Once through the large sliding door, Maria came running toward me. As she got closer, I could see she was crying. When she reached me, she grabbed me, and we began kissing, I dropped the cane and held her tightly.

I couldn't help but think I hadn't seen one dirty look here. We were standing in the middle of the doorway. Everyone walked around, giving us our space. Maybe it's a California thing, and not an entire-country thing. I'll never know. When I get home and out of my uniform, I don't plan on ever wearing it again.

We came up for air. Maria, "Let's continue this in the back seat." Trying to get a laugh out of her I kidded, "We're blocking the door, and I need a towel to dry off." No laugh, but a nice, weak smile.

Hand in hand we walked to the limo. Vince had put my duffle in the trunk and held the door. I was about to follow Maria in but spotted Tony sitting by the opposite door. I made my way around the limo, yanked open the door, and grabbed Tony. Seconds passed before I could speak. "I am so glad to see you. I missed you, more than you'll ever know."

I stepped back, took a better look, and then leaned over and whispered, "T, what the fuck happened to you? You look like shit."

Tony told me the uniform suited me and I looked great in it.

"Yeah, yeah. Cut the crap. That doesn't answer my question."

"A doctor told me I have gout that will come and go. Each episode will get worse. The medical field is working on it, but nothing yet. Last night's episode was a killer. It's just swelling and pain. It will pass, and I'll be fine."

"Tony, whatever it costs, we're gonna get answers about this shit, and a cure, and not wait for anybody."

On the way home, I asked Tony if he and Gloria were still together. "Yes, closer than ever. She felt this should be just the three of us. That's how great a woman she is."

As Maria and I were getting out of the car, Tony said, "Early tomorrow let's meet up at the office. We have a couple of important things to discuss."

As soon as we were in the house Maria and I began kissing. I cupped her face between my hands, couldn't stop looking at her. We decided to go out to the patio and have some of our favorite iced tea. After a couple of hours of talking I told Maria I didn't plan on ever wearing this uniform again. "But for now, I have to keep a promise I made and need the uniform for a short while longer. I'm driving to Dix. I don't know when I'll be home. I can't wait to spend the night with you."

At Dix the MP at the gate passed me through. I drove to headquarters, told a sergeant I was trying to locate an old friend, Sergeant Moore. "He was barrack sergeant and DI of a basic training unit. I had been told he's still here."

After checking a lengthy roster, he told me Moore was in Alpha Company, and he's a corporal now. "I'll have a driver take you. It's easier than my giving you directions, and easier on you with the cane. Sarg, the jeep will pick you up in front." I thanked him.

The minute I reached the curb a jeep pulled up. We drove down streets with the same old fucked-up barracks. The driver stopped, pointed to a barracks and told me I could find Alpha Company's top on the first floor. In the barracks I found the first sergeant's office, I knocked on the door and walked in.

He told me Moore was at the NCO club. "How about joining me, drinks are on me." When we walked into the club, the place became quiet, most likely because of my dress uniform and cane. Moore was sitting at a table with a sergeant. We joined them. After we ordered a couple of Buds, the first sergeant asked about the 25th and Special Forces. I told him I had been in a unit of Special Forces assigned to the 25th. The unit's mission was tunnel rats.

I nodded to Moore and asked if he remembered me. He said he didn't. I suggested we go back to the barracks and get caught up on old times. I put a twenty on the table; then we left.

On the way to the barracks I asked, "You really don't remember me?" He told me he didn't. "It's been awhile now; it looks like you fucked up. When I knew you, you were a sergeant. I made you a promise in a latrine. I keep my promises."

All he could say was, "Shit, fucking shit."

In the barracks four GIs were sitting around, one a spec4. I told Moore to get his toothbrush – we were going into the latrine. I told the spec4 not to let anyone into this latrine, to tell them to use the crapper upstairs.

When Moore and I were alone in the latrine, he started blabbering excuses: he had been drunk, he didn't know what he was doing.

"That doesn't cut it. When you told everybody about what happened, why'd you leave off pissing on the floor? This is an order. You will dip your toothbrush in a bowl and clean the urinals, and then the base of the bowls. They are to be spotless. When I return, they better be, immaculate or you will do it till they are."

I went outside and smoked a cigarette. I was thinking the army changed. The latrine was filthy. We could never have gotten away with it. I decided I wasn't going to keep this shit up. Being home was more important.

I went in and told Moore, "That's enough. Stand by the sink and brush your teeth with that brush." He did. After a while I instructed: "Lift the seat up, get on your knees and hang your dick in the bowl." I slammed the seat down on his dick and walked out. I told the spec4 Moore needed his help.

Maria was asleep when I got home. I joined her. She kissed me awake, telling me I had to get up for work, the vacation was over. I pulled her to me. We were locked in a tight embrace. I told her she was right, except about the vacation. "Maria, I'm sorry about last night. I'll make it up to you for the rest of your life."

# *CHAPTER 59*

Maria and I drove to Muraso in our own cars. After we kissed in the parking lot, Maria walked over to this big building that made Muraso look runty. In Muraso the guard in the booth told me he couldn't let me go further without an ID card. After checking out my name on the phone, he told me to please go in. I told him, he should have had someone come out and verify who I was.

I looked in Mario's office – he wasn't there. I looked in mine – it was the same as I left it. I went to Tony's office. Mario jumped up and began hugging me – that Italian thing, telling me how good it was to see me. I told him it was good to see him, and I really missed him.

"Mario you'd be proud of me. I beat this guy in chess. He used to be on chess and checkers teams in college. You taught me well; I nailed him hard."

I asked Tony how he felt today. He told me a lot better. The only problem he had was whatever happened to respect, "Good morning Mr. D, how are you?"

"I asked how you felt. What more do you want from me?" We were kidding.

"We have two problems we need to talk out, and then decide how to handle them."

Mario began with: "Our federal senator has been probing Tony. He wants to put him away for a long time. The word we got is Juan is behind it, with the Sicilians. Juan wants all of the automotive and amalgamated; the Sicilians would get everything else."

I sat quietly taking in and analyzing what he told me. Tony asked if I had any thoughts about it. I told him yes and asked if he had anything to add to it. He said Mario told me everything they know.

"The senator is new shit. Juan and the Sicilians – we knew would happen eventually. It's just coming too fast and too soon. I have some suggestions on how to handle the senator and Sicilians. If you agree with me, we'll act on it."

"With the Sicilians, there's nothing we can do except give them the Bronx and the dope, and that's it. We need to move the family and everything we can to Vegas. We move the inventory from Royal Auto Sales to Vegas and set up a new Royal Auto Sales. We move the equipment from Waste, Beacon, Bruckner, and what we can from Astro, and set up new facilities."

"We buy three office complexes: one for us, one for Dawson, and one for Amalgamated. We build a warehouse for Dawson. We move our banking to Vegas.

I can sell Bruckner, Beacon and the other two yards to Juan. Tony, you need to sell the other families the Astro business, and the waste business."

"Vegas is booming. We could cash in on it. Asphalt, concrete, trash. We can get back into auto sales. Let's stay out of the fuckin' dope. We need to build back the Family in Vegas. We should get started now, before the fuckers catch us holding our balls. If you agree with the way I want to do it, good. If not, we'll talk about it."

"As far as the senator, I'll set up a meet with the senator at Palisades Park, under the Washington. I 'm going to lead him on. That the meeting is going to be me ratting you out for immunity for myself. We'll meet alone: no one watching, no one listening, no communications with anyone. If he agrees, we'll do it, and meet in his car. I know the fucker is going to tape our conversation. When I get in his car I'm going to set a small block of C4 with a ten second timer against the seat, out of sight. When I leave, I'll pull the pin and run to my car. When all the bullshit dies down and they replace him, you buy the guy off, no matter how much. That will give us the time we need."

Mario said, "Its fuckin' genius. The senator and Vegas. I agree with everything you've said."

Tony agreed as well. "I like the Vegas move. As far as the senator, it sounds OK, but you be careful with the C4." Saying I would, I didn't tell him I had handled it so much this was a cakewalk.

"As for Juan, he and I are going to have dinner together. I want to find out firsthand if he's behind this and learn more about him. If he's behind this, he's going to try to talk me into running it. When I figure out how to off him, we'll get together and talk about it. For the Sicilians, I have an idea, but that's down the road. I'll tell you this: we will get our vendetta."

I reminded Tony he built an empire by taking the advice of my grandmother and Hyman. In his own words, he didn't want to be old-school mafia. "Us putting out contracts or going to the mattress gets us nothing. We can handle this in house, smartly, and move on."

I went to my office and spoke to Maria on the phone, asking if she would do me the honor of having lunch with me. "Or we could go home and start the long process of having a family... long because I want to take my time doing it" She told me tonight. For now, we'd go to lunch.

As we were eating, I suggested she get ahold of my mother and begin the wedding preparations. "I can't wait to see you walking down the aisle. You're going to be the most beautiful bride in the world."

Maria said she'd contact my mother, arrange going to Vegas so the two of them could plan the wedding.

I told her I had some urgent business to take care of and advised her to fly out to Vegas that night. We would catch up when she got back. "This job-thing is bothering me so bad, I won't be any good till I handle it."

Maria, being Tony's daughter, knew better than to ask me what is was. I felt if things went to shit, she'd be safe in Vegas.

Back in my office I asked Cleo to get Senator Block on the phone, and then Juan Hernandez. All through lunch, and even now, I had this feeling the world was coming down on us. I spoke to Block. When I told him what I wanted, he got excited. He agreed to the rules and the place. We'd meet at eleven tomorrow morning. I knew he was going to set up security and surveillance, probably bug his car. The fucker gave me no credit for intelligence.

Juan who was glad to hear from me, and offered to have prepared the best dinner I ever ate. There were a couple of things to discuss while we dined. I was to arrive about five.

I made a contact for the C4 and timer, and asked Vince to pick it up for me. Warning him the package contained an explosive. I sat back, crossing my t's and dotting my i's. I got ahead of myself, probably because of the C4. In planning the vendetta, I had to insure no one was to be within two square blocks of Muraso. We would bring in flatbeds and trailers, move Dawson coffee and whatever else we wanted. We would leave the offices at Muraso as much intact as we could. When the Sicilians took over their new headquarters, they would be blown to shit.

I went downtown to the Waldorf. The same fag clerk was there. He got the key and opened the elevator. Before I could push the up button, he stepped in and told me he thinks about me a lot and had been wondering where I was., "Please, pretty please. Can I suck on your cock?"

I told him I was in a hurry. "Next time we'd get it on good."

He left in a flurry, waving his hand, saying, "Till next time."

In the elevator I was thinking, "Thank you, Bryant, for teaching me patience. The next time, I'm going to castrate the fuckin' fag." The elevator door opened, and there was Juan... with his usual, predictable, phony graciousness. He invited me to join him on the patio to relax, talk, smoke a Cuban, and drink before dinner. Alongside the lounge chair, on a small table, was a bottle of Chianti and a Cuban. In front of us, behind a glass enclosure, was his pool, with a naked girl playing in the water. She was young, with black straight hair, great tits, and a terrific body. I thought she was his girlfriend, and he was showing her off to me.

The opening conversation was a lot of small talk. Then Juan asked about the army. I wanted to get on with this, so I gave him an in. I told him the army taught me one thing. From now on I look out for me, no one else, and I will never take orders again. If he didn't bite on that, I would be hard-pressed to come up with something else.

"Paul, that's one of the things I want to talk to you about. I'm going to take over the automotive business of the Family and Amalgamated Insurance. The Sicilians are taking over the rest. I want you to run everything for me." I told him it sounds great, just what I want, but I won't take orders.

"The Sicilians won't give you orders. They're too fucking stupid. They're along for the ride. This is all me, and I won't ever give you orders." I told him OK, we have a deal.

"The second thing – "

Before he could say more, I said, "Let's stay with the first. You taking over the automotive is a good move. I'm not sure how you plan on doing it. If you plan to do it by force, the DeAngelo family will destroy you and the Sicilians. If you plan to get rid of Tony, it wouldn't matter. I have a much easier and neater way. Write me a check to the DeAngelo family for $10 million. I will see to it that all the automotive is transferred to you. The property at Bruckner, Royal Auto Sales, Beacon, and Brooklyn is worth that much."

"Deal. Let me get a check right now."

Handing me the check he said, "I want to talk to you about the bitch in the pool. I want you to take her out in my boat, the same one you captained a few times, pop her and let her swim with the fish."

"I could do that for you, but why waste a great piece of ass like that?"

"She knows way too much about our business and me. This wouldn't be bad if she didn't have a big mouth. I told her you just got out of the army, and I wanted her to give you the best time of your life."

I told him OK, I'd do it after dinner.

While we ate, the girl kept glancing in my direction. Me, being the gentleman that I am, I couldn't take my eyes off her tits.

We were moving through the bay with the running lights on. I was at the controls and decided to put it in automatic. The girlfriend who was standing very close to me, told me her name was Carmen and she knew mine. I asked her if she knew why we were on the boat ride. She answered Juan wanted her to do whatever I wanted so I could have the best time of my life. I asked if she understood what he meant. She answered sex, any way I wanted it.

"You're his girlfriend! I can't understand how any guy would think so little of his girlfriend to do this."

"I'm not his girlfriend; I'm his showpiece. When he's with friends or businessmen he wants to impress, I'm invited. He can't bring out his boy bitch. Yes, Paul, Juan is a homosexual. On a lot of occasions, he's said he'd give a lot to suck your cock.

When Juan told me what he wanted, I agreed without hesitation. Even though he got me drunk, I remembered the time we were in the pool. Then tonight, seeing you on the lounge, and at dinner, I got so excited. I'm a virgin, have never even kissed a man. Juan has kept me under lock and key."

The boat started to sway. We were out of the bay and in deep water. I told her I was going to drop anchor, so we could go on the deck, relax on the lounge chairs and talk. She asked if we could talk naked to our waists. "Later. For now, I just want to talk." I asked where she was from and how she got together with Juan.

"I'm from Bolivia. My father and Juan worked out a deal. Juan bought me. It's not as bad as it sounds. In Bolivia, there are the wealthy and the poor, nothing in-between." "My family is large and very poor. It wouldn't have been long before we starved to death. My father and I talked. I told him I was willing to do it. The money Juan gave my father meant my family could have a good life."

I suggested we could now get undressed to the waist. While I stared at her tits, she ran her hands over my shoulders and chest. After a while she stopped and asked if I was like Juan. Far from it. She asked why I didn't I touch her. "I will. For now, I'd like to be the first man to kiss you. We can have a nice, friendly kiss, or we can have a kiss you'll remember for a long time." She wanted a kiss to remember. Our kiss was passionate. I wondered if she had practiced kissing a mirror. My hand went to her tit. I held it gently. Her nipple was rock hard.

"Let's go down and continue this in bed, so you won't be cold." I told her hold onto the railings and take her time. With the boat moving like this she could easily fall.

Once we were in bed, I told her she was no dummy. "You need to think out carefully what I'm about to say. The reason we're here is not for you to show me a good time. We're here because Juan wants you dead. I'm supposed to do him a favor and off you, weight you down, and throw you overboard. Juan's afraid you know too much about him and his business, and someday he'll get hurt because you have a big mouth."

She started crying and tried to get out of the bed. I grabbed her and told her I wasn't finished.

"I told you to think out what I tell you. You can't think straight while crying like a baby." She stopped and was looking at me with the saddest eyes I've ever seen. "If that's what you want, we'll fuck, and you can give me a blow job. We'll kiss again, and I'll off you. Juan will be happy. I want you to tell me everything you know about Juan and his business. Most important, what he's so afraid you might tell someone. If you do that for me, I'll relocate you home with enough money, so you and your family will be considered wealthy."

"He'll find me and kill me!"

"Good, now you're thinking. Juan won't be around." She told me she'd do it my way, except first she wanted me to fuck her. Then she wanted to suck my dick. And finally, she wanted a kiss. If I agreed to that we had a deal.

"You start talking. We'll see about that later." She began telling me about Juan, his family, what he had, the men and boys he had all over. She went into detail about Juan and his boyfriend here. When she got to his plans with the ugly Italians, I was pissed but didn't let on.

Juan bragged to the Italians he was going to get me into a position where he'd suck on my cock. When he got tired of it, they could kill me. She continued telling me all the plans Juan laid out, every detail.

"Afterward he would say those stupid bastards didn't understand a word. He'd have to go over it again tomorrow." She kept talking about the Sicilians. At one point, she said, "That night we were in the pool – you and Tony looked like movie stars compared to these guys."

"Speaking of the pool, what was the what-kind-of-name-is-Pauly shit?"

She said she was sorry she ever opened her mouth – she was drunk. She wanted me so bad, but I was with that other girl. She had a hard time controlling herself.

"This is what I'm going to do. I'll get you a nice place for tonight. Someone will contact you tomorrow and make the arrangements."

Carmen wanted to go on deck and finish where we left off. When we got to the chairs, she picked up her purse from the table, took out a gun, and pointed it at me. "You're not as smart as you think you are. In fact, you're a stupid ass. This was never about you offing me. It was a plan for me to kill you."

"They should give you an academy award for your acting. There is one detail you missed in your plan. I'm stronger than you." With that I grabbed her hand, and pointed the barrel away from me. She pulled the trigger. Nothing. Juan had given her an empty gun. I pulled it out of her hand, put it in my pants pocket. I dragged her to the weight and flipped it to the other side of the railing. Lifting her over, I attached the ropes to her ankles and kicked the weight overboard. I grabbed her and shoved her gun down her throat. "Suck on this, bitch," I snarled before I let go.

I returned the boat to the pier, got in my car, and went home. I called Tony and told him what went down. "We should get rid of Hernandez before the senator. If he realizes what happened, he'll move up his timetable and we'll be fucked." Tony agreed. I also told Tony I would drop off a check for ten million from Juan. "He bought our automotive. Have someone cash it first thing."

The next morning, after I stopped at Muraso, I was at the Waldorf. I told the parking attendant I wasn't going to be long.

The clerk behind the desk was my fag friend. I told him I needed to go up. When we reached the elevator, I suggested we go up together. He'll be able to suck on a lot of cocks. The door opened into Juan's lobby. I stepped to one side and told the fag to call out Mr. Hernandez. Juan came out of a room, asked what he wanted. I stepped around the corner, "He wants to suck your cock." Pointing my gun at him, I said, "I want you."

The three of us went into the bedroom. The boyfriend was in bed. I closed and locked the door behind me. I told the bitch to get out of the bed. "Everybody get undressed. Fast. Juan, get on your hands and knees. Fag, lay on your back and suck Juan's dick. Bitch, mount Juan and fuck him in the ass."

The two were working Juan good. "Juan, you're going to suck. Open your fuckin' mouth." I shoved my gun down his throat and pulled the trigger. He went straight down. The gay guy tried to push Juan off. He couldn't. Juan's cock was still hard and must have been way down his throat. I thought for a second: this is more than you bargained for, fag.

The bitch had gone down with Juan, and still had his cock embedded. He was a feminine-looking guy. I shoved my hand in his mouth and said, "Suck, bitch, I want you to go out with a smile on your face," as I put two below his left ear. I put my gun on the toy-boy's head and put two in him. I felt bad about it, but he was a witness. I took the elevator down and broke the key off in the lock.

There was still plenty of time, so I went to the office and phoned Maria. I apologized for waking her, and explained it was important. "Put the wedding preparations on hold. We've got some trouble. We've decided to move everything to Vegas and get out of the Bronx. I need you to locate offices along with a warehouse for Dawson Coffee.

Lease or buy a facility that we can move Amalgamated into and ask Hyman to coordinate the move. I love you. And tell my mother I love her. I'll see both of you soon.

I drove to Jersey. There was still plenty of time. Instead of driving to the Park, I drove to the lookout. The lookout was above the Park, almost at the top of the Palisades. The view of the city over the railing was spectacular. I was leaning on the rail taking it all in. A black van pulled up. A guy got out with a bunch of equipment and set it by the railing.

"Good morning," I greeted. "What a great day to take pictures of the city! Can I buy a couple from you?" I knew it wasn't a camera – it was a listening device. I couldn't wait for the bullshit.

"This isn't a camera. It's the latest in voice detection. Some big shot guinea is going to spill his guts to a senator. We'll hear everything and record it."

"That sounds very exciting. Can I listen in?"

"You can't. This is undercover work. No one is supposed to know we're here."

I drove to the park, concealed the car under a tree, out of sight. I took off my sport coat and tie, sat back and smoked a cigarette. I put it out and got out of my car and lit up a Denobli. These fuckers tasted like shit and smelled like it. I figured I'd get into his car smoking. If he objected, I'd get out, make a big deal of putting it out on the ground while I was setting the C4. If he didn't object, I'd still be able to set the C4. He'd be so sick and wanting to get over with it. He'd be focusing on taking himself and the car to be fumigated. My thought was he'd be happy, re-lieved to meet his Maker. I was glad I wasn't in my car smoking this shit. The only good thing about the Denobli was they were great for lighting a torch in the junkyard.

A limo pulled into the park. The senator got out from be-hind the driver's seat and sat in the back, leaving the door open. I walked over, and climbed in, taking some puffs. I said, I'm sorry. "Does this bother you?" He told me no. If it made me comfort-able talking, he was all for it. I closed the door. After a couple more puffs, the fucker started getting pale. I told him I needed him to reaffirm our agreement, that this talk was confidential, and I would receive immunity. He swore he was a man of his word and would most certainly honor our agreement.

"My name is Paul Watson. Tony DeAngelo and I are co-boss-es of the Bronx Mafia Family. We're only figureheads, don't have no authority. The true boss is Juan Hernandez. He gives the or-ders and calls all the shots. Juan's the largest producer and dis-tributor of cocaine in the country. He brings it in from South America, distributes it to the Mafia Families across the country. Juan has his own crew that does all the hits. Juan is in a war with the Sicilians who want to take everything he has. Tony and I do nothing. We're there only for show."

My rope finally got to him. Block was sick. He told me to follow him to the Federal Building, so he can record our conversation. Going to the Fed Building was to have me arrested and dummy up what I told him. I got out, pulled the pin on the timer, and turned for my car. I was in my car when the limo lifted off the ground with a roar, then burst into flames.

# *CHAPTER 60*

The next afternoon Tony set up a meeting for us with the *capo* and the other bosses. There was plenty of time, so I told Tony about my night with the cunt and about offing Hernandez. I was almost finished when the TV started beeping. An announcer said, "Senator John Block and Mafia boss Paul Watson were killed in a car bombing at the Palisades Park at eleven-fifteen this morning. The station has been able to acquire their conversation prior to the bombing."

Those guys must have been contractors and didn't work for the government. They saw an opportunity to make big bucks and took it. The recording started from the beginning. I explained to Tony I was smoking a rope to fuck Block up. When the announcement was over, Tony told me I hadn't lost it. I was still the smartest fucker he knew.

Tony got a kick out of everything I told him, especially how I offed Juan and the other two fags. He said the meeting this afternoon is to sell off everything. I asked if we wanted to sell to get rid of it, or if we wanted to make as much as we can. Tony didn't think we should give it away, but he didn't want the cost to be an obstacle to getting rid of it. Who's the smart fucker now?

We were in a high-rise office building, sitting in a conference room with the *capo*, Vito, Carmine, Piagio, and Boscato. Tony started it off with the reason he requested the meeting – to retire and move to Vegas. He wanted to sell off his businesses. It was only right for them to have his businesses rather than outsiders. It was going to be interesting to see how Tony handled Boscato, who was Sicilian. I wondered how he would manage his dislike when it came to business.

Tony put the concrete and asphalt businesses on the table with a price. Boscato said, "Sold," and they shook hands. Vito bought the dealerships and yards except for the body shop. Carmine bought the docks and unions, and the *capo* bought the waste business, excluding the manufacturing and some trucks.

Boscato settled with Tony first. As he was leaving I met him in the hallway, introduced myself, and said I thought he might be able to answer some questions for me. I told him it was only a shot in the dark, and he might not know anything. Did he have any information about the Sicilian family that took over Naples?

It was his, but there was nothing personal, it was business. I told him I understood. I mentioned that I heard a gardener who had nothing to do with the family was killed. Boscato remembered that. It was a shame. That gardener was in the wrong place at the wrong time. We parted.

I figured out how Tony and I were going to have our vendetta. Back at the office I told Tony about my call to Maria. Although it wouldn't be necessary to buy off Block's replacement, he needed to get to the senator from Nevada. Tony said it had been done a long time ago.

"Mario needs to handle the manufacturing and trucks to Vegas and finish up anything he has here. He'll need to help Luca move what he wants and take anyone he wants. And Benny the same. Sam needs to handle the move of Dawson Coffee and then go to Vegas. You should handle your and Gloria's personal things and take her to Vegas. Establish a new base for us, not in or near the hotel – the same as we have here. You need to take with you anyone you want from here. After I introduce Boscato to the city, I'll get what they owe us, clean up any loose ends. Once we have our vendetta, I'll join you."

Tony beamed. "Good. That's how we'll do it."

"I'm going to tell you about a talk I had with Boscato after the two of you settled up. I don't want any emotion from you! I'll handle it my way." While describing the talk, I could see the anger build up in Tony. I pointed out, "The only good thing about this guy is I got the opportunity to be here and with you."

In ten days, I was the only Family member in the Bronx. Everybody else chose to go, even Cleo. I introduced Boscato to the people he needed in the city. I suggested he pay off as much as he could and as high as he could. He'd get it back in spades.

I was told it would take the city thirty days to get our money. I asked to have the check made out to Astro Concrete and Paving. I said I'd be back. It was a huge amount they owed us for the concrete and asphalt. I told Boscato this is what your purchase will bring you. Buscato and I did a lot of talking. I told him we were leaving our complex in the Bronx. He should become the boss of the Bronx – a lot better than Staten Island. All he'd have there is farmers. "Good idea. Why don't you stay here? We'll run the family business together."

"Something to think about. We'll see. After I handle some personal things and get the city money, I don't want to live in Tony's house anymore. You should live there. It's big, furnished, and has all the luxuries of a mansion. I'm clearing up a bunch of little shit in the house and offices. After I get the city money, we can decide what to do with it, get it to Tony or look at it as part of the sale.

"I'll call. You can bring the whole family to your new headquarters. And while they're getting settled in, we can go to Tony's house. If you and I are still gonna do this together, I keep my office." Boscato said yes to everything.

I spent my days planning the vendetta, calling Tony and calling Maria several times a day. On one of those calls I told

Maria I was going to have a courier bring her the wedding ring, jewelry, and cash. Was there anything else she wanted? She said no. I asked her for the bank account she had in Vegas, so I could have the bank here transfer her accounts. Also, I was going to pack and ship all her belongings, and have her car transported.

I was a busy little beaver, but the days dragged by. One day at Muraso I got a bug up my ass and called Bryant. When I got him, I asked if he missed me yet. I got a long hesitation. I said, "Jesus Christ, you really are a dickhead."

He started screaming my name. I told him to shut up – he sounded like a broad.

Bryant said it had been all over the news – the car bombing of the senator and Paul Watson. When he heard the recording, he knew it was me. He's been so fucked-up; Pam and Beth had been distraught. I told him I was sorry for that. He told me he was glad I called, and that his good friend wasn't dead.

"What was all that Hernandez stuff?" I told him Hernandez was pulling the senator's strings to get Tony out of the way. He wanted to take over the Family.

"What about everything you said about him?"

I told Bryant the dope was true as far as the Family was concerned. I tried to get Tony out of the limelight. I knew they were taping our conversation. Bryant said it sounded great, and his friend was one deviously smart guy.

"How did you do your death?" I told him I didn't. "Because they had the two of us on tape, they assumed we were both in the car."

He asked if I did it. I reminded him that I had told him once how the death in Nam bothered me because people who didn't deserve it were killed. This prick deserved it. He asked about Hernandez. I told him he met his Maker before the senator.

"All of us are in the process of moving to Vegas. By the time you come to visit, I'll be married. We'll take bets on who's the better looker, Beth or Maria."

"Last thing, Paul. Did you do Hernandez or did the Sicilians do him?" I told him he taught me a valuable lesson – not to react but think things out rationally. Hernandez was a rational decision.

"I'll be in touch. Say hello to Pam and Beth. And you'd better take care of Beth, or I'll rationalize your ass, Sir."

I spent my days at Muraso taking calls and doing a lot of thinking. I felt free – no pressure, no one to report to. I thought about Moore. That had been a long time in coming, but I kept my promise. I always said, "Payback is fuckin' hell."

I still had a lot of time till I could get the city money. During one of my calls to Tony, he told me he had been approached by an investment group. They wanted to form a conglomerate and build six hotels and casinos on the Strip. We would share the profits and be paid a fee to manage the hotels and casinos. The Family would be equal shareholders in the conglomerate but not have to invest any money. The group wanted to meet with everyone in authority to explain the arrangement. Everyone would hear it firsthand and get answers to any questions they might have. Also, these guys wanted to see who they would be partners with. Tony asked me what I thought.

"At first glance," I told him, "It sounds too good to be true. But you have nothing to lose by listening to them." He told me he was going to have Maria there because she had a good mind. The investment group wanted to have the meeting the first of next month. Tony asked if I could fly out for it.

"Sounds good. We'll see. I'm going to call Santo and tell him about Juan. He can set up his own connection for the shit. I've been telling the families that have been calling for Al that we are no longer in the business, so they need to make a new connection. I don't give a shit what happens to Juan's crap. Last, the city insists I pick up the check in person and sign for it."

I spent the next weeks having the few people that were in the two square blocks around Muraso moved. I was lucky – the neighborhood had gone to shit. It was mostly vacant lots where homes used to be, or abandoned homes that were vandalized and looked like shit. I spent my time redirecting incoming calls. When that petered out, I decided to fly to Vegas.

# *CHAPTER 61*

Tony picked me up at the airport in the limo. Vince was driving, just like old times. We went on a tour. We passed a five-story, all-glass building that had an Amalgamated Insurance sign. Next, we passed a complex of buildings with a sign saying Dawson Coffee. Later we passed a great-looking building – it was TPM Enterprises. We drove to the Strip. Not far from the casino was a large used car lot; the sign on it was Royal Auto Sales.

We drove out of town. We came to a large chain-link fenced-in area, the location of Astro Concrete and Paving. Next to it was another sign: Waste Management. A couple of miles away a neat-looking metal-fenced, good-sized lot. The sign read Royal Auto Parts. I was amazed at how much had been accomplished in such a short time. Tony had Hyman bring a lot of the offshore money to Vegas. They were spending it as fast as they could.

We drove back to TPM and walked into the lobby of the building. Behind a small counter was a guy in a uniform and Cleo. A door flew open and Maria ran to me. She told me how wonderful it was to see me, and she planned on us spending a lot of time together. She apologized that for now she had to get back to work.

Tony took me on a tour of the building. The first floor had conference rooms, a large cafeteria, and lounges. We took the elevator to the second floor. It was the same as Muraso:  a bullpen and glass-enclosed offices. The third floor had three offices, a conference room and an elegant dining room. The offices had hand-carved entry doors.

Tony opened a door and told me, "This is yours." I looked in. The office was large, with an entire wall of glass looking out on the Vegas landscape. He opened the next door. Mario saw me, hurriedly got up from his desk, and hugged me.

Tony said, "Let's go to my office. We've got a lot to catch up on." The three offices were identical. Tony began filling me in on all the businesses. "We're not going to be in the dope business or any other business that is illegitimate. We're going to keep the offshore accounts to minimize our taxes."

Mario started telling me about our waste business. "The thing took off like a bat out of hell the minute we opened the door. We bought a large tract of land in the desert and set up a station like the one at Bruckner. We're building a landfill. The only thing I regret is we won't be in the junk business."

Tony told me he had my mother close the Italian restaurant that night to the hotel customers. "We're all going to have a private dinner together. Tomorrow you should visit with each of the businesses. And you need to get together with Sam and Maria to go over the coffee supply. When that's finished, Vince will take you to your new house."

I told them it was hard to believe all that they've done – I felt left out. Tony told me, "Bullshit! There's no fuckin' way you should feel left out. You're too much a part of it all."

I told them about my plan for the vendetta. "Tony, it's the only way I could figure how to do it. I'm sorry about destroying your memories."

"No problem. They're only buildings. It's a good plan."

While we were driving, Vince told me I wouldn't believe what Tony did out here. We drove for a while and came upon an area with beautiful houses and well-manicured landscaping, surrounded by a tall wrought-iron fence. A little further away a small subdivision. Vince drove to a gate, hit a button, and the gate opened. As he was driving in, he pointed, "That's Tony's house, yours is over there, and Mario's is on the other side. Hyman's house is close to Tony's. My house is in the subdivision along with everyone else from the *famiglia* and all of the staff for the main houses."

Vince pulled up in front of a beautiful house and told me, "This is yours." He was going back to TPM and would be back at six-thirty to take Maria, Hyman, and me to the restaurant. Tony planned on taking Gloria, Mario and his wife in his car. I walked to the front door. Before I could reach for the knob, it opened. A distinguished-looking guy in a suit greeted me and said, "My name is Carmine. I am the house butler. If you would like, I can show you to the master bedroom." I nodded yes and followed him into the house. It was impressive.

We went upstairs. Carmine opened a door and asked if there was anything I needed. I told him no and he left. I looked around, thinking, *This is some fuckin' room.*

I found and read a note left on the dresser. "Look in the closet. I bought you a new wardrobe. All the toiletries you will need are in the bathroom. There is a box of Cubans in the top dresser drawer. Love you. See you in a while."

I picked up a Cuban and went downstairs. Carmine met me at the foot of the stairs. I said, "I know this place has a patio. Point me in the right direction. And does Maria have a pitcher of her iced tea in the refrigerator?"

"She does, and I'll bring you a glass. The patio is through those double doors."

I was relaxing, drinking my tea, and enjoying the cigar. I don't know how long I had been there when Maria was standing beside me. I got up and we kissed. She started telling me how much she loved me, "But now we have to get going. We're running late."

Vince picked us up. Hyman was already in the limo. We went to the hotel. The minute we walked in my mother grabbed and hugged me. It was almost like she had a death grip on me. I kissed her on the forehead and told her I loved her. The meal was great; the conversation was lively. I sat back thinking, *How wonderful my life is to be with a group of people I love more than anything in the world.*

Once home Maria asked if we could just shower and go to bed. "Sure, as long as we shower together." Later, we were in bed kissing. Maria said she wanted to start our family now! The sex was wonderful, exactly how I envisioned it for so many years. I told Maria, "I hope our first-born is a girl, a daughter just like you."

The next morning Maria drove me to Dawson Coffee. After a cup of Sam's great coffee, we began talking business. They decided to open two hundred coffee shops in metropolitan areas across the country. Once they were running well, they would franchise a thousand more. I asked if their coffee supply was still from the Columbian plantation. Sam said Dawson Coffee used the best beans available. I asked if Hernandez had been involved.

Sam told me no. "Tony didn't want Hernandez involved. He sent me to Columbia with an interpreter. I bought a plantation and lucked out. I have the greatest coffee expert in the world running it."

I told him Tony is a smart guy, and Hernandez is deceased. I borrowed Maria's car and drove to Astro. Benny and I talked, and I asked for the Astro bank account number. "When I get back, I'll be signing for the city check for $684,000. I'll have Manufacturers wire it to the account." I went next door and visited with Waste, and then to Royal Auto Parts and Luca. I drove back to Dawson, picked up Maria, and went home. We enjoyed a leisurely evening together. Later in bed, it was the same as the night before, beautiful and loving.

The next morning, I drove Maria to work before heading for TPM. I wanted to spend more time with Tony and Mario. They filled me in on all the plans they wanted to put in motion and wanted my feedback. That made me feel good. I told them we ought to consider building two more large hotels and casinos.

"I know what you told me about the meeting you're going to have. I think you should pass on it. There's something fishy about what you told me. It's a waste of your time. I have a feeling this is bad."

Tony told me. "Like you said, it can't hurt to listen. I think you're right. We will build two hotels and casinos. When you get back we'll start on it."

I asked Tony what ever happened with Shaffer? Shaffer had the equipment delivered, setup and serviced. Maria and Hyman were satisfied with everything. I thought about Shaffer and Hyman and decided not to open that old wound. I contacted an organization that was hunting guys like him, gave them all the info. We didn't have the time to mess with him.

After a while I told them Maria was working late. I was going to the hotel to spend some time with my mother. I planned on going to the Bronx tomorrow, finish up, and get back there for good.

I asked the front desk clerk to page Mrs. Walker. I invited my mother to have dinner with me. We could catch up on things and spend time together. She suggested I include Hyman and asked if I could join her in the auditorium, now.

When I got to the auditorium my mother greeted me with a hug and a kiss on the cheek and then told me to follow her.

There are a couple of young ladies who will be happy to say hello to you. We walked to the auditorium and backstage. I could see Kathy sitting at a desk talking to a showgirl. As soon as Kathy saw me, she jumped up, screamed "Pauly," and ran to me. The showgirl in costume and full makeup was right behind her. Both were hugging me and kept thanking me. I told Terri she made a great-looking showgirl.

Kathy said, "Pauly, you have the greatest mother in the world."

I told her I knew and asked how married life was? She said wonderful.

My mother, Hyman and I were in the Jewish Delicatessen. I love Jewish food. We talked about everything. Old and new – it was all good. I told them Tony mentioned the meeting he wanted both of them to attend. I asked what they thought about it.

Hyman said, "If it comes about, it would be very good for us. We will own Vegas."

My mother said she didn't like it. "No one in this world gives you something for nothing. The whole thing is wrong!"

I told my mother it must be something in our genes, because I didn't like it either, had a bad feeling about it. I picked up Maria and went home. When we went to bed, Maria asked if we could take a hiatus tonight.

She sighed, "Pauly, my love, you have worn me out."

I told her I understood. "Tomorrow morning I'm taking the first flight out. I need to finish up some things. When I get back we can continue where we left off."

# *CHAPTER 62*

In New York I drove to City Hall. I saw Leon in procurement, got Astros' check, and headed for the bank. The wire transfer was easy. Back home I got a beer, a Cuban, and headed for the patio lounge chair. I began thinking this place sucks with just me here. My mind went back to Vegas. Life is great when I'm a part of everything and with the people I truly love.

Over the next couple of days, I sorted out the few things I wanted to take to Vegas and packed them in my car. My plan was to drive to Vegas. I made my contact and picked up the C4 and timers. I already had a five-gallon can of gas at the house. While I was at the office taking things I wanted, I called Santo. I told him about Vegas and invited him and Meyer to come out. We'd show them a great time. We also talked about the dope deal.

After I hung up, the phone rang. It was Sam. He was crying so hysterically that I couldn't understand what he was saying. I told him to calm down, take a deep breath and speak slowly.

He gasped, "They're dead. They're all dead...your mother, Tony, Maria, Mario, Hyman...they're all dead.

He continued blubbering. I was numb. I said, "Stop! Tell me what happened."

"The meeting they had was a phony, he wept. "Salassi and five guys gunned them down."

I told him, "You have a lot to do now. You can grieve later. I want you to get ahold of Howard in accounting. If he doesn't know what happened, tell him. I want him to transfer money from all the accounts in Vegas to Dawson Coffee. He's to shift Hyman's and my account from the Caymans to my Bronx bank.

Tony's goes to an account for Gloria in Vegas. The DeAngelo family account to you and the other two to Dawson Coffee.

When Howard's finished, I want him to go to my place and Hyman's. At Hyman's I want his valuables, specifically a Sondrio watch. At mine I want all of Maria's jewelry, specifically her wedding set. Have it sent to Muraso. Tony's and Maria's personal accounts transfer to Gloria. When Howard's done, you stash him somewhere and then have him work for you. Give him a very healthy bonus for all this, and pay him well.

"I've got a few more things I need you to do for me. Get a hold of Vincent, he was head of security at the hotel. Tell him the hotel and casino are his if he wants them. If he doesn't, sell them. Benny at Astro and Pietro at Waste, the same. Aside from that, sell everything the family owned.

"Sam, we are back at the beginning. We're partners.

I want you to set up a funeral. The best coffins you can buy. Headstones to match my father's. Everyone in plots together. I'll be coming to Vegas. I need to handle Salassi. But I can't go to a funeral. At the funeral, I want you to place a rose on my mother's and on Maria's coffins. Tell them for me that I loved them, I'll miss them, rest in peace. For Tony, Hyman and Mario, tell them the same for me.

"I won't see you again. I want you to distance yourself and the company from the Family as much as you can. Build Dawson Coffee into a megacompany to honor Maria.

"We were friends. We were good friends. I'm gonna miss you. You're the only one I have left in this whole fuckin' world. Good-bye."

I went into a rage … and then thought, *Later. I've got things to do.* I sat down and tried to get my head on straight. I felt this wasn't all Salassi. He had to have someone backing this deal. I called Mr. G. The guy who answered the phone told me Vito is no longer here. Joseph Colombo is *capo famiglia*. I asked for Mr. Salassi and was told Mr. Salassi is out of town on business.

I called Buscoto,and told him I had a great idea. "When you and your *famiglia* come to the Bronx, invite Mr. Colombo and his *famiglia*. We've got great food and a wine cellar. Everyone can have a good time. You and Mr. Colombo can discuss a joint venture in an olive oil distributing business. Every pizzeria uses olive oil. It's big and going to get bigger. Tony built two large warehouses behind the office. The sign on one is Muraso Distributing. It's a front. The two of you can use it as your distribution warehouse."

He told me it sounded great. "I'll invite Joe and tell him to wait for my call. I'll call him after I hear from you."

I waited a couple of days before I called Boscato to set up the meeting. I set the timers on the C4. I had them follow me to the offices, then I took Boscato to Tony's house. Boscato was sitting in Tony's easy chair. I put two rounds in his head. I said, sarcastically, "Sorry about this. It's personal, not business." I doused him and the house with gasoline, set it on fire, and drove to the airport.

When I got to La Guardia, the terminal TV screens showed extensive devastation in the Bronx, comparing it to a war zone. Gas mains were spewing flames everywhere and water mains had ruptured and shoot cascading waterfalls six foot high. And a home in Yonkers was in flames. Firemen were trying to contain the fire and protect neighboring homes.

I took a taxi from the Vegas airport to the hotel. At the front desk, I asked for Mr. Salassi's office and was told he was in a meeting. I told her I was a very close friend. If she would point me to his office, I would appreciate it.

I took out a submachine gun from a bag I was carrying, threw the bag on the floor, and went into his office firing. I swept the office back and forth. I stood over Salassi and raked his body up and down till he looked like ground beef. I threw the gun at him and walked out. A taxi brought me to the airport. I caught a red-eye back to New York.

I drove to the Waldorf and told the desk clerk I wanted a penthouse for ten days. She ran my card and asked if I had luggage. I pointed to the bellboy. She said, "Right this way." We took the elevator to the penthouse. She showed me around, asked if I needed anything. I handed her a hundred-dollar bill and told her I didn't want maid service. She thanked me and left. The bellboy asked if I wanted him to put my things away. I told him no and handed him a hundred. I got undressed to my shorts, hung up everything, and began grieving and crying. Then I began a ten-day binge of drunken rage.

I became a rabid animal. The penthouse didn't look the same after I broke or smashed everything. I didn't sleep. All I could do was go over and over everyone. When I thought about Maria, I sat up, and could only yell her name and cry. My mother, Tony, Hyman, and Mario being gone was overwhelming. I walked out to the balcony, leaned over the railing and contemplated suicide. I thought about it for a while but knew that's the last thing any of them would want of me. I went back to the room, continued crying and raging, cursing in every language I knew.

For the first time in my life I was scared. I feared being alone. I was afraid of living without them for the rest of my life. After ten days of agonizing shit, I was exhausted and fell asleep. I woke up and called down for coffee, a lot of it. They brought me a large coffee urn. I drank cup after cup of coffee, showered, shaved and went to a restaurant to eat.

Back in my room I called Bryant. I asked if he could fly to New York. I needed him. He said he couldn't get away right now. Feeling like a lost soul, I hung up. I tried to reach my God. Nothing there. I just sat for hours, depressed.

For some reason, I don't know why my mind cleared. I began to think rationally. After everything that transpired I needed a new identity. I remembered a few years ago Tony needed a new identity for someone. He made a contact, and the woman was a pro. I found her telephone number and set up an appointment.

In her office I told her I wanted a new driver's license, social security number and passport. I also wanted her to change the names on my birth certificate and military identification card. I handed her all my stuff and asked her to keep it intact in case I needed it again.

She took a picture of my driver's license and gave it back to me saying I might need it, also this wasn't going to be cheap. "I'll be finished a week from today."

I told her I didn't think it would be cheap.

My next move was to see Steve at the bank. I told him about Vegas and that I needed to change my identity. If I gave him a new name, and showed him a driver's license with that name, could he change my accounts? He told me he would, just tell him the name, I didn't need to prove it.

I asked Steve to contact Josh Morganstern and tell him his old friend and everyone else was murdered in Vegas. The hospital and foundation was his and Ely's. I thanked him and asked if he'd open my safe-deposit box with me. I took some cash out and headed for the hotel.

At the front desk I told the clerk I needed to change my penthouse. I had a problem with the one I was in, and I'd be more than happy to pay for the damages. She told me that would be alright, would I care to go to my new penthouse now, yes.

In the penthouse she told me this is the same as the one I was in. Then she said, "I guess you don't remember me?"

I told her I didn't, I'm sorry, I had a few bad days. She told me she was the clerk that showed me the first penthouse. She appreciated the tip I gave her, and made sure the damages to the other penthouse were not charged back to me. She asked if I wanted a bell-hop to move my belongings. I told her yes.

In the elevator going down I gave her a five-hundred-dollar tip, and a hundred for the bell-hop. At the front desk I asked her to break two one hundred-dollar bills into twenties for me.

I spent the week as a tourist; the city had so many great sites that I never took the time to see. On one of the days I spent it in the penthouse. Swimming, sunbathing, and smoking Cubans, just relaxing.

It was finally my new identity day. As I was about to enter her office I noticed a small sign I missed the first time. "Lewis Realty." She had everything laid out on her desk and told me from now on I was going to be John Lewis. She explained John was her husband who had recently passed away.

"I copied your passport picture for your driver's license and made some changes. I used his birth certificate and made some changes. Your passport I changed the name. The social security number was his. He had a military ID; I made some changes. He had an American Express credit card; it's now yours. I never notified them he was deceased."

She asked if I wanted to look everything over. I told her I had while she was going through it. She placed everything in a large envelope and told me that would be ten thousand.

At the hotel I called Steve at the bank and told him my new name and asked him to hold onto the new checks.

554

# *CHAPTER 63*

Nam came to me. I thought about all the families and loved ones of those I killed. The agony and grief they endured. I remember as a kid, when there were things people didn't understand, it was always "God has a plan. You must believe." I can't believe a God would put so much grief and agony on people.

I thought about Chua. I booked reservations for Saigon. I was told I could travel there. At the front desk, I checked out.

I went to the bank, closed out my accounts, and had them give me cash. I filled the safe deposit box and got a second. The remainder I put in my luggage. I put the second key with the gold key.

For most of the flight I thought about Chua and Hoai Mi. Maybe my thinking was wrong. They might have gotten caught up in something and couldn't contact us. Maybe the VC threatened them. I hoped I was wrong about it all being bullshit. I was thinking about Hoai Mi and Hawk getting married. I wondered if she had been looking forward to it as much as Hawk. I kept hoping it wasn't bullshit. I was asking my God for help. I need it to have a life. I didn't feel I could do it alone.

After a very long flight, we landed. I took a taxi to the house. I asked the driver to wait. I knocked. Chua came to the door, saw me, and began crying. I lifted her face and kissed her on the forehead. In Vietnamese I told her not to cry. A Vietnamese man rushed toward us and asked Chua if she was all right. He told her to get in the house – he would get rid of the American scum. Chua said I was an old friend.

"You do not have American friends. Did you suck his cock? Did he fuck you? You are nothing but a slut!"

I asked her in English who is this guy? "He is my husband and the father of my son."

I asked if he supported her. She said no, she supports herself and her son as well as him. I asked if he was always like this, and, did he hit her. Her reply was yes and yes. She stayed with him because it was the law. I asked if she would come with me. She told me she couldn't.

Her husband ordered her to get in the house and make food – he was hungry and he would deal with me. She ran into the house.

In broken English, he said, "You have lot of money. I sell her to you to fuck her."

I told him good and extended my hand. He took it with a toothy smile. The sight of a guy with a cane gives some guys balls.

I shook his hand. It felt like shit. I began to squeeze lightly. He reached over with the other hand to pry our hands apart. I told him in Vietnamese to put his hand down. He did. I asked him where Hoai Mi was. He said she lives in the basement of the hotel where she works. I asked if she ever married. He replied no.

I snarled at him. "You will never prostitute your wife again, you fuckin' pimp. Never hit or hurt her again." I was squeezing harder. "Do you understand?"

He said, "Yes, you hurt … Let hand go."

"In Vietnamese I said, "Where does a stupid, fuckin' prick like you get off calling me American scum?" I broke his hand. He screamed. I left.

I told the driver the Rex Hotel. A bellboy got my bags and followed me to the desk. I told the clerk I wanted the best room in the hotel for two days. I inquired if Hoai Mi, the massage lady, still worked here. Yes. "I want a massage from her ten minutes after I get to my room."

I put my things away, took off my shirt and tee, left the door slightly open. I stretched out on the bed on my stomach. A knock on the door was followed by "massage." I told her to come in and close the door. She straddled me and began massaging. I told her the massage she gave me several years ago was much better than this. She told me she has gotten old and tired. I asked her if I gave her a hundred a night for two nights would she stay with me. She asked what we would do. I said what do you think? She told me OK. I told her I wanted to turn around, so she could massage my front.

I looked at her. She looked drunk and didn't recognize me. I asked her what was wrong with her. She said she was high and does coke. That's why she agreed to the hundred a night.

"Does Chua and the man do coke?"

"Yes, he's not a good man. We were getting high, he grabbed my tit, squeezed, and told me to get out of the house."

"Was Chua with him when we were together?"

"No, right after you left he forced himself on her. That's why we were not able to contact you."

"Who is the father of the boy?"

"You are. He has some kind of problem and can't fuck."

She could see my dick and asked if I wanted to start now. I told her I wanted her to take a shower, shampoo her hair, and wash well. "Because you're dirty and you fuckin' stink! How long has it been since you bathed?" She didn't remember.

I heard the shower, got undressed, and stepped in. "I figured I'd hold you so you don't fall and break your ass." We were face-to-face. She still had great tits. They glistened with beads of water and her nipples were hard. I was holding them.

"Wash your face and neck. You're fuckin' filthy. Turn around; I'll wash your back." I got to her waist, washed her ass, then told her she could do her legs. She turned around, bent over. Those beautiful tits were hanging. My cock was hitting her in the face. She opened her mouth and was going to suck. I stopped her and told her, "I'm getting out. I feel like a prune."

I was sitting in the chair, naked. She sat in the chair next to me, with a bath towel wrapped around her. She was drying her face with a small towel. She asked why I was so angry with her. "I didn't say or do anything to make you angry."

"I don't like dopeheads, and you sure as fuck are one."

"I can't help it. Doing dope gives me a little relief from my misery."

I asked if she was still high, because she didn't sound like she was. She told me she wasn't. "Between the shower and time, it wore off. I feel fine."

I told her to look at me, really look at me. She glanced, squinted, then stared. Her expression changed. She smiled, jumped on me, kissing my face all over. I gently pushed her back to the chair and told her I was angry because of what she did to herself.

"They told me you and Duwayne were dead. Then my mother died. I didn't want to live. I had nothing to live for. Chua had been doing coke for a long time – she got me hooked. When Chua would tell me about you, I would die inside. You loved her far more than she loved you. She had a plan to get money from you. She wanted to be the largest dealer in Vietnam with her now husband.

"I grieved for Duwayne … I loved Duwayne. Please don't get angry with me, but I was also in love with you. Duwayne and I would make love – in my mind he was you. I felt very bad when we got the news, but I grieved for you. If the truth be known, you're the cause of what I am today."

I asked her if I helped her, would she kick it? She answered yes.

We were in bed relaxing. I was looking at her, thinking we're both grieving. She took one path to try and deal with it. I took a different path. Maybe hers was the right one. At least I could have a brief time free of the agony. Suicide or coke, they both sucked. I took her in my arms and kissed her passionately.

"We're going to kick this. We'll both get over our demons and then make a good life together."

We talked. I decided to buy her a car because I couldn't drive with the maniacs here. "We'll stay in the hotel for as long as it takes for you to get straight. I'll buy you an outfit in the hotel. We'll get the rest in the city later."

In the shop, she modeled a dress for me. I told her she looked great. "Don't forget a bra and throw your old clothes in the trash." After a good meal in the dining room we went back to the room. We were in bed kissing. Hoai Mi asked if she could please do me. I told her she doesn't ever have to get my permission. She went down on me. It was good. I lifted her off, laid her on her back, and got on top. That was good, too. We kissed. I really liked kissing her because it seemed she couldn't get enough. I was lying against the headboard with her in my arms. I asked her how she felt. She told me wonderful, she never felt this good in her life.

"Why weren't we able to make contact? Hawk was looking forward to the wedding. You really fucked him up." I didn't get an answer. I knew then this was all bullshit. We spent our days together. I had a thought – *I want to drive to Long Binh and see Brown.*

We drove to the base. An MP stopped us at the gate. I showed him my ID, he waved us on. We drove to headquarters and went to the Special Forces Command. An MP asked if he could help us. I told him I was looking for Sergeant Brown. He told me Sergeant Brown had been killed in action on the same mission as Colonel Bolton.

As I turned to leave, I noticed on a wall a glass-enclosed box about five feet by three feet. Large brass letters across the top read, "In Memoria." Beneath it, two plaques, one for the Colonel and one for Hawk. Then there were two rows of 3x4 brass strips with officers' names. Beneath that were rows of smaller strips for enlisted men. I found Brown, and after searching for a while I found Michael Ritchie, my buddy Mickey.

The Colonel's plaque read:  For Heroism and Selfless Ethic. He had helped two wounded men to safety. He repeated the action twice more before he was killed. The Medal of Honor was presented posthumously.

Hawk's tribute read: His selfless regard as he covered a mine with his body to save a fellow Gl. First Sergeant Hawkins was the most decorated soldier of the Vietnamese conflict.

At the bottom center was a brass plaque etched with the *ma guy* ace, with a story of the ghost devil card.

The next two days were quiet but good. On the third I went to see Chua. I took a taxi to the house and told him to wait. Chua answered my knock and opened the door. I asked if her husband was home. She told me no. I told her about my meeting Hoai Mi and what she told me.

Chua began crying and told me she had no choice. Her husband is VC. "He came to our house and told me we were collaborating with the enemy. Everyone in the house would be executed unless I married him."

I told her, "I know the boy is mine.: The three of us could go to the States and start a new life.

She told me she couldn't leave Vietnam. "Please don't take my son. He is all I have; he is all that matters to me."

I told her, "I'll be back when this is over. I want the three of us to be together."

When I got back, Hoai MI was sprawled on the couch, high. Coke was all over the place. I packed my things and took a taxi to the airport. How could this fuckin' dopehead bitch degrade Hawk's memory the way she did! I considered going back there to fuck her up but changed my mind. It would be a waste of time. A new life was in the fuckin' shitter.

# *CHAPTER 64*

I got a ticket and flew home. Landing at Kennedy, I realized my car was at La Guardia. I took a taxi. On the way, we passed a Royal Auto Sales Dealership. It looked the same, but the name had been changed.

I drove my Vette to the bank and spoke to Steve, the manager. He said the bank had received a wire transfer from Vegas for seven million for me. I told him to cash in my CDs, add that money to the seven and make me out three checks. "I want whatever check is the safest and easiest for me to deposit." I emptied my safe deposit boxes into a duffle bag and left.

I had no place in particular I wanted to go. I got on Route 70 and drove west. I was in a bad way – tense, unable to focus. I'd lose my concentration and had a couple of close calls. All this fuckin' money … .what good is it when you're alone? I'd give it all to somebody if they'd give me back the ones I loved. I spent the night in a motel, drunk, shit-faced, wasted.

The next day I drove bleary-eyed. My hangover-driving made me a menace on the interstate. I don't know how many birdies I got. I didn't give a fuck.

I drove past Indianapolis and got off Route 70. I was aimlessly wandering around the countryside. Lunch was in a cafe in a small, old, agricultural town. About five miles from town I passed a "For Sale" sign on a farm. I inquired about it, met with the realtor, and bought it. Vietnam was still going on and there was no way I could get there. I realized Chua and the boy were better off without me.

In time, I married, raised a family. I didn't have the capacity to feel, give, or show love. I imagine my wife rationalized it that I loved her and the kids, just didn't know how to show it. I was a fucked-up husband and a fucked-up father. I enjoyed farming, planting and harvesting crops, and taking care of our livestock. It really was a good life. As the family grew, I built a new house.

One evening my wife and I were in bed. She was sleeping, but I couldn't get to sleep. Suddenly it felt like someone threw a bucket of water on me. My life came crashing down. Everyone I lost kept moving back and forth in my brain. I was in bed crying and couldn't stop. I had no idea what brought it on. It just happened.

The next day I went through my chores half-assed. I didn't give a shit. I couldn't get the night before off my mind. Night came, and we were in bed. Again, I couldn't get to sleep. I was thinking about my father passing – it was the best thing for him; he was out of pain. Hyman was old and would have passed soon anyhow. I missed both. Then I began thinking about Maria, my mother, Tony and Mario. All I wanted was to be with them again. I needed them and missed them so badly. Different than the night before. I didn't cry. I spent the night in gut-wrenching agony.

The next day was the same as before. I decided to make an appointment with the family doctor. I was concerned about my lack of sleep and my sanity. The doctor and I spoke for quite a while. She prescribed an antidepressant and a sleep aid. She told me to try them, and if they didn't help in a week, to call her – she had another idea.

What she prescribed didn't do shit. I called. She suggested I voluntarily go into a psychiatric ward in the regional hospital in Avon, the next town to us. She set it up and I checked in. The first thing I was told was to take off my belt and shoe laces, and I was assigned a room. The room was dingy, barren except for a bed. I was sitting on the bed thinking, *What the fuck am I doing here? I feel worse than I did before I came here.*

A nurse walked into my room and told me the policy and procedures. She gave me a sheet of paper which was a schedule I had to follow and left. I looked over the schedule. Breakfast, group meeting, arts and crafts, then lunch, followed by individual meeting, then free time till dinner. The second day was the same. The third day was similar except I was to see a psychiatrist.

They showed me to an examination room and told me the doctor would see me soon. It was one-thirty. A guy with a stethoscope around his neck walked in. He put the ear plugs in and told me he wanted to listen to my heart. He bent over and was listening. Then he stood up and said, "You have a murmur. I'm running very late for a tee off time. I'll see you next visit." He left.

I was sitting there thinking, *This is one fucked-up place. I'm getting out of here.* I went to the desk, told the person I was leaving, and needed a phone for my ride.

I began seeing one of those chain-operated shrink places. I'd spend one day a week talking to a sociologist, and one day a month with a psychiatrist. The weekly talk was good, but not very helpful. The shrink prescribed different antidepressants. I did it for three months. I decided to make an appointment with my primary at the VA for a referral to the VA psychiatrist. I met with her. She told me she had read my records. As far as Vietnam was concerned, she could do nothing, I had to handle that myself. She wanted to talk about the deaths of Bolton and Hawkins.

"They were Colonel Bolton and First Sergeant Duwayne Hawkins. They most certainly deserve respect from you." She prescribed an antidepressant and told me she'd see me in three weeks. I told her I didn't think so and left.

By this time, my wife had given up on me. She was sleeping in another room. We had little to no communication unless she needed money for something. I took a job in a plant on third shift. I left for work in the dark and came home in the dark. I slept a little during the day.

One day my son came to visit. His son had enlisted in the Marines. He tried to get me to talk about myself and Vietnam. I told my son I was sorry, I couldn't talk about Nam. Instead of getting into my personal life in Nam, I vented all the shit I had suppressed for decades. I told him I felt Nam was the stupidest war America had ever fought. "It probably will go down as the greatest tragedy of all time. No one ever heard of Vietnam. None of us ever knew what we were fighting for."

"After Kennedy got hit, LBJ was president. He relieved Westmoreland because Westmoreland was determined to win the war. He proposed hitting the VC strongholds in Cambodia, the area they would retreat to after nailing us. He wanted to take the army into an aggressive mode instead of the defensive mode they were in. The atmosphere in this country, the media who fed on it, and all the protests persuaded LBJ. He rejected everything Westmoreland wanted. He was nothing more than a fucked-up politician. Americans died. Their hands were tied.

"Just before Nixon was elected, LBJ wanted to send fifty thousand infantry to Nam. Nixon's campaign was about ending the war, but he never told how. The fifty thousand were never sent to Nam. In fact, he began withdrawing troops. The army had never pulled out, so it was fucked-up, too."

"The lives this war took, the devastation, the misery people had to endure, all of it was for absolutely nothing. My concern is Danny getting caught up in another politician-created war. I hope I'm wrong. The military could be a good career."

My son left. I was sitting in my rocking chair on the porch admiring my cornfield. It was about two in the afternoon. I had spent a lifetime on this farm. Often, I thought about people I had loved and some I hadn't. Here I was … sitting on this porch … thinking about my life. Perhaps people do this, reflect, when they get old.

For most people life is like a road that meanders over small hills and shallow valleys. My first thirty-five years were a roller coaster of towering heights and profound depths. I thought of the first part of my life as a pendulum swinging. One direction brought so much joy – I'd be flying high. A swing to the other side brought the severest agony and depression imaginable.

I've spent the past forty years on this farm. It seemed everything that went on in the world passed us by. The lows I had were the death of a beloved pet, the market price of our grain or livestock falling. Outwardly I'm a laid-back farmer. Inwardly, a day doesn't pass that I don't relive my first thirty-five years. I never spoke of any of it to anyone.

I have never gotten over my disdain and loathing for politicians and for the army. I choose not to vote. It doesn't matter to me. One is as bad as the other. I could never get over missing all the people in my life. Looking back, all I've had is agony since that call from Sam.

I sit back in my chair and enjoy the sun's warmth. Suddenly I feel a severe pain in my chest, and it is getting dark. *What is happening? Am I having a heart attack? It's fucking painful. Ugh! I am having a heart attack – right here on my porch! Fuck, I'm actually having a fatal heart attack!*

For the first time in all these years I am with the people I loved. Standing in front of me are my mother and Maria; both are exceptionally beautiful. In the background, I can see Bolton and Brown in fatigues, saluting me. Off to the side is Hawk giving me a high five. Now, I see Hyman and my father – both looked good. Tony and Mario are standing together. They seem happy to see me.

Suddenly I have Maria in my arms; all the wonderful feelings I had for her are bubbling in my brain. I am staring at the most beautiful woman in the world. Maria takes my hand, and we begin to walk towards a bright white light as everyone follows. It's wonderful.

# *WHAT READERS ARE SAYING*

*Ma Guy: Ghost Devil* is powerful, fast moving and completely absorbing as a journey told by a young man of principal growing up in the gritty world of the Bronx in the 50's who goes on to distinguish himself in Vietnam and then suffer tragic consequences as a result of his childhood associations. His war scenes are large scale and completely believable, his characters vivid and compelling if sometimes somewhat salty. We will surely hear from this first time author again with his next novel, and soon is not soon enough!

*C.K. Robinson, Editor, The Tiverton Review*

*Ma Guy, Ghost Devil* translated from the Vietnamese, is an easy, interesting and entertaining read that amazingly allocates approximately equal text to the mafia in New York City and US "tunnel rats" in South Vietnam. Pauley Walker, the central character, is part James Bond and part Einstein as women adore him, he kills bad guys and Vietcong soldiers, and ALWAYS seems to have the cute bad-guy putdown while recognizing and solving all problems.

*Dr. B.E. Hutch, Professor, University of Tennessee*

Tells a gritty, uncensored, look into the early rise of the mafia in the Bronx, New York, and Las Vegas, Nevada. This story, of a one man wrecking machine, paints a picture of the single most influential figure the history books have never known, wrapping himself into various important ideas and innovations of the 1900s. The protagonist, Pauly Walker, enjoys the benefits of growing up in the mafia with the consequences that are always lurking in the shadows.

*Charles Michael, Attorney, Baltimore Maryland*